SCANDAL *at*
the HOUSE OF RUSSELL

Never Kiss a Rake

ALSO BY ANNE STUART

Summer Love

New Year's Resolution: Baby

New Year's Resolution: Husband

One Night with a Rogue

Strangers in the Night

Highland Fling

To Love and To Honor

My Valentine

Silhouette Shadows

CATEGORY ROMANCE

Wild Thing

The Right Man

A Dark and Stormy Night

The Soldier and the Baby

Cinderman

Falling Angel

One More Valentine

Rafe's Revenge

Heat Lightning

Chasing Trouble

Night of the Phantom

Lazarus Rising / reprint as Here
    Come the Grooms

Angel's Wings

Rancho Diablo / reprint as Western
    Lovers

Crazy Like a Fox / reprint as Born in
    the USA

Glass Houses / reprint as Men at Work

Cry for the Moon

Partners in Crime

Blue Sage / reprint as Western Lovers

Bewitching Hour

Rocky Road / reprint in Men Made in
    America #19

Banish Misfortune

Housebound

Museum Piece

Heart's Ease

Chain of Love

The Fall of Maggie Brown

Winter's Edge

Catspaw II

Hand in Glove

Catspaw

Tangled Lies / reprint in Men Made in
    America #11

Now You See Him

Special Gifts

Break the Night

Against the Wind

NOVELLAS

The Wicked House of Rohan

Married to It (prequel to Fire and Ice)

Risk the Night

Married to It

SCANDAL *at*
the HOUSE OF RUSSELL

Never Kiss
a Rake

ANNE STUART

 Montlake
Romance

Published by Montlake Romance

PO Box 400818
Las Vegas, NV 89140

ISBN-13: 9781477807323
ISBN-10: 1477807322

To
Jane and Miriam
For always watching my back

1869

CHAPTER ONE

M ISS B RYONY R USSELL SAT in front of the dismal fire in the tiny terrace apartment on the very edge of Whitechapel. It was a dangerous area, and well she knew it, but with the small amount of money left the three sisters hadn't had much choice. Lodgings in London weren't to be had cheaply in the thirty-second year of Queen Victoria's reign.

Bryony looked at her sisters and cleared her throat. "I believe there's no choice for it, we'll have to go into service."

Her sisters looked at her with a mixture of interest and horror. "Service?" her youngest sister Sophia echoed faintly. "As in, work? As a maid?"

"What else does 'service' mean, you silly goose," her middle sister Madeleine said. "I think it's a brilliant idea."

"I don't," Sophia said decidedly.

Bryony surveyed them impatiently. "Not you, Sophie. You'd get fired within a fortnight. And I'm not saying you should do it either, Maddy, if you don't wish to. But the only way we're going to find out the truth about what really happened to Papa is to get inside the households of those we most suspect, and I can think of no better way."

It had all happened so swiftly. One day they were the pampered daughters of a wealthy shipping magnate, the next they were destitute, orphaned, and under a cloud of shame. Eustace Russell had been a self-made man, amassing a fortune through the shipping company that had started out a mere fledgling business and ended up being the foremost company in England and half of Europe. He'd married a great and titled beauty who'd given him three daughters; he lived life well.

And six weeks ago he'd supposedly embezzled a massive amount of Russell Shipping's finances and then died in a carriage accident as he raced for the Continent, plunging to his death over the high cliffs on the southwest corner of England. His three daughters were finally beginning to emerge from the shock and grief that had overwhelmed them, only to find they were in social disgrace as well.

Two banks had failed immediately following the discovery of their father's perfidy, setting off a financial panic that had wide-reaching effects. It was no wonder the name of Russell was viewed with scorn and mistrust nowadays.

For the past six weeks Bryony and her sisters had been in a fog, numbed by grief and confusion. Everything was gone—the money, their good name, their faith in their father. Their former town house on Curzon Street had been set on fire, presumably by Eustace to cover his tracks, and the ruined shell of it remained, mute testament to the shame that had come to their family. Even Renwick, the vast country estate in Somerset, had been taken, the entailed property returned to the heir upon Russell's death. The three daughters had arrived from the country with no place to stay, and it had taken all Bryony's force of character to keep her sisters from feeling the shame and hopelessness that was crushing her. It was a blessing that their delicate, high-strung mother wasn't still alive to endure the public recoil. It was hard enough on Bryony, and she accounted herself far sturdier than their mother had ever been.

It hadn't taken long for Bryony to pull herself together, take a clear look at the so-called proof of her father's iniquity, and realize it was all a lie. The scribbled note, in her father's own hand, had further convinced her.

Don't trust any of them. Someone's stealing money, and it looks like Kilmartyn's in league with them, no matter what excuses he makes. Don't trust Morgan either. Never trust a pirate. Something's going on, and I'll get to the bottom of it, or

Don't trust anyone. That's what her father had dashed off, a note to himself, but for Bryony it was something else. It was purpose. The idea that there was actually something that could be done was a tonic to her soul. There was no way she could bring her father back, but if she could ensure whoever was truly behind this met justice it would give them all some kind of peace, or, at the very least, resolution.

"We don't even know that he was murdered," Sophie protested. "Simply because you found an odd note among Father's papers doesn't mean we should pay it any heed. Carriage accidents do happen, you know. And who's to say that Father didn't take that money?"

"Because Papa was almost maddeningly honest, and he instilled those values in all of us," Bryony said firmly. "I simply cannot believe he would ever do such a thing."

"I told you," Maddy snapped at her younger sister. "If you ever used your brain to think about anything but fashion and food . . ."

"We aren't getting to enjoy any fashion," Sophie shot back, plucking at her black-dyed mourning dress. "And since I'm the only one who can cook around here we're not getting to enjoy the food either."

"Stop fighting!" Bryony said wearily, not for the first time. "I swear, the two of you are like angry cats. If we're to get through this with any kind of success we have to work together."

"Sorry," Sophie muttered, casting a half-resentful, half-apologetic look at Maddy.

"I'm sorry, Bryony," Maddy said with a degree more sincerity. "Where do you propose we start?"

Bryony sat back, pouring herself another cup of the strong, cheap tea they were subsisting on. "I can think of three suspects—Papa named two of them. The Earl of Kilmartyn was his business partner and made a fortune at Papa's side. Papa distrusted him, and for some reason the bank panic didn't affect him in the slightest. He's the most logical choice. He's a well-known rake, despite his beautiful wife, and he's got the morals of an alley cat, or so I've been told."

"He's too obvious," Maddy said. "What about Captain Morgan? Father had just removed him from his command, and he was on his way to Devonport when the accident happened. When our choice is between a peer of the realm and a former pirate the answer seems logical."

"Privateer," Bryony corrected firmly. Maddy had a tendency to be overdramatic. "You're right, though. Captain Morgan appears to be a man who wouldn't blink at the thought of murder. I don't believe Father ever trusted him completely. Although there are a number of reasons to drive to Devonport—visiting Captain Morgan being only one of them. There did appear to be bad blood between them."

"There was bad blood between Father and almost everyone he ever met," Sophie scoffed. "Honest or not, he was hardly the most convivial of individuals. Surely you're not suggesting Captain Morgan embezzled a fortune and killed our father out of pique?"

"It's something you would do," Maddy said pointedly.

Sophie shrugged with surprising good nature. "I suppose I might, if someone annoyed me enough. But what about Viscount Blackhurst? With our father's death he regained ownership of Renwick, no small treasure. He already murdered his wife. Why hesitate to kill a total stranger if you stand to gain that much?"

"We don't know that he murdered his wife," Bryony corrected her. "It's just rumor. And of the three I admit he seems the least likely. The man was already wealthy, and he owned several estates. Besides, Father didn't seem to suspect him."

"Clearly Father didn't know everything, if he ended up dead," Sophie replied, sinking back on the window seat and staring out into the rain-drenched city, the sheen of her unshed tears barely noticeable. She looked like a gorgeous, shining doll amidst the trappings of a black crow. Mourning clothes had been expensive, even using the cheapest of worsted, but instead of diminishing Sophie's vibrant beauty the stark black only made her more stunning. "Why don't we simply go with our original plan? I'll marry someone fabulously wealthy and very handsome and support the two of you."

"This mythical husband of yours has yet to materialize," Maddy pointed out. "And may I remind you that my suitor discovered a pressing need to travel to South America when all of this came out?"

"Just because you couldn't hold on to Tarkington doesn't mean I'll have similar problems."

"Stop it!" Bryony said sharply. "This is difficult enough. If we spend all our time arguing with each other we'll never find out what happened! Surely you don't want our father's murderer to go scot-free?"

"We don't know for sure that he was murdered," Sophie said in a sulky voice.

"No, we have no proof. A hasty note in Father's hand that tells us not to trust anyone. Not to mention the fact that every penny of his fortune has disappeared, leaving us on the streets," Maddy pointed out in a caustic voice.

"Not on the streets," Bryony said, a stickler for accuracy. "These rooms are warm and comfortable, and there are relatives who have offered us a home any time we choose. In fact, we were just about to leave when I found the note in a box of his papers." She glanced over at the stained piece of paper on the small table. No matter how many times she read it, it still failed to make any sense.

"Of course there are," Maddy shot back. "I could live with second cousin Rosalie and take care of her seven ghastly children in between running errands."

"And how is that different from going into service?" Sophie countered.

"Because there's no way out from Cousin Rosalie's," Maddy said gloomily. "No answers to be found, and not even a farthing to show for it. I'd rather be an honest maid than a slavey for Cousin Rosalie."

"I thought the whole point was not being particularly honest," Sophie pointed out.

"That's enough," Bryony said firmly. "Neither of you is required to do anything. I came up with the idea, and I'll follow through. If I can get a job in Lord Kilmartyn's household it would give me access to his papers. No man can keep secrets from his domestics. Within a matter of days, weeks at the most, I should have my answer, and if he proves innocent I can move on to the viscount or Captain Morgan."

"What do you intend to do?" Maddy asked, putting her own cold tea down with a grimace. "Could we even pass muster as maids?"

"I'm going to apply for the post of housekeeper. Apparently Lord Kilmartyn is always in need of one—the last stayed less than a month. Given his reputation, he probably drives them away with his reprehensible behavior. I don't know how his wife can bear it. But I'm not going to be driven away. You know that I'm much better suited to being a housekeeper. Maids are supposed to be pleasant to look upon. Have you ever seen a maid who looks like me?" Bryony said evenly.

"Don't be ridiculous!" Maddy snapped. "You're beautiful!"

"My face is covered with pox scars, Maddy."

"Only half of it," Sophie piped up with devastating loyalty. "And the other side is very pretty. Of course you're not as pretty as I am—no one is—but you're still well enough."

Bryony laughed, used to her sister's backhanded compliments. "I also know more about running a household than I do about cleaning and dusting. I ran both the town house and Renwick for years, ever since Mama died. I think I'd be perfectly prepared to be a housekeeper. And I already have the right clothes." She plucked at her plain, ugly dress.

"And when would this start?" Maddy said dubiously.

"I have an interview tomorrow."

Her two sisters stared at her in dismay. "Don't you think you should have brought this up earlier?" Maddy said finally.

Bryony managed to smile. "I was afraid you might talk me out of it."

"And so we should," Sophie said. "This is absurd."

"At least I feel I'm doing something," she shot back. "Not just sitting around waiting . . . waiting for God knows what." She sighed. "In the meantime I want the two of you to go stay with Nanny Gruen while I'm working in the Kilmartyn household. I'm old enough to stand as chaperone to the two of you and keep your reputations intact, but you cannot stay together without someone to look out for you. Nanny Gruen has been begging us to come ever since Father died, and I've written to tell her you'll be on your way."

"Awfully high-handed of you, Bryony," Maddy said sternly. "Just because you're the eldest doesn't mean you have say over our actions."

"I don't want to stay with our old nanny," Sophie broke in. "Her cottage is too close to Renwick, and if you think I can sit by and watch that . . . that wife-murdering usurper swan around *our* house then you're mistaken."

"Renwick isn't our house anymore, Sophie," Maddy said with more kindness than she usually showed her spoiled baby sister. "And it wasn't ours in the first place—Father won it from the current viscount's father in a card game. We only had lifetime rights to it, rights that vanished when Father died. We need to accept that."

Sophie glared mutinously, obviously not prepared to accept anything, and Bryony spoke before another battle could erupt.

"I've bought tickets on tomorrow's stage to Somerset and I've written Nanny to expect you. Don't fight me on this, please. I hate the thought of separating." Bryony gave Maddy a rueful smile. "You would have left me soon enough, if Tarkington had come up to scratch."

Maddy shrugged. "Who can blame him for running scared? In place of an heiress he was confronted with a pauper with a cloud over her head. And it wasn't as if I were in love with him."

"Of course not," Bryony said firmly, knowing how Maddy had wept bitter tears over the faithless Tarkington.

"He was a weak-chinned idiot who didn't deserve you," said Sophie, who held the strong belief that no one should criticize Maddy but her younger sister. Maddy smiled at her, and Bryony sighed in relief. For all their squabbling, her sisters loved each other, and Nanny Gruen would keep them safe.

"Then we're agreed," she said briskly. "Tomorrow you two travel to Somerset and I will go to my interview."

"But what if they don't hire you, Bryony?" Sophie inquired.

"As I said, they've had a great deal of trouble maintaining a decent staff at their house in Berkeley Square, though I'm not sure why. In any case, my forged credentials are impeccable, and I'm quiet, forceful, yet unassuming. They'll take me."

Neither Maddy nor Sophie protested this self-assured statement. Indeed, they believed their older sister capable of anything she set her mind to, Bryony thought. She only wished this were more a matter of fact than bravado.

"Then we're decided," she continued. "I think we should break into Sophie's supply of tea cakes. They're sinfully good for only your second attempt at baking."

Sophie preened. "Let's eat them all," she said recklessly. "I'm ready to tackle bread next."

"I'm sure Nanny will give you plenty of scope for your culinary genius," Maddy said, not without kindness. She looked at her older sister. "There's no chance at changing your mind, Bryony?"

"None at all," she said.

"Then tea cakes it is."

CHAPTER TWO

BRYONY STOOD OUTSIDE the large town house on Berkeley Square that was home to the notorious Adrian Bruton, Earl of Kilmartyn, and his beautiful wife. Bryony had never stepped foot inside it—indeed, she had shunned society completely for her entire adult life, a fact which now served her well. Standing on the street, her drab mourning garb washed and faded to a dull brown, the ugly hat pulled down over her tightly braided hair, she felt as if she were entering into battle.

She straightened her back and squared her shoulders. This had been her idea, and a good one it was. She was more than capable of carrying off the role of housekeeper—that was all she'd been since she'd left the schoolroom. Most of her life she'd been immured in the countryside, and no one in London would recognize her, despite the distinctive scars. With her light hair pulled back tight against her scalp, her too-generous mouth pulled into a grim expression, she could pass muster with the best of them.

She'd seen her sisters off less than an hour ago, and it had taken the brisk walk from the staging house to Berkeley Square to put the ramrod back into her spine, to let the tears dry. She had a mission, and she was never one to shirk a responsibility. It was time to start her new life.

Opening the iron gate, she started down the alleyway beside the large stone house. How did people know which alleyway belonged to which house, she wondered. There was no plaque to signify. She would simply have to hope this would lead her to the servants' entrance of the earl's town house.

For once her luck held. She descended the narrow steps and rapped firmly on the door.

No one came. Did servants and delivery persons simply enter a kitchen unannounced? Or need she wait for someone to open to her?

She rapped again, tapping her foot. A moment later the door opened, revealing a young woman in a maid's uniform, her hair awry, her eyes running over Bryony's form with thinly veiled contempt. "Yes?" she said impatiently. The woman was pretty enough, though the sullen turn of her mouth rather spoiled the effect. Her apron and cap were gone, and she looked as if she'd just left her bed. "What do you want?" she demanded of Bryony. "We don't allow no Reformers in this household."

Bryony drew herself up straight. Best to start as she meant to go on. "I am Mrs. Greaves," she said calmly. She'd chosen the false name with a certain amount of irony. "I have an appointment with Lady Kilmartyn. Please tell her I await her pleasure." And without another word she moved past the woman, making her way into the overwarm basement kitchen.

It was a shambles. Dirty dishes littered the table where a footman sat, sprawling, his long legs stuck out, his neckcloth awry. There was a stain on his livery, and he looked at her for a moment, his practiced eye raking her body, moving up to her face and then dismissing her as unworthy. "Who's this, then, Ruby?" he demanded.

Ruby didn't have time to answer before an older, cheerful-looking woman scurried into the kitchen, her plump figure and stained apron attesting to her role. "Beg pardon, miss," she said hurriedly, wiping her hands on the grubby apron. "I'm Mrs. Harkins, the cook. You must be here about the new position."

At least this one was polite, though something would have to be done about the general cleanliness of both the kitchen and Mrs. Harkins's aprons. Bryony nodded graciously, a housekeeper-gracious, not a lady of the manor–gracious. "I'm Mrs. Greaves," she said composedly. "I hope I'm not too early." In fact, she hoped no such thing. She'd wanted a chance to get the lay of the land before she had her interview. Clearly her work here would be cut out for her.

"Don't you worry about it, Mrs. Greaves," the cook said. "You have a seat and I'll bring you a nice cup of tea while Alfred goes to inform her ladyship that you're here." She turned to the indolent footman. "Get your lumpen arse off that chair, Alfred, and do your duty."

Alfred was unimpressed. He rose with slow insolence, reaching up to straighten his neckcloth. It still wasn't right, but apparently it was good enough for this household. He strolled out of the room; slow enough to make it clear he was going because he wanted to, not because Mrs. Harkins had ordered him.

"And you, Ruby! Don't you go be leaving Emma with all the upstairs work. Get a move on."

"Emma can handle it," Ruby said rudely.

"If she can then there's no need for you on staff, now is there?" Mrs. Harkins replied.

A moment later Ruby was gone, and Mrs. Harkins put a cup of very strong tea in front of Bryony, sighing. "You can see we're at sixes and sevens here, Mrs. Greaves. I do my best, but I'm not cut out for managing a household this size, and that's the truth of it."

Bryony put sugar and milk into the inky tea, then managed to take a sip without shuddering. She sincerely hoped Mrs. Harkins's cooking was better than her tea. "It's a difficult task if you've been thrust into the midst of it," she said. "Particularly if things have gotten lax." She resisted the temptation to glance at the littered table.

But Mrs. Harkins recognized her own failings. "We need more staff," she said with a gusty sigh. "Ruby and Emma are the upstairs maids, but Emma doubles as my helper, and the two footmen, Alfred and Bertie, aren't worth spit, though at least Bertie tries. Mademoiselle Hortense's only task is to take care of Lady Kilmartyn, but Bertie occasionally doubles as his lordship's valet when his lordship lets him, and the boy who hauls the coal and such ran off weeks ago."

A household this size should have four upstairs maids, a scullery maid, and a kitchen maid. Two footmen might suffice, but a butler would do better at overseeing them, and the idea that a gentleman of Lord Kilmartyn's stature didn't have a dedicated valet was a surprise indeed. "If they hire me I'll do my best to get things sorted out," she said pleasantly, not disguising the iron determination in her voice.

"They'll hire you, mark my words," Mrs. Harkins said. "Lord Kilmartyn doesn't concern himself with household matters, but things have come to such a pass that he's put his foot down. It just remains to be seen if you'll stay the course. This b'aint an easy job."

There was a trace of Yorkshire in Mrs. Harkins's comfortable voice, reminding Bryony of cool summers and dark hills and laughter. But the house in Yorkshire was gone, along with everything else. "I'm not in the habit of quitting," she said coolly.

At that moment Alfred sauntered back in. "Her ladyship will see you now," he said, dropping back down at the table.

"You could see to the silver, young man," Mrs. Harkins said sternly. "It hasn't been polished in weeks."

"Nobody notices," he said lazily, reaching past Bryony to pour himself a cup of tea.

"Aren't you going to escort Mrs. Greaves to her ladyship?"

"In a moment," he said, not making any attempt to move.

Bryony rose. "I'm ready to go now."

He looked up at her with perfect indifference. "Are you, now?"

"Yes, I am," she said, her voice like steel. "Get up."

He rose, much to his own surprise, she expected. She had the voice of command, one he would be used to. She had been dealing with servants her entire life, with fairness and compassion, and despite the laxness of the household Alfred instinctively responded to it.

"All right," he said, still sounding sullen. "I suppose the sooner I take you the sooner I can have a peaceful cup of tea."

It was going to be the last peaceful cup of tea he had for a long time, Bryony thought, as she followed him up the narrow servants' staircase. For the first time in months she felt a faint glimmer in the darkness of her soul.

At last she was on her way to discovering what lay behind that strange note her father had left, a note that had turned grief and shame to fury and resolution. Finally she had something she could do.

The room she was ushered into was dimly lit, the curtains pulled against the bright sunlight, and for a moment she blinked, peering into the shadows. A faint voice drifted toward her, soft and gentle. "Please come in, Mrs. Greaves. You'll have to excuse the dim light—I am afflicted with the migraine and sunlight positively cripples me."

Her eyes were growing accustomed to the darkness, and she could see Lady Kilmartyn now, draped across a chaise longue, an icon of frail beauty. Bryony moved toward her, stopped and gave a dignified bow. She'd considered it long and hard, and she and her sisters had decided that a curtsy was too demeaning for an august housekeeper. "Your ladyship," she said in a quiet voice. She was intimately acquainted with migraines—her mother had suffered from them, and Maddy had inherited the dreadful tendency. Loud voices were almost as bad as sunlight. "Would you prefer I come back later?"

Heavens, she hoped not. She had counted on this working out so completely that she had informed their landlord they would no longer have need of the shabby rooms that had housed them for the last six weeks.

"You're very kind, Mrs. Greaves, but there is no assurance that I will feel any better tomorrow. Please sit."

Should she, or shouldn't she? When she had asked a servant or housekeeper to sit her in presence they usually did, but she had always been a comfortable mistress. On instinct she took the seat Lady Kilmartyn waved her toward, keeping her back straight, her knees together, and her lips pursed.

Cecily, Countess of Kilmartyn, was one of the most acclaimed beauties in England. The daughter of a minor baronet, she'd reigned over her first season, and if people were astonished she'd married an Irish earl when she could have set her sights higher they had only to consider that the earl was Adrian Bruton and they understood. They were a beautiful couple, moving through their world on a cloud of adoration, and even Bryony understood the perfection of the match. Lady Kilmartyn had smooth, delicate skin, luminous dark eyes, a small, willful chin, and a mass of dark hair that was dressed in loose curls around her beautiful face, and she surveyed Bryony with a critical eye.

"Your references are impeccable, Mrs. Greaves," she said finally. "Perhaps you might tell me about your last position and why you left?"

Bryony had been prepared for this. Of course her references were magnificent—she'd written them herself, and she'd worked up a complicated history that would convince anyone. "I was working in Italy with the late Lady Margrave," she said, keeping her voice soft and servile. "She kept a large household, and I oversaw both the Italian and English servants, while maintaining order and the serenity she required as she suffered through her fatal illness. Needless to say I returned to England upon her death and immediately sought a new position."

"And didn't Lady Margrave reward such devotion? I would think she would be generous enough to see you didn't have to work for quite a bit."

Bryony had anticipated this. "Lady Margrave was indeed very generous. Unfortunately I have family in Dorset who depend on my assistance."

Lady Kilmartyn frowned. "I hope they don't make too many demands upon your time, Mrs. Greaves. I would expect you to be here."

"My responsibility to them is only financial," she said smoothly.

Lady Kilmartyn was watching her closely, and she suddenly sat up, peering at her in the darkness. "You know, I'm not sure but that an older woman might be more suitable," she said suddenly. "You seem too young to be able to run a household."

"I assure you, Lady Kilmartyn, that I am more than capable of ordering a full staff of servants and seeing to the smooth running of your home." Bryony struggled to keep her voice calm as panic filled her. What had she said to change Lady Kilmartyn's mind?

"Take off your bonnet and move into the light, if you please," Lady Kilmartyn said, her voice sharp.

Bryony didn't dare hesitate. She rose, pulling off her bonnet to expose the tightly braided hair, then moved toward the pool of light that escaped one dark curtain.

"What's wrong with your face?" the woman demanded.

For a moment Bryony considered not responding to her rude question. Then again, if one was a servant then there was no such thing as rude behavior from an employer. "Smallpox, your ladyship. I had it when I was quite young."

Lady Kilmartyn considered her for a long moment. "No," she said abruptly. "Your face distresses me. I don't like to be surrounded by ugly things."

Ugly things. The words should have stung, but Bryony had heard them before. From her mother. From her own mouth as she stared into a mirror.

She stood frozen. She could hardly change her face, and begging would do no good. She nodded, temporarily accepting defeat, when there was a sudden shaft of light into the room, and Lady Kilmartyn let out a cry of pain that was as beautiful as she was.

"Close that door!" she demanded. "You know how much the light hurts me."

"Indeed I do, my love," came a smooth, elegant voice. "But I'm afraid I'm going to have to override you."

CHAPTER THREE

LIGHT FLOODED THE SALON, and Bryony almost clapped her hat back on her head, but something stopped her. If she was going to work here he would see her face soon enough, and there was no chance in the world he would recognize her. Few people even knew there were three Russell daughters.

"Don't be ridiculous, Adrian." There was just the hint of a snap in his wife's voice. "You've given me run of the household and promised not to interfere. Mrs. Greaves will not suit—"

"Mrs. Greaves will suit very well, my darling," he said softly, but there was no mistaking the steel in his charming voice. "I'm afraid your delicate health is simply not up to the strain of ordering the household. Things are in such disarray that either something must be done or I'll be forced to take rooms of my own and spare the household the added strain of my presence."

Lady Kilmartyn reacted quickly. "You're too thoughtful, my love. Of course there can be no question of you removing yourself. Alas, you're right, I've been too indisposed to see to the household. If you believe Mrs. Greaves will suit then I wouldn't think to suggest otherwise."

"Mrs. Greaves will be a treasure, my love. When can you start?"

It took Bryony a moment to realize he had turned his attention to her. "As soon as you wish, Lord Kilmartyn." Her voice was cool, unaffected, and she allowed herself a covert glance at him.

And she felt her breath stop.

He was beautiful, there was no other word for it. Tall and lean, with a slightly disheveled elegance that was both charming and impudent, he had eyes of such a deep green she could see them from across the room. He had high cheekbones, slightly slanted brows, and golden hair just a bit too long in a manner that looked dashing rather than unkempt, and his mouth was mesmerizing. A laughing, mocking mouth, made for wickedness. He looked every inch the charming rake he was purported to be, the seducer of beautiful women, yet he was looking at her with no sign of disdain for her ugliness.

She deliberately turned the scarred side of her face toward him, though she wasn't quite sure why. The lord and master of the house would hardly trifle with the hired help when clearly a man like that could have any woman in London. And he already had one of the most beautiful in his bed.

He was watching her, that lazy smile on his face, with no reaction at all to the scarring on her face, and the light from the open doorway was merciless. Could the man possibly be a liar, a thief, and a murderer? Her own father had doubted him.

She met his gaze for a moment, then lowered her eyes politely, the perfect housekeeper.

"Then we would have you come to us immediately, Mrs. Greaves," he said in that enticing voice. "You should take one of our carriages to collect your things."

"There's no need, my lord. It's not a long walk."

"Indulge me," he said softly, and the words rippled down her spine. Her stiff, unbending spine, she reminded herself. He wasn't looking at her anymore, and indeed, he'd probably never really *seen* her. Few people of their class actually looked at servants. It was little wonder the scarring hadn't caused him to react.

"Thank you, my lord," she said in the voice she had worked hard to perfect. Neither meek nor arrogant, upper class nor working class, it was a perfect blend of each, and it had been difficult to master just the right note of subservience without sounding weak. It wasn't that she was naturally arrogant, but humility had definitely never been her strong point.

She stood there for a moment. "Go along then, Mrs. Greaves," he said lightly, dismissing her. "The sooner you get your hands on this wretched hovel the better."

"Adrian!" the countess objected. "It's hardly that."

"You have my permission to spend whatever you need, hire whatever servants you deem necessary," he continued, flashing her his devastating smile, ignoring his wife. "And if you have any problems you may bring them directly to me."

That was never going to happen. She'd underestimated the power of a beautiful man. Being around a devious charmer like the Earl of Kilmartyn was going to be the most difficult part of this entire venture, she realized with a shock. He most certainly gave that wicked, seductive smile to everyone without thinking. She managed the slight bow that befitted her station in the hierarchy of servitude. "Thank you, my lord," she said again, and made her escape.

• •

Adrian Bruton, Earl of Kilmartyn, turned to look at his frail, beautiful wife, laid out so temptingly on the rose-colored chaise that set off her dark beauty to perfection. She was looking at him mutinously, and he knew he was going to pay for his interference.

"She's hideous, Adrian! I don't want her around me. You know how sensitive I am!"

Sensitive as one of the water buffalo he'd seen in India when he'd travelled there. "Don't be absurd, my darling." He always used extravagantly affectionate names for her. It was his small indulgence, a needle to her overweening vanity, when she knew she was the furthest thing from his darling. "There's nothing wrong with Mrs. Greaves."

"Nothing wrong! Did you see her face?"

"Of course I did. She has a few scars from the pox. So does half of England. It hardly signifies."

"Well, you might not mind being surrounded by ugliness, but I do," she snapped.

He was already surrounded by ugliness, the ugliness of human nature at its worst, and he'd been chained to her for close to a decade. He gave her his most loving smile. "Then I'll have her report directly to me on all matters and you won't have to see her," he said softly, knowing it would goad her.

"No!" Her voice shook. "I know you too well. You lust after her."

His smile was derisive. "Either she's abominably ugly or so irresistible a piece that I want her the moment I see her. Make up your mind, Cecily. She can't be both."

Cecily looked up at him, her lower lip trembling. She seemed to have forgotten her manufactured headache.

He should have known it wouldn't last. "Why won't you come to me, Adrian?" she murmured, attempting a winning smile. "I miss you in my bed."

"You surprise me, my love. There are usually so many occupying it that I wouldn't have thought you'd notice." The retort wasn't a wise move on his part, but there were times he couldn't resist.

"You're such a bastard," she snapped, forgetting her headache. "If you won't satisfy me you can hardly blame me for looking elsewhere. Since I have no intention of letting you out of this marriage you might at least take advantage of its pleasures." She stretched one leg out on the chaise, her rich skirts riding up over her perfect, plump ankles. Ten years ago it would have driven him mad with desire.

Today it simply seemed like an absurd affectation. He could find pleasure anywhere he turned, and without the poisonous afterbite of this black widow spider. "I wouldn't think to trouble you when you have the headache, my precious," he said, pressing a soft kiss to her forehead. And he walked from the room, closing the door quietly behind him.

He headed straight for his study on the first floor, as far away from her as he could get, barring the kitchens in the basement and the servants' quarters at the top of the house. He went to the cabinet he always insisted be kept full, reaching for the bottle of Irish whiskey. It was eleven in the morning and he didn't give a damn. He could do what he bloody well pleased and today it pleased him to get drunk. He poured himself a glass, then drank it down without ceremony. He felt unsettled, uneasy, and he couldn't pin down why.

And then it came to him. The new housekeeper, with the pulled-back hair, the prim mouth, and downcast eyes. She hadn't the faintest idea how oddly tempting she was. There was something about her that had struck an odd chord inside him. Was it lust? He was accustomed to that. He found many women desirable, and while the stiff Mrs. Greaves was hardly his usual sort, he found himself wondering what kind of body she had under that hideous dress. And whether he was going to ignore convention long enough to find out.

He poured himself a second glass, taking the time to savor its smoky flavor, the warm afterburn of it against his tongue, and then he dropped down on the sofa where he'd slept many a night, stretching his long legs out in front of him. He had a great deal to think about. There was the usual—how to divest himself of his despised wife before he strangled her. How to end this tedious existence without having his entire life be brought to ruin around his ears for one stupid mistake, one idiot act of trust.

And now one more question to trouble his mind. Who the hell was the woman he'd been fool enough to hire as his housekeeper?

He'd always liked a challenge, and she was so tightly buttoned up she might as well be wearing armor. How hard would it be to strip off that armor?

She was a little thin for his tastes, when he liked women to have curves, but he could overlook that. The few pockmarks were scarcely noticeable, and he didn't give a damn about them. It was her eyes that drew him, the eyes she tried to keep hidden, downcast like a proper servant. Dark blue, almost indigo, and while she tried to look subservient he could sense her impatience.

She wasn't a proper servant—he'd guessed that immediately. It was clear in the way she carried herself, the tilt of her head, her manner of speaking. She was no down-on-her-luck widow looking for a job, he was willing to bet his life on it. And she had no intention of letting him get anywhere near her.

Yes, he did like a challenge. He wasn't sure whether he was going to seduce Mrs. Greaves, or simply see if he could make her smile, but he was always interested in a challenge.

Who the hell was she? And why had he invited her into his house, a house filled with so many secrets? Keep your friends close and your enemies closer was an adage that had been drilled into him from early on; perhaps that was the reason.

His wife didn't want her here. That should have been recommendation enough, for he had no greater enemy than the beautiful woman he'd once loved to distraction.

Perhaps he'd been imagining danger where none existed. She might simply be a gentlewoman, forced to earn her living by catering to the whims of people who should have been her equal in this bloody, convoluted society that ruled England and therefore the Ireland of his birth and his soul. Why should her sudden appearance have anything to do with the dark stain on his honor?

There was no harm in erring on the side of caution—he would have to keep an eye on her. Though in truth the cautious thing would have been to let Cecily simply dismiss her. But there was something about the mysterious Mrs. Greaves that interested, no, fascinated him. Despite the unflattering hair, the prim expression of her mouth, she was a pretty woman trying to look plain. Not a beauty—the marked side of her face would always preclude that—but a far cry from Cecily's horror.

But she was so tempting, and he seldom bothered to resist temptation. Besides, any attention he paid her would infuriate his wife, always a benefit.

He rose, crossing the room to pour himself his third glass of Irish, then glanced at his reflection in one of the many mirrors Cecily had placed in the house. The man he saw was a stranger, a charming, golden, slightly drunken English lord. He raised a mocking toast to the man. "Here's to you, lad," he said, slipping into the lilting Irish of his forebears. The ones he'd tried to honor, and instead shamed.

He drained the glass, and turned away.

CHAPTER FOUR

IT WAS INFINITELY REASSURING how well things seemed to come together, Bryony thought later that evening, sipping at her delicious cup of smoky China tea Mrs. Harkins had unearthed. Alfred and Ruby had been dismissed, departing in a huff, but Bertie and Emma had filled in admirably, and Bryony had pitched in, ensuring that the meal was presented and served as it should be, even if most of it was returned untouched.

She took a deep sip of the wonderful tea. She was right where she needed to be, with her sisters safely stowed in the countryside while Bryony did her investigating.

And so she was—starting with the Earl of Kilmartyn. He was the majority stockholder of Russell Shipping. The embezzlement scheme had left his share of the company oddly untouched, and the ensuing bank panic hadn't affected him.

Her father's lawyer had been no help in looking into things—he'd known he wouldn't be paid, and he'd been brutally clear with what little information he had. Her father was a criminal who had stolen everything and left them destitute.

Not that Bryony could ever believe it. Her new employer was the logical villain. He was her father's partner—who better than he to embezzle the fortune that Eustace Russell had spent his life amassing? A house on Berkeley Square cost a great deal to maintain, and the jewels around Lady Kilmartyn's slender throat were impressive indeed.

Was he really capable of such a heinous act? To be sure, he was reputed to have the morals of an alley cat when it came to affairs of the heart—that much gossip had been simple enough to acquire. He also had an extraordinary gift for making the right investments, amassing a fortune so impressive it made society overlook his Irish heritage.

Bryony leaned back in her chair. There was a tiny office just off the kitchen, and her predecessor had left it in a shambles. She had cleaned it herself, had even found a comfortable chair in a storeroom that would definitely need clearing out. The material that covered it was ripped, but it didn't take her more than a few moments to mend it with invisible stitches. Her feet hurt, her shoulders ached, her hands were raw. Given the wretched state of the household, even the housekeeper had to do her part, and the office had needed a thorough scrub.

She could only hope most days wouldn't be so tiring. Housekeepers kept long hours, but they weren't usually responsible for the rough work. Things were so disastrous in Kilmartyn's house that today it was necessary, and perhaps tomorrow as well, until she managed to hire more help. But hard work never did a soul harm, and it kept her mind off things. Such as the darkness in Kilmartyn's eyes, the lines of dissipation around his mouth and forehead.

Dissipation, or guilt gnawing at him?

"Mrs. Greaves?" Emma appeared in the open doorway, looking nervous. "Lord Kilmartyn's asking for you."

The tea immediately curdled in Bryony's stomach. "For heaven's sake, why?" she said, and then could have cursed herself. That wasn't a proper housekeeper's response. She quickly recovered. "Wouldn't you know, just when I've gotten my feet up," she said with a small laugh. She rose. She looked like a mess—her hair had come loose, her ugly worsted dress was wrinkled and spotted, she'd managed to roll up the sleeves and unfasten the neck. She needed to put herself in order, but she could hardly be caught primping. "Could you tell him I'll be there momentarily? I can hardly present myself to my employer in this state." She unfastened the apron she'd found and placed it on the desk.

"I'm sorry, Mrs. Greaves, but he said you was to come immediately. He's in the music room on the third floor and he says it can't wait."

This time she stifled her instinctive curse. Five blasted flights of stairs, from basement, ground floor, first floor through the third, when her feet were killing her. At least she'd been able to keep her own shoes and underclothes when they'd been brought back to London, though the soft, expensive leather was hardly made for such rough treatment. "Then I shall go," she said calmly, rolling down her sleeves.

She had time enough to work on her toilette as she trudged up the servants' stairs. There were no railings to help her—most servants were carrying things when they moved between floors—so she went slowly, refastening her sleeves at her wrist, fighting with her open neckline. The button there was missing, but the tiny bit of throat exposed was hardly noticeable. At least she was blessed in one matter—employers never really looked at servants. They were part of the furniture, existing solely to make the master's life effortless.

She was out of breath by the time she reached the third floor. She moved swiftly through the back corridors into the dimly lit hallway. The double doors to the music room were closed, and for a moment she wondered whether Emma had been mistaken. Bryony would have given anything to simply walk up one more flight to her attic bedroom and curl up.

She stiffened her back. She was a Russell, she reminded herself. She was on a mission, and her father's reputation and her sisters' futures depended on her. She strode forward and knocked quietly on the door.

CHAPTER FIVE

THE EARL OF KILMARTYN knew he was getting drunk. Not as drunk as he could be, and he hadn't indulged in absinthe for almost a week now. The Irish whiskey worked almost as well, though he wasn't sure if the headache was worse than the aftereffects of the green fairy. He stretched out on a sofa, glass in one hand, waiting for his mysterious new housekeeper to come in and lie to him.

Other men might be annoyed. He was perversely pleased. After all, everyone lied; it was only to be expected. And he was damnably bored with life right now. Having a gently bred young woman wait on him was a novelty not to be missed.

She looked familiar, but he couldn't imagine where he would have seen her before. Granted, the scattering of pox scars on one side of her face should have made her memorable, but he couldn't place her. It was something about her eyes, perhaps. The dark, almost indigo eyes she tried to make cool and detached. Maybe she was a wandering lunatic, bringing danger into his household.

Wouldn't that be delightful? he thought with cynical amusement. *One could only hope.*

He heard the quiet knock. Most servants scratched at the door, not wanting to intrude on their masters' lives more than necessary. They were supposed to be like fairies, managing everything while they were unseen, invisible. It was simply unfortunate that he always noticed things.

It must be part of his bloody Irish heritage. Another thing to thank an absent God for. He was far too fanciful—what other grown man would even remember the notion of fairies?

"Come," he said.

She slipped inside the room, the proper shadow of a servant. She looked different, though. Her hair was coming loose from its rigid arrangement of braids, curling slightly around her face. She was rumpled, and tired, and he knew he should feel guilty. She shouldn't have worked herself into exhaustion in his household.

Then again, for some distant reason she had sought this out. He intended to find out why.

"Lord Kilmartyn?" she said, polite and professional, not like a damned spy at all.

He didn't bother to sit up. "What color is your hair?"

She stiffened. "I beg your pardon?"

"I asked you what color your hair was."

She frowned at him. "Is that why you sent for me, sir? It could hardly matter."

A little saucy for a housekeeper, he thought with approval. *This could be fun.* "Does it matter why the master of the house sends for you?" he said loftily. "I wasn't aware I needed to justify my request."

She flushed. "Of course not. I beg your pardon, Lord Kilmartyn."

"Pardon is granted. What color is your hair?"

"Brown," she said flatly.

"Not it's not. I distinctly see some lighter shades in there, now that it's coming loose from that damnable arrangement you showed up in."

She put a nervous hand to her hair, trying to smooth the escaping tendrils back. It was a lost cause—they had a mind of their own. "Sir, if I might be so bold, I have had a long and tiring day. Your household is in dismal condition, and I've barely put a dent in it."

He waved a dismissive hand. "You're right; this place is abominable. If you're tired then sit. It's just you and me. No one to spy on us. We can do anything we please, break any rules we want to."

She jerked, clearly unsettled. Was it the word "spy" or his very mild suggestion of bad behavior? "I believe I will stand, sir."

Such dignity! She was playing her part very well, and it was a part. He wasn't quite sure how he knew it, but nothing could shake his conviction. He smiled at her lazily. She could play the housekeeper, he could play the drunk. He could hold his liquor far too well, but she wouldn't know that. "I must admit, Mrs. Greaves, that I have, in fact, forgotten why I sent for you," he confessed, deliberately adding a faint slur to his voice. The Irish was more noticeable as well—it came out when he was drinking. "But you might oblige me by fetching me another bottle of this lovely stuff."

She started, realization dawning on her. "You're drunk."

"That should be, 'you're drunk, my lord,'" he said reprovingly. "Or, 'you're drunk, Kilmartyn' if you wish to be familiar. Or 'you're drunk, Adrian' if you want to be more than familiar. And indeed I am," he lied. "Very drunk. These things come up from behind and surprise you, and since I'm already almost entirely castaway I may as well finish the job."

She stared at him for a long moment. She had very fine eyes as well, though he probably shouldn't mention them. She moved across the room, picked up one of the small bamboo-style chairs, and sat in front of him. He smiled at her with deliberately boozy benevolence. He could see her shoes, and very fine shoes they were indeed. Not the shoes of a house-keeper.

"I believe, Lord Kilmartyn, that you'd be better served by going to bed. You're going to feel miserable in the morning as it is."

He laughed. "My dear Mrs. Greaves, I'm well acquainted with the bloody aftereffects of a night of debauchery. I barely notice it anymore."

There was an odd expression in those dark blue eyes of hers. Presumably contempt, though he could fancy it looked like something else. She was most likely some sort of spy, he told himself, though for the life of him he couldn't imagine who would have sent her. His worst enemy already had proof of all his secrets. And he was married to her.

"So tell me, Mrs. Greaves," he said with an attempt to sound business-like, "you started the day in my appalling household and found it dread-fully understaffed with a complement of six servants. By the end of the day we have only four. How is that progress?"

He was expecting faint color to blossom in her pale cheeks, but he'd underestimated her sangfroid. "The two servants I dismissed were unpro-ductive and having a most unfortunate effect on the atmosphere."

"And whom did you sack, Mrs. Greaves? I hope not that pretty, buxom creature who always gives me such welcoming glances?"

"Ruby? Yes, she was the first to go," she said, and he could hear faint disgust in her voice. "Alfred, your very handsome footman, was the other. Unless he was the one giving you welcoming glances."

Damn, she was saucy! "Not my style, Mrs. Greaves. My wife, however, might be upset."

That startled her. So, she hadn't yet realized that the beautiful Lady Kilmartyn was a libidinous harpy. It would be a happy surprise.

"I'm afraid that in my household the servants aren't available to their employers for sexual trysts," she continued primly.

"Are you included in that edict, Mrs. Greaves?"

For a moment she didn't understand his meaning. And then she did color, just slightly, and he counted it a triumph. She was playing her part so well, so rigidly in control that he was determined to break her.

He smiled at her. She was pretty and she didn't know it, which was always an enchanting combination. He pulled his attention back to the topic at hand, not giving her a chance to answer his purposefully outra-geous question. "So, do you think you have a chance in hell of putting this wretched household in order?"

She wasn't used to cursing, he noticed by the faint flicker in her eyes. So she'd had a sheltered upbringing. That made the whole farce even more intriguing.

"Of course," she said calmly. "I am used to running far larger house-holds. For a house this size I would expect no less than four footmen, a boy for lugging things, at least three parlor maids, perhaps more, a maid for the mistress, a scullery maid, and a valet for the master."

"Absolutely no valet," he said quickly, a little too quickly for someone supposed to be castaway. "I'm not some fey Englishman who can't dress himself. I've done so since I was six years old—I don't need someone fussing at me. If society doesn't like the way I dress then they can go fuck themselves."

He'd shocked her with his language, but she didn't waver. He saw the almost imperceptible rise of one eyebrow as she chose to ignore his deliberate crudeness. "Aren't you English, my lord?"

"It's an Irish title. I'm a fish out of water in this bloody place." He shouldn't tell her that. She was a spy, and he was confiding in her. That was the trouble with drinking too much, he thought.

"Nevertheless, right now you are a gentleman living in London society. A valet will simplify matters, and if you end the evening . . . indisposed he'll be able to help you retire."

Oh, lovely, he thought, hiding his expression behind half-lowered eyelids. It hadn't even occurred to him until she mentioned it. Mrs. Greaves was going to have to help his supposedly drunken carcass to bed. That was full of possibilities. "I'll consider it. As for the rest of the staff, do as you please. I trust you." Now there was a lie of monumental proportions.

She nodded, all dignity. "I won't betray that trust."

A magnificent lie in return. They were well matched. "I'm afraid my wife can prove difficult. If you have any problem simply come to me."

"I will endeavor not to give cause for disturbing her."

"She already has cause. She's a jealous woman."

The woman . . . what was her name . . . Brianna? Bryony? Something like that. She just stared at him. "You've had even more to drink than I thought, my lord. I'm hardly the sort of woman men are attracted to."

He laughed, just a soft sound, but said nothing. He cocked his head, surveying her. Beneath that astonishingly frowsy dress she was a little thin, but even in his slightly inebriated state he could see curves. Respectable breasts, the faint flare of hips. He wondered how the late Mr. Greaves performed in bed. Not well, he suspected. She held herself like a spinster.

A sudden thought struck him, and he frowned. "Are you a widow, Mrs. Greaves? Or is the 'Mrs.' merely a courtesy title taken on by house-keepers?"

He could see her flash of hesitation. "A widow, my lord. My husband died."

"How?"

He'd flustered her. "A carriage accident."

Another mistake. It was unlikely the husband of a housekeeper would be riding in a carriage. A coach or a wagon, perhaps, but carriages were mostly reserved for the upper classes.

To which this woman clearly belonged. He managed to focus on her. Definitely a spinster. In which case a virgin. Too bad—virgins were best left entirely alone.

"You're going to have to take me to bed, Mrs. Greaves," he said. It was difficult to hide his amusement as a look of shock and horror washed over her face. "Don't jump to conclusions, my dear. While I'm never too drunk to perform, I suppose I ought to leave the staff alone. It's damned hard to find a decent housekeeper."

She rose, effectively shielding her reactions now. "I'll call Bertie."

"I want to go to bed now, Mrs. Greaves. I don't wish to wait for the footman, and if my memory serves me Bertie has never been remarkably swift. If we wait I'll pass out and be too heavy even for him to move. I've fallen asleep on this settee before and it's damned uncomfortable. I'm going to feel miserable enough in the morning—I want the comfort of my own bed. I'm not going to molest you, my dear woman. I merely need your support." And to emphasize his demand, he pushed himself up to his feet, weaving slightly. Deliberately.

She caught him, and he draped his arm around her shoulder as she braced his waist. "Just . . . guide me to my rooms," he said, letting himself slur, "and then you can leave me to suffer the results of my indulgence."

"Overindulgence, more like," she muttered beneath her breath, and the slight northern accent she'd been using had vanished, giving her the same clear tones of society he was used to. *Caught you, my girl.*

He tried not to put his weight on her—she was stronger than she looked, but he weighed a good amount more, and if he was going to knock her over beneath him he wanted to wait until there was a mattress handy. He concentrated on the warmth of her, the feel of her as she slowly guided him down the hall.

His rooms were on that floor, while Cecily kept quarters on the floor below, so they didn't have to navigate the stairs. Like a good housekeeper she already knew which were his rooms, and she guided him into them.

He was expecting cold and darkness. Instead the gaslight had already been lit and there was a fire burning in his bedroom for the first time in months, taking the damnable spring chill off the place.

Christ, he didn't care if she were a spy; as long as she was this good at seeing to his comfort she could have all his secrets.

Except for the one, he reminded himself. Couldn't let that one go—too many people depended upon him. Cecily had managed to find out, and used that knowledge to try to control him ever since, but he was too old and too cynical to risk letting that dark knowledge out to anyone else. He hadn't been careful enough. He wouldn't make the same mistake again.

The darkness was closing in as they approached the bed. Damn, he'd drunk more than he realized. For a brief moment he wondered if he could manage to hold on to her as he fell, and what she would do. She smelled . . . delectable. He wanted her beneath him, he wanted to kiss that prim mouth into soft acquiescence. He wanted a thousand things he couldn't have.

He let go of her, falling onto the mattress, his grasp slipping free, and he closed his eyes.

• •

Bryony looked down at the Earl of Kilmartyn. He was half on, half off the bed, and she managed to push him onto the mattress with an undignified grunt. The man weighed a ton, for all that he seemed too lean. She stared down at him then, trying to summon the appropriate disgust for an inebriate. She'd seen servants the worse for wear, but never a gentleman, and she had to admit he held his liquor well. Even on the edge of passing out he had barely slurred his words, and it had taken the brightness of his eyes, the deliberateness of his gestures to realize just how drunk he was.

He should have looked revolting, lying there on the bed. Instead he looked beautiful, like a young boy, his overlong hair tousled around his face, the lines momentarily relaxed, the cynical tilt of his mouth softened.

Did you kill my father? she thought, keeping the words silent. *Did you betray his trust, rob him blind, and then have him murdered? All for the sake of money?* She reached down and brushed the hair away from his face. He didn't move—she could probably get on the bed and jump up and down on it and he wouldn't awaken.

She looked at him and tried to summon hatred. Anger, disgust, contempt. All she could feel was sorrow for the darkness that infused him. He looked like a boy, despite the lines around his eyes and mouth, like a man who'd lost his way. And she was being ridiculously romantic. At best he was a drunkard and a lecher. At worst, a man who would betray and murder his friend.

She knew what she wanted the answer to be. She didn't want this man to have taken everything from her. He was probably like every other aristocrat in London society, interested in women and wine and gaming and little else.

She unfastened his cravat, pulling it loose, then plucked the gold studs from his shirt, placing them on the table beside the bed. As she removed each one the white shirt fell away, exposing his chest, and she stared at it, momentarily mesmerized.

She'd occasionally glimpsed shirtless men—farmworkers at her father's estate in Somerset. They'd been burly men, covered with hair.

Kilmartyn's chest was different. His skin was smooth, a white gold, with just a faint tracing of hair. His nipples were dark, flat . . . and she flushed. Why was she doing this? She'd never even considered nipples before. She removed the last stud, then pulled the shirt free from his trousers. He needed to eat more, she told herself, trying to be professional. He was too thin.

ANNE STUART

But she could see why one of the most acclaimed beauties of the London season had married him. A woman would throw away almost anything for a man who looked like this, she thought. She found herself reaching out to touch the skin of his stomach, her hand seeming to have a will of its own. His flesh was smooth, warm, alive, and for a moment she let her fingers slide across the skin in an unthinking caress. And then she pulled her hand back as if burned.

Shoes, she told herself, practicality rearing its head. She was hardly going to be rhapsodizing about his toes. She yanked them off, dropping them on the floor, leaving his hose alone. There. He looked as comfortable as he was going to be.

She glanced around the room with a practical eye. The man was clearly drunk, and imbibing too much had certain well-known effects. There was a bowl of fruit, untouched, on a table near the fire. She dumped everything out of it and brought it back to the bed. If he were going to cast up his accounts at least he might manage to use the bowl. It would make cleaning up easier on the servants, and they had far too much to do right now while they were understaffed and trying to catch up with months or perhaps years of neglect.

She took one last look at him, trying to steel herself. He could be the man she hated most in the world, the author of all the pain and sorrow life had visited on her sisters. Instead he looked like a fallen angel, doomed and sad.

If she'd ever managed to conjure up a dream lover he would look like Kilmartyn, with the warm skin and the haunted eyes and beautiful, cynical face.

But she was never going to have a lover, conjured up or real. She was never going to feel the touch of a man's lips against hers, never feel him cover her in the darkness, take the love and ease she could offer. She couldn't move, staring down at him. He was drunk. Unconscious. He would never know if she gave in to temptation.

She had kissed her sisters, kissed her father. She had barely spoken to men, living in seclusion as she had. And she would go back into seclusion once she restored her father's name and his fortune.

34

But she could take this. No one was watching, he'd said. No spies here. Take just this much, and no one would ever know.

The bed was high, but she was tall, and she pulled herself up to kneel on the mattress. He was breathing softly, steadily, in a drunken stupor, she reminded herself. And she leaned over and pressed her lips against his.

His lips were firm beneath hers, almost as if he wasn't in a drunken stupor. It must be very close to what a real kiss felt like.

But she'd read more than her share of French novels over the years. She could let her lips trail down the side of his face, nibble at the edge of his mouth. She could taste the smoky flavor of the whiskey, feel the warmth of his breath against her, and she wanted to kiss him again, harder.

For a moment she almost imagined a response, as if he were reaching up for her with only his mouth, and she pulled back in a panic. He lay as he had been, unconscious, unknowing. She scrambled off the bed and practically ran for the door. What an idiot she'd been! He was married, he was the enemy. Why had she risked everything with that one moment?

She closed the door very quietly behind her, even though slamming it wouldn't have woken the drunken earl, and she moved toward the back stairs. She was exhausted, every bone and muscle of her body aching with weariness, but she had to go back down to the kitchens to ensure everything was finished for the night, everything was set for the morning. Her bed called to her, and she wanted to weep with tiredness.

Squaring her shoulders, she started down the stairs.

Kilmartyn slowly sat up in bed, rubbing his fingers against his mouth, as if he could hold the kiss there. How very odd of Mrs. Greaves. How very delightful of her. He'd had her totally convinced of his inebriation, and he'd felt her hand touch his chest. It had taken all his concentration to lie still, hoping she'd investigate further. The soft, feathering touch of her mouth, with its delightful innocence, was almost obscenely arousing. One shouldn't lust after an innocent. He'd lifted his hand, prepared to slide it behind her neck and hold her still for a kiss of complexity and desire, but he'd let it drop, continuing on in his feigned stupor. He'd have time. Most clearly he'd have time enough to savor Mrs. Greaves.

Now if only his wife would fall off some convenient cliff.

CHAPTER SIX

HE YAWNED. IT WAS EARLY, far too early to be awake, but Cecily, Countess of Kilmartyn, was at heart a ridiculously provincial woman, despite her aristocratic heritage, and she always wanted him out of the house before the world was up and about. The man calling himself Rufus Brown pulled on his clothes lazily, refusing to be hurried. She looked deliciously sated, as she ought to, and she rolled over to admire him as he dressed. He was an inventive man, and he knew how to keep her enthralled. Obsessed, even.

"I fail to understand, my darling," he said as he sat down on the bed to finish dressing, "why you're even interested in what your husband thinks? He couldn't care less whether I spent the entire day in your bed, or fucked you on the steps of Saint Paul's. It would be one thing if you were prey to the softer emotions, but you and I both know that neither of us are capable of something as maudlin as love. So why do you make such a fuss about the man?"

She looked at him from her dark, sharp eyes. "I despise losing anything I consider my own. Including my husband. Oh, in terms of power I have him where I want him, where any woman should have her husband, firmly under my heel. One misstep and I could crush him, and he knows it, and hates me for it. Which is something I quite enjoy. What I can't bear is his ability to ignore me."

"No man could possibly ignore you, my sweet." Rufus took his cue promptly, wondering how quickly he could escape. "He's simply pretending he's indifferent, filling his time with women of no consequence. Have you seen him maintain a mistress for more than a few months? Your husband seems more interested in variety than constancy. And that, my darling, is because he still fancies you." It was an absurd lie, but Cecily was neither remarkably bright nor terribly observant, and she took it as her due.

"It's not that I mind his affairs," she confided, leaning back and letting her eyes run over him. He knew she would want him to come back to bed with her after talking, thinking about her unattainable husband, but he really couldn't afford the time. She was a venal woman, though, and he had to tread carefully. A house of cards could collapse with one strong puff of wind.

"No?" he questioned politely, using Cecily's silver shoehorn to put his own footwear on.

"After all, there is no one in London whose sheer physical beauty can possibly compare to mine, and I don't mind if he settles for less. It's just that woman . . ."

Rufus was getting bored, but then, Cecily had always bored him. She was simply a beautiful, annoying means to an end. "What woman?" he said wearily.

"The new housekeeper. She's a tall, skinny, washed-out creature with a hideous face! He hired her deliberately. It was an affront, a deliberate one, to insist the creature join my household. And he's insisting on dealing with her, telling me the strain is too much for me."

She was sounding positively disgruntled, and he controlled his urge to laugh. She must have backed herself into that mess with her protestations of exhaustion and pain. Considering their active night he could testify that the only exhaustion Cecily, Countess of Kilmartyn, suffered was from a surfeit of fucking.

But his job was to placate her. "Kilmartyn is doing it to annoy you, darling. How could he possibly prefer her to you? It sounds as if she's perfectly ghastly. Of course, the pathetic woman is undoubtedly grateful for any attention Kilmartyn might toss her way, but he would hardly lower his standards to sleep with her when he can have anyone in London."

"He can't have me," Cecily said promptly, which he knew was an outright lie. "Whether he beds her or not, I want her gone. She got rid of my favorite footman."

"Ah, yes, the esteemed Alfred."

"I won't have it, Rufus! The woman would fall into his bed in a welter of gratitude, and do anything he required of her. Anything! He's only doing it to spite me."

"Are you hatching evil plans, my love?" Rufus murmured as he buttoned his waistcoat.

She smiled up at him demurely. "Always."

He made himself smile back. "I'm here to help you, my love. Is there something you need taken care of? A throat to slit, a reputation to ruin? You know I'm your man."

"Get rid of my housekeeper."

Rufus glanced at himself in one of Cecily's many mirrors. He had trained the most adorable curl to fall to the middle of his forehead, and he arranged it carefully before turning back to her. "Fire the woman."

"I can't. I didn't hire her—Adrian did."

"How did you let that happen? You've always held the running of the household, haven't you?"

Cecily looked sullen. "No longer. He hired the wretched woman over my objections, and I know he's planning on seducing her, just to spite me."

Rufus allowed himself a small smile. "That's not very wise, considering the trouble you've had maintaining a housekeeper. Trifling with the servants leads to nothing but trouble. Besides, I thought you told me she was hideous?"

Cecily sniffed. "Not exactly hideous. One side of her face has pox scars, which I find most distressing. You know what a sensitive creature I am—I need to be surrounded by beauty. Ugliness makes me melancholy." She gave him a doleful look. "Unfortunately my wretched husband is an insensitive brute. He had the temerity to tell me she was pretty!"

Rufus laughed. "Darling Cecily, we're all insensitive brutes when it comes to pussy. We take what's available."

Cecily sat up, affronted. "I beg your pardon?"

"Not you, my pet. You make your lovers work for it." He gave her his most charming smile. "The greater the challenge, the greater the reward, and you are magnificent."

"You redeem yourself, Rufus, but just barely," she purred, a faint hint of menace in her voice. "I want you to get rid of the housekeeper for me."

"And how do you propose I do that? Shall I simply strangle her and dump her in the Thames?"

Cecily laughed uneasily. She had no idea what he was capable of, and he preferred to keep it that way. "Of course not."

"Will she be hiring new staff?" he asked, doing his best to sound only randomly interested.

She shrugged. "I suppose so. We need more footmen, and Mademoiselle told me that the maid told her that the woman thinks she can hire a valet for him. As if my husband would be gentleman enough to use the services of a valet. He's bog-Irish and always will be, and I was a fool to marry him."

"Bog-Irish or not, he's got a gift for making great pots of money, darling. Yes, I know, money isn't everything but it does solve a multitude of problems. And pays for all that lovely jewelry you like to adorn yourself with." He leaned down and pinched her willful little chin. "Leave it to me, my precious. I'll take care of things."

* * *

Bryony woke early, the gray sunlight coming in her newly cleaned windows, and she groaned. The tiny space under the eaves wasn't that bad, considering the state of the household. The bed was small and narrow but there was a comfortable chair, a desk, a washstand with decent china. The cupboard held her two cheap mourning gowns as well as one dress she'd managed to hold on to when they had left the house they'd grown up in.

There was even a rug beneath her feet, a rug she'd had to hold out one of the windows and shake fiercely. And the windows were wonderful, now that they were clean, letting in a view of the rooftops of Mayfair. She was like a bird, she thought, perching high overhead, looking down on everything.

The bed had seen better days, but it wasn't any worse than their previous accommodations. That made her think of her sisters, and for a moment she felt such longing, such worry. They would be fine, of course. Nanny Gruen would look after them, and sooner or later some nice young man would show up and fall in love with Maddy. A rich young man would be perfect—he could see to Sophie as well—but if she had to choose she'd prefer kindness.

Not that her sisters would be amenable to her choosing their husbands. They were both strong-minded, though Sophie was more interested in playing prospective suitors one against the other. In her first season she'd evinced not the slightest interest in any of the young men flocking around her.

Maddy was different, more sober, sensible beneath her pretty exterior. Tarkington had been on the verge of offering when the news of their father's disgrace came, and he'd beat a hasty retreat. So had everybody else. No one had any interest in associating with the impoverished daughters of a dead thief who'd almost brought the financial structure of a nation to a standstill.

Of course, it could simply be a matter of the very strict rules governing mourning periods. In six months' time, with their fortune restored and their father's name cleared, the girls could begin to emerge from the shroud propriety demanded of them. Within a year they could reenter society and even entertain offers, though some might frown at the haste.

She needed her sisters taken care of. She needed not to lie awake in this narrow, uncomfortable bed and worry about them, as she worried about so many things.

It would be about five in the morning, she guessed. Something had woken her—voices, perhaps, though she couldn't imagine who else might be awake at such an ungodly hour. She might as well get up. Perhaps when this household was better ordered she could sleep in one slothful hour later, but right now she had work to do. The sooner she got this household running properly the sooner she could start concentrating on finding out the truth about her employer. He was hiding something, she just knew it. But was it something evil, or simply the normal secrets that seem to creep into one's life?

The kitchen was a bustle of activity, and the wide table was spotless. Mrs. Harkins was in the midst of kneading dough, and she looked up when Bryony came in.

"I sent a message to one of the girls who used to work here," she said. "Begging your pardon for being so forward, but since Becky knows this kitchen and my work habits, and she was in need of a job I thought . . ."

"Very resourceful, Mrs. Harkins," she said in a soothing voice, glancing over at the wide copper sink where a young woman was scrubbing pots. "I'm sure you're the best judge of your own kitchen."

The cook beamed at her, clearly pleased her own area of power wasn't threatened. Bryony continued. "Would you like me to present the menus to Lady Kilmartyn or would you prefer to do it?"

Mrs. Harkins looked skeptical. "Her ladyship usually just waves me away when I try. She says the thought of all that food makes her ill." There was no disguising the hurt in Mrs. Harkins's voice. "I've been taking it to the master the last few weeks. At least he looks at it, and I know I'm not going to lose my place for ordering venison from Scotland and oranges from Spain."

"You won't lose your place—this household is lucky to have you," Bryony said firmly. "Let's start with her ladyship. When does she usually wake?"

"She's already had her first tray. We bring her hot cocoa first, then follow it with a breakfast tray that she never touches. Emma was just about to carry it up."

"Then I'll go with her," Bryony said decisively.

Facing the haughty countess was not high on her list of preferred duties but anything was preferable to the fascinating earl. She doubted she could look at him without remembering the forbidden feel of his skin beneath her hand, his mouth beneath hers. What kind of madness had filled her last night? One would have thought she was the one who was drunk, not Kilmartyn.

The countess was reclining in state in the sitting room Bryony had first been taken to when she arrived there, following the dutiful Emma. It was on the second floor, and her first impression was heat and cloying perfume. It took all her strength not to cough.

Mademoiselle Hortense, the countess's haughty maid, barred her way, her thin body rigid. "Her ladyship has not asked for you," she said in her heavily accented English.

"Oh, never mind, Hortense," Lady Kilmartyn's airy voice floated to the door. "I may as well see her. Come in, Mrs. Greaves. How can I help you?"

Cecily, Lady Kilmartyn, looked as beautiful as ever. Today the dark curtains were pulled back, and Bryony could see her quite clearly. It was little wonder Kilmartyn had fallen in love with her.

Cecily was staring at her with cool disdain, though she was keeping her gaze carefully focused on Bryony's right ear, the furthest part of her face from the scars that marred her, and suddenly Bryony thought of her mother. Her mother had managed to never look at her directly once she'd recovered.

She took a deep breath and managed a pleasant smile. "I've brought the menus for the week. Mrs. Harkins did an excellent job of planning, but we need your approval, and it would help to know if we're to expect any guests in the next fortnight."

"I fail to see why that's any of your concern."

"We want the household to be ready if you do have guests. So you can take pride in your surroundings."

Cecily Bruton's eyes narrowed. "I don't give a tinker's damn about my surroundings. You think you have me fooled, Mrs. Greaves, but I wasn't born yesterday. I know why you're here."

Sudden tension ripped through Bryony. How could the woman know? Was Kilmartyn the true villain, and his wife his accomplice? And was her disguise so poor that it took less than a day to penetrate it? She kept her face impassive, saying nothing.

"You're here for my husband, aren't you?" Lady Kilmartyn said accusingly.

Well, in fact, that was the truth, though certainly not in the way Cecily Bruton meant it. "I'm here to serve you, my lady." The words burned her tongue, but her tone was just the right side of servile.

Lady Kilmartyn had shifted her gaze to Bryony's shoulder. "Women love my husband," she said, as if she hadn't heard Bryony's words. "He's irresistible, and I'm afraid servants have always been fair game for the master of the house. If you haven't come to seduce my husband then you'd be far better off leaving. Today. We can do very well without a housekeeper, and you'll be generously compensated."

"Your ladyship mistakes the matter," Bryony said. "His lordship has no interest in me, or, in fact, any of the staff. I came here looking for nothing but a job, and trust me, I am eminently qualified to handle your household."

"I don' t like you." The words were flat, unequivocal, and Bryony wanted nothing more than to return the sentiment.

"I'm sorry, your ladyship. I'll do my best to keep out of your way. If you would just sign the papers approving the menus then I'll leave you . . ."

Lady Kilmartyn took the papers in her thin, bejeweled hand, and slowly, methodically ripped them in two. She dropped them on the floor and then looked Bryony full in the face, wincing dramatically as she took in the scars. "I do believe these menus are unacceptable. Make up new ones. And I want you to do it, not Mrs. Harkins. I recognize her semiliterate scrawl. In fact, Mrs. Greaves, I want you to make up complete menus for the next three weeks, so I have something to choose from. Assuming, of course, you stay that long."

Bryony didn't blink. This woman was her enemy, and she had no idea why. She did, however, have enough sense not to react. "Of course, Lady Kilmartyn."

"You're not wanted here," the woman added in a low, scathing voice. "The sooner you realize it the better."

The animosity was bewildering, and Bryony broke the cardinal rule of servitude. She asked a question. "Why do you dislike me, Lady Kilmartyn?"

The woman was momentarily taken aback. "Because my husband likes you. He never would have interfered if he wasn't attracted to you. He wants to bring his affairs into my house and I won't have it."

"Lady Kilmartyn, have you taken a close look at me?" Bryony knew she had, of course, but she seemed to have forgotten one essential fact. "Why would any gentleman, in particular a gentleman who could presumably have anyone he wanted, be interested in the likes of me? You're worried for nothing." It was too familiar of her, but she was at a loss.

"You think he could have anyone he wants? Because he's so handsome, so charming, so wickedly appealing? I knew you wanted him—I could see it in your eyes the moment you looked at him." The woman's voice was rising, moving toward hysteria, and the maid rushed over, flashing a furious glance at Bryony.

"Now, now, my lady, don't let that one disturb you," she murmured soothingly. "She will be gone soon enough, and you will have nothing to worry about."

Bryony desperately wanted to point out she had nothing to worry about now, but Hortense glared at her, and she decided retreat was her best course. "If your ladyship will excuse me . . ." she began.

But Cecily Bruton's voice rose to a scream. "Get out, get out, get out," she shrieked, as Hortense put her skinny arms around her and began to soothe her in French.

Bryony decamped.

She made her way back to the kitchen, slowly enough, giving herself time to consider the unpleasant interview. Clearly she was going to have to deal with Kilmartyn after all.

Mrs. Harkins looked up hopefully when Bryony returned to the kitchen, but one look at her face and her empty hands told her what she needed to know. She sighed. "Should have gone to the master first," she said.

"I had decided as much myself," she said composedly, ignoring her apprehension. "When did he last approve the menus?"

"Not for weeks, Mrs. Greaves. Bertie will take his tray up and he can tell you when his lordship might be ready to see you."

"It won't be for a while," Bryony said caustically. "And I have errands to do."

"I beg your pardon?"

"He was quite the worse for drink last night. He barely made it into his rooms. Tell me, is that a common occurrence in this household?"

"Not common, but not unheard of," Mrs. Harkins said carefully, clearly not wanting to malign her employer, and Bryony immediately realized her mistake. She should never have mentioned it, never have questioned, but tact had never been her strong point.

"Of course," she said, dismissing it. "That's not unusual. It was an impertinent question, but I need to visit the employment agency to find us new help and I planned to hire a valet for his lordship today as well. If he was frequently . . . indisposed that could alter my choice."

Everyone turned to look at her in astonishment. Bertie was busy shining shoes, Emma gathering a mop and bucket, but the sudden silence was broken only by the sound of Becky, soldiering on at the sink.

"His lordship doesn't wish to have a valet," Mrs. Harkins said finally. "He refuses."

"Which is why I will have to be extremely resourceful in hiring one," Bryony said, unperturbed. "In the meantime, follow the menu you had planned. I'll deal with his lordship later."

She didn't hesitate any longer. After her unpleasant interview with Lady Kilmartyn she found she was in desperate need of fresh air, and there were servants to be hired. She wrapped her cloak around her and stepped out into the cool morning air to make her way to the employment agency.

Bryony had mastered the circuitous paths surrounding Berkeley Square and their old home on Curzon Street, and she arrived at Lawson's Agency for Domestics in a good amount of time. They greeted her arrival with appropriate delight, plying her with tea and small cakes.

"I have a most startling suggestion, Mrs. Greaves," Mr. Lawson himself said when she finished listing her requirements. "I beg you will hear me out."

"Certainly, Mr. Lawson," she agreed. He was a kindly man, slightly patronizing, but with a good heart.

"Just today the perfect man to serve as valet to his lordship arrived on our doorstep like a gift from heaven. I do think you should consider him."

"It would be extremely shortsighted to ignore a gift from heaven, Mr. Lawson," Bryony said, reaching for her cup of tea. "Tell me about him."

The Earl of Kilmartyn never liked coming home. He always rose early, no matter how much he'd imbibed the night before, and he was out of the house before his loving wife could arise. He'd spent the early morning at the stables, watching the horses being put through their paces in light of the upcoming derby. Then his club provided a quiet place to read the paper and pick at the excellent food offered, and in the afternoon he played cards at Ridgely, the latest in a line of popular houses that offered both gambling and available women. He ignored the women, left the table nine hundred pounds to the good, and decided to walk home. The longer it took him the better—he had a great deal to think about. His brand-new live-in spy wouldn't have time to be a problem—the house was in too much disarray. He could always go out, but he wasn't in the mood for loud voices and bright lights; he wasn't interested in willing women and inventive sex. He was in the mood to play games.

He climbed the front steps, two at a time, and was astonished to see it open before he had to apply his cane. Mrs. Greaves had already improved things.

A strange man stood there, dressed in the sober black of an upper servant, his head lowered as he ushered Adrian in. "Your lordship," the man said smoothly, and automatically Adrian handed him his gloves and hat. "I hope you had a most pleasant day."

"And just who the hell are you?" Kilmartyn demanded irritably. He never liked surprises—they were usually unpleasant.

The man reacted with perfect calm. "I am Smyth, my lord. Your new factotum."

Kilmartyn raised an eyebrow. "And what is a factotum, may I ask?"

"It is Mrs. Greaves's term. I am here to oversee the male servants, act as butler and majordomo, sommelier, dogsbody, and, I'm afraid, your valet. Mrs. Greaves thought you might not object too strongly."

Kilmartyn looked at him. "I distinctly told Mrs. Greaves I do not want a valet."

"And indeed, sir, I understand that most thoroughly. Don't think of me as a valet, think of me as . . . as an assistant. I have already put your clothes in decent order, and I've arranged things to be just a bit more useful. I hope I've done so to your satisfaction." His voice was the flat, expressionless tone of a good servant, his eyes were lowered, but something was different about Mr. Smyth, and Kilmartyn couldn't pinpoint it. Jesus, had she brought another spy in?

"We'll see," he grumbled. "I won't want you hovering around, scrubbing my back while I'm in the tub or watching me put my underwear on."

"Indeed not, sir. I am here to make your life more comfortable, not more difficult."

Kilmartyn heard it then, just the faintest echo in the man's voice. He had a good ear, though, and could pick an accent from a handful of words. "You're Irish. County Sligo," he said suddenly. "And your name's not Smyth."

That broke through the automaton's demeanor. His head jerked up, looking at Kilmartyn in surprise. "Collins, my lord. From Ballymote."

"And was it my housekeeper's suggestion that you change your name?"

"No, my lord."

The man wasn't about to offer more unless Kilmartyn prodded him. He prodded. "Then explain why you don't use your own name like an honest man."

"I am an honest man!" he said, a trifle too sharply for a servant. "My lord," he added a moment later. "The great households of London have no particular fondness for Irish servants. I'm more likely to get work if I'm assumed to be English."

Kilmartyn's laugh was without amusement. "While you're with us you'll be Collins," he said. "Not that I expect you to be here long. My wife has a habit of driving servants away."

"My lord, if may speak frankly, I need this job. It will take a great deal to drive me off."

Kilmartyn tilted his head to survey him, just as his new housekeeper bustled into the entrance hall. She looked ruffled, her hair escaping those braids again, her pale cheeks flushed. In fact, she looked delectable, proving to Kilmartyn that perhaps the games he had in mind might be a bit too dangerous. For both of them.

"I beg your pardon, my lord," she said hastily, her proper accent slipping out. "I meant to introduce you to Mr. Smyth."

"Collins," Kilmartyn corrected. "We use our real names in this household." He wanted to laugh at the notion. He doubted his housekeeper was using the name she was born with.

"Yes, well, Collins, then. I know you said you didn't wish to hire a valet, but Mr. Collins seemed too well qualified on every level, and I required help. You did say I was free to hire whatever staff I deemed necessary."

"And I did say no valet."

"You may use Mr. Collins as much or as little as you require, my lord," she said smoothly, so smoothly he knew that Collins's real name had come as no surprise. In fact, he had little doubt the devious creature had hired him deliberately, knowing that a second-rate Irish lord would find a second-rate Irish servant more palatable. He had the pleasant suspicion that Mrs. Greaves was going to prove a formidable opponent.

And she *was* looking pretty today. Her eyes were sparkling, her cheeks were rosy, and she really did have a tempting mouth, a cupid's bow on top with a full lower lip he wanted to nip at. He wanted to see what kind of shape her body was beneath those dark, baggy clothes. Not that he should. He never had sex with courtesans or servants. He wanted to be sure his women were willing, not forced to his bed by financial considerations. But for the mysterious Mrs. Greaves he might allow an exception to his personal rule.

"You're a very clever woman, Mrs. Greaves," he said in a silky voice.

She wasn't foolish enough to take that as a compliment. She maintained her starchy demeanor, one at odds with her rumpled appearance. She'd been working too hard on his house again, he thought. "I hope I provide good service, my lord."

His smile widened, and he wondered if she recognized the wickedness in it. "Oh, you will, Mrs. Greaves."

She did. She stiffened even more, then relaxed, as if she thought she'd misread his intention. Foolish girl.

And she was a girl. Even if her years on earth were close to thirty there was a certain innocence about her. Mrs. Greaves was no widow. She was a virgin. And he liked unsettling her. He hadn't made up his mind whether he'd do anything about his odd, powerful attraction to her. Bedding servants was bad enough; bedding a spy could be disastrous.

But there was that lovely mouth.

Not now, unfortunately. "I'll be in my library," he said abruptly. "I have work to do."

"Very good, my lord," Collins said. "Will you be going out later?"

He glanced at his housekeeper. Bryony. That was too uncommon a name to take—it was more than likely her own. Just as Greaves most certainly wasn't. "Nothing for now. In fact, the two of you can go off and leave me alone." He sounded bad-tempered and he didn't care. For some reason the woman irritated him. Fascinated him. Aroused him. And he had to decide just what he was going to do about it.

She didn't blink. She wasn't a servant, but she was a damned good actress. That might be why he found her slightly familiar. He must have seen her onstage at some point. For some reason he'd assumed she was here on her own volition, but now he realized the unlikelihood of that. Women were seldom bent on spying, his wife being the exception. Mrs. Greaves must have been hired by someone to infiltrate his household. He wondered if those scars were even real.

But who could have hired her? He was outspoken in his views about independence for Ireland, and those views were very unpopular, particularly since the latest outrage caused by the Fenian rebels. More than thirty people had died in the explosion at Clerkenwell Jail, and a hundred were injured, and the call for redress had been immediate and fierce. If the police had caught any of the Irish Republican Brotherhood, the group behind the bombing, the rebels would have been torn apart by the angry mob.

But there was no one to heap the blame on. No one knew it had been his money that had financed that plot, a plot he'd been told would be a peaceful distraction to get their leader out of jail. It didn't matter that they'd lied to him—he wasn't born yesterday. His money had paid for a bomb that killed people. It was on his head.

And his secret. Only Cecily knew, and she used her knowledge like a whip to keep him in line. He had no idea what would happen if he were found out. Whether he'd be up for charges in the House of Lords or treated like a common criminal. Barrett, the man who'd set the bomb, had been publicly hanged last year. Who was to say he wouldn't follow? He had no seat in Parliament, those being relegated to only the oldest of the Irish peerages, but he had friends who could vote, wastrel friends who could be influenced, political friends who were sympathetic. But not if they found out he had been involved in the Fenian Outrage.

There were any number of politicians with opposing views who might be looking for ways to discredit him. They wouldn't find any cause in his household. He'd severed all connection with the Irish Republican Brotherhood, and there should be no trace of his generous donation. Nowadays he kept his excesses in full view, and while they were notorious, he was no worse than many of the less upright members of society, simply less discreet. Being a lord, even an Irish one, excused any amount of misbehavior, be it gaming, sexual indulgences, or a surfeit of alcohol.

There was no way in hell they could find out the one thing that would discredit him entirely. Cecily was the keeper of that secret, and if it were out it would be worthless to her. The value was in the holding of it, and she would protect it with her cold, black heart.

Mrs. Greaves had vanished into the cavernous hallway without a word, and he knew a moment's regret. Collins remained, still holding his gloves and hat. Kilmartyn glared at him. "Go away," he snapped.

"As you wish, my lord," Collins murmured.

Kilmartyn stared down the hallway where Bryony Greaves had disappeared. After a moment he headed for his library, trying to ignore temptation for the very first time in his life.

CHAPTER SEVEN

NOW DIDN'T THAT SABOTAGE all her plans, Bryony thought as she headed back down to the kitchens. She'd been busy every single moment since she'd risen at that ungodly hour—once she'd returned from the employment agency she'd assisted with the cleaning, with the intention of taking sole responsibility for Kilmartyn's study and whatever papers might be there, but Emily had insisted on helping her, and all her efforts to dislodge the girl had been fruitless. So instead she'd spent hours scrubbing fireplace bricks and polishing doorknobs, cleaning windows and shaking out rugs. She hadn't wasted time looking for a bathing room, but tonight she had no choice. She was filthy.

She'd hoped to make it back to the study when they'd finished cleaning for the day, but the new employees arrived, and Mr. Lawson's suggestion had been brilliant. Hiring an Irishman to serve Lord Kilmartyn was positively inspired, and Mr. Lawson had assured her how rare it was to have found a qualified candidate. His arrival at the agency that very day had been most opportune, and Bryony could only agree.

The others, a new footman and two new maids, were exceptionally well chosen. Interviewing them, getting them settled, and instructing them in their duties had taken the rest of the day, and she had devoutly hoped that she could slip away during dinner, having been told that the earl never returned home until the small hours of the morning.

Apparently they'd been wrong. Now he was ensconced in the library, the most logical place for her to find any evidence of wrongdoing, and there was no way she could search the place.

Belowstairs they had already eaten their supper. Becky was scrubbing dishes while Mrs. Harkins sat by the stove with a disheartened expression.

"What's wrong?" Bryony asked, shoving her disordered hair away from her face.

"Not a thing, Mrs. Greaves. At least, nothing I'm not used to. I made *truite meunière*, followed by the most succulent of lamb chops, some fresh spring potatoes with mint and parsley, a baked turnip with watercress glacé, and they won't eat." Her torture of the French made Bryony hide her smile. "Her ladyship says she requires nothing but toast and tea, and his lordship—"

"His lordship says he is not to be disturbed," Collins spoke from behind her.

Mrs. Harkin's face crumpled. "It's a waste of my time and genius! It fair to breaks my heart, working so hard over a meal only to have it tossed back in my face."

There was an awkward silence in the kitchen. They all knew that the vagaries of their employers were sacred and that life was unfair, and there was no comfort to offer the poor woman.

The hell there wasn't, Bryony thought. "Mrs. Harkins, please make up a tray."

The woman brightened slightly. "Would you be wishing to try this, Mrs. Greaves? If I'd known the quality weren't going to be eating I could have fed it to the staff, but everyone's eaten a full meal."

"Thanks to your most excellent cooking I'm sure that the staff is as full as I am. No, I'm bringing it to his lordship."

"If he's in a mood he might throw something at you," Emma said, worry in her voice. "He doesn't like to be disturbed."

"I can duck."

"Allow me carry it for you, Mrs. Greaves," Collins said. "I expect it'll be right heavy." The Irish was coming out now, and Mrs. Harkins was eying him with fascination.

Bryony hesitated, then nodded. "You may carry it to the door for me, but I'll be the one to bring it in. He's less likely to chuck something at me than you."

"I wouldn't want you to think his lordship is not a good master," Emma continued earnestly. "You'll never see him raging like the countess. Sometimes, though, he's ... er ... not well when he's home."

"Three sheets to the wind, you mean," Mrs. Harkins snapped, her annoyance with her lord and master overcoming her natural discretion.

"I'd still rather face him in a towering black mood than her ladyship," Emma said stoutly.

Mrs. Harkins peered at her. "Why, lass, do you have a weakness for his lordship? That's a very bad idea, that is, and I'd be more worried except that I know Ruby never got anywhere with him, and she just about threw herself naked at his feet to try to get his attention. He doesn't trifle with those beneath him. So you just get any such foolish notions out of your head. There's nothing that will lead to disaster surer than thinking you're in love with the quality."

Emma had flushed a beet red. "I know my place, Mrs. Harkins."

"See that you remember it," the cook said gravely.

Bryony decided it was time to intervene, ignoring the odd pang that had struck her. In truth, it was her place to warn Emma, not the cook's, but she hadn't wanted to get involved in any kind of discussion about the Earl of Kilmartyn.

"I think Emma understands your concern, Mrs. Harkins," she said gently. "And I believe she's wise enough to know what's proper in a good servant. She has you for an example."

They both looked gratified rather than offended, and Bryony breathed a silent sigh of relief. While she'd dealt with staff issues, their own housekeeper had handled tricky situations like this one, so Bryony simply had to rely on her instincts. Then again, she'd had plenty of practice with her argumentative sisters.

The heavy silver covers were set on the tray, and Collins picked it up. "If the sight of such a magnificent meal makes his lordship violent then I vote we put him on a diet of bread and water."

Mrs. Harkins blushed prettily at the compliment. "Happen he might prefer it."

"Never, my dear Mrs. Harkins," he said, and the lady practically beamed.

They moved through the hallways at a calm, decorous pace. At one point Collins spoke. "Should I have brought a bottle of wine, Mrs. Greaves?"

"He drinks too much already," she said tartly.

A moment's silence. "Is there anything else you should acquaint me with concerning his lordship?"

Bryony sighed. Discretion was one thing; necessary knowledge was another. "I imagine you'll have to help him to bed, though as yet I don't know how often. There have been a number of comments that have led me to believe this is a fairly common occurrence. As you've doubtless noticed, the earl and the countess do not share a room, or even a floor. You have yet to meet her ladyship, but I suggest you be wary."

"Is she truly the tartar they suggest she is?"

Bryony instinctively shrugged, then froze as she remembered that a proper housekeeper is not likely to shrug, or to have such conversations with her underlings. Fortunately Collins was concentrating on his passage through the halls without knocking over any of the delicately balanced silver cutlery and he hadn't noticed.

Bryony considered her words. "I've dealt with her ladyship twice, and I would call her high-strung, perhaps. She doesn't like me much, but I don't think she'd have anything against you."

He nodded. "So I am to assume his lordship and his wife do not get along?"

Bryony thought about it. "He was nothing but charming toward her, even as he overruled her when she was not entirely enthusiastic about taking me on. He did threaten to move out if she didn't capitulate, but that was simply a joke. I can't imagine a man turning his back on her." For some reason she found that thought intensely depressing. She should be used to it by now.

Her mother had made it clear—the only value a woman had was her beauty. Once Bryony had lost hers at age twelve she became worthless in her mother's eyes, a useless appendage to a wealthy family. Her mother had forced any number of cosmetic treatments on her, from cold buttermilk compresses to steam baths, but nothing helped. The cosmetics her mother had insisted upon cracked the first time Bryony had laughed, and her mother had slapped her, the brittle stuff crumbling beneath her hand.

She could still remember her mother's words. "You may find this amusing but I don't. You're a leper, and you're doing nothing to improve things. You'll have no choice but to stay hidden away like some mad relative, out of sight and out of mind. People won't be able to bear the sight of you."

"Because you can't bear the sight of me," she'd responded.

Her mother didn't waste time denying it. "There's a new doctor in Basil—"

"No more treatments," Bryony had said sharply. "The scars aren't going away, Mama." She looked into her mother's beautiful face, the face she'd passed on to her three daughters, looking for any sign of love or affection. All she saw was thinly veiled disgust.

She reached up and pushed the crumbling makeup off her face, and it dusted the plain, slightly oversize dress she wore. "I suppose I'm simply going to be the madwoman in your attic, Mama."

She'd embraced that role with enthusiasm, locking herself in her rooms, refusing to come out despite her sisters' blandishments, despite her father's pleas. She'd sat and stared at her reflection in the mirror, until something inside of her broke, and she took up her fire poker and smashed every mirror in the room. She had been sixteen at the time.

There had been three mirrors. Twenty-one years of bad luck, Bryony mused, and she'd barely made it through the first twelve.

They'd reached the library door, and she lifted her hand to knock sharply when she heard Collins's swift intake of breath. "What is it?" she whispered as alarm spread through her.

Mr. Collins cleared his throat. "I think perhaps this isn't a wise idea. His lordship is clearly—"

"Clearly what? You can't see beyond a closed door," she hissed.

"I have a particularly strong sense of smell."

She looked at him in frustration. "And what do you smell?"

"Anise. Fennel. Flames. Burning sugar."

"Good God," Bryony said. "He must have thrown something into the fire..." Her voice trailed off, as she realized on such a warm evening no fire had been laid in the library. "More reason for us to intervene." And before Collins could stop her she rapped sharply on the door, then pushed it open.

Just as the Earl of Kilmartyn ordered her to go away. She paid no attention, trying to take the heavy tray from Collins's strong hands, but the man simply shrugged, entering the room and setting it down carefully on the desk where Kilmartyn sat. He had a tall glass in front of him, filled with an odd, milky-looking mixture that was slowly turning green.

"Mrs. Harkins has prepared a marvelous dinner for you, Lord Kilmartyn, and I know you would never think of offending her by ignoring her efforts."

He just looked at her, his face impassive. Then he turned to Collins. "If you ever barge into my library again I'll throw you out the window," he said in a deceptively charming voice.

"Yes, my lord," Collins said meekly, not missing the menace beneath that tone. He started to back out, then paused, as he realized Bryony hadn't moved from her place beside the earl's desk.

"You may go, Collins," she said calmly. "There's no need to protect me from his lordship. He's hardly likely to throw me out the window."

"I might be tempted," he muttered, letting his green eyes move over her in an oddly assessing manner.

She made a shooing gesture, and Collins left, clearly reluctant, closing the door behind him. She removed the covers from the dishes, and the odors were wonderful, filling the room, overcoming the strong, not unpleasant scent of anise. What in the world had he been eating before they came in? Some sort of confection?

He looked at her, then down at the tray. "You brought enough to feed a horse," he observed.

"You're too thin." The moment the words were out of her mouth she realized her mistake. No servant should ever comment on her employer's physicality, except in discreet praise.

He didn't seem surprised at her slip. "So are you," he said. "I have little appetite. I eat when it pleases me."

"As do I," she said, bitterly aware of her own body. She wasn't precisely skinny, but she was a far cry from the lush curves popular nowadays. She had breasts and hips, but her flesh was undimpled. Maddy had described her as "coltish" in an effort to ameliorate her frustration, and in return Bryony had simply neighed.

His lids drooped over lazy eyes. "I'll make a bargain with you, Mrs. Greaves. You've guaranteed that Cook's meal is outstanding enough to interrupt me in my library. If you expect me to partake of it, then you'll have to share it too."

"I've already eaten. And her name is Mrs. Harkins, not 'Cook.'" She didn't bother to keep the note of censure out of her voice.

Instead of being offended, Kilmartyn looked amused. "I'll do my best. I suppose that means I'm to call John Coachman by his real name."

"Do you have a coachman?" she asked, startled. One more person to oversee.

"He lives back in the mews and takes care of his own meals, and for that matter his name is Taggart. He's an extremely bad-tempered soul, so I suggest you steer clear of him. He's under my authority, not yours. Pull up a chair, Mrs. Greaves."

She considered it, and him, for a moment. He was a very unsettling employer, alternating a devastating charm with flashes of brooding temper. In her relatively sheltered life she had met few Irishmen, and they were notoriously volatile.

She could walk away, but one was supposed to acquiesce to an employer's demands, even the unreasonable ones. She turned, found the smallest, most uncomfortable chair, and brought it over to the other side of the desk, facing him across the heavily laden tray. "I've already eaten, my lord," she said again, her patience wearing thin.

He was watching her, a cynical amusement in his eyes. "Not much, I wager. You need fattening up." He handed her a delicate silver utensil. "You'll have to make do with the cake fork, I'm afraid since Cook . . . beg pardon, Mrs. Harkins . . . didn't realize you'd be dining with me. In the future would you please have her set two places on my dinner trays."

"Your wife will join you?" she said hopefully.

"My wife would rather eat dead rats than look at me while she eats. And I'm bored—I require company if I'm to eat regular meals. So just add that to your list of onerous duties, Mrs. Greaves."

She looked at him, startled. "You expect me to take my meals with you?"

"Just supper. If I happen to be home. Don't worry—it will be all business. My wife is too . . . delicate to deal with the running of the household, so you'll need to report to me. Do you like fish?"

The added question startled her. "Yes."

"Good." He took the bread plate and placed a healthy portion of the *truite meunière* on it, along with the turnip and minted potatoes. The smell was divine, and Bryony realized she hadn't eaten very much of Mrs. Harkins's nourishing but bland stew.

She couldn't sit there and eat his dinner. It was simply . . . wrong. She tried again. "I'm really not hungry . . ."

"And I really don't care. Eat." Beneath all that affability there was a note of steel in his voice, at odds with his well-honed charm, and Bryony picked up her fork.

It was delicious. Meltingly so, and Bryony let out a soft moan of appreciation as she savored it. And then she realized Kilmartyn hadn't touched his food, he was watching her with hooded eyes and a faint smile. There was an odd heat in his eyes, something she didn't recognize.

"Do you realize you look and sound positively orgasmic when you eat something wonderful?" he said softly.

She shouldn't ask, she knew it, but she couldn't let it go. "Orgasmic? I'm not familiar with that term."

NEVER KISS A RAKE

For a moment he stared at her blankly, then he leaned back in the chair and hooted with laughter. Bryony's back stiffened, and she set down her fork, thoroughly annoyed. "I'm glad you find me so entertaining, my lord. I'm gratified to know I've relieved your boredom."

He was still laughing when he sat forward, tears in his eyes. "I think I'll wait and explain that term a little later in our relationship, Miss Greaves."

"Mrs. Greaves, my lord," she corrected him gravely.

He merely smiled, and took a bite of the fish left on his plate. He closed his eyes for a moment, then looked at her. "Definitely orgasmic. Pray give Mrs. Harkins my compliments."

"I will, my lord."

"Could you cease all the 'my lord'-ing?" he said. "I've told you to stop. It's becoming tiresome."

"I could say 'your lordship,'" she offered.

"Jesus, no. That's even worse," he said, and she flinched at his casual curse. "Don't call me anything."

"Whatever you wish, my—" She stopped herself with an effort. There was a reason to use titles in any conversations. It made the class distinctions clear, and she didn't want to slip and start talking to him like an equal.

"Whatever I wish, eh?" he murmured. "Eat your trout—it's too good to waste."

She finished the portion on her plate, being careful not to make any more signs of appreciation that he could comment on. He ate lazily, leaning back in his chair, picking at his food, then finally set the plate back on the tray. "That's enough," he said. "It's more than I usually eat."

His portion had been smaller than hers, and he had a goodly amount left. "You didn't like the fish?" she said with a sinking heart. After all, overseeing the food was her responsibility.

"The fish was delightful. I just don't eat much."

"You should make an effort. It's not healthy to live off your own nervous energy."

"Worried about me already, Miss Greaves? I'm touched. If I need to eat I will. Food is easy enough to come by if people have the means."

"And if they don't?"

"Then they beg on the streets, sell their bodies for a pittance, rot their brains with gin, and give their children away. They die young, and the next generation takes their place, disease-ridden and desperate. And the English government does nothing about it, both here and in Ireland."

She was momentarily shocked by both his words and the intensity behind them. "And what are you doing about it?"

He blinked, as if realizing he'd said too much. "Doing?" He shrugged. "I give to charity, I charm a few politicians, but my main pursuit is pleasure. Fortunately that's as easy to find as a starving orphan."

There was no missing the faint bitterness in his voice. "And in your own house, my lord. You have a beautiful wife." Her voice was stiff.

Once more he was amused. "The pleasure I intend to pursue in my own house isn't my wife, Miss Greaves. And don't call me 'my lord.'"

"Then why do you insist on calling me 'Miss' instead of 'Mrs'?" She knew no servant would address their employer in that tone, but she couldn't help it.

He leaned forward, and his smile was devastating, lighting his dark green eyes, the kind of smile to mesmerize some vulnerable young girl who didn't have better sense. Fortunately she was neither young nor vulnerable, and her common sense was excellent. She was immune to that charm of his, even as she felt her skin warm.

"Because, *mo chuisle*," he said softly, sounding very Irish indeed, "You're as sure a virgin as I am Irish. There was no Mr. Greaves, there was no anyone. You're untouched, and that's a crying shame."

She froze, her skin heating. He was having the strangest effect on her normally obedient body. At his words she felt her stomach tighten, as strange, warm sensations moved through the lower part of her body in a most disconcerting manner. What was wrong with her? She finally found her voice. "I don't think that's any of your concern, my—" She stopped in the nick of time.

"Don't you, now?" He smiled at her, but his eyes were steady, gazing into hers. "We'll have to see about that."

"I really should check on the kitchen," she said hastily, suddenly desperate to escape. "The new maids and the scullery girl seem very capable, but I should—"

"I have complete faith in your judgment. I think they'll be perfectly fine. Their work should be done—most of them have probably been enjoying themselves."

"I'm exhausted," she said quickly, no lie. And this verbal sparring was making things worse. "I should retire."

"It's only nine."

She looked at him suspiciously. This was going all wrong, and she had no idea how to put things back on the proper footing. He wasn't treating her like a housekeeper, and she wasn't responding like a proper servant. "What does 'macushla' mean?"

"Nothing so terrible, Bryony. I'll tell you later."

She wondered how he even knew her first name. She'd had to sign papers, but he should hardly have been interested in such a triviality, not enough to remember it. She straightened her back. This had to stop. "I believe you should call me Mrs. Greaves, not by my given name. Those are reserved for housemaids, not upper servants, and I believe I've earned the honor."

"You may have earned the honor, my heart's delight, but you most definitely haven't earned the Mrs."

Enough was enough. She stood up, so abruptly she knocked the dishes, and she caught them before they fell on the floor. "I believe I'll retire, your lordship," she said sternly. "Bertie will remove the dishes." He didn't rise. Of course he didn't, she was a servant, she reminded herself. "I haven't dismissed you, Bryony." It was a challenge, with a charming smile and eyes of forest green.

Servility could only carry her so far. "But I've dismissed you, my lord," she said serenely, and sailed from the room, closing the door behind her.

She should have been horrified by her temerity, shocked by her boldness. But she heard his laughter behind the heavy door, and breathed a sigh of relief. The Earl of Kilmartyn was proving to be far more of a challenge than she'd expected, but she could deal with him.

She'd been a fool to think this was going to be easy. She had expected he'd be gone, that she'd be able to search his office and any other place that might hold critical information while she directed the servants to work in other areas of the house, but so far she'd been run ragged, and he'd been home, when he should have been off somewhere. She'd also imagined she'd be invisible, as a good servant should be. But the Earl of Kilmartyn insisted on looking at her, at *her*, not her scars, and his attention was most unsettling. It caused her stomach to flip around in a ridiculous manner, it caused an odd, not unpleasant cramping sensation lower down. It even made her . . . chest area . . . feel sensitive. If she didn't know better she would say he was trying to seduce her. Not that she had any experience with seduction, but she'd read a lot.

It was his form of amusement, she thought, pushing away from the door and starting down the servants' staircase. But she could deal with it. Still, if there was anything she could do to speed up her investigations it would be a good thing. Once she was assured of his innocence she would simply decamp in the night. The Kilmartyns would once more be left without a housekeeper, but they'd muddled through before.

She wasn't quite certain what she'd do if she found proof of his guilt. There was something wrong here, she had no doubt of it, but for some reason she didn't want to think this beautiful, unexpected man had had anything to do with her father's disgrace. Could he really be a cold-blooded murderer and embezzler? She was a fool not to consider such a thing, considering her father's hasty note to himself.

She couldn't afford to ignore it, and she couldn't afford to assume Kilmartyn was innocent. There were secrets in this house, dark secrets; she could practically breathe them in. Whether they had to do with her father or something else, she didn't dare leave until she knew the truth.

Even if the truth wasn't what she wanted to believe.

CHAPTER EIGHT

BRYONY WOKE EARLY, after a nearly sleepless night. For some reason she kept thinking of the Earl of Kilmartyn, the heat in his eyes when he looked at her, and it made her skin feel uncomfortably warm. She would rise and throw open the window, letting in the cool night air, and then grow chilly, and rise to close it again. When she dreamed the images were confused and disturbing, sensual dreams of touching and tasting, so that when she finally awoke the sheets were twisted about her and she was covered with a film of sweat.

Fortunately she'd already requested that a bath be prepared for her, and she'd heard Bertie clumping up and down the stairs, hauling the tins of water. Poor man, and his day had only begun, but he was good-natured and hard-working. As the senior servant, Bryony would be the first to enjoy the bath, and the maids would have to make do in her water, but with such hard toil, so much dust, and the craziness of her disordered dreams, she would have carried the water herself if necessary.

The bath improved her mood exponentially. She braided her wet hair in tight plaits and fastened it in a bun at the back of her neck. She put on her second dress, the one that clung to her curves a little more closely and bared too much of her throat, but she covered it up with a capacious apron and hoped for the best. She was going to have to institute regular bath nights for everyone, and see if she could hire a laundry maid rather than have those duties devolve onto the housemaids, or even worse, their over-worked housekeeper. More and more often small, forgotten tasks had come to her attention, with no one to attend to them but herself. In the two days she'd been in residence she'd laundered and even mangled linens; she'd polished silver that Bertie and the new footman, Jacob, hadn't gotten around to; she had laid fires, emptied ashes, dusted bookshelves, washed windows, and peeled potatoes when the other servants were already busy; and while a part of her found the hard work and her ability to do it and do it well curiously satisfying, it was a far cry from what she'd imagined she'd be doing as a housekeeper. Her back ached, her hands were rough and red, and her legs were a mass of bruises from bumping into things, but she felt a certain buoyancy from the healthy weariness that covered her. More people should engage in physical work, she thought, and then was momen-tarily ashamed of herself. Most people had no choice in the matter. But truly, the idle rich didn't know what they were missing.

Their father had always tried to imbue a strong work ethic in his chil-dren, and he'd been far too successful with his eldest daughter, as well as a complete failure with his youngest. Sophie never stirred herself if she could help it.

But at least her father's puritanical views about work had served Bryony well in the long run.

"His lordship's already up and about," Mrs. Harkins greeted her. "That, or he went out late and hasn't returned home. When Mr. Collins went in with his breakfast he'd already left."

Bryony frowned. "That's odd. He made no mention of plans to go out."

"What did he say to you when you brought him his tray?"

He had said a great deal, but nothing she was prepared to share with Mrs. Harkins. "Oh, this and that," she said in an abstracted voice. "I did notice the library was very untidy. Perhaps I'll work on that while the maids concentrate on hauling out the third-floor bedrooms. They seem nothing more than a repository for old furniture and bric-a-brac." She hesitated. If she was going to discover papers of some sort, wouldn't she be more likely to find them tucked into a drawer in an unused room, rather than the obvious place, his office? "On second thought, I think they should work on windows on such a fine day. Windows and laundry. I've sent a note to Mr. Lawson, telling him we need at least one laundry maid and another footman to wait at table."

"I'm able to wait at table," Mr. Collins volunteered from his seat to her right, putting down the newspaper he'd been engrossed in. An Irish newspaper, in fact, when Bryony didn't realize they printed them in England.

"Thank you, Mr. Collins, but I don't think that will be necessary. You're already stretched too thin as it is. If we need you in an emergency we will call on you, but in the meantime it isn't your place." Servants were incredibly mindful and jealous of their status, Bryony had discovered, much more so than in society. Any democratic ideas she'd tried to institute at Renwick and the town house had been quickly rebuffed.

"Yes, Mrs. Greaves. And what would you have me do today? I made significant progress sorting through his lordship's clothes, pulling out that which needed to be laundered or mended."

"Don't worry none about the mending, Mr. Collins," Bertie said cheerfully. "The gentry don't like mended clothes—they just throw them out and have new freshly made. We usually share the old stuff amongst ourselves, though somes of us resell 'em."

It was a common enough practice, one of the few advantages of the serving class. "And you do the same with Lady Kilmartyn's?"

Mrs. Harkins laughed. "Lord love you, we wouldn't dare. None of us could hardly wear them, and her ladyship worries that some of her more distinctive dresses might be recognizable if someone buys it from a rag merchant. She has that mademoiselle destroy everything she's finished with."

"Destroys them?" Bryony echoed, aghast. "All her expensive wardrobe?"

"Seems to me you could at least take some of the trim off, reuse that," Mrs. Harkins said with a sniff.

"It must be very extravagant," Bryony said tentatively, fishing for information.

"Indeed it is. Not that money's an object. His lordship's rich as Croesus, and Lady Kilmartyn lives to spend it."

"No one has unlimited money," Bryony said.

Mrs. Harkins shrugged. "Well, he just inherited ownership of the ship-building business he started with some cit. Things seem to happen like that—money just falls in his lap. I don't think Lady Kilmartyn needs to worry."

"If she did, I doubt she'd be here," Emma said from her spot across the table, draining her cup of tea.

"Don't let Mademoiselle hear you say that," Mrs. Harkins warned her. "You know she carries tales, and you'd be out on your arse in a moment's notice."

"No, she wouldn't," Bryony said. "The hiring and the firing of the staff has been left up to me, with his lordship having the final word." Unbidden the memory of his objection to the term "your lordship" came back to her, and she could feel her face heat. "Though I will agree we need to treat our employers with the respect they are due."

"I was, Mrs. Greaves," Emma said with a wry grin.

Bryony had to cough to hide her answering smile. Clearly Lady Kilmartyn may have managed to fool most of society, but the members of her household weren't as easily hoodwinked.

"Windows today," she announced, ignoring the faint groan from Emma and her new assistants, Grace and Allie. "I haven't had a chance to check his lordship's room, to see if anything needs replacing. You say he left early today?"

"He did," Mr. Collins affirmed. "Her ladyship has gone out as well. Would you like me to accompany you, Mrs. Greaves?"

"No need," she said airily. "I merely want to check the curtains, upholstery, and such. I've only had a brief glimpse of it on my first tour of the house, and I'm responsible for it." Not to mention a darkened glance when she helped him into bed two nights ago. In fact, she was responsible for everything, a curse and a blessing. No one would ever question why she should ferret around in the earl's bedroom.

If Lady Kilmartyn was out she probably ought to start with her rooms, but she really didn't wish to. And it made sense that if there was some sort of proof to be hidden it was far more likely in Kilmartyn's rooms than those of his despised wife.

She waited until the staff had started on their daily tasks before climbing the servants' stairs again to the third floor where Kilmartyn slept. She was slowly getting used to her many trips up and down the narrow flights, and when she came out into the third-floor corridor this time she wasn't out of breath.

A good thing, since the first thing she saw was a perfect stranger in the middle of the hall, standing at the door to the ballroom, looking for all the world as if he belonged there.

Maybe he did. The morning sunlight came directly in from the windows to the east, illuminating his elegant figure, and she dropped into her customary bow automatically as he strode toward her, entirely at home.

"You must be the estimable Mrs. Greaves," he purred, his voice soft and seductive. "My cousin has told me a great deal about you, but she failed to mention how pretty you are."

Bryony's pleasant smile didn't falter, and she didn't automatically touch her face, much as she was tempted to. "I may assume Lady Kilmartyn is your cousin, is she not? Then the reason she failed to mention my purported beauty is because she considers me . . ." She wanted to say "a hag from hell" but that would hardly be appropriate. ". . . unaesthetic," she said.

He tipped his head to one side, eyeing her, and then he smiled, a winsome, lovely smile. "I expect she was jealous. My cousin is exquisite, one of the great beauties of England, and yet she can't keep from feeling threatened whenever another pretty woman enters her world."

Hardly pretty, Bryony wanted to say, but she was silent. One didn't correct the employers or their friends.

He took a step closer, and the sun glinted off his chestnut hair, and his brown eyes were merry. "Yes, I know, you think I'm flattering you, but you're being tolerant of the silly man. I'm Brown, you know. Rufus Brown."

"Indeed, sir," she answered politely. "Is there some way I may assist you?"

He took another step toward her, but she held her ground, surveying him calmly. He really was quite handsome—beauty must run in Lady Kilmartyn's family. He had a dark curl that rested on the center of his forehead, a seemingly artless foible that she suspected was well honed. He was also doing his best to charm her, but she'd been up against the best. Against the Earl of Kilmartyn, in fact, and she'd managed to resist him. Mr. Brown was child's play compared to him.

He cocked his head, that lovely smile playing around his lips, but the smile didn't quite reach his eyes. "I suspect you are going to be a difficult conquest, Mrs. Greaves."

"I beg your pardon?" Her voice was cold enough to freeze water.

"I always like to have the staff on my side," he added, and for a moment she felt like a fool. He could hardly have meant what she thought he had. "I have a habit of coming and going at odd hours, and I don't like to disturb the household. Lady Kilmartyn and I are . . . very close, and there are times when Adrian can be ridiculously provincial."

He was sleeping with his cousin, she realized with shock. It wasn't unheard of for cousins to marry—in some families it was even encouraged. Queen Victoria herself had married her first cousin, but Bryony had spent her long, empty days in scholarship, and she'd been particularly fond of Egyptian civilization. A civilization that had been destroyed by inbreeding as much as any other influence.

But she was a servant, she reminded herself. It was hardly her place to judge. And if, despite all appearances, the Earl of Kilmartyn really had killed her father then he deserved everything he got. "Very good, sir," she said politely. "Is there anything else?"

"Why in such a hurry to get away from me, Mrs. Greaves?" he said, moving closer. "I might get the feeling you don't like me."

Enough was enough. He was so close she could feel his body heat, smell the scent of sweat and stale perfume that wasn't his. Plus something else she couldn't identify, didn't want to identify. And why was he here in the house when both lord and lady of the house were out? "It's hardly my place to like you, Mr. Brown. It is merely to provide excellent service and see to your needs." Bad wording, she thought belatedly.

"Oh, I have no doubt you will," he said softly. "Good day, Mrs. Greaves."

She stifled her sigh of relief. "Good day, sir," she said in the perfectly neutral, modulated voice she'd perfected for the fictional Mrs. Greaves. She and her sisters had always enjoyed amateur theatricals, and Bryony had excelled as the villain. She had mastered any number of accents, walks, and styles of speaking, which was only one reason she was sure she'd succeed in her masquerade.

The other reason being that she had no choice.

She watched Mr. Brown saunter down the hall, a man certain of his own irresistibility. And indeed, he had reason to be. It wasn't his fault she was entirely immune to it. At another time, another place she would have been trembling and grateful for his faint, sexual innuendos.

But compared with the powerhouse that was Kilmartyn, he seemed like a boy. Kilmartyn must know that no woman could possibly resist him, and yet he didn't walk with that offensive swagger.

No woman apart from herself, of course, she thought quickly.

She waited until she heard his footsteps all the way down the stairs. And then she headed for Kilmartyn's bedroom and slipped inside, closing the door silently behind her.

There was no reason for her to be secretive—she'd already announced to the staff what she was doing. But stealth seemed ingrained, and she leaned back against the door and surveyed the room with the eyes of a housekeeper before she used the eyes of a spy.

It was a large room, with massive windows on the front of the house, though the hideous red curtains were shut tight against the light. The fabric was ugly, gaudy, and it hung around the bed, covered the chairs, covered the walls, and for a moment she was startled. Did Kilmartyn really have such bad taste?

There were two other doors leading from the room, one on each side, and she went to the left first, expecting to find a sitting room. Instead there was nothing but a surprisingly small dressing room, with barely enough room for a chair. There would be no chance for Collins to sleep there, awaiting his master's return after a night of carousing.

The clothing was in perfect order, though she expected it would have been an entirely different matter before Collins had arrived on the scene. Closing the door behind her, she crossed to check the other adjoining room. It was dark, shuttered, the furniture shrouded in linen covers. Odd. The master of the house usually had much more spacious quarters.

And better taste in curtains, she thought, looking at them in disgust. The color was particularly displeasing—garish, jarring. She couldn't imagine how anyone could sleep in here. It would give her nightmares. She crossed the room and pulled the heavy drapes aside, flooding the room with the sunlight of a rare clear day, then turned to look at the room.

It was clearly meant to be a guest room, or perhaps space for an extraneous relative. There were at least six larger bedrooms on the second floor, currently uninhabited, though Bryony had seen to their cleaning. Why was he up here? To get away from his wife?

For that matter, why was Lady Kilmartyn's cousin up here? That made no sense at all.

If it were up to her she would strip the curtains, the wall hangings, everything of this noxious color and put something more soothing in its place. But that was the least of her worries. She wasn't here to make life more pleasant for Kilmartyn, she was here to discover whether he was innocent or guilty of collusion in her father's disgrace and death. There was a small gilt desk in one corner, and she headed for it. In the top drawer there was nothing but a stack of invitations and cards, carelessly discarded, and she doubted she'd find anything of interest there. She sat down anyway, going through them, looking for something out of place, a name, an event that might spark something. But everything was deadly dull—it was no wonder he'd simply tossed them in the desk. Collins would see to clearing out such things in the future.

Indeed, she had no reason to feel guilty for spying. After all, she would be leaving this house and its inhabitants in a much better state than the chaos she'd walked into. Assuming she didn't leave this house with its master in prison.

She pulled open the next drawer, to find cuff links and studs, a gold watch carelessly discarded, a silver brush that had come apart, and a peculiar pin, made of the kind of curling lettering she associated with medieval monks. There were letters—I, R, and B. His last name was Bruton— perhaps this had belonged to someone in his family. The silver looked new, though, and heavy. What was he doing with such a thing?

She closed the drawer, leaving everything intact, and turned, reluctantly, toward the unmade bed.

There should be no reason why she could picture the Earl of Kilmartyn lying in that bed, sheets twined around him, the ugly covers pushed to the floor, wearing nothing but his golden skin. She put her hands to her lips, remembering how his mouth felt beneath hers, and she shivered.

She could remember his chest, smooth, the light dusting of hair in the middle, the heat of his skin. So different from the farm workers. She'd seen them in the fields on blisteringly hot days, and she'd watched in fascination, the way muscles played beneath skin, at backs and arms and strong legs clad only in rough breeches. It had been a purely intellectual interest, she'd told herself. Nothing worse than looking at some of the magnificent paintings and statues in the British Museum, and there she'd seen a great deal more. That strange arrangement of little parts between their legs that no lady should ever observe fascinated her. She knew the mechanics of sexual congress—one couldn't live in the countryside and be unaware of it—but she still couldn't quite figure out how something so small could manage the trick.

Not that she was about to be deflowered by one of the Elgin Marbles, she thought absently. She wasn't going to be touched, deflowered by anyone. So why was she looking at Kilmartyn's bed and thinking about men's parts and deflowering?

She knew why, and her skin grew warm.

She had no idea why no one had made up the master's bedroom yet—she would have to speak to the girls about it. She rose and began to pull the sheets together, yanking them up and smoothing them so that they lay, flat and neat against the mattress, followed by the heavy brocade counterpane. Tucking the sheets underneath the mattress, she suddenly froze as her fingers touched something. A journal, a book of some sort, the leather of the thin spine soft against her questing fingers, and she began to tug it toward her, excitement rippling through her, when she heard a noise.

The Earl of Kilmartyn stood in the open doorway, an unreadable expression on his handsome, saturnine face, and she froze, knowing she was the picture of guilt.

CHAPTER NINE

"LOOKING FOR SOMETHING, Mrs. Greaves?" Kilmartyn said in a lazy voice. And then, to Bryony's horror, he closed the door behind him and leaned against it, all catlike elegance.

She stiffened, as she knew she should. "Of course," she said briskly. "This entire household is under my care, and I wished to make certain your rooms were cleaned and comfortable. I'm afraid the maids have yet to get to your room, and I thought I should help."

"The staff know to leave my room alone," he said, not moving. "They are to come in when I tell them to, and at no other time. I don't like spies."

There was no way she could control the heat that flooded her face, but she pulled herself together, banishing inconvenient things like guilt. "You've hired me to be the housekeeper here, my lord, and it's my responsibility to make certain the rooms are clean and comfortable. If you have a problem with that perhaps you don't need my services."

He seemed amused. "Oh, I most definitely need your services, my dear Miss Greaves. If it would make you happy to have my rooms cleaned daily then feel free to arrange it. In fact, if you wished to do it yourself I could hardly make an objection, and I must admit the sight of your hands tending my bedding is curiously arousing. As for the room, nothing in hell could make it comfortable. The walls and the hangings look like pig vomit, and letting in sunlight only makes it worse. I use this room for sleep and nothing more."

Except for the book beneath the mattress. "I trust my staff to take care of your quarters, my lord. Though I agree these are quite distasteful. Why do you stay here if you hate it so much? There are other more pleasantly outfitted bedrooms on the second floor." She shouldn't be asking so many impertinent questions, but if she didn't, how would she ever discover the truth?

"I like it up here. I just don't like the way the previous owners decorated it. My wife went through and spent a fortune on everything she could, but by the time she got to these smaller rooms she lost interest. After all, they're for poor relatives and unimportant guests, and they should simply make do. Or so she said."

"Previous owners?" she echoed.

"Did you think this was a family manse, passed down by generations of Brutons? We're Irish, Miss Greaves. I'm only tolerated because I'm an aristocrat—I'm sure they'd send me back to the bogs if they could. I bought it from a businessman who lost a fortune in a slight miscalculation. Fortunes are won and lost that way, you know, my dear Miss Greaves. Just one mistake, and everything can disappear."

Was he talking about her father? Thinking about him? Did he think Eustace Russell had truly brought the shipping company to the edge of ruin by embezzlement and then run away to escape the consequences? It could hardly be termed a mistake, if true, and she knew it wasn't. What small mistake could he have made that left him dead and his family destitute? Trusting the Earl of Kilmartyn?

"I wouldn't know, sir," she said in a polite voice, hiding the emotion that surged beneath her faded black dress. "High finance is hardly my concern. This household is."

He was making no sign that he was going to move away from the door anytime soon, and if she approached him there was a good chance that he'd hold his place, putting them in much too great a proximity. Instinct told her that would be a very bad idea.

"So it is," he said softly. "Then what do you intend to do about this monstrosity of a bedroom? Do you have any idea how to make it a more inviting place? As you can see, the bed is large and comfortable. I could happily fit at least one more person in with me." His eyes ran over her body, and she felt a sudden heat. "But I wouldn't want to subject a woman to those curtains."

"I would think your wife would be used to them."

"Don't be disingenuous, Miss Greaves. You know I wasn't talking about my wife."

She didn't blush. She was getting used to him, used to his unsettling ways. "Curtains and bed hangings are easy enough to change. So are wall coverings. And the furniture could be moved to a more pleasing aspect. Since you have no sitting room attached, you need a better place to sit, assuming you prefer to be here and not in the library."

"Considering my propensity for drinking a great deal too much, it might be better to end up here sooner rather than later. We don't want you having to help me to bed again. Next time I might not be so drunk that I'd let you go. Why, I might even go so far as to kiss you."

Bryony froze in horror. He'd been unconscious—he couldn't possibly remember her impulsive action. But he was looking entirely innocent, as if there were no hidden meaning beneath his outrageous words.

She stiffened her back, managing a polite smile. "Indeed, and that is one of the many reasons why I hired Collins. As to whether you decide to kiss him, that will be between the two of you."

Kilmartyn hooted with laughter. "I don't think I'd ever get that drunk, Mrs. Greaves. And I thought you put out an edict that no member of the family bed the staff."

"I did."

"Tell me, Miss Greaves, does that apply to you?" His voice was soft, almost a purr, and she wanted to drift closer, into the warmth he seemed to emanate. Yes, the man was very dangerous to her peace of mind.

She stayed right where she was. "Of course."

He smiled. "Good to know. In the meantime, may I count on you to make my bedroom more habitable?"

Startled, she looked around her again. "If you wish, sir."

"Oh, I wish. So tell me, what kind of colors do you prefer?"

"That should hardly signify."

He looked at her dreamily, his eyes half-closed, a lazy expression on his face. "You have very pale skin, with just a hint of soft rose. I could see you surrounded by a shade of blue. Perhaps a rich, indigo blue to set off all that lovely, creamy skin and your beautiful eyes." He paused, looking positively lascivious. "Yes, make them blue. And every time I slip into bed I'll be thinking of you."

She managed a frosty look, her insides roiling at the image, and he laughed.

"In gratitude, Miss Greaves. God forbid I should think of you in any other way."

She managed a nod. "It will be seen to, sir." There was no way she was going to oversee the transformation of his sleeping quarters, his huge bed. It would be too unsettling. She really should make Collins deal with it. But she knew she wouldn't. "It can be arranged fairly quickly, but I'm afraid the actual work will take a number of days. Where will you sleep while the workers are here?"

"As you pointed out, there are any number of available bedrooms in this household. Who knows, I may even make a few conjugal visits. It's been a while since I've sampled my wife's abundant charms, and she's been making demands."

This time Bryony did blush. She suspected he'd said it simply to see her reaction, but that didn't mean she could control her normal bodily reactions. In fact, her normal bodily reactions were in a turmoil any time he was near, whether he was saying outrageous things or not, and she was having a hard time pulling herself together. "That's hardly any of my concern, my lord," she said in a stilted voice.

"I beg you pardon, my dear Miss Greaves. I've embarrassed you. Consider me all repentance."

He looked about as repentant as a jackdaw. She bowed her head again. "Certainly, my lord."

"How many times are you going to bow at me? How many times are you going to call me 'my lord' when I've directed you to call me Adrian?" he said, that soft, seductive note in his voice once more. And for some wicked reason she thought of the bed behind her.

"When I am no longer employed in your household, sir. At which point there will be no reason for our paths to cross, so in truth, I expect the answer is never."

"You are so bracingly forthright for such a young woman, Miss Greaves. And you are young, aren't you? Your papers said you were thirty-five, but I calculate you're about ten years younger. And yet you seem to be able to manage the servants and the household much more efficiently that any of my previous employees have. What accounts for your frightening maturity?"

"I beg your pardon, sir, but this has nothing to do with my duties, which are being neglected as we speak. If you don't mind I should go check on the kitchen . . ." She moved toward the door, all determination, but of course he remained where he was. Leaving her close, much too close.

"Your first duty is pleasing me," he said, and she felt a little frisson of uncertainty run down her backbone. His half-closed eyes opened suddenly, green meeting her own dark blue, and for a moment she froze, staring up at him, unable to move.

And yet how could she say she froze, when she was suffused with such heat? Never had she felt anything like this. He wasn't even touching her, and yet she felt invaded, taken, seduced, and enraptured, all from the deep, piercing look that caught between them, pulling her like a riptide, and she swayed toward him, wanting to feel his body against hers. Her breasts were hot, there was a tight feeling in her belly, and she wanted . . . she wanted . . . she couldn't name what she wanted. She could only feel it.

And he was feeling it too, she knew it. That look was holding him captive as well, unable to move, staring down at her with fathomless emotion, need and doubt and surprise. Need won out, and he moved his head down toward hers, and she knew he was going to kiss her, really kiss her, going to take her, and she would let him, God, she would let him, and . . .

The sharp rap on the door was a shock to them both, and the tension broke. She fell back, almost stumbling, and he moved away from the door, barking out a sharp "What?"

"Begging your pardon, my lord," came Emma's breathless voice. "But we're looking for Mrs. Greaves. There's been a calamity in the kitchen."

"I'll be right there, Emma," Bryony said, shocked at how normal her voice sounded. She reached up to smooth her hair, but it was still neatly coiffed, she touched the neck of her dress, expecting it to be unbuttoned half to her waist, but it was intact. It had been the most erotic moment of her life, and he hadn't even touched her.

He said nothing, watching her out of his intense green eyes, so different from the languid ones he presented to the world. She opened the door, and it seemed as if sanity rushed back in with the light from the hallway. "If there's nothing else you need, my lord, I'll go see to the kitchen. And you can be assured your drapery and wall coverings will be changed to your satisfaction."

"There's that word again," he murmured, so low that Emma couldn't hear. "Satisfaction. And there's a great deal I still need from you, Mrs. Greaves. But we'll attend to that later."

She didn't show her reaction, the frisson of heat that rushed through her body. Stone-faced, she nodded, and left for the blessed relief of a kitchen catastrophe.

Kilmartyn watched her departure, at a dead run, and laughed softly. This was much more fun than he'd expected it to be. He was doing everything he could to unsettle the cuckoo in his nest, the interloper, the spy, whatever she was.

All he had to do was come close, make some sexual innuendo, and she'd panic delightfully. More proof that the girl was the upright British virgin he knew her to be. Unfortunate, because virgins were not fair game, particularly upright British ones. When he'd so much rather see her horizontal.

He laughed again at his own wicked thoughts. She really was quite lovely. The scars on her face were a trifle—he'd seen worse on aristocrats who'd suffered from a surfeit of spots when they were young. That tawny hair of hers fascinated him, her dark blue eyes nagged at his memory. In fact, his enjoyment of this little game of cat and mouse warred with his discomfort. He was becoming a little too obsessed with her. Despite his reputation he wasn't the heartless rake he was painted, and he didn't like innocents.

But he found he was liking Miss Greaves. Bryony. Very much indeed.

• •
....

"Rats!" Mrs. Harkins announced tragically when Bryony breezed in the door. "Rats in the cupboards, getting into me flour and meal, gnawing on the joint I planned to roast for dinner. I've had the rat catcher in half a dozen times and it does no good, and now there seem to be hundreds of them."

"They do tend to breed," Bryony said smoothly. She'd take rats over the Earl of Kilmartyn any day. "What we need is a cat."

"An animal in my kitchen?" Mrs. Harkins said. "Never!"

"And a dog. The dog will catch the larger ones, the cat will take care of the mice."

"Now I don't mind a dog so much," Mrs. Harkins said, softening. "But cats are nasty creatures. They look at you as if you're put on earth to serve them, instead of the other way around."

Bryony laughed. "That's part of their charm." She glanced around the kitchen. Bertie was polishing silver industriously, Mr. Collins was entering something in the wine ledger, and Becky, the scullery maid, was lurking in the corner.

"So, gentlemen," she continued, "which do you prefer, cats or dogs?"

"Cats," Mr. Collins announced. "They're cleaner, and they hunt for the fun of it."

"Dogs," Bertie said, casting an apologetic glance at Collins. "They're more friendly-like, and they'll take out a rat quick as you please."

"I likes 'em both," piped up Jem, the new boy, as he came in lugging a huge brass kettle of coal. He set it down, taking a deep breath. The coal scuttle was almost as big as he was, and probably weighed as much.

"Jem, I think you should carry lighter loads," Bryony said.

Jem straightened his shoulders, looking affronted. "Lighter? Mrs. Greaves, this is nuffin. I can carry twice as much and not break a sweat, I can."

Tact, she reminded herself. "I'm sure you can, Jem. But we count on you so strongly that we'd be in disastrous straits if you happened to hurt yourself by overdoing."

The grubby face looked slightly mollified. She'd have to see to baths for him as well, though to give him his due he had been mucking about in the coal cellar. "I won't let you down, missus," he said. "And I just happens to know of a dog what needs a home."

Bryony raised an eyebrow. "Really?"

"Happen I do," Jem said. "He's a bit of a stray, but he's a good boy, real friendly-like, and I've seen him catch rats big as cats themselves."

Bryony hid her smile. "And do you know where we'd find this most excellent canine?"

"I can bring him to you, missus. I think I may have seen him in the stables." He was trying to look innocent and failing.

Bryony had already heard the complaints from the coachman about the dog who'd seemed to arrive at the same time Jem did, though he did grudgingly say the dog wasn't half-bad, which for Taggart was rare praise. But she decided not to mention it.

"That would be excellent, Jem. Thank you. You may fetch him when Mrs. Harkins can spare you."

Mrs. Harkins sighed. "You might's well go now then, boy," she said. "Just leave the coal here for now—it's a warm day and no one will be wanting a fire until later tonight, if then."

"I don't suppose anyone has a cat stashed someplace?" she asked idly.

"I can see to that, Mrs. Greaves," Mr. Collins volunteered.

Bryony nodded. "There. Catastrophe averted. Mrs. Harkins, do you have something you can serve instead of the joint, or do you need me to go to the butcher's for you?"

"Oh, no," Mrs. Harkins said cheerfully. "I'll just cut off the part they gnawed on and feed it to the staff."

Bryony opened her mouth to express her horror but stopped as the other servants expressed their delight in such a treat. Belowstairs didn't usually enjoy the luxury of a joint of beef, and clearly they would take it any way they could. She quietly shuddered at the thought. She'd forgo supper entirely, and . . .

Just then she remembered Kilmartyn's casual words. That he expected her to join him for dinner each night, to report on the day's work. Had he really meant it? Dear God, she hoped not. The longer she put off seeing him again the better she'd deal with him. She was still feeling flustered about the oddness of their last encounter.

She shook off the memory. He couldn't have meant it. "Bertie, when Jem returns with the dog would you see that they both have a bath. We don't want fleas invading the household—they're almost as bad as rats."

"I'll help," Mr. Collins volunteered. "I don't expect it's going to be an easy task."

"I'm going out for a bit," she announced. Maybe fresh air would clear her head, exercise would rinse the strange feeling from her body. "His lordship's room needs new curtains and bed hangings, and I'm off to the draper's to make arrangements. I presume everything is calm now and I'm not needed?"

"We'll be fine, Mrs. Greaves," Mrs. Harkins announced. "But do you want one of the men to accompany you? I wouldn't like to think of someone accosting a pretty thing like yourself, all alone out there."

Bryony looked at her in astonishment. Why in the world would Mrs. Harkins say such a cruel thing to her? But Mrs. Harkins was looking her bland, cheerful self, with not a drop of malice in her.

The woman was clearly in need of glasses.

Bryony forced a laugh. "I'll be perfectly fine. I've been out on my own for years."

In fact, she hadn't. Not until her father's death and the ensuing scandal. Before then she'd had a footman or maid with her wherever she went, and the new freedom was one of the few good things to come of the tragedy. Once she managed to clear things up, restore her father's reputation and their privileged lives, she wasn't going to give this up. She wasn't going back to the polite prison that society, even the limited society she'd lived in, dictated.

Her shawl and hat were in her office, and it was the work of a moment to grab them, plunk the ugly bonnet on her head, and start out into the bright sunshine of a spring morning. Weather in London was seldom this glorious—she would enjoy it while it lasted. A nice long walk to the draper's would be good for her.

Rufus lounged against the wall, well out of sight. He didn't mind waiting—he was basically an indolent man, and he knew that sooner or later his patience would be rewarded.

It was sooner. The woman emerged from the alleyway beside Cecily's house, a shawl bundled around her, a ghastly hat on her head, but he'd know her anywhere. Cecily's new housekeeper, wandering where she shouldn't, in the wrong place at the wrong time.

She shouldn't have seen him. No one, not even Cecily's maid, had ever seen him, and he intended to keep it that way. He couldn't afford to have curious servants start spouting nonsense about a man they'd seen, lurking on an uninhabited floor of the Kilmartyn town house.

He'd already promised Cecily he'd do something about the housekeeper. It was a shame—she was a pretty little thing if you didn't see the scarring, and a man could make sure she kept her face turned away from him. All cats are gray in the dark, and she looked lithe and strong, able to withstand a great deal. While he was catholic in his tastes when it came to gender and class, he liked a resilient partner in bed.

But alas, she'd sealed her own fate, simply by getting a good look at him. Too bad. He'd gone to so much trouble to get his own help settled inside the household that any disruption could disturb his careful house of cards. Then again, he'd always liked risk.

It would take but a moment, a brush, a slight push, and Cecily's despised housekeeper would go tumbling beneath the hooves of a horse, the wheels of a carriage. After all, accidents happened all the time, and he knew how easy it was to sabotage a carriage. He'd done so recently. If he continued to walk swiftly no one would ever connect him with the poor young woman lying in the road.

It was the practical thing to do. Pushing away from the wall, he started after her.

It was truly a glorious day, Bryony thought. If she'd been in the country, at Renwick, she could have thrown off her bonnet and danced in the sunlight, with no one to watch or disapprove. On such a warm day she could even slip off her stockings and shoes and go barefoot in the thick grass, with the heady smell of roses surrounding her. The rose gardens at Renwick were renowned, and sometimes it seemed that she missed the flowers more than anything else.

She tilted her head up to the sun, letting the warm rays bathe her face. She'd end up with freckles the moment the sun hit her skin, but since her face was already ruined she never minded the spatter of gold across her nose.

There was no scent of roses in the streets of London. In Mayfair it was relatively clean, but the street reeked of horse droppings and urine, and even in the distance the manufactories were puffing out smoke. She needed to keep her eyes on her destination, not looking upward into an endless horizon that promised nothing. She needed . . .

Something bumped against her, hard. She put out her hands, but it was too late, and she felt herself falling, falling, into the street, the carriages moving dangerously fast, bearing down on her, and she was going to land beneath the deadly hooves ...

A strong hand clasped her arm, yanking her back, and she fell against him as she overtipped her balance. It was all she could do not to fling her arms around the stranger and sob in relief, but she managed to swallow her panic and look up to thank her rescuer.

"Don't you know better than to daydream on a busy London street, Mrs. Greaves?"

It was the Earl of Kilmartyn's lazy voice in her ears, his dancing green eyes looking down at hers, his hand still clasped around her arm.

"Bugger," she said, and then slapped her hands over her mouth.

CHAPTER TEN

KILMARTYN LET HER GO, laughing. "Why, my dear Mrs. Greaves," he said, "wherever did you learn such a word?"

His housekeeper stiffened her shoulders, and he wanted to touch her again. Really, that dress was too dreadful, and the bright sunlight only proved it. It was shapeless, the cloth shiny in worn places, and the hat was an atrocity. He wanted to strip everything off her, down to her doubtless plain underdrawers and chemise. He wanted her naked, bare of any of the things she used to hide from the world. He wanted her hair down around her pale shoulders, he wanted it wrapped around him.

And he'd better damned well stop thinking such thoughts or he'd embarrass himself in the middle of Saint James's Street. The poor darling spy was looking apoplectic, and he wondered what kind of excuse she was going to come up with for her delightfully shocking word. So far she'd been absolutely silent.

She took a deep, audible breath. "I do beg your pardon, my lord. I can only cite the extremity of the circumstance that caused me to utter such an inappropriate word. I'd almost been killed, and I was overwrought."

"You only said it when you saw it was me, Mrs. Greaves," he pointed out gently.

There was a faint stain of color on her cheeks. "Delayed reaction," she said firmly. "As for where I heard the word, I must assure you that I haven't lived a rarified life, and during my work with tradesmen and such I've heard any number of words, including some even you might not know. But it was unforgivable of me to have uttered it."

He tucked her arm under his, not without a small fight on her part, and began steering her down the street once more. They were attracting a great deal of attention, and if it got back to Cecily she could make life miserable indeed for her housekeeper. "First," he said, "it wasn't unforgivable. I'm the only one who was the recipient of it, and I forgive you."

She was regaining her amour propre, and she made the most quiet noise of derision possible. Damn, he liked this woman. "Secondly," he continued, "I sincerely doubt you know any naughty words that I don't. We can have a contest over dinner tonight, but it probably wouldn't do to try it in the street. Someone might overhear and get the wrong idea."

She gave a small tug, but he held her fast. "Don't bother," he murmured. "I'm not going to risk you taking a tumble beneath a carriage again. They drive much too fast down Saint James's Street, and I'd rather not end up beneath the wheels of a coach while trying to rescue you."

She gave up fighting, and he was almost sorry. Until he looked into her dark blue eyes and saw the fury she was trying to hide. "I wouldn't think of bothering you, my lord. I'm certain you have a great many important things to do and you can hardly waste time shepherding a clumsy housekeeper through the streets of London."

"It's odd," he mused, "but you never struck me as particularly clumsy. In fact, you have a certain delicious grace about you, the way you move, the way you scowl at me."

She rose to the bait like a sun-dappled fish. "I don't scowl!"

"You do, particularly when you think I'm not looking. The problem with that, my dear Miss Greaves, is that I always find myself looking at you."

He could feel the tension in her arm, the way she tried to hold herself away from him. He could feel the slight tremor that washed over her at his words. So she wasn't immune to him.

Then again, he already knew that. He knew women well enough to read the signs that they usually didn't bother to hide. The faint wash of color, the sudden intake of breath, the heat of their bodies, even their scent. But Bryony Greaves wasn't like those women, none of them, not the cheerful, inventive whores or the randy duchesses. He'd had a great many women, both before and after his disastrous marriage. He was a man of strong appetites, and carnality was simply a part of him.

He doubted his deceptive, innocent housekeeper had ever had a carnal thought in her life. At least, not until she met him.

"*Mrs.* Greaves," she corrected in a frosty tone. "And you didn't answer my question. Don't you have more important things to do than find yourself consorting with a servant in the middle of Mayfair?"

"Is that what we're doing? Consorting? Would that make you my consort? The idea has a certain appeal. I wonder if the Queen would approve of having both a wife and a consort."

"You know perfectly well what I meant," she snapped, all attempts at servility vanishing. "Even if you don't have anything to do, I am not similarly blessed. Now if you will please excuse me, your lordship." It was a good push this time, but he'd felt her muscles tense a moment before she shoved, and he simply tightened his grip.

"You're on your way to Mr. Peach, the draper, to choose new coverings for my room, and it seemed only logical that I accompany you. I wouldn't want to end up with poison green walls, and I imagine when you think of me the thought of poison dances longingly through your head."

"How well you know me in such a short time."

"I'm very discerning." He was having the best time he could remember in years. She was such a delicious, contrary little bundle, and in truth, he wanted nothing more than to lead her into an alley, slam her up against a wall, and take her, hard and fast, breathless completion for both of them until they returned home to continue their mutual exploration in leisure.

That would have to remain a fond fantasy. For one thing he knew damned well she was a virgin, and you didn't introduce a novice to the art of making love by hard and fast and semipublic. And she wasn't ready to fall. She was at that delicious point where she didn't know which end was up. She despised him, yet she trembled at his touch, and her eyes grew heavy as she watched him, and maybe the alley wasn't such a bad idea after all.

"You're woolgathering," she said sharply. "You're the one more likely to steer us both in the path of a carriage. Why don't you return home or retire to your club or something while I deal with the draper? I promise I won't put up anything worse than what's already there."

"You couldn't find anything worse." He steered her around the corner to the equally crowded Piccadilly. "And I find I have a sudden interest in what my bed contains."

He thought he heard a low snarl coming from somewhere inside that horrible dress. She had her head down, trying to hide her face, and he took pity on her. "My dear Mrs. Greaves, you needn't worry about anyone jumping to the wrong conclusion about my escort. You look like an ancient crone in that shapeless dress and oversize bonnet. People will simply assume I'm being a gentleman for once, and mistake you for an indigent relation." His eyes narrowed. "In fact, that's what that dress looks like. Not the sort of dress worn by housekeepers and their ilk, but more like a well-brought-up young lady in penurious circumstances, forced to earn her living catering to the insidious likes of me."

"Bugger," she said succinctly, deliberately. "That's not a word proper young ladies know."

"Oh, I don't think you're proper at all, Mrs. Greaves." He made his voice low and caressing, and he could feel another shiver run through her. Delicious. "I think all you need is the right encouragement."

"All I need is to get to the draper's, take care of my business, and return to the house. The staff isn't used to behaving like proper servants, and I need to keep an eye on them. In another month it should be so ingrained that it'll be second nature to them."

"Are you planning to leave us in a month?"

To his surprise she colored. "Of course not!"

So whatever she was up to, she expected it to be done in a month. Why had she picked a deadline, and what exactly was she hoping to find? If she knew who he was all she had to do was announce it—once suspicions were aroused the police would be able to find proof no matter how well he'd covered things up. No matter how hard he tried to atone.

If the woman beside him knew who he was it would explain her highly entertaining lack of respect for him, but he didn't think that was the case. She was simply chafing at the restraints of servitude, and he was doing his best to needle her. It was working beautifully.

"You can take a deep breath and relax, my dear Mrs. Greaves," he said lightly. "I have no intention of assaulting your honor on a public street. Truth be told, I'm bored, and I'd rather accompany you to the draper than deal with business."

"Business, my lord? I can't imagine an aristocrat would have anything to do with business."

"Then you'd be surprised. I find business quite fascinating, and I have an odd gift for making money. Unfortunately one of the businesses I had a partnership in has hit a difficult patch. The founder embezzled a fortune from the place, and then was killed in a carriage accident as he tried to make his escape. I've been trying to shore things up, make certain the investors are satisfied, see to it that any money left by the wily old fox gets returned to the company."

"Interesting," Bryony Greaves said in a neutral voice, and he got the sense that she meant it. "What about the man's heirs?"

"His heirs don't matter," he said, "because he left nothing to inherit. Everything was confiscated by the crown. So not only has Russell destroyed his business and his good name, he's ruined his family as well."

She was even stiffer than she had been before, but she didn't try to pull away. "Russell? Was that the man's name?"

"Don't you read newspapers, Mrs. Greaves? You strike me as someone who would. If so, I'm certain you heard of the nine-day's wonder that was the Russell case and the ensuing bank panic?"

"It sounds vaguely familiar. So did you lose a great deal of money in all this? I would think you'd be very angry at . . . Mr. Russell, did you say?"

"I didn't have time to be angry with him—I heard of his death before we realized he'd embezzled such a vast sum of money from the company that he left it on the edge of ruin, destroying two banks in the process and nearly causing a panic. By then it was too late."

"What about his heirs? Couldn't you have extracted your pound of flesh from them?"

"You like Shakespeare, Mrs. Greaves? Now why doesn't that surprise me? And you're perfectly suited to the *Merchant of Venice*. You're such a stern, judgmental creature."

She opened her mouth to refute him, then snapped it shut again, and he wondered what she'd do if he simply leaned down and tasted that luscious mouth as he so wanted to. "I most certainly am not," she said finally.

He just laughed. "And I hold no personal grudge—if anything my finances are in better heart thanks to Russell. For some reason he left my shares completely untouched. The other investors weren't quite so fortunate."

"For some reason," she echoed, sounding skeptical. "And did the police look into that? I do assume the police were involved?"

"Of course they were. Did they scrutinize my finances? Of course not—I'm a peer of the realm."

"Not this realm, apparently. I didn't know Irish lords received the same careful treatment from Scotland Yard."

"You're forgetting my charm."

"I'm—" She stifled herself, and he wondered exactly what insult she'd been about to hurl at him. The bonds of servitude certainly chafed.

"Oh, don't hold back, Mrs. Greaves. I assure you, I don't mind if you speak freely. I find it quite refreshing."

"I beg your pardon, my lord. I wouldn't think of insulting you."

Oh, you'd think it, my girl, he thought cynically. *It's killing you not to lash out at me with that sharp tongue.* "Always the perfect servant," he murmured.

She knew a goad when she heard one, but she had mastered her reactions. "I do my best to please, my lord."

Oh, that he couldn't resist. He leaned down, and his mouth brushed her ear. "Oh, my sweetness, you most certainly will." He pulled back, looking ahead of them on the noisy street. "I believe we're here, Miss Greaves."

Peach's Emporium was just a few doors away, the word *Drapers* written beneath the sign in neat, gold ink. She pulled her arm free, and this time he let her go, watching with amusement as she struggled to pull herself together. She turned to face him, her expression a mask of politesse. "I thank you so much for accompanying me, your lordship. I should have no trouble from here on."

"Of course you won't, my dear Mrs. Greaves, because I'll be with you." The door to the shop had already been opened by one of Mr. Peach's subordinates, and he waved her in.

She looked up at him, all stubborn defiance. She was a charming woman but a terrible spy. Didn't she know her best bet was to encourage his advances instead of trying to drive him away? She was much more likely to ferret out his secrets by curling up next to him. There was nothing to be gained by searching the house or questioning the servants. Only old Taggart knew the truth about the money he'd sent, and he'd go to the stake before he'd utter a word.

He didn't move. It was a contest of wills, but they were on an uneven playing field. She could scarcely defy her employer in front of witnesses and expect to continue in her job. And she knew it.

Her shrug was almost imperceptible, and she preceded him into Mr. Peach's emporium.

· ·
· ·

Why in heaven's name was he doing this? Bryony fumed. He had absolutely no real interest in her, only the enjoyment in thwarting her. She should learn her lesson, gracefully agree to everything—total compliance—and he'd grow tired. She hadn't yet mastered servility, at least, not with the man she suspected of orchestrating her father's destruction, but she'd need to try harder. So, as she'd suspected, he hadn't suffered any unfortunate financial effects from the so-called embezzlement? Hadn't anyone else thought that significant?

Little Mr. Peach was busy fawning all over his damned lordship, ignoring her. But then, she'd dressed to be ignored, and clearly the Earl of Kilmartyn was his client, not the frumpy little woman at his side.

"We want blue, Mr. Peach," he was saying. "Dark, I think, rather than pastels or bright shades."

"Certainly, your lordship," Mr. Peach said, snapping his fingers at his assistants as they rushed to do his bidding. "We have a dozen shades of dark blue, from a soft slate to the deepest indigo."

"I've brought my housekeeper, Miss Greaves," Kilmartyn continued, using "Miss" just to annoy her, she thought. "She'll see to the details, of course, but I wanted to make sure we ended up with just the right shade. About the color of her eyes, I think."

Oh, damn the man! Bryony thought, keeping her face impassive as Mr. Peach peered beneath her bonnet.

"I hesitate to ask, Mrs. Greaves," Mr. Peach said, automatically giving her the married status that housekeepers, by tradition, earned, "but could you possibly remove your bonnet and move toward the window? That way I can best judge the shade his lordship has in mind."

"His lordship is being fanciful. I don't think—" she began.

But Kilmartyn interrupted her. "His lordship is never fanciful, as Mr. Peach well knows."

Bryony began to untie her ribbons, resigned, as she moved closer to the windows.

"And will this be for your pied-à-terre near Bloomsbury Street, perhaps?" Mr. Peach inquired, peering into Bryony's face. "I believe we already have the measurements on record."

"Why do you have a place in Bloomsbury Street?" she blurted out. Too late she realized why.

"To house my mistress of the moment, of course," Kilmartyn replied. "But alas, Mr. Peach, my housekeeper is not currently in my keeping—I sold the house. This will be for my own rather spartan bedroom in the house on Berkeley Square."

Not currently? She was going to kill him.

"I see," said Mr. Peach, running a practiced eye down her body. He turned and called over his shoulder, "The Andalusian blue, I think, Jeffries." He glanced back at her. "It would look spectacular on you as well, Mrs. Greaves."

"I don't wear blue." It was the truth. Her mother had told her blue washed her out and Bryony had believed her. After all, if her French mother didn't know about fashion then who did?

"You should," Mr. Peach said briefly before turning his attention back to Kilmartyn. Once more she was dismissed, and she took a step back, listening as Mr. Peach fawned all over Kilmartyn.

She hadn't seen him in broad daylight before, hadn't had a chance to observe him. He was quite tall—next to Mr. Peach he seemed almost a giant, and his lean build only accentuated it. He had faint lines around his eyes and mouth, though whether they were signs of laughter or dissipation she couldn't be sure. Knowing him, probably both.

Given her cloistered life, it was little wonder that she would find herself reacting inappropriately. She'd never been around men anywhere near her age or station. Even when she'd visited London to oversee the household there she'd remained out of sight, only leaving the house in the early hours of daylight, long before the fashionable left their beds, and always heavily veiled. She had never been the recipient of attention from a beautiful man, and she wasn't quite sure what to do about it.

Because he was beautiful in broad daylight. Despite Collins's best efforts he was still casually dressed, though his clothes were pressed, and his tawny hair was too long. His face was clean-shaven, unlike the fashion of the day, and she liked it. Liked the high cheekbones and the firm jaw and the teasing mouth.

Blast. Damn. Bugger. She had experimented with cursing one summer, with Maddy's amused help, but it still didn't come out naturally. Except at the worst time of all, in front of the Earl of Kilmartyn.

His eyes met hers suddenly, and she wanted to kick herself. He'd caught her staring at him, and that infuriating smile played around his infuriating mouth. "What do you think of this shade, Miss Greaves?"

Mr. Peach had unearthed a really luscious shade of blue, with just a hint of purple in it, almost a blueberry color, rich without being bright. Bright colors in a bedroom never suited. "I like it," she said.

"Come here."

She didn't move. She found she had managed to wander a comfortable distance from him, far enough to breathe more easily. "I can see the color quite well from here, my lord," she said in a dulcet tone.

"Come here." The repeated command was quiet, but she didn't make the mistake of thinking it was an option. If she didn't move closer he would move her himself.

"Certainly, my lord," she said with patently false meekness, and came back to him, shoulders braced.

He took the bolt of fabric and tossed a length of it over her shoulder, startling her, and then pulled her closer, lifting the fabric to cradle her face. He was looking down at her with a totally unreadable expression in his forest green eyes. Such deep, unfathomable eyes—she could fall right into them if she wasn't careful. She stood very still, feeling like a cornered animal.

He tilted his head to one side, surveying her. "Yes, it suits her. An excellent match for her eyes, Peach. We'll take enough for the room, the hangings, and the counterpane, and I want, oh, five ells extra for Miss Greaves."

"No," Bryony said.

His lips twitched. "You can't stop me from buying fabric for you, Miss Greaves. If we're refurbishing my surroundings then we may as well refurbish you."

"That wasn't what I was saying no to," she said. "My lord," she added belatedly. "If you do the room in just the one color it will be as if you crawled inside a blueberry tart. It will be suffocating. You need varying shades." She shrugged the fabric off her shoulders, back into his hands, and moved to the counter, picking out a complementary shade with gray undertones, a lighter one, and an indigo so dark it was almost black. "There," she said. "A combination of these will suit better. I would suggest the lighter shade for the walls, the darker for the bed hangings, and the . . . favored color for the curtains."

"The lady has excellent taste," Mr. Peach pronounced, clearly impressed.

"The lady is very wise. However, we'll have the darker shade for the curtains and the rich blue for the bed." His eyes slid down over her, and it almost felt as if he were touching her. "To better complement anyone who might find herself in it."

He couldn't mean what she thought he meant. But it was so blatant there could be no doubt. Mr. Peach coughed, and she wanted to slap Kilmartyn's face, hard. She wanted to take her small fist and punch him in the stomach. She wanted to strip off her clothes and climb into that bed with him. And she suspected he knew it.

She kept her face expressionless, for what good it did her. "As you wish, my lord," she said, all humble servitude, but he wasn't fooled.

"Peach, if you can send your minions over to take measurements as soon as possible we'd be most grateful," he said, not taking his eyes from her.

"Your lordship, I will come myself," Peach said grandly. "And do you wish us to measure Mrs. Greaves? I can recommend any number of excellent dressmakers . . ."

Before Bryony could protest Kilmartyn shook his head. "I'd prefer everyone else keep their hands off her."

She could feel the heat in her face. He was practically announcing to the world that she was his mistress, or at least his plaything. "I prefer *everyone* to keep their hands off me," she said grimly.

"If wishes were horses . . ." he murmured. He picked up her discarded bonnet, then looked at it with ill-concealed dislike. "Is this really the best you can do?"

Looking at it with fresh eyes, she had to agree it was phenomenally ugly. It also shielded most of her face from curious eyes, and she'd kept it for years, even though the current fashion was for smaller hats, close to the head. Dying it black hadn't been a complete success, and it looked rather like it was covered with a molting snake skin. "Yes," she said, and clamped it onto her head defiantly, fumbling with the ribbons.

He shook his head, then brushed her hands aside. "Allow me."

She had to fist her hands rather than fight with him. She held still as he slowly tied the heavy silk ribbons that had begun to fray. He'd taken off his gloves, and his long fingers brushed her skin, setting off all sorts of unexpected feelings rushing through her body, heat and longing and a deep sorrow she couldn't define.

He stepped away. "I suppose it will have to do for now. Peach, we look forward to seeing you."

They were back out on the street before she realized it, and he'd drawn her hand through his arm. When she finally found her voice her words were incautious. "You are a truly terrible man."

He laughed. "Not really. Only a slightly terrible man. When you get to know me you'll find that I can be quite charming."

"I've already seen your charm. I was not impressed." The moment the words left her mouth she halted, shocked. This was much worse than "bugger." No employer could be spoken to in that way. She suspected even a cherished mistress wouldn't be allowed such liberties.

But Kilmartyn didn't appear surprised. "You need to remember your role, Miss Greaves. No one is going to believe you're simply an overzealous housekeeper if you keep baiting me. Mind you, I find it quite delightful, but for your sake you might confine your insults to times when we're alone." He tugged at her, but she didn't move. There were just so many disturbing things in his words that she felt sick.

"What do you mean?" Her voice came out raw and anxious.

The smile that played around his mouth had nothing to do with the dark intensity of his eyes. "Do you really wish to have this discussion standing still in the midst of Regent Street, my very dear Miss Greaves?" She said nothing, and he continued. "No? I thought not."

He started walking, and this time she didn't pull back, or try to break free. She had more important things to concentrate on. Did he suspect she was something other than a housekeeper? If so, why in the world did he allow her to remain in his household?

There was no answer to that, and Bryony considered herself to be a pragmatic woman. She would put it in the back of her mind and think about it later. There was no value in worrying about it now.

They walked back toward Berkeley Square in a surprisingly comfortable silence. It was a rare, beautiful day in spring, and the feel of the sun shining down was almost a blessing. She could see the trees with their fresh buds blooming against the bright blue sky, and she allowed herself a small moment of peace, and for some reason the strong arm beneath her hand, the tall, warm body beside her, was part of that peace.

"I'll leave you here." His voice broke through her reverie, and she looked up, startled. They were on the edge of Berkeley Square, and the house was in sight, halfway up the street. "My wife has her maid spy out the windows, and we don't want to make your situation in my household any more difficult."

"It's not difficult now, my lord," she said, glad her calm voice was back. She needed to remember to use his title more often. It reminded her to keep her temper under control and her role intact. "A challenge, perhaps, but not difficult."

He released her, and for all that she'd fought his polite hold on her, she suddenly felt . . . bereft. She gave him her official bow. "May we expect you home for dinner, my lord?"

"It depends. If I find something more entertaining I might spare you the exquisite pleasure of my company."

"I beg your pardon?"

"We have an appointment, Miss Greaves. You share my dinner, and we trade obscure curses. I'd be hard-pressed to find anything that could possibly compare. On a purely intellectual level, that is."

"Bugger," said Bryony, and walked away from him down the street.

She could feel his eyes follow her all the way to the house.

CHAPTER ELEVEN

Rufus didn't enjoy making mistakes. In truth, it put him in a perfectly foul mood, and once he'd decided to finish the interfering Mrs. Greaves he wanted it done with. It had been simple enough to brush past her at just the right moment, to give her a shove that should have sent her flailing beneath the murderous hooves of one of those reckless carriage drivers. He hadn't realized that he wasn't the only one following her.

It was careless of him, when he was usually the most precise of men. He hadn't even noticed Kilmartyn behind him, close to him, moving in to whisk her out of harm's way.

It could have been quite disastrous, if the streets weren't so busy, if Kilmartyn had recognized him and started to become suspicious. He was a very clever man, Kilmartyn was, though it pained Rufus to admit it. Not nearly as smart as Rufus himself, but then, who was? Fortunately Kilmartyn had only the faintest idea who he was, and had no hint that Rufus was one of many who enjoyed the countess's favors.

However, it didn't do to underestimate his opponents. The housekeeper was negligible—she simply had the misfortune to see his face, and for that she was doomed. And she'd be easy to deal with, as long as he made sure no knights in tarnished armor like Kilmartyn were there to rescue her and then take her away with him.

He didn't bother to follow—he could tell by the way they looked at each other, the way Kilmartyn kept hold of her that there was something between the two. They weren't lovers yet—he could recognize the difference in the way people moved with each other, the hidden touches, the looks. No, these two were antagonists of the best sort, wanting to rip each other's clothes off and hating each other at the same time.

It would keep the two of them completely occupied for a good while. Once Kilmartyn had shagged her he'd lose interest, but as long as the hunt was on he'd be fully distracted.

Rufus wondered whether he ought to head back to Berkeley Square and inform the delightful Cecily of what he'd observed. She would explode with rage, and he rather liked her when she exploded. But no, he had other things to do, things to arrange, and he needed to be careful. That information could wait.

He would walk to his rooms, change, and go out to dinner as if he hadn't a care in the world. And in truth, he didn't. All would fall into place as it was supposed to. He could take his time, stroll by the burned-out shell of a house on Curzon Street, and remind himself of all that he had wrought. This was only a minor setback, one he was sure would be taken care of in time. He would get rid of the too-observant Mrs. Greaves, as well as clinging, venal Cecily. He could do the rest on his own.

• •

Kilmartyn didn't end up returning for dinner that night, for which Bryony could only be grateful, she assured herself. The new staff were settling in. Mr. Collins was proving invaluable in overseeing them, and Mrs. Harkins's culinary genius was beginning to approach French levels. Normally staff ate early, before the quality, but given how little the masters of the household enjoyed Mrs. Harkins's food, Bryony came up with the notion that the staff should have a substantial tea and then supper later on. That way they could enjoy at least a taste of the fruits of Mrs. Harkins's labor, and the cook wouldn't be cast into the slough of despair.

As the day wore on spirits grew lighter, and there was laughter at the table as the staff devoured coq au vin, fresh Dover sole, and the most delicate trifle imaginable. And then, eventually, Bryony was alone, the house shut down for the night, though Bertie would doze by the front door in case his lordship decided to return. According to Bertie on nights like these his lordship usually ended up spending the night in the arms of a courtesan, one of several who enjoyed his favors.

Her father had never kept a mistress, even after her mother's death. But then, her father had been too obsessed with making money to be distracted by carnality, and thank God for that. She truly didn't want to even consider her father having those kinds of needs.

Of course there was always the off-chance Kilmartyn might return in the middle of the night. If he had a late-night card game, or if he preferred not to spend the night in a bed of pleasure but only a few hours then he might come back to torment her.

Perhaps he'd leave her alone, once his . . . his beastly cravings were satisfied. Her main source of knowledge on such things came from her sisters, and she suspected their information was somewhat incomplete, given that they'd received it from their school friends. But it only made sense that if one . . . itched, then one would be more likely to torment the people around one. Once scratched, peace of mind should settle down, and the Earl of Kilmartyn would no longer seek to torment her. He wouldn't look at her with those unfathomable dark green eyes, as green as a forest after rain. She'd be invisible to him, as all good servants should be.

She could only hope so, she told herself, sitting at the desk in her little office by the deserted kitchen, going over her accounts. Mr. Peach had arrived promptly, measurements taken, orders prepared. He didn't say a word about the extra fabric Kilmartyn had decreed, and she kept silent as well. No doubt Mr. Peach understood how uneven an aristocrat's attention might be. He would forget all about his absurd suggestion. Particularly after having spent the night in the arms of a courtesan.

And why did she keep thinking about that? It was none of her business, except as it affected the running of the household, and Bertie was used to sleeping in a chair in the front foyer. So why did the very thought of Kilmartyn's elegant hands, sliding over smooth, bare skin, make her edgy and anxious and ready to explode?

She shook her head, disgusted with herself. She knew the disastrous truth, and she had never been one to avoid such things. She'd developed a . . . weakness for him, after a mere three days in his presence. Not exactly a *tendre*—he was much too complicated a man to inspire such a sweet emotion. It was more like a schoolgirl crush, though she was as far removed from the schoolroom as she could be. There was nothing to be ashamed of. He was a very beautiful man—that mane of hair, the high cheekbones and smiling mouth, and dark, dark green eyes. And she liked his height, the way she felt walking beside him, glancing up at him, feeling both threatened and protected at the same time.

He was the first man she'd ever been close enough to flirt with. At least, that appeared to be what he was trying to do, though she was giving him no encouragement. She would have felt the same for that man she'd come across in the upstairs hallway—Mr. Brown? She would have felt that way for Bertie, a well-set-up young man, or the muscular butcher, or any of her father's business acquaintances and cronies she'd seen from a distance over the years.

It was simply her misfortune to have been thrown together with one of God's own creatures. He looked like a fallen angel, all raffish charm and seraphic good looks. And she was understandably vulnerable.

Not that he was going to know it. He might suspect, but in no way was she going to give any hint that she found him to be other than an employer, an aristocrat so far above her touch that they may as well be separate species.

And she'd tell him that, if she ever got the chance. Not that she would—he was a master of innuendo, not of plain talk, and it was so desperately hard to fight innuendo.

But if he'd spent a night making love that should improve the situation. When he eventually returned he'd be in better spirits, and when he looked at her he'd see a scarred, plain housekeeper and nothing more. To quote her beloved Shakespeare, "it was a consummation devoutly to be wished."

Of course it was.

Searching the study was out of the question tonight—it was too near the front hall and Bertie. She could try the bedroom again—he'd interrupted her before she could finish, and she was desperate to find what the slim volume beneath his mattress held. Proof of a conspiracy of theft and murder? Or something harmless? She could risk it. If Kilmartyn returned home and saw a light up there he might reasonably assume it was Collins, not his errant housekeeper.

Though his last words earlier in the day had been disturbing. Why had he suggested she was playing a role, and needed to be believable? Was he simply trying to find ways to disturb her? He might suspect she was a gentlewoman down on her luck—there was no crime in that. In fact, perhaps she should embellish a bit of history to Mr. Collins in hopes that he'd pass it on. She could be the impoverished third daughter of a baronet or something, forced to earn her own way after her father's untimely death. Or the widow of a missionary who'd been cast off by her well-to-do family for the mésalliance. Anything would do, as long as he believed it and it quieted his suspicions.

Or maybe she was paying it too much attention. Kilmartyn was a man who liked to push, to disturb. At least, he did in her case. It was probably no more than mischief and boredom. It meant nothing.

She closed the account book. Mr. Peach had been prepared to charge Kilmartyn a fortune for his services, but Bryony had simply fixed him with her calm, cool stare and he ended up taking twenty-five percent off the total. The only uncomfortable part was when he handed her an envelope full of money, her kickback. She'd shoved it back at him in horror. In truth, tips and bribes were the one part of servitude that she couldn't abide. People had seldom made that mistake when she'd served as housekeeper for her father and if they did they'd quickly learned the error of their ways. Even if it made her role more believable there was no way she was going to take a handful of greasy bills from Mr. Peach, no matter how much her sisters might need it.

She rose, stretching. It had been a desperately long day, well after midnight, and the next day would start far too early. At least she could sleep until the sinfully late hour of six a.m.—the servants had mastered the breakfast rituals, and only Lady Kilmartyn would require a morning tray. The woman had only left her rooms once since Bryony had moved in, something Bryony attributed to either a monumental case of sulks or the fact that her handsome cousin kept her well occupied. Either way, it was none of her concern. As long as the staff responded to the mistress's needs in a timely fashion Bryony didn't need to waste her time thinking about her. In fact, she ought to have told everyone to sleep in, but they were just growing accustomed to the new discipline, and if there was only one breakfast tray to prepare there were a thousand more things to clean.

She passed the storeroom, glancing in longingly. It had usually served as the housekeeper's bedroom, but in the intervening years it had simply been turned into a repository for cast-off chairs. The thought of climbing those endless flights of stairs made her want to weep.

She could manage it for a month. She'd promised her sisters it would be no more than that, and she never broke her promises, at least not to the people most important to her. If she didn't find any proof of his guilt or innocence within the month she would move on to Captain Morgan, disappear from London like a wraith.

Right now she was so tired she thought if she stopped to rest on the narrow stairs she'd probably go to sleep on her feet. She finally made it back to her room, kicking off her shoes, stripping off her clothes, and washing thoroughly in the now-tepid water. Her head ached, and she unfastened her braids, letting her hair hang down her back as she pulled on her cotton nightdress.

It had been a mistake to bring it, as well as her undergarments. They were remnants of her past life, silk and the softest linen, decorated in the finest lace. She'd told Emma, who worked on the laundry with the new girls, that they'd been gifts from her old mistress. But they reminded her of the life that was gone forever, the loss of her father, the loss of safety for her sisters.

She climbed into bed. She ought to rebraid her hair, but she simply didn't have the energy. She needed to sleep, now, immediately. She'd deal with tangled hair in the morning.

Two hours later she was still staring wide-eyed into the shadows, ready to weep with frustration. The full moon coming in her attic window was beautiful; it was also fiendishly bright. She was going to have to find something to tack up, to blot out the light that shone directly into her eyes. She'd even tried getting up and dragging her narrow iron bed out of the direct path, but that didn't help.

When she heard the clock chime three she pushed up, sitting on the side of the bed. It was chilly now, the bright warmth of the sun having worn off, and she shivered as she reached for her knitted black shawl, wrapping it around her shoulders. Warm milk was a well-known cure for sleeplessness. In order to get warm milk she'd have to climb down five flights of stairs and somehow get a fire started in Mrs. Harkin's massive cookstove, hope to God there was milk in the larder, and then hope the home remedy was a cure.

She closed her eyes again with a weary groan. She couldn't do it, any more than she could lie back and fall asleep. All she could think about was the slender book in Kilmartyn's bedroom. It haunted her. If she just dared to creep down the one flight of stairs and fetch it then she'd be able to sleep. Her entire future might very well rest with that book, whatever it was. It would contain proof, she was sure of it. Proof of his guilt or his innocence was the question, and she told herself she didn't care. She simply had to find out, before this . . . this weakness of hers got entirely out of hand.

It would be perfectly safe. The earl was out for the night—if he returned unexpectedly Bertie would make enough noise to alert her. She was a fool to miss this chance.

Her entire body ached. She was slowly, slowly getting used to the unaccustomed physical work the disaster of a house demanded, and if she wanted things done to her satisfaction then she had no choice but to demonstrate. Her wrists stung, her back ached, her legs throbbed, and her head hurt from all the unanswered questions. She couldn't do much about the other issues, but she could find out the truth that had so far eluded her. And once she did, she could be gone from this house in an hour or less, never having to see Kilmartyn again.

The shawl she'd draped over her nightdress left her decently covered if she happened to run into another servant. The moon was setting, plunging everything into darkness, and she lit the candle beside her bed. There was no way she was going to light the gaslights for her clandestine adventure.

It would be harmless enough. If anyone caught her she would simply say she was in search of laudanum to help her sleep. She despised the stuff—she'd been forced to drink it when she'd been so ill with smallpox, and she'd vowed never to touch it again. She'd seen how it affected people.

People could be dangerously fond of their laudanum, she knew from bitter experience. Her mother was one who had a great affection for it, and when she misplaced it she reacted with all the sweetness of a demented virago. Her employers might not appreciate that their new housekeeper was rummaging in search of drugs. Lady Kilmartyn would do anything she could to get rid of her, and this would give her the perfect excuse.

That was better than the truth, however, and as a transgression it was relatively minor. And that was only if she was caught.

Pausing by the stairs, she looked down the three landings to the foyer below. She could see Bertie's feet where he slept, proof that Kilmartyn had found another bed to spend the night in. And she was very glad of it, she assured herself as she headed down the darkened hallway to his bedroom.

She blew out the candle and opened the door, slipping inside and leaning back against it. Her heart was thudding, which was ridiculous. There was no one to see her, no one to guess at her nighttime activities. She was safe.

It took a moment for her eyes to grow accustomed to the darkness. She could see the outline of furniture in the shadows—the huge old bed, the chair, the small table. She could either relight the candle or go by sense of feel, which was going to make it impossible to read the ledger or whatever it was. She could always take the thing away with her and return it at first light. If Kilmartyn was spending the night in riotous licentiousness he was hardly likely to drag himself out of bed at a decent hour. While of course she had no firsthand knowledge of sexual congress she imagined it could be quite exhausting. Not that Kilmartyn, with his sleek, almost catlike grace, seemed overly energetic. He'd be more likely to provide stamina, which should have seemed rather unpleasant. It didn't.

She moved into the center of the room, carefully avoiding the chair that was out of place. She bumped into the small bedside table, and cursed beneath her breath as she steadied it. Her fumbling hands found the drawers, and she pulled one open, reaching inside. Her fingers closed around a small glass vial. Laudanum, no doubt, her excuse for her nighttime ramblings if anyone should catch her. She breathed a sigh of relief, pulling it out and tucking it in her pocket, and then turned to the huge dark cavern of the bed.

She sank to her knees on the floor beside it, pushing up the disordered covers, sliding her questing hands under the mattress. And then it hit her—the covers were disordered, when she herself had made the bed. Her fingers found the journal just as hands clamped around her wrists, pulling them free, and she felt herself hauled through the air to land on a hard, male body. A moment later she was beneath him, and he was very heavy, pressing her down into the bed. She opened her mouth to scream.

"I wouldn't make a sound if I were you, my dear Miss Greaves." His voice was a soft, dangerous purr in the darkness. "You wouldn't want the other servants to find out what you were doing in the middle of the night. Not if you want to maintain discipline."

For a moment she was completely frozen in horror as her brain rushed to remember her excuse. "I was looking for laudanum," she said in not much more than a whisper.

She could feel the laugh shake his body as it pressed against her. He was huge, overwhelming, warm skin everywhere. He was so solid, not soft like her at all, not soft like anyone she'd ever been close to. His chest was hard against her, his stomach flat, his . . . Shock hit her, as she realized what else she was feeling. She shouldn't even know what it was, but she did. That didn't feel like anything she'd seen on the Elgin Marbles.

"So my new housekeeper has a fondness for drugs?" he murmured in her ear, his breath as warm as his skin. "You should have told me sooner. I could find all sorts of things for you to try."

"I couldn't sleep," she said, holding herself very still. Not that she had much choice. He was so much bigger than she was, so much stronger, with all that hot, sleek flesh. And she certainly didn't want to do anything that would put her in closer contact with *that* part of him. "And I was in pain."

His soft laugh should have annoyed her. Instead it only increased that treacherous stirring deep and low inside her. "I'm sure you were, my precious. You don't mind me calling you my precious, do you? I tend to use endearments to anyone who's lying beneath me in my bed."

"I'd just as soon not be in your bed, my lord." Her voice came out slightly strangled but there was nothing she could do about it.

He laughed again. "No, I imagine so. Don't worry, my pet. There are plenty of other places we could do it."

"Do what?" she said, mystified, before she realized what he meant. She started to struggle then, not caring what part she hit. "Let me up."

He caught both her wrists in one hand and hauled them above her head, his hips pinned hers, and his legs trapped her own. "I didn't invite you here," he pointed out. "You simply waltzed in, in the middle of the night, and I'm never a man to turn down such a generous offer."

"I told you, I was looking for laudanum!" She was trapped beneath him, even more thoroughly than she had been before, and she knew she should be terrified. She couldn't decipher what she was feeling. Fear was part of it, certainly. But so was a strange sense of longing she didn't quite recognize. Her breasts were pressed against him, and they ached. Everything was aching in an entirely different way than it had been before. Her entire body felt hot, restless, edgy.

"Beneath my mattress?" His voice was like a purr. "I promise you, my very dear Miss Greaves, I don't hide my vices. I keep them in plain sight for any curious housekeeper to come across."

"Your laudanum was in the drawer," she said before she could consider the wisdom of it.

"I don't like laudanum. It's a watered-down drug for ladies. Is that what's digging into my hip?" Before she realized it he'd reached between their bodies, his hands brushing against her stomach as he searched for the pilfered bottle, and heat and shock exploded through her. He found her pocket and pulled out the bottle, holding it up to the tiny shaft of moonlight that speared in through the curtains. And then he really did laugh, so hard that he released her, falling against her, convulsed in such mirth that she was able to shove him off her, almost able to escape before he caught one wrist and hauled her back.

"That's not laudanum, my precious. That's something else entirely, and you would have been very sorry if you'd tried to drink it."

She wasn't going to ask him. Damn it, she wasn't going to say a word. "Then what is it?"

"It's an interesting oil from the Far East that helps intensify certain . . . pleasures. I'd be more than happy to demonstrate, but with such a puritanical virgin I think a simple fucking would be more than enough for the first time."

She froze at his offhand words. She tried to speak, but when the words came they were shamefully weak. "Are you going to rape me?"

"Of course not. I wouldn't have to. I could have you eating out of my hand if I set my mind to it."

She ground her teeth. "I am not a virgin, I am not puritanical, we are not going to have any kind of . . . carnal debauchery at all. Now let me up."

He didn't laugh at her this time. He fell back against the mattress with a weary sigh, still holding on to her wrist. "Now that's the damnable problem, my angel. I'm all set to play the villain, have my disgusting, delicious way with you to both your pleasure and mine, and you say something completely adorable like 'carnal debauchery.' How is a man to react to something like that?"

"He's supposed to release me."

"I ought to," he said. "If I had any scrap of decency left in me." He turned his face, and she could see him in the shaft of moonlight, his skin white gold. It was then she realized he wasn't wearing a shirt. Realized that he wasn't wearing anything at all. "Fortunately," he added, "any decency is long gone." And he pulled her over on top of him.

"If you keep this up I'm going to get dizzy." This time she managed a satisfactorily dry, cautious tone.

He put his lips to her ear, and she could feel his hot breath against her skin. "You already are dizzy, my dear Miss Greaves. Your heart is pounding, your pulses are racing, and your nipples are hard. I'm willing to bet my sweet little virgin is wet."

She frowned, ignoring the nipple part. "Wet?"

"Between your legs. It's a sign of arousal, your body readying itself for mine."

"That's disgusting."

"That's delicious," he corrected her. "Shall I see?" And his hand slid down her thigh to the hem of her nightdress. She slapped at him, but he simply caught that hand with her other. "This isn't going to hurt, precious. I just want a taste. A forfeit, since you were the one who decided to come to my bed."

"Your bedroom," she corrected, "and I told you, I was looking for—"

"Yes, you told me, and I don't believe you."

"Let me up," she said fiercely.

"Not yet. I require two things before I release you."

"Name them." She would make a bargain with the devil to get away from him. Before she didn't want to leave at all.

The bed was so warm, and soft beneath her. It smelled wonderful, of spice and wood and Kilmartyn, some scent all his own, and it would be so easy to lie back and let him do what he wanted. There was even a certain sense to it—if she had relations with him he might lower his guard. It wasn't as if she ever planned to marry—the loss of her virtue would be no loss at all, and it would slake her endless curiosity.

She was mad! She needed to get away from him—these thoughts were insane.

Before she realized what he was doing he'd slid one arm around her waist, pulling her against him, and his other hand moved up to her throat, his long fingers cupping her chin, stroking. He moved closer, blotting out the fitful light, and she thought, now I am going to be kissed, really kissed, and she closed her eyes, preparing herself.

Instead, his mouth moved to her ear, and his teeth bit down on her earlobe. Instead of pain, warmth flooded her body, and her eyes flew open again. "Just so you know there are other, surprising places that can be almost as much fun as lips," he whispered, before his mouth closed over hers.

She'd been expecting the kind of kiss she'd given him that first night when he had passed out, the pressing of lips against lips, with the possible addition of some excited grinding. This was entirely different.

His mouth merely brushed hers, so softly it was feather light, and she knew a moment of disappointment. Until he did it again with a mere touch, so tantalizing that her body began to rise to meet his. She kept herself still, as his lips traveled over her jaw, her cheek, across her closed eyes, and then back to her mouth again, so softly, like a butterfly exploring a flower. And she was forgetting to breathe, entranced.

She could feel his breath against her, and then the totally surprising touch of his tongue against her lips. Why? But his hand was still cupping her chin, holding her gently, and his long finger caressed her jaw. She automatically opened at his urging, just as his mouth covered hers again, his tongue swept inside her, wet and hot and seeking, and she knew she should be disgusted, knew it as her tongue slid against his, tasting him. This was what she'd been waiting for, though she hadn't known it. This was what she had needed.

It wasn't a kiss of domination, strange as it was, it was a kiss of discovery, of tasting and touching and teasing, of utter joy and promises of oh, so much more, and she sank into it, danced into it, reveling in its unexpected delight. She didn't want it to end. She couldn't breathe, and she didn't care. He was everywhere, all around her in the warm bed. He'd slid his hands down to her shoulders, holding her, and then they moved down her arms, and she didn't care. She wanted him to touch her, touch her everywhere. In the darkness her scars were invisible, in the darkness this beautiful man wanted her, and she would endure anything for the bizarre glory of this deep, draining kiss. She made a low moan of protest as he lifted his head, and she realized that at some point she'd reached up to clutch his shoulders. Naked shoulders, strong and well muscled, naked as the rest of him. He was looking at her now, breathing heavily, a surprised expression on his face. "Well," he said in rough voice. "Well, now."

Before she could say anything he kissed her again, no teasing this time, just a hungry demand, and she felt her body tremble with longing that she didn't understand, could only feel. She wanted this man. She wanted to stay here, lie beneath him, have him push between her legs and take her as a man took a woman. It was wrong, it was selfish, and it didn't matter. Everything about her ached with need, and she slid her hands up his arms, clutching his shoulders, arching into him. She wanted to tell him not to stop, it didn't matter if she couldn't breathe, if he was crushing her, and she felt his hands sliding down her legs.

Her nightdress had ridden up, bunching around her thighs, and he moved his hand and pressed it, low and flat across her stomach. She liked that too, the warmth from his big hand filling her, soothing her, and for the barest moment she relaxed, sliding into the wonderful feeling. Safe. Wanted, when it seemed no one had ever wanted her. Protected.

And then he moved his hand down between her legs.

She tried to let out a shriek of protest but his mouth still covered hers. She tried to buck at him, but he simply lifted his head and smiled at her lazily.

"You might actually like it, my precious."

She tried to kick him, but he stilled her thrashing legs with one of his. She could feel the strong, warm, hair-dusted leg holding her still, the sensation momentarily distracting, and he used that distraction, stroking her, until she felt a powerful sizzle of reaction blaze through her.

It took more strength of will than she would have thought she had to shove him away. "No!"

"No?" he repeated gently. "You don't know what you're missing."

She was breathless, aroused, and she knew she should be ashamed. She wasn't. "I'm not supposed to know what I'm missing," she said tartly.

"And you a widow?" He laughed softly, but she was past worry about a slip of the tongue.

"We had a very restrained marriage," she snapped.

"I imagine you did," he said. Before she could stop him he'd cupped her face, sliding his long fingers into her hair, and kissed her again.

How could there be so many different kinds of kisses? This time it was a claiming, pure and simple, except there was nothing pure about it. She hadn't even realized she'd put her arms back around him, moving underneath him, kissing him back without any hesitancy, tongue and teeth and lips, and she wanted him to slide his hand down again, this time she wouldn't stop him, she wanted him to touch her there again.

But then he stopped, suddenly, and a moment later he lifted his head and rolled off her, sitting up in the bed. "Now that," he said, "is going to cause a very great deal of trouble." His voice was dazed, speculative, and reality came crashing in.

He'd been playing some sort of game, of course. Even in the darkness she was imperfect. She started to scramble out of the bed, but he caught her arm and hauled her back, staring down at her, an unreadable expression on his face.

She swallowed. She wanted him to kiss her again, to strip off her clothes and kiss her everywhere. She wanted him to let her go. "Was there anything else, my lord?" she inquired, the perfect servant.

For a moment he said nothing, just watched her out of oddly troubled eyes. Then he spoke. "One more thing. Ask me nicely."

She stared at him in shock. More games? Of course—that was all he ever did. Still, could it be that simple?

"All right," she said. "Let me go. Please." She ground out the last word, hating it.

He released her. "If you insist." And he slid his arm away, turned over and proceeded to fall asleep.

Or at least she assumed as much—she wasn't waiting to find out. She scrambled off the bed, almost falling on the floor, and she was across the room in a matter of moments. She opened the door silently, slipping through. And then, at the very last moment, she slammed it as hard as she could.

••••••••••••••••••••••••••••••
....

The Earl of Kilmartyn rolled onto his back, amusement still fighting with arousal over his endearingly clumsy spy. Really, if he had to have someone infiltrate his house to try to find out his secrets he couldn't have chosen a better one. There was no question who would win their little battle of wills. She was going to find nothing about his darkest secret. But she was going to give herself to him, body and soul.

As well as the name of the man who'd hired her.

He suspected it was one of Cecily's many lovers. Not that he should complain—he'd hardly been monogamous. He had no illusions that his wife really wanted him—it was simply that she couldn't have him that made her wild.

He set the small bottle of oil on the table. He was going to introduce Miss Bryony Greaves to the Oriental pleasures provided by the balm. He was going to talk her into everything and anything he wanted. And she would be quite willing by the time he got through with her. She was half-willing already, and he'd barely kissed her.

She'd discovered the leather-bound volume of erotic engravings beneath the mattress—she'd probably come back for that later. He had to ensure that the best one was there. He had several masterpieces down in the library, more collector's items than pleasure enhancers, but for a young woman who seemed to know very little about the process it could cover a lot of ground.

He was hard as a rock, and he lazily considered bringing himself off, thinking of her, then changed his mind. He liked the edge frustration brought him. By the time he finally sank into her he was going to be voracious. And so, by God, was she.

•••••••••••••••••••••••••••••
....

He was right, Bryony thought miserably. She was wet between the legs, and the knowledge horrified her. The sky was growing light by the time she'd finished scouring her body with the cold water, scrubbing her teeth to wipe away the distracting taste of him, and she knew sleep was out of the question. She dressed, groaning as she put her shoes on. Once she found out who had destroyed her father she was going to spend a week in bed, being waited on, and she was going to be even more considerate of whoever did the waiting. She would plead with someone to rub her feet, her back, her calves, and she would never think of Kilmartyn again, unless it was to see him hang for his crimes.

The longer she stayed here the less sure she was. He didn't seem to have the soul of a murderer. But how would she know—she'd never met any murderers in her life.

Even so, there was definitely something going on here, something secret, even something evil, and she couldn't leave until she discovered exactly what it was, until she was certain it had nothing to do with her father's destruction. Whether it was Kilmartyn himself, or his spoiled wife, she had no idea, and she was too tired to think about it. All she had to do was get through the day and she would sleep like the dead that night. And she wouldn't go after that leather-bound volume beneath his mattress until she was absolutely certain he was out of the house. Which had better be soon. The longer she stayed here the more trouble she was in. If she had stayed in his bed one moment longer she would have stayed there all night.

She had to hope that Captain Thomas Morgan was a troll.

CHAPTER TWELVE

THE KITCHEN WAS SPOTLESS when Bryony managed to drag herself down there at the shockingly late hour of six-thirty. There were fresh cinnamon rolls baking—she could smell them, and there was only one tray set out. At least they had no idea that Kilmartyn had returned in the middle of the night. They wouldn't know what she'd been doing in his bedroom. In his bed.

"You poor lass," Mrs. Harkins greeted her familiarly. "You look so tired. Begging your pardon, Mrs. Greaves," she added, remembering the hierarchy that seemed to matter so much.

She managed a weary smile. "I didn't sleep well, I must confess."

"Well, you just go on into your office and I'll bring you a nice strong pot of tea and the cinnamon buns when they're done. That'll put some heart into you. We won't need to see the master for a few hours yet."

"See the master?" she echoed faintly. She glanced back at the single tray. "Has he returned?"

"Some time in the night, apparently. And her ladyship has up and left on one of her long rounds of visits, taking that snooty French maid with her. You never know what's going to happen in this household, and that's the Lord's truth. Her ladyship's rooms are in a shamble, with no word to the staff."

"How do you know she's gone on a visit?"

Mrs. Harkins shrugged. "What else would she be doing? She goes off every now and then, usually after there's some row with the master. He keeps his distance from her but sometimes . . . well, her ladyship is the sort who looks for trouble. If you'll pardon my saying so."

"And was there a row with the master?" Bryony knew she shouldn't ask such an intimate question, but she couldn't help it.

"Bertie says he might have heard some to-do, but he doesn't remember much." Mrs. Harkins made a disgusted noise. "It's not like that boy. He slept like the dead, he did. Didn't wake when his lordship practically tripped over his feet, and he never saw Lady Kilmartyn and her maid when they left. Doesn't know if she went before or after his lordship returned."

"Does it matter?"

For a moment Mrs. Harkins looked uncomfortable, and a strange sense of dread began to coil in Bryony's stomach. "Happen it might. The two of them don't do too well together, you know. And her room was in such a mess." She shifted her impressive weight. "I just don't understand why Bertie didn't wake up."

"He's been working very hard, Mrs. Harkins," Collins said from the doorway. "It's no wonder he fell asleep. We shouldn't be so hard on him."

Mrs. Harkins managed to sniff in disagreement while she cast Collins a covert glance. "Young Bertie's a light sleeper, and always has been. He's been in the household for ten years now, starting out as the boy who brought the coal in, and he's always been someone who could be counted on."

Mr. Collins moved farther into the room. "Everyone makes mistakes, my dear Mrs. Harkins."

The cook's face flushed becomingly. "Aye," she said. "No need to go over it. In the meantime, though, I'm that worried about her ladyship. Her room looked like a storm hit it."

"I'm sure there's no reason to be troubled about it," Collins said smoothly, "but if you'd like I can go tidy it up a bit before anyone takes notice. We shouldn't want her ladyship's room looking like a pigsty, and my duties at present are very light."

Bryony frowned, shaking her head. "Certainly not, Mr. Collins. That's hardly in your purview. One of the maids can tidy it, but there's no particular hurry if, as it appears, her ladyship has departed for a lengthy visit. How long does she usually stay away, Mrs. Harkins?"

"Two weeks at the very least. Sometimes a month or more, with no word to the master or anyone."

"Then clearly we can get our usual daily duties taken care of first before we set her ladyship's rooms to right." At Mrs. Harkins's doubtful look she continued, "I'll go and check on it, see if it requires more than a simple tidying. If it's that bad Emma can take the two new maids and they'll get through it in no time."

"You can't go now, Mrs. Greaves. His lordship has left word. He wants to go over the menus with us." Mrs. Harkins looked pleased at the prospect of someone finally caring about her culinary genius.

"But why? He never has before." Realizing how she sounded, she quickly softened her voice to hide her sudden panic. "And he doesn't need me for that. You present him with the menus while I see to Lady Kilmartyn's rooms."

Mrs. Harkins shrugged her shoulders. "I could always tell him you're busy, but the master isn't someone to be denied when he wants something."

Bryony felt a tension in her stomach at Mrs. Harkins's artless words, and it had nothing to do with household duties. Those moments in his bed, his hand between her legs, were emblazoned in her mind. She managed a tight smile. In fact, seeing him in Mrs. Harkins's company would most likely be easier. He couldn't very well refer to her midnight ramblings in front of the cook.

Could he?

And why hadn't she noticed that Lady Kilmartyn had made an unexpected departure sometime during the night? It sounded like a Restoration comedy—the three of them wandering the halls, with no one bumping into each other. She'd heard nothing when she'd lain in Kilmartyn's bed, but then, hearing was the sense least involved with those few minutes. She could remember the feel of his warm body, pressing her down, the taste of his mouth on hers, his tongue. His hand, touching her so intimately, and the shockingly powerful reactions that touch had provoked. So odd, and yet so . . . interesting. The smell of his skin, his sheets, the scent of soap and some citrusy herb and just Kilmartyn. She could see him, the intensity in his eyes as he bent over her. It was little wonder she'd heard nothing. Lady Kilmartyn could have been murdered on the floor beneath her and she wouldn't have even noticed.

And that was an odd thought. Why would the idea of murder even enter her mind? Well, not so odd after all, considering that her own father had been murdered.

It was after eleven o'clock when the summons finally came. She'd consumed an entire pot of strong tea, not to mention three sugary cinnamon rolls in an effort to keep awake. She'd found herself dozing over her books twice, and she'd cursed the Earl of Kilmartyn every spare minute. She couldn't stop thinking of him. She'd been a fool to assume he was sleeping elsewhere, and she'd been far too eager to get her hands on that ledger. She wouldn't make that mistake again. She wasn't going anywhere near his bedroom until she'd actually seen him leave the house.

Collins returned to the kitchen and set the heavy silver tray on Mrs. Harkins's spotless table. "He's in a rare mood this morning," he announced. "He's wanting to see you in the library, Mrs. Harkins." He turned as Bryony entered the room. "And he said as how you were to see him afterwards."

Bryony managed a tight smile. "Very thoughtful of his lordship, but we may as well make his life easier and both see him now," she announced. "I have too many things to do to sit around and wait upon his pleasure."

Everyone turned to stare at her in shock, even Becky. "But that's what we do, Mrs. Greaves," one of the new maids said finally. "It's our job."

Bryony controlled her instinctive snarl, plastering a pleasant smile on her face. "Indeed. But another part of my job is seeing to his wife's rooms before she makes a sudden return and finds everything in disarray. There's no need to argue about it. If his lordship is ready for us now then we may as well go."

Collins frowned. "Mrs. Greaves, he particularly asked—"

"Don't worry about it, Mr. Collins. If his lordship has any objections I'll make certain he knows it was my decision. And what, precisely, did you mean by 'a rare mood'?" Not very housekeeperly of her. Instead of asking she should have chastised Collins for commenting on his employer, but after last night she was too wary to walk in on him unprepared.

"Hard to explain, Mrs. Greaves. Like a man about to embark on a load of trouble and excited to do so. I've seen that look on gamblers when they're about to risk everything. Perhaps his lordship has got some wager at one of his clubs?"

"It's a possibility," she said glumly. She had a very good idea of the trouble he was wanting to get into, and that trouble was his new house-keeper. A good look at her in broad daylight should put him off. She'd skinned her hair back, wetting it so it clung to her scalp, though she could feel little tendrils beginning to escape. She'd worn the uglier of her two dresses, buttoning it up tight to her throat, and the black apron she wore made things even worse. She wished she'd gone ahead and found clear eye-glasses to complete her initial appearance, but she'd thought her scars would scare off anybody.

It was starting out to be a sunny day, and she would make certain the curtains were open and the right side of her face was in full view, reminding him that he had better things to do while his wife was out of the way. Not that her presence seemed to have much effect on him.

Her heart was hammering as she led the way upstairs. She would have much preferred to lurk behind Mrs. Harkins's impressive bulk, but that would have involved breaking precedence, and as housekeeper she was expected to maintain it. By the time she reached his door she felt almost faint with exhaustion and anxiety, but she was reasonably certain she showed neither. She lifted her hand to knock on the door when she heard Mrs. Harkins's shocked sound, and turned.

"Begging your pardon, Mrs. Greaves, but tha' shouldna knock. It disturbs the master. Most of us just scratches on the door."

Bryony felt herself flush. Of course she was right—her own servants had made only a faint sound of warning before entering a room, never knocking. "You're absolutely right, Mrs. Harkins," she said. "My last employer was an elderly woman who would hear nothing less than a loud rap on the door, and I'm afraid I forgot myself. Would you please alert his lordship that we're here?" She'd never scratched on a door in her life—it reminded her of cats—and she needed to study Mrs. Harkins's technique.

It was actually quite simple; more of a backhanded rub than an actual scratch, but the sound of Kilmartyn's voice made the knot in her stomach tighten even further.

"Come in, Mrs. Harkins." He sounded so normal. Just a lordly aristocrat going through his daily chores, checking on menus in the absence of the mistress of the house. Though, according to Mrs. Harkins, Lady Kilmartyn never showed the faintest interest in menus either.

I can do this, Bryony thought, squaring her shoulders. *If not for me, for father and the girls.* She opened the door and walked in, Mrs. Harkins following closely behind.

He was sitting at the huge desk, the one she'd had yet to search, and he looked . . . almost normal. Clearly the advent of Mr. Collins had made a difference—instead of his casual disarray he was now neatly dressed, a perfect example of an aristocrat tending to his daily duties. His long hair was brushed back from his face and while he wore no jacket, his brick-colored double-breasted waistcoat with silver buttons lent just the right touch of elegance to his attire, and his dark silver cravat made his green eyes almost iridescent. His smooth shave accentuated the line of his jaw, and not for the first time she wondered why he went without facial hair. A beard or at least a mustache would have covered up some of that almost irresistible beauty.

But he probably knew exactly how his smooth, glorious face affected the female population, even one as unlikely as she. She gave him her dignified bow as Mrs. Harkins joined her, flushed and excited. "I believe you wished to see us, sir?"

He glanced at her, impassive, before turning to Mrs. Harkins, and it was like a blow. She didn't know what she'd expected, but hardly this total lack of reaction. "Indeed," he said. "Mrs. Harkins, I believe you had menus to present?"

Beaming with pleasure, Mrs. Harkins started forward, handing her lord and master the neatly plotted menu for the week. He took it, and instead of glancing at it and dismissing her he looked down at it for a long moment. Then he squinted. Then he did the most shocking thing of all. He reached into the top drawer of his desk and pulled out a pair of spectacles and placed them on his nose.

Bryony stifled her gasp of shock. No wonder he mistook her for a beauty. He was close-sighted!

He must have heard her anyway, for he looked up, directly at her as she stood in the sunlight that was pouring in the library windows, her face in full view. He looked at her, seeing her absolutely clearly, and then pulled off the glasses.

"Wretched things," he said casually. "I only need them when I have to read very small writing. You'd oblige me, Mrs. Harkins, if in the future you wrote your menus in a broader hand."

"Of course, my lord," Mrs. Harkins said, sounding agonized, and Bryony was immediately protective, her anger overriding her reticence.

"Mrs. Harkins went to a great deal to provide the most glorious menus for the week," she said sharply. "If you like I'll read them to you." She'd said it to shame him, but the moment the words were out of her mouth she regretted them.

"An excellent idea," he said, handing her the sheet of paper. "Mrs. Harkins, why don't you leave us and Mrs. Greaves can report on my comments."

Ooooh, no! "Of course Mrs. Harkins should stay," she said quickly. "Much better to get your decisions and comments directly, rather than have me repeating them. That way there can be no miscommunication."

He raised an eyebrow. "But isn't that your job, my dear Mrs. Greaves? To pass on my orders to the other servants? Do you feel you're not up to it?"

Good God, was he looking for a reason to fire her? Not that she could blame him—a housekeeper who searched the master's bedroom in the middle of the night was hardly the thing, and in retrospect the specious excuse of laudanum only made things worse. He had every reason to dismiss her. Not to mention the embarrassing situation—he'd kissed his ugly housekeeper, covered her in his bed, pushing her down into the mattress.

He'd . . . used his tongue. Touched her, more intimately than anyone else ever had. In daylight the very thought horrified her, and it most likely embarrassed him. Chances were he would want to get rid of her as quickly and efficiently as possible. She couldn't let that happen.

Before she could answer Mrs. Harkins spoke up. "Mrs. Greaves does an excellent job, my lord. She's already got the new maids trained to the needs of the household and they're working beautifully, she found us Mr. Collins and the new footman, and she's going to rid the house of rats. If you don't mind me being so bold, sir."

His dark green eyes swept over her figure in the bright sunlight, and nothing was hidden. "Rid the house of rats, is she? That would be quite a formidable feat."

Did he consider himself a rat? Or was he referring to his wife's lovers, like the gentleman she found prowling the halls yesterday? "The new boy, Jem, has an excellent dog that should take care of the rats. I'm planning on securing a cat or two to look after the mice."

There was just the faintest quirk of a smile on his mouth, and she remembered those lips, brushing against her face, her skin, her mouth, and she suddenly grew hot. "Ah," he murmured. "The rats and the mice. Large, wicked rats and quiet, shy little mice. I expect the rats will win any battle between the two."

She was no fool. He was comparing her to a quiet mouse, while he was the wicked rat. But she was no meek and gentle mouse, and she wasn't going to play his game. "There won't be any battle—the dog and the cats will take care of them."

He sighed. "Yes, it's always the larger outside forces that ruin many a rat's well-thought-out plan. Read me the menus, would you, Mrs. Greaves? And Mrs. Harkins, if you wish to stay you most certainly may do so."

Mrs. Harkins looked at her helplessly, but Bryony gave her a faint nod. She needed her presence, even if she didn't want sweet Pauline Harkins caught in the middle of whatever odd game they were playing. And it wasn't rat and mouse, it was cat and mouse. Though she wondered why Kilmartyn equated himself with a rat, one of the vilest creatures on earth.

Bryony picked up the paper and began to read the menus in a clear voice, growing hungrier as each menu was read and then elaborated upon by the cook. She'd stuffed herself that morning, and yet Mrs. Harkins's creations were making her ravenous. In fact, it seemed as if all her appetites had been awakened. Things tasted better, music sounded sweeter, the sky was a brighter blue. And the man in front of her was more devastating than she'd ever found anyone before.

"It all sounds divine, Mrs. Harkins," Kilmartyn said in a soft voice. "Clearly I'll have to have supper at home more often."

And that was all she needed, Bryony thought miserably. She should never help Mrs. Harkins with her menus again.

"Very good, my lord," the cook said, beaming as she sketched a faint curtsy.

"Then we'd best get to the rest of our duties," Bryony said briskly. "Do you have any idea when her ladyship is expected to return home?"

If he was surprised to hear of his wife's departure he didn't show it. "I neither know nor care. Nothing would please me more than if she'd simply fall off the face of the earth, never to be seen or heard from again."

The flat, cold tone of his voice shocked her, as much as the belief that he meant every word. He clearly despised the woman he married.

"Then we'll simply make certain her room is put back in proper order for her eventual return," she said evenly. "Come along, Mrs. Harkins." She moved fast, hurrying the woman along, and she'd almost made it to the door when Kilmartyn spoke up. "Not so fast, my dear Mrs. Greaves. We have yet to discuss the household."

She wanted to gnash her teeth, but she'd forgotten she had actual news to impart. She could have always handled it in a note to his wretched lordship, but status would dictate that any disclosures should be made in person. She came forward to stand in front of his desk obediently, as Mrs. Harkins gently closed the door behind her. Kilmartyn's expression didn't change. He still had that polite, faintly disinterested look on his face, identical to the one he showed to Mrs. Harkins. That, at least, was a relief. Wasn't it?

"I did have news for you, my lord," she said, before he could start with a list of her deficiencies. "Mr. Peach will start work on your bedroom today, and promises he should be finished by Saturday. I will need to make arrangements for an alternative bedroom for you, and I wondered if you have a preference."

He was shuffling papers absently, like any employer forced to deal with the humdrum matters of everyday life. "Yours," he said.

It took her a moment to grasp the import of his words, but he continued on quite smoothly. "I expect you'd probably raise a fuss, so I'll make do with the violent-yellow chamber at the end of the hallway." He raised his eyes to meet hers, and his expression was absolutely serene.

Bryony took a breath. "You, my lord, are absolutely outrageous."

He smiled then, an innocent, almost angelic smile that went well with his beautiful face. "Hadn't you realized that, my dear Miss Greaves? My very dear Miss Greaves?"

There was a gnawing feeling in the pit of her stomach that she told herself was hunger. But hunger for what? For the attention and flirtation of a beautiful man? This was very bad. This was very bad indeed.

If he could be businesslike despite their odd banter then so could she. She cleared her throat unnecessarily. "The household is slowly becoming ordered. The new maids are working out extremely well. Jem, the kitchen boy, is lively and energetic and occasionally respectful, and you know that Mr. Collins has been a gift from the gods."

"A gift from you, Miss Greaves. Do you consider yourself a goddess?" He leaned back in his chair, putting his fingertips together in a motion that simply called attention to the beauty of his hands. "Let me see, which would you be?"

"Hestia," she said promptly. At least this was a safe topic of conversation. "Goddess of hearth and home."

"Oh, no," he said. "You're much more interesting than that. You're more like Diana, the chaste huntress. Then again, what are you hunting?"

That managed to unsettle her further. How in the world could he guess that she was looking for something? "I would hardly qualify as a goddess, my lord." She didn't bother to gesture to her face—it was there to see quite plainly in the bright sunlight.

For some reason he didn't seem horrified by it. In fact, he didn't seem to notice it at all. "You might qualify as Ariadne, for all the clever webs you're trying to spin. Or you might be Persephone, trapped with an ogre like me."

"You're hardly an ogre, my lord, and I'm not trapped. I can leave anytime I choose."

"Can you?" He sounded doubtful, and that troubled her even more. "I think the closest you could come is Demeter, worried about her lost children. But you're too young to have children, and besides, you're a virgin. It must be your . . . sisters you're worried about. Brothers would be on their own, but sisters usually require someone to look after them, and I presume your parents are dead."

He was getting hideously close to the truth. He was a clever man, and he could put clues together. If she wasn't careful he'd guess who she was before the month was up. She couldn't let that happen.

"My parents are dead, and I have neither sisters nor brothers. I was an only child."

"Then who are the people you send your salary to?"

"I beg your pardon?"

His smile was catlike, no longer the dispassionate employer. "You told my wife you were still in service because the money your previous employer left you went to your family. What family?"

Bugger. The forbidden word danced in her head, and she wanted to groan. She should have been more careful.

But she rallied quickly. "My uncle, my great-aunt, and an unending series of young cousins all rely on my help," she replied. "I can give you their direction if you doubt me." She flung the last at him, a dangerous offer.

"Oh, there's no need, my darling Miss Greaves. I know as much as I need to know about your personal life."

It felt like a slap in the face. Of course the personal life of a servant was of no interest. Even the family life of a courtesan would be unimportant.

"Certainly, my lord," she said, trying to sound meek and almost succeeding. "Did you have any questions? About the household," she added hurriedly.

"None at all. You manage things quite beautifully, Miss Greaves. I don't know how we shall manage without you."

She froze. "I wasn't aware you were about to face such an eventuality. Have I somehow failed to give satisfaction?"

Something about her commonplace phrase amused him. "You have been admirable, my dear Miss Greaves. So admirable, in fact, that I doubt you'll wish to stay with us for long. But our household will delight in your presence for as long as you care to grace us."

She blinked at his flowery words. Too flowery. Unease trickled down her spine and then danced up again, making her throat tighten beneath the stiff, choking collar. "You are too kind, my lord."

"Oh, my dear," he said softly. "I'm afraid I'm not very kind at all."

For some reason that phrase sounded blatantly sexual, and she remembered the vial she had found.

As she remembered the leather folio beneath the mattress. Mr. Peach's men would be dismantling the place in a few hours, and she needed a chance to get her hands on whatever lay there, assuming he hadn't removed it, but there was no reason for him to think last night was anything other than a search for something to help her sleep. He'd be much more likely to consider it an approach on her part, but she'd disabused him of that notion, at least for now. He could have no idea how he affected her.

"If your lordship will excuse me, I have a great deal to do. Are you certain you want the yellow chamber? It's quite small."

"Yes, but the bed is big, and I'm a tall man. And I certainly want room for a companion. Or two."

She wasn't about to rise to *that* bait. "Certainly, my lord. And I'm sure Collins will let Mrs. Harkins know if she needs to provide an extra breakfast tray. Or two." Her tone was dulcet.

"Oh, they don't stay till morning. I fuck women, I don't sleep with them."

She stiffened. "I'm afraid I find that word offensive, my lord. I'm not used to language of that sort."

He smiled at her. "Well, I could say I bugger them, but that's not true. Usually," he added blithely.

All right, she conceded. Bantering words with him was a waste of time—he was far too good at saying things to startle her and she had no experience talking to men.

"Shocked you, didn't I, my very dear Miss Greaves? Do you even know the meaning of the bad words you occasionally spout when you're caught unawares? I'd suggest you ask someone."

She gave him the same steely gaze she used to subdue her sisters. "If you're finished with me, my lord, I have to oversee the maids, have them move your belongings to the yellow room. Mr. Peach and his men should be arriving shortly."

"I'm not finished with you by a long shot, my pet. But if you want to go make my bed, feel perfectly free."

She gave him a glacial nod and moved to pick up the breakfast tray. It wasn't her place to do such menial labor, but then, she'd done far worse in the few days she'd been in residence. Unfortunately she had nothing to show for her great subterfuge but cracked, blistered hands, a spotless house, an inexplicable ache in her heart with no proof at all of the man's guilt or innocence. She was going to need to work harder.

She leaned across the desk and caught the handles of the heavy silver tray, about to lift it when his hands gripped her wrists, stopping her. He lifted her hands, and though she tried to yank them away he was holding her tight.

She was used to wearing gloves. Last night had been a strange, dream-like interlude, one she could pretend hadn't happened. For some reason the broad daylight on her poor hands made everything more intimate, his skin on hers. "What in God's name have you been doing to your hands?" he demanded.

"Cleaning your house."

"That's the maids' work."

"It is. But when I first arrived we didn't have enough staff, and the place was a disaster. We had to make a start on it."

He'd turned her hand over, his thumbs rubbing the soft spot in her palms, and he said another foul word. "You need to do something about them."

"I will. It's the housekeeper's place to see to the care of minor wounds and such. When I get a chance I'll use some salve and wear gloves if your lordship doesn't mind."

"His lordship doesn't mind." The indolent master had returned, releasing her hands and leaning back in his chair. "Go and do it now. Unless you'd rather I take care of you."

"No, my lord." She started to pick the tray up again but he brushed her away. "Yes, my lord."

"Send someone else in. Send the new boy so I can take a look at him. It would be a good idea if I knew just who had free run of my household."

Like that handsome man outside the ballroom, Bryony thought, and almost opened her mouth to say something. But then, he was clearly there as an intimate guest of Lady Kilmartyn, and it would hardly be politic to mention him.

"Yes, my lord. Do you know when we may expect the return of your wife?"

He shrugged, completely unabashed, as if he hadn't had her in his bed last night, hadn't been kissing her so thoroughly she doubted her mouth would ever forget the feel and taste of it.

"I have no idea. If she stays true to form she won't return for weeks. No need to bother with cleaning up in there. Save your hands."

She was getting to the point where she didn't believe a word he said. The unpleasant Lady Kilmartyn could return anytime now. If she was to get a chance to search her rooms that chance would be now.

"Of course, my lord," she murmured. She was getting so very good at lying.

Kilmartyn sat where he was, staring at the closed door to his study, considering matters. Things were becoming a bit clearer, but for every answer two more questions sprung up.

Such as, why had one of Russell's daughters infiltrated his household?

It had come to him in a moment, when he'd randomly mentioned sisters, and then everything had fallen into place. The reason her eyes looked so familiar. Not the shape of them, but the deep blue color that he'd only seen in one other person. Eustace Russell was a far cry from the pretty woman who was trying so hard to look plain—it was little wonder he hadn't recognized the eyes he was used to seeing in a heavy, aging face. But once he had made the connection he was shocked it had taken so long.

His little spy had nothing to do with his own secrets—she would have no reason to be interested in the fact that he'd supported a doomed and dangerous cause, something that could get him arrested and possibly even hanged for treason.

But Eustace Russell was another matter entirely. Her father had committed a crime and been caught at it, and died trying to escape the country. He was disgraced, his entire estate confiscated by the crown, and at the time Kilmartyn hadn't remembered his three daughters, much less felt a moment's concern for their well-being. His own solicitor had assured him the girls were well cared for by their late mother's estate, and they had no need of money earned the old-fashioned way, by hard work.

He hadn't even bothered to revisit Russell's peculiar accusation, ascribing it to an attempt to divert suspicion from his own nefarious activities. Now he wasn't so sure.

Why was Russell's daughter here? He was almost positive she was the eldest, the one he'd never met. Supposedly a childhood illness had left her weak. Obviously a lie, to cover up the fact that she had a few trifling scars from a bout with smallpox. It was hard to believe that was the reason she'd been hidden away, but he could think of no other.

He might be mistaken, but he didn't think so. Russell had not been a pretty man, but those uncommon blue eyes were a giveaway. And their mother had been an acclaimed beauty, which explained where Miss Greaves had gotten her looks.

Miss Greaves? Miss Grieves! Now that he thought about it everything was incredibly obvious, and he was tempted to go after her and demand what the hell she was doing. What she wanted from him.

Because he knew what he wanted from her.

That was another matter entirely, one he needed to put out of his mind until he found out why she was here. He couldn't afford to think with his cock right now. That could come later.

The first thing he needed to check was the status of the daughters' finances. He trusted his solicitor completely, but there had been a great deal to sort through at the time, what with Russell's supposed absconding with such a huge amount of investors' money, and the welfare of the criminal's offspring had hardly been of monumental importance. It was possible they didn't have enough money to support themselves, and with the cloud over Eustace Russell's name the girls would be hard put to make decent marriages. But no matter how destitute they might actually be, there was no reason for them to do manual labor.

Now one of them had landed in his lap. He had an unfortunate tendency to remember almost everything people said to him, and he instantly remembered Russell's talk of his three daughters. He'd even had miniatures of two of them on his desk. With the third he'd had only a silhouette.

He shook his head in disbelief. Was her family blind? Had they been the ones to turn her into a pariah, or had she chosen that way herself? He knew enough about her strength of will to guess that it had been mostly her choice.

The pseudonymous Mrs. Greaves was Bryony. She'd given her name as Bryony Greaves, and it was an easy jump. If she was going to take as obvious a last name as Greaves then she probably wouldn't go far from her given name, no matter how unusual it was. People who were pretending to be someone other than who they were—and he had far too much experience in that regard—would be wise to stay as close to their given name as possible. And Miss Bryony Russell was a very wise young woman.

He leaned back in his chair and laughed softly. This was even better than he expected. She could have only one reason to be in his household. She must believe her father innocent, and she was looking either for a scapegoat or the missing fortune, or both.

He himself had little doubt that Russell had done it. The evidence had been clear—there had been no other possible conclusion. Then again, perhaps that evidence had been just a little too clear. He'd known Russell since he'd first come to England, had considered the man a mentor as well as a business partner. Not that Russell was a particularly warm man. In fact, he was gruff and practical and rigidly honest . . .

Kilmartyn slammed his hand down on the desk with a muttered oath, and the dishes jumped. God, he'd been a fool! Russell had always been so scrupulous about matters of business—insisting on refunds if he considered there had been an error on the part of his employees, despite his concern for his stockholders. He never would have stolen money and tried to run away with it, abandoning his daughters, nor destroyed the company he was so proud of, the company that bore his name. His coach had gone over the cliffs near Devonport, his daughters left behind in Somerset to fend for themselves. The one weakness Russell had had was for his children. He would never have abandoned them.

Rising, he paced toward the window, pushing the curtain aside to stare out at the damp spring day. This changed everything. No wonder they hadn't found a trace of the fortune that had gone missing. Russell had never had it. Though why he'd been heading toward Devonport was anybody's guess. Unless he was going after Captain Thomas Morgan.

Morgan was a reprobate, and it took one to know one. He'd lived hard for his thirty-some years, including a stint as a privateer down in the Indian Ocean. His ethics and morals had always been highly questionable, but he'd been a damned good captain, and up until a week before Russell had died he'd commanded the best ship in the fleet.

Kilmartyn had had very little to do with the day-to-day running of the business—he sat on the board of directors and Russell would consult him about the financial end of things. Kilmartyn had an exceptional mind for business, a fact that had always amused him. Since he'd come to

London he'd made ridiculous amounts of money, and even after sending the bulk back to the estate in Ireland he still managed to live in luxury. So much that he hadn't paid proper attention when the Fenians had come to him for help, calling on his Irish blood. He wouldn't be making that mistake again, if he managed to survive the first one.

He hadn't known that Russell had sent orders to remove Morgan from his command at the last minute, beaching him like a fish. Or, remembering Morgan, a shark. That came out in the inquest, but Morgan had insisted he had no idea why.

If Russell had been heading toward Morgan then the man must be involved, or at least Russell had had very good reason to believe so.

Had his little spy deduced that? Apparently not, since she was busy snooping around his house and not Morgan's. Of course, he had the advantage of knowing he had nothing to do with the huge mess, whereas Bryony Russell thought he might be a murderer.

He turned back, smiling faintly. If he were a good man he would call her into the library, tell her he'd seen through her charade, and explain to her why Morgan was the logical culprit.

But then, he wasn't a good man, he knew that. He was a liar, a cheat, a shallow, conscienceless cad.

He was also a very handsome man; his mirror, his horrible wife, and the female half of society made that very clear. He could have just about anyone he wanted, with little or no effort. But for some damned reason he wanted Bryony Russell, thorns and all.

Maybe it was simply the challenge she offered, the sheer delight of playing her ridiculous game, confounding her even more. In the end, when he was ready to let her go, he'd tell her the truth. And then she could run off to Devonport and see if Thomas Morgan was in need of a housekeeper. And if that thought bothered him he'd soon get over it.

At least Cecily had decided to disappear without a trace. She had a habit of doing so, ever since the first time, when he'd gone into a panic, afraid she'd thrown herself in the river. Nowadays he couldn't care less. For the time being he didn't have to worry about her and what kind of trouble she might be stirring up for him, a small blessing. He didn't have to deal with her threats or her tantrums. She was gone and she could stay that way.

He'd much rather concentrate on Miss Bryony Russell. Bryony. First off, it would behoove him to find out where the other two sisters were, and what their financial situation really was. Then, and only then would he start in on the cuckoo in his nest.

There was only one problem with all this. Seducing well-born virgins was universally frowned upon by society. It was just lucky he didn't give a tinker's damn about society. Because he meant to have her, and he was getting tired of waiting. Last night he'd had a taste, and that taste lingered in his senses, driving him mad. He would have her, and soon.

The question was, would he ever be ready to let her go?

CHAPTER THIRTEEN

IN THE END, Bryony had no choice in the matter. Much as she wanted to inspect Lady Kilmartyn's apartment, Mr. Peach and his crew were arriving after lunch to begin work on Kilmartyn's room, and she needed to get his belongings out of there. More important, she needed to get the leather book from beneath the mattress.

It had been easier than she expected. Mr. Collins was an excellent taskmaster, and he kept the men busy making room for the new furniture. She could hear the girls chattering away cheerfully from down the hall, and there were no eyes to watch her as she stepped back into his bedchamber once more.

She was perfectly composed looking out the tall windows, glancing at the pretty rug, the door to the empty dressing room. It wasn't until she looked down at the unmade bed that her body felt suffused with heat.

She needed fresh air, she thought, making no move to go to the window. She simply stood and stared at the bed. *Your heart is pounding, your pulses are racing, and your nipples are hard. I'm willing to bet my sweet little virgin is wet.* His soft, seductive words echoed in her mind, as she felt her body responding to the memory of those moments in the bed with him, the fierce surge of pleasure at the touch of his hand between her legs.

She gave herself an impatient shake. She was no young debutante to be all atremble over a man. She was simply . . . unused to such attentions. It was no wonder it had upset her. But she was strong-willed, and she would deal with it.

The girls hadn't made the bed, knowing it was going to be dismantled, and she looked at the tangled sheets. Remembering them twisted around his naked body.

"Oh, God," she whispered out loud, though whether it was a curse or a prayer she had no idea. Gritting her teeth, she touched the soft, wrinkled sheets, then slid her hands beneath the mattress.

For a moment she thought it was gone. She could have sworn it was closer to the foot of the bed, but instead it was toward the head. It didn't matter—when her fingers finally touched it she drew it out with a sigh of relief.

It didn't look particularly prepossessing. It was simply an oversize, leather-bound book, with no title on the cover and an unexpected lock holding it closed. She was about to fiddle with it when she heard Mr. Collins's voice nearby, and she quickly yanked the sheets off the bed, wrapping them around the book a moment before he walked in the door.

He didn't seem to find it odd that she was kneeling by Kilmartyn's bed. "We're ready to move the furniture if you wish, Mrs. Greaves."

She rose, still clutching her treasure beneath the heap of sheets. They smelled like him. Not in a bad way—the scent was a combination of skin and spice and leather, and she belatedly thought of the bedside table and its odd contents.

"That's excellent, Mr. Collins," she replied. "Do this room first, since it's the most important, and then go on to the adjoining one. Do you think there's room for all the furniture in the room across the hall?" She sounded so calm and smooth she wanted to crow in triumph.

"Everything but the armoire," he replied, looking at the bundle of sheets she was clasping to her bosom. "May I assist you with the laundry, Mrs. Greaves? That's hardly your responsibility."

She resisted the impulse to grasp it more tightly and shriek no. She simply shook her head. "No, thank you. There are a few tears that need mending and I thought it would be something soothing to keep me busy after supper."

"Tears?" Collins echoed, shocked. "In Irish linen sheets?"

She managed not to choke. "Not in the sheets themselves," she amended. "In the embroidered crest."

"Not to question your judgment, Mrs. Greaves, but surely that should be given to a professional needlewoman?"

She smiled tightly. "Normally, but I happen to have a particular gift for needlework, and I find it soothing. When I'm done no one will even be able to see that there was fraying." *Mainly because the sheets were in excellent shape,* she added silently.

Mr. Collins swallowed the dodgy excuse. "Shall I have someone carry them up to your room, then?"

"No need. I'll be back in just a moment." Before he could ask any more questions she was out the door and racing up the narrow staircase to the servants' quarters. She didn't dare take time to look at the journal, she simply dumped everything under her bed and went back down. There'd be time enough to deal with it later on.

She went directly to Lady Kilmartyn's apartment. The hallway was deserted, which came as no surprise. The entire second story was the domain of the countess, and apart from a cursory inspection, one that fell short of the countess's bedroom, Bryony had kept her distance. In fact, she felt uneasy walking down the hallway, past the tightly closed doors. She couldn't rid herself of the feeling that hidden eyes were watching her, which was ridiculous. Lady Kilmartyn had disappeared, probably with her handsome cousin, and was unlikely to return for weeks. She might as well take the time to acquaint herself with the one part of the house she'd previously been denied before setting the maids to work on it.

Not that she expected Kilmartyn would have hidden anything incriminating in the vicinity of his wife. It was clear he despised the woman he married, and the feeling appeared to be mutual. If there was any way Lady Kilmartyn could betray her husband she would have already done it.

Still, there was such a thing as hiding in plain sight. While this would be the last place she would expect to find something incriminating, she couldn't afford to be careless. She turned the highly polished brass door-knob and stepped into the bedroom.

She was immediately seized by a fit of sneezing. The room was very dark, the heavy curtains pulled against the daylight, the stench of clashing perfumes hanging heavy in the air. Closing the door behind her, she started toward the windows, then caught herself as she immediately tripped over something on the floor. She took another step, then caught herself again, finally making it to the curtains by dint of shuffling her legs so that nothing else could threaten to send her tumbling to her knees.

The early promise of a bright day had faded, but even the fitful sunlight illuminated such a shambles that even though she'd been warned Bryony was shocked. It looked as if there'd been a boxing match held in the midst of the elegant rooms. Furniture was upended, the bed was torn apart, feathers floated in the air, presumably from a pillow having been ripped apart. She could see the glitter of broken glass on the floor, smashed perfume bottles, no doubt, and one of the curtains was ripped halfway off the curtain rod. She stared around her in dismay. How could all this destruction have occurred without anyone hearing anything? Surely Kilmartyn, being only one story above, would have been disturbed by some of the clamor? Though perhaps it had happened before he returned home last night.

It would take the girls several days to bring this place back into order, but in the meantime she could get a start on things. Anything to keep her mind occupied until she could sneak away and search through that ledger with its ancient leather binding.

Of course Lady Kilmartyn's rooms held nothing as useful as a broom. Bryony waded into the midst of it all, uncertain where to begin, when she looked at the bed. The counterpane was ripped and clawed by some sharp instrument, possibly a knife, but the sheet half on, half off the mattress looked to be in one piece, though she suspected that was the source of some of the rancid perfume. She yanked it off the bed, hearing the glass crunch beneath her shoes, and stretched it out on the floor. Another Irish linen, with a fine, tight weave, it would hold things admirably, and heaven knew if the stink of the perfume could ever be removed. It was probably beyond salvage.

She tossed broken bits of perfume bottles, shards of mirrors, smashed bits of furniture into the center of the sheet, catching up stained, discarded dresses, torn books, all manner of detritus. The dressing table was littered with spilled powder and hairpins, and she dusted it off, setting the pieces of broken jewelry on the marble surface. She had no idea whether Lady Kilmartyn had a similar destructive policy toward her jewelry as well as her clothing, but there was no way a thrifty soul like Bryony Russell could countenance tossing out three links of a diamond-studded bracelet or a single emerald earring with a broken clasp. She worked steadily, moving around the room in a counterclockwise motion. When the sheet was filled she tied the corners together and dragged it out into the hall, then went back in and ripped down the torn curtain, starting a new pile in the center of it. Dust motes danced in the air, and Bryony had the suspicion that these rooms hadn't had a thorough cleaning in a shockingly long time, given the amount of dust she was unsettling. Her ladyship wouldn't recognize the place when she finally returned, a fact that should have filled Bryony with trepidation. Lady Kilmartyn wasn't the type to view any major change to her comfort with equanimity, and she'd take any excuse she could find to dismiss Bryony.

However, there was the very real possibility that Bryony would be long gone before Kilmartyn's wife returned, and she would never have to see the wretched woman again.

Her back was beginning to ache and her enthusiasm for hard work flag when she finally reached the corner under the far window that overlooked the small formal garden between the house and the mews. At first she thought the dark patch on the floor was simply a shadow. Moving between the window and the patch made no change in its irregular shape, and on impulse she leaned down and touched it. Her fingers came away wet, sticky, and she yanked her hand back, rubbing it against her now-filthy white apron, leaving streaks behind. The maids were going to have to give the entire room a solid scrubbing, and whatever had spilled onto the floor had spread into the Aubusson carpet, probably ruining it.

She brought her fingers to her nose, sniffing at it, and the smell was oddly familiar, though she couldn't place it. There was a metallic tang to it, almost like that of copper, but she could think of nothing that would fit that description.

Yanking off her apron, she dropped to her knees beside the puddled stain and began trying to soak it up. In moments the grubby cotton was soaked, and the stuff seemed to ooze out of the carpet. She rose and moved to the window to stare at the stain, holding it up to the light.

She let out horrified cry, dropping it to the floor as she fell back from the vile thing. In the clear light of day it could be one thing and one thing only. Blood.

The knock on the door shocked her, and she whirled around, just as Emma poked her head inside the room. "Do you want some help, Mrs. Greaves? Mrs. Harkins said things are a rare mess."

Bryony had shoved her hands behind her back, acting on pure instinct, and she could only hope the shadows in the room hid what was likely her greenish pallor. "No need," she managed to say in a relatively brisk tone. "I'll finish up in here by myself."

"Are you certain, Mrs. Greaves? Because I could—"

"Absolutely certain," she said, unable to keep a note of grimness out of her voice. "I'm sure you have other things that will keep you busy."

If her tone surprised Emma she didn't show it. "Yes, ma'am," she said, and a moment later she was gone. Bryony sank to her knees then, holding on to the wide sill of the window for balance, then snatched her hands back when she saw the bloody marks she was leaving. She sat back on her heels, shuddering.

What had Kilmartyn said? *Nothing would please me more than if she'd simply fall off the face of the earth, never to be seen or heard from again.* And in Bertie's drugged-like stupor he'd heard what he called a tremendous row. Had Kilmartyn fought with his wife one last time? Had he lost his temper?

She shivered in the cool, damp room. The thought was abhorrent, so bizarre she couldn't believe she was even considering the possibility. And yet, she was already wondering whether he'd killed her father in cold blood. Just what kind of monster was he?

Had he killed his wife, disposed of her body, and then taken to his bed only to end up with Bryony in his arms? Surely if he'd killed his wife he would have gotten rid of all evidence. He was a very thorough man. And what about Lady Kilmartyn's French maid? Where had she gone during all this?

She should leave the room as she'd found it and send word to Scotland Yard. They'd flatly ignored her suspicions about her father's death, refusing to look into it, but if the Earl of Kilmartyn was suspected in a second death then the first one would be more likely to come to light. If he was a cold-blooded killer then this time he would have signed his own death warrant. All she had to do was lay charges against him and take off, waiting for the wheels of justice to grind.

But could she trust Scotland Yard? No one had her motivation, and as far as she could see the only one who'd care about Lady Kilmartyn's demise would be her handsome cousin. Given the circumstances he could scarcely come forward.

She pushed herself to her feet. Her legs were stronger now, and her hands weren't shaking as much. Her stomach still felt a bit queasy, and she glanced over at the dark, viscous stain. What else could it be? One of Mrs. Harkins's rapacious rats? She had no sense of how much blood a human or a rodent contained—the mess might simply be the result of someone dispatching a rat with a fire poker. The elegant mademoiselle might be willing to wield the weapon—she was French, after all—but soaking up blood might be a little too much to ask. It was a reasonable scenario. A revolting rat appears in the countess's bedroom, she shrieks, and her maid does battle, leaving the room in a shambles and covered in blood, and the two of them take off rather than deal with the mess.

Reasonable enough. She could convince herself that was what happened, couldn't she? Except what kind of rat had that much blood in him?

She wasn't going to consider any other possibility, at least, not at the moment. Lady Kilmartyn would show up in a week or two, that smug smile on her perfect mouth. If Bryony were to make a fuss over a little blood it would simply distract from what she was here to accomplish.

There was simply no way that Kilmartyn could have had anything to do with this. The wickedly playful man she'd tumbled into bed with hadn't come from a scene of carnage or a violent crime, nor would he have arisen in the predawn hours to go commit such a heinous act. It was impossible, unless he was far greater a villain than even she could imagine. And he wasn't. He was a great deal of dangerous talk, but beneath it she doubted he could ever hurt something weaker than he was, even his despised wife.

• •

She'd never been so grateful for the wonders of hot, plumbed water. She'd found an empty ewer and climbed the stair to fill it from the bathing room on the third floor, then carried it back down to the ruined bedroom. It took four trips to get the majority of the blood up, and even then the ominous brownish stain lingered on the edge of the pale pink carpet.

She'd ended up using some of Lady Kilmartyn's white lawn chemises, then wrapped them all in a dark wool cape and tucked the whole thing into the middle of the second pile of discards. The weave of the wool was tight enough that the drying blood shouldn't leak through, and all this should end up in the ocean or the Thames by day's end. There would be nothing to tie all that blood with the countess of Kilmartyn. She pulled the curtains again, plunging the room back into darkness, and at the last minute found a small, woven rug on the floor of the dressing room. It would look odd, pushed up against the windows and covering part of the Aubusson, but it would be better than nothing.

She would have given anything to go upstairs to bathe and change. The smell of blood seemed to cling to her, and her stomach was still unsteady after the day's work, but she didn't dare. Instead she managed to sneak into the bathing room, strip down to her waist and scrub most of the blood off her. Some lingered in the cracked skin around her fingers, beneath her short nails, and she was so ruthless in scrubbing that she caused her own damaged skin to bleed. She dried her hands on her own petticoats, dropping the dark skirts back down over them, and pulled her clothes back around her before splashing water in her face.

There was a large mirror opposite the huge copper tub, which struck Bryony as odd. There would be no way to avoid looking at one's unclothed body, and she couldn't think of any possible benefit to such an embarrassing encounter. It was one thing to check one's reflection to ensure that one's clothes fit correctly, one's hair was neat. There was absolutely no reason to look at an unclothed body. Was there?

She glanced back at the huge tub. The house on Curzon Street hadn't yet been fitted with hot water—her father had always held a deep mistrust of excessive bathing, and there were always plenty of servants to lug hot water for her and her sisters. If it had been up to her this would have been the first improvement she would have made to their London house, the house that was now a burned-out shell. If they ever regained ownership of Renwick she would have hot water piped all the way up to the servants' quarters—these past few days had reinforced her love for the incredible luxury of a hot bath.

She still looked a little chalky, and she reached up and pinched her cheeks, forcing color back into them. Her hair had come loose, and she pinned it back in place. *It was going to be just fine,* she told herself. *Everything would be just fine.*

The huge bundles she'd left in the hallway were gone by the time she opened the bathroom door, and the gaslights had been lit against the increasing gloom of the day. The noise overhead was silenced, and she moved up the inner staircase to the third floor and poked her head into Kilmartyn's bedroom.

The progress was impressive. The walls had been stripped of their gloomy fabric, the curtains were down, and the woodwork had a fresh coat of paint. If Mr. Peach's men could replace the wall coverings by tomorrow Kilmartyn would be able to return to his room by the following day. She moved through the inner doorway, peering into the adjoining room. That was even further along, with two of the four walls already covered in the gray-blue damask that brightened the area. The late spring afternoon was beginning to settle down, and she moved to the window, staring out into the gathering dusk. Where in the world had the day gone? Scrubbing the blood of a murdered woman, or cleaning up after a dead rat? She wasn't sure she wanted to know the answer.

"I got rid of them parcels, Mrs. Greaves," Bertie announced when she made her way into the kitchen. "Mr. Collins thought we ought to go through things, see what we might save, but I told him her ladyship don't like to keep things around and she don't like other people using her things. Dustman's already taken everything up on his cart as well as piles from three other houses, so I'm hoping you haven't changed your mind about it. There won't be getting any of it back."

She considered feigning a look of disappointment, then decided not to bother. "Thank you, Bertie. We're well rid of it all."

"I still say it's a Christian shame," Mr. Collins announced. "Such good things going to waste."

"It's not our place to question our employers," Bryony said in a reproving tone. She'd almost used the more common phrase, "our betters," but something stopped her at the last minute. There was no way she could reasonably refer to a reprobate like the Earl of Kilmartyn as her better—she'd choke on the very words.

She didn't want time to stop and think, nor did she want the other servants to start wondering. The more she thought about it the more convinced she was. Blood had been everywhere in that room. No one could lose that much blood and survive. She had never been prone to dramatics—she left that up to her younger sisters. Common sense had always seemed to serve her best, but she couldn't rid herself of the hideous certainty that someone had died in that room. Was there any possible alternative?

Lady Kilmartyn had disappeared, leaving everything, her jewels included, behind. Leaving nothing but blood-splattered clothes and sheets. Her maid was gone as well. There had been stories, of course, of servants driven mad who'd turned on their employer, and even this short taste of life belowstairs made it seem more than reasonable. Not that she was tempted to take a butcher knife to Kilmartyn. A good solid broom against the side of his head, however, might knock some sense into him.

But if someone had murdered either Lady Kilmartyn or her maid or both, then where were the bodies? The blood was telltale enough.

Like a moth drawn to a flame she'd been pulled back to the room, over and over again, checking to make certain there was no sign of violence, of bloodshed left to the casual eye.

In the end, Kilmartyn didn't return, and there was no way she could look into his dark green eyes and know for sure whether he'd committed a horrific crime. Or two of them. She picked at the venison pie Mrs. Harkins had made for her absent employer, and it wasn't until late that she finally managed to crawl up the endless flights of stairs to her room beneath the eaves, and she was so weary she almost forgot about her hidden cache under her narrow bed. She'd waited until everyone else had retired, insisting she had work to do on her housekeeping books, and it was all she could do to stay awake long enough to be certain that each and every one of the servants was sound asleep. Bertie had been relieved of hallway duty, both because he'd failed so dismally the night before and because Kilmartyn had left word not to expect him home. Bryony could only thank the heavens for that small blessing. She wasn't sure she could look at him again, not after having spent the day cleaning blood from his wife's bedroom. His despised wife's bedroom. No matter how often she told herself it meant nothing, a strange feeling lingered between her shoulder blades, a feeling she didn't want to examine too closely.

She also had no intention of going to bed with dried blood caked beneath her fingernails. She waited as long as she possibly dared before creeping back up to the second floor, the floor of bloodstains and no living soul around. Her understanding of plumbing had its limitations, and by the time the copper tub was six inches deep with water the stuff coming out of the tap was cold, so she simply stripped off her clothes and climbed in, letting the water lap around her hips. It still felt wonderful, even if she had to duck and bend and turn, even if she had to rinse her hair in icy water, even if she panicked every two minutes, thinking she heard footsteps. It wasn't until she'd finished that she realized she'd forgotten something as mundane as toweling, so she simply dried herself off as best she could with the cleaner bits of her clothing, wrapped it around her body and then sped up the two narrow flights of stairs to her bedroom, all without anyone catching her. By the time she closed the door behind her, dropped her soiled clothing, and fell naked on her bed, she was shivering and laughing at the same time, thrilled with having gotten away with it. It wasn't until she reached for her nightdress that hung in the small armoire that she remembered what had happened to her the last time she wore it, and her momentary sense of triumph vanished.

There was no gaslight on the top story of the town house, but the oil lamp provided more than enough illumination. Once she was dressed she hauled her cache out from under the bed, dumped it on the mattress and set to work on the lock. It seemed to be meant more for fashion than function, because she easily opened the ledger that would provide proof of Kilmartyn's guilt or innocence.

She slammed it shut again with a horrified gasp. It wasn't a ledger, a journal, any kind of proof at all, unless you considered it a proof of moral depravity, and she hadn't needed proof of that. The book was very old, filled with engravings that were detailed, delicate, hand-tinted. And startlingly obscene.

The men and women in the drawings were in various stages of undress, though the clothing, or lack thereof, was the least shocking thing about it. It was what those men and women were doing that was so astonishing.

At least it answered her question about the Elgin Marbles. These men were possessed of body parts that were very different from those she'd seen in the British Museum, and after one close look she immediately slammed the heavy leather covers closed again as she felt the heat rise in her face. She wasn't so naive that she doubted that's what people actually did to each other. She'd spent enough time in the country to understand the rudiments of animal congress, though the sketches in this book seemed to suggest that humans use a great deal more variety in their amorous pursuits. And surely the . . . appendages must be exaggerated.

She opened the book again, steeling herself to look down at the drawings. There was text as well, in old Italian, and she suspected the book was both old and valuable. Perhaps people didn't do such things anymore. Perhaps this was aberrant behavior practiced by Italians, or members of some cult.

She closed it again, scrambled off the bed, and shoved the book underneath the mattress, blowing out the lamp before climbing back under the covers. If Kilmartyn could sleep on it so could she. Tomorrow she would burn the wretched thing.

Five minutes later she sat up, lit the lamp, and pulled out the book once more. The oddest thing about the drawings was how happy everyone appeared to be. The women who were being pleasured most outrageously were laughing in delight, the men equally pleased with the world. She didn't equate copulation with such open joy. Carefully she began to read through the book again, distracting herself by translating until she began to understand what the words were saying. She almost slammed the book closed again, but she steadied herself, studying each page with care. In fact, now that her initial shock had faded, it seemed more like some wicked chapbook, with careful instructions for degrees of intimacy if her limited grasp of Italian served her. She stopped at the strangest engraving of all. A man was standing by an open window, his breeches unfastened, and a woman knelt in front of him. All she could see was the back of the female's head, but she had a strong suspicion about what that woman was doing. And indeed, when she turned the next page the view was from a different angle, and the activity was far too clear.

Bryony told herself she should feel horror, disgust, shock. Instead she stared at the drawing for long moments, wondering what would cause a woman to do such a strange thing. Wondering what it would taste like. Feel like. Wondering why she felt heat begin to pool low inside her.

She shoved the book away again. Nanny Gruen would tell her it ought to be burned, but even Bryony, despite her innocence, knew better. The sketches had been done by a master's hand, and the sheer inventiveness and joy in the pages should never be obliterated. Kept out of sight of innocents, of course, but it really was the most extraordinary document.

She lay still in her bed, fighting her curiosity. Her long thick hair was still damp, and she shivered slightly in the cool night air. She needed to sleep. She'd worked abominably hard today, tomorrow would bring new challenges, and she was exhausted.

She lay on her back, and yet the covers seemed to caress her body, including the fine lawn nightdress she'd brought with her. It was almost as if there'd been some sort of magic elixir in the bathwater that had made her skin sensitive to the feel of everything. Perhaps her father had been correct about the dangers of excessive bathing.

Or perhaps he'd known nothing at all. It wasn't the hot water caressing her skin, the scent of lavender from the fine-milled soap that had roused such a strange reaction in her body. It was the book hidden beneath her bed, the drawings. The suggestions of possibilities that seemed to have slid beneath her skin like some wicked itch.

She suddenly realized her hand had drifted to her stomach, and she pulled it away, shocked at herself. Women didn't touch themselves. Pleasure themselves. Unless, of course, they were the women in the sketches, who seemed just as happy using their own hands or cylindrical objects provided by their partners.

She sat up. Her skin was on fire, the secret place between her legs felt heavy, aching. She needed to think of something else, something to wipe the erotic images from her brain.

The answer was clear, obvious, and unacceptable. She could think about what happened in the room two flights beneath her. The struggle, the blood, the death she didn't want to believe had happened. Or she could think of the men in the book, the clever hands touching places no gentleman should touch, the body parts that were much larger than seemed possible, and slumberous pleasure on the women's classic faces.

She lay back down again. She could think of it in scholarly terms. Artistic ones. She had a certain talent with brush and ink, but the delineation of muscle, the smoothness of flank, the delicacy of expression clearly showed the hand of a master. What artist had spent such time crafting naughty drawings? And had he experienced everything he'd drawn? She suspected he had, and more than once, if he'd been able to capture it so faithfully, and then she realized her hand was stroking her pebbled breast and she yanked it away again, keeping her arms rigidly by her side.

She couldn't think about those drawings, not with the peculiar effect they were having on her own flesh. And she wouldn't think of Lady Kilmartyn's devastated room and whatever disaster she had covered up.

She could think of Renwick, its vast, sprawling lands, the house that went back to the time of Good Queen Bess, the dairies and honey house and gardens, all tended with loving care. But the longing that had always suffused her seemed muted now. Renwick was in the past, no longer hers to watch over. This was her home now, as disordered as it was.

Was it feminine nature, to claim wherever one lived as home? Was it normal to cleave to the new household, dismissing the old? Or was there something else about this place that drew her? Not just the mysteries, the questions, the unproven hints of violence. Why did this suddenly feel as if this was where she belonged?

She knew the answer, of course. Knew it, and refused to think about or dissect it. Adrian Bruton, fourth Earl of Kilmartyn, degenerate, sensualist, rake, and reprobate, had as powerful an attraction for her as the wicked drawings beneath her bed. No matter what crimes she thought him capable of, she was still drawn to him in a way no Christian woman ought to be. And as she let sleep claim her, her drifting mind saw herself on her knees in front of him, the taste and size of him in her mouth, the delight on her face with her half-closed eyes.

• •

It had been a hell of a day, Adrian thought as he stumbled through the darkened hallways of his town house. There was no one waiting up for him this time—little wonder, since his footman had been sound asleep when he'd come in the night before.

Of course, that hadn't been an accident. Bertie wasn't the brightest of lads but he was usually reliable. He expected someone had drugged the boy.

He hadn't even thought more about it, heading up to bed until he'd woken up with the delightful surprise of Bryony rummaging underneath his mattress. Hadn't thought of anything at all until he'd been sitting at his desk, thinking of his housekeeper, Russell's daughter, and he'd finally decided he'd had enough of his blackmailing harridan of a wife.

If he was going to be tried for treason so be it. He'd be gone before they put him in the dock—he had enough money to disappear. He had little reason to trust the British government, and he'd done his best to find peaceful ways to change the current iron control of Ireland since the debacle of the first Fenian Outrage. If he had to leave he would, and never look back.

But he was damned if he was going to spend one more day married to a woman who paraded her lovers in front of him and toyed with him when she grew bored. Those damnably few moments with the sweetly delectable Bryony in his bed had done something to him. Changed him in some immutable way.

He hadn't thought the world could get much darker, but it had. It was pure luck that he'd found the blood-soaked clothes, *his* clothes, before his unwanted but acceptable valet did. He had little doubt that violence had been done in his house, and that his despised wife was dead. And someone was trying to make certain he was the one who'd be blamed for it.

He'd had no idea he had such a powerful enemy. Or maybe it was simply Cecily who had enemies, and whoever had killed her needed a scapegoat.

He should feel grief. Feel *something*. But instead he simply felt dazed, empty of everything, even relief. The only thing he could concentrate on was trying to figure out who was his enemy? Who would want Cecily dead? Who would want him dead as well, because surely he'd hang for it if they convicted him. Being a lord would do nothing to help him.

He was nobody's scapegoat. The clothes were hidden at the back of his cupboard, where even the inquisitive Collins wouldn't find them, and he'd deal with them later.

Cecily's rooms, at first glance, had looked normal, despite the stench of spilled perfume. And then he recognized the coppery tang of spilled blood beneath the thick, flowery scent, and on closer inspection he'd seen signs of a struggle. Someone had cleaned up after whatever violence had been done to her, though he couldn't imagine whom.

Yes, he could. Bryony could have done it, though he wasn't certain why she'd bother. If she'd called the police it wouldn't take long before she'd be exposed, but if she truly believed he was responsible for her father's death he would have thought that would be exactly what she wanted.

And yet everything had been wiped clean. He was half-tempted to find his way back into those rooms, see if he could discover any sign left behind of what had happened, but something stopped him. If he was going anywhere he was going up to the servants' quarters to see what the proper Miss Russell thought of his erotic engravings, and he couldn't do that. Not given who she was. She was now officially off-limits.

Or was she? She'd destroyed her reputation by moving into his household. If word got out she'd never marry, never be able to hold her head up. But she'd said she had no intention of marrying, and she'd never been in society before—she would hardly start now, after her father's disgrace. So who would know or care if he partook of such a tempting morsel?

She'd know. Bryony, for all her stern behavior, had a fragile heart beneath everything. She'd deny it as strongly as she'd deny who she was, but he knew women. He could scarcely seduce and then discard her like a demimondaine.

And he'd know. He didn't have much of a conscience left, but what remained seemed to belong to Bryony.

He reached his temporary bedroom in the darkness, not bothering with the gaslight or even a candle. Collins was nowhere around, thank God. He stripped off his cravat and coat, undid his waistcoat and dropped it on the floor. He was bone-tired, and he didn't want to think about blood or death or sex or anything pleasant or unpleasant. He just wanted to sleep.

He heard the footsteps, and cursed his damnably acute hearing. Someone was descending the servants' stairs, too near his room, and he recognized the sound. Bryony Russell was heading downstairs, and there was the excellent chance he'd catch her just as she was rummaging through his desk.

That would be more than interesting. With a sigh he rose from his bed and moved into the darkened hallway.

The crash had woken her up. At least, she thought it was a crash—in the suddenness of her nighttime awakening she couldn't be sure it was anything more than a bad dream. She heard it again, a muffled noise, and she sat up, reaching for her wrapper. It hadn't come from directly beneath the servants' floor, which should rule out Kilmartyn trying to find his drunken way to his new bedroom.

She slipped from the covers, her bare feet silent on the plain wood floor. She ought to go wake up one of the men. She moved to the cupboard and reached for her apron, and then pulled her hand back. She didn't have her keys, and the door between the attics that housed the male and female servants was stoutly locked. There was no way she could rouse any of the men.

She could see a light coming from the gap under her door, and she froze. Whoever was approaching was silent, ominously so, and for a moment she was tempted to try to shove the wardrobe in front of the door to keep out whatever monster lurked there. And then she stiffened her back. There was no way she was going to cower in her room, leaving the other women to the mercy of whoever was roaming the house. She pulled open the door before she could think better of it, and both she and Emma shrieked in unison.

"Hush!" Bryony said firmly, as if she hadn't been equally loud. "What are you doing here?"

"Oh, Mrs. Greaves, we heard the most dreadful noise coming from downstairs, and we thought you ought to know about it."

"I heard it," she said dryly. "It was probably nothing, but I think we'd best investigate, don't you?"

Emma's pale face looked aghast. "Oh, no, missus! I'm right terrified. I can't go down there."

Bryony stifled a sigh of irritation. "There's nothing to hurt you, Emma. It was most likely his lordship returning home."

"Most likely," Emma said with alacrity. "And if it's anyone else they're hardly likely to want to bother the servants, even if they could find the back staircase. I'll just go and tell the other girls not to worry about it." She had already started to back down the hallway, leaving Bryony alone and in the dark.

"Wait a moment," she said. "At least give me your lamp. I intend to investigate."

Emma offered no token protest, simply handing the lamp to Bryony. "You be careful, missus."

I'd be a great deal more careful if I had someone to watch my back, my girl, Bryony thought, irritation almost managing to wipe out her nervousness. "There's absolutely nothing to worry about," she said in the voice that had always convinced her younger sisters she was afraid of nothing. "But in the meantime you lock your door and stay in your room until morning. I don't want to be running into you in the dark again and frightening the life out of me."

"Yes, miss." Emma bobbed a curtsy, and before Bryony could think of another way to make her stay the girl had disappeared into the darkness, followed by the closing of the door and the scrape of a lock.

Idiot, Bryony chided herself. Emma was a servant; she was her mistress, or at least as close as you could get. She could have simply ordered the girl to go with her.

Except she understood very well why the girl was so nervous. And she had no intention of ordering anyone to do something that she herself wasn't willing to do.

Squaring her shoulders, she shut the door to her room behind her before starting down the narrow hallway, resisting the strong impulse to follow Emma's lead and dive back into the safety of her bed. Emma was right—the servants' staircase was hidden behind a series of baize doors, and no casual visitor to the house would easily discover it. She would make her way carefully down into the basement kitchen and equip herself with one of Mrs. Harkins's stout butcher knives. She was also possessed of a most impressive scream, one that could rouse the entire household and scare away all but the most determined villain. If things got really bad she could hurl the lamp at him, but since that might end up with the house going up in flames, just as their house on Curzon Street had, that would be only as a last resort.

She could be as silent as she could be loud, and she barely made a sound as she crept down the endless flights of stairs to the kitchen, stopping on each landing to listen for any telltale noise. The house was quiet once more, and she wondered whether that crashing noise had been next door, or out in the streets. After all, she slept with her windows ajar, no matter how chill the spring weather, and she could have easily heard the sound of dustbins crashing over, or an amorous catfight.

She paused on the second floor, about to move on, when she heard a muffled curse, and she froze, suddenly terrified. The curse came again, and she sank back against the wall in relief, recognizing Kilmartyn's deep voice. He'd come home after all, and he was probably so drunk he didn't realize he wasn't on the third floor but the second. If she were truly a good Christian she would rescue him, lead him to his bedroom, and dump him on his bed as she had the first night she'd been here. And she was going to do no such thing.

If she had any sense at all she'd go right back upstairs and lock herself in her bedroom. But apparently she was both a heathen and a dullard, because she was going to continue down to the ground floor kitchen and find that butcher knife before she did another thing. Bad things had happened in this house, very bad things, and she wasn't going to make the mistake of going about without some sort of protection.

The kitchen was still warm from the banked stove, and she set the lamp down on the big wooden table, looking around her. The night was still and quiet but her nerves were raw, and there was no way she was going to fall back asleep anytime soon. She reached a hand out to the stove, but it would take far too much time to start a fire hot enough to boil water for tea. Picking up the lamp, she headed into the butler's pantry. The heavy silver tray lay where Mr. Collins had left it, the cut glass decanter and delicate, globe-shaped glasses waiting. She picked up the heavy tray and carried it back into the kitchen, leaving the lamp in the other room, a pool of light spreading into the room.

Drinking the master's brandy was an offense punishable by instant dismissal and even a charge of stealing, but there were times when the rules simply didn't matter. She sat down at the table, poured herself half a glass of the amber-colored liquid and tossed it back as she'd seen her father do with whiskey.

She immediately began coughing and choking, her throat on fire as she struggled to regain her breath. Only to have it frightened out of her again, as a firm hand slapped her in the middle of her back.

"Now that's a truly criminal way to treat my best cognac, Miss Greaves," came Kilmartyn's smooth, not at all drunken voice.

"Bugger," said Bryony.

CHAPTER FOURTEEN

SHE IMMEDIATELY TRIED TO rise, but he put his hand on her shoulder, holding her back down in the chair, and she decided to stay where she was, simply because she had no choice.

"That's better," he murmured as he sensed her acquiescence, and he moved around into the shadowy kitchen, pulling a chair out with one foot and dropping down into it with perfect ease.

She couldn't read his expression in the shadows, and she sat there, flushed from her coughing fit, cursing her stupidity. The filtered light gave the ordinary room an intimate air. She was sitting there in her nightdress and shawl and bare feet; he was beside her in shirtsleeves, the buttons undone to leave an expanse of golden skin open. She'd touched that warm, sleek skin the first night she'd been here, when he'd been sleeping. She'd felt it press down on her the night before, crushing her breasts, and for some awful reason she felt those small, previously ignored breasts become almost unbearably sensitive against the soft fabric of her nightdress. And then she remembered the book, and she knew her face flamed. Fortunately the dark that hid his expression also shielded her own.

"Now what has brought my inestimable housekeeper down to the kitchen in the middle of the night in desperate search of my cognac?" he murmured. "Trouble sleeping again?"

He *would* bring that up, she thought, trying to summon indignation to fight the curling heat in her body. She used her best housekeeperly voice, but she was having a hard time getting the accent right. "I thought I heard a noise, and I came down to investigate it."

"Alone? I don't think that was a very wise idea." His voice was light, but there was a hard note beneath it.

"The door is kept locked between the rooms that house the male and female servants, and I left the keys downstairs. In fact, I was coming down to get them so I could summon assistance."

"And none of the female servants could at least accompany you?" Again that note of steel beneath his soft, charming voice.

If she told him Emma had refused he might very well fire the girl, even though he'd given her final say over the staff. She lied. "I didn't want to frighten them. And besides, by the time I reached the second floor I heard your voice and realized you'd come home unexpectedly and there was nothing to worry about."

"Nothing to worry about? You flatter me, Miss Greaves."

Again that twist in her stomach, an odd, clenching feeling that wasn't particularly unpleasant, just disturbing. She needed to pull herself together, and fast. "I do apologize for taking some of your brandy, my lord, but as you know I have difficulty sleeping and I decided to continue on down to the kitchen to brew myself a soothing cup of tea. Unfortunately the stove wasn't hot enough, and I gave in to temptation. I realize it was unpardonable, but—"

"Oh, I rather like the idea of you giving into temptation. And that isn't brandy, it's the finest French cognac. Haven't you ever had any before?"

"A lady doesn't drink hard spirits," she said stiffly.

He simply smiled at her. "But you're not a lady, my very dear Miss Greaves, you're a housekeeper. Or had you forgotten?"

"Of course not, my lord," she shot back, mentally cursing herself. She wasn't going to give in to this strange lassitude that was spreading over her.

She had a job to do and she would do it. "I was merely using the term 'lady' to apply to any properly brought-up female, whether she comes from the aristocracy or the serving class."

"And you were a properly brought-up young female? Tell me about it."

She watched, hypnotized, while he reached out for her brandy snifter and poured a scant inch of the fiery liquid into it, then poured the same into the other glass. She stared at his hands, beautiful hands, with long fingers. He had a heavy signet ring on one hand, and it gleamed dully in the diffused lamplight, and for a moment she couldn't tear her gaze away.

It took her a moment to remember she'd already worked this out, committed it to memory as well as her forged letters of recommendation. "My father was a shopkeeper, my lord. My mother had been in service before she married and I was their only child. After my parents died it seemed only natural that I follow in my mother's footsteps."

"I see," he murmured, lifting the glass to the light to admire the color. "And you come from the north, do you not? Occasionally I hear a bit of Yorkshire in your voice."

It should have been more than occasionally, but she accepted that. "Yes, my lord."

"I told you to stop calling me 'my lord.'" His tone was almost lazy.

"And what do you expect me to call you?" she replied with some asperity.

"Use your imagination. Pay attention, my sweet. I'm about to give you a lesson in the proper way to drink cognac."

"I'm hardly likely to partake of it again."

"Oh, you never know when you might be tempted to sneak down and pilfer the good stuff again," he said lightly. "Of course I can always ask Collins to put it under lock and key from my tippling housekeeper, but that would be unkind. I'm more than willing to share."

"I don't—"

"Pick up the glass, Miss Greaves," he said, and she did so.

"That's right," he continued in a softer, almost seductive tone. "Now, you cradle the globe in your hand, sliding your fingers around the stem of the glass. That way your body heat warms the liquid, just slightly, bringing it to the same temperature as your body."

"That's assuming the room isn't freezing cold," she pointed out.

"Are you cold, Miss Greaves? It feels quite cozy to me—the heat of the day's cooking remains, but if you're chilled I can think of a number of ways to warm you."

His words alone could do that, she thought as she felt the heat rise in her face. She picked up the glass, letting her fingers wrap around the base, and he frowned.

"Why are you wearing gloves? Were you planning on going out in your nightdress?"

He *would* have to mention what she was wearing, she thought mutinously. A gentleman would have ignored it. A gentleman wouldn't have put his hands on her and made her sit with him in the kitchen and drink cognac.

A gentleman would have fired her.

She immediately set the glass down again, trying to put her hands in her lap. "My hands were hurting—I was trying an old cure."

She should have known he wouldn't let her get away with it. He caught her arm and pulled her hand out, then proceeded to slowly peel away the white cotton glove, then reached for the other and did the same. He surveyed her hands with a critical eye, turning them over, and Bryony could feel herself blush. They were looking better—not as cracked and painful, but still rough. There was a long silence as he looked at them, and then, to her horror he caressed her hands with his, running his thumbs against her palms, his fingers stroking hers, entwining with them. "Much better," he murmured softly.

She tried to tug them away, but he held them, almost a battle of wills, before he released them. "I'm pleased to know you're so concerned with my welfare, *my lord*." There was just the faintest emphasis on the last, and she did it to annoy him, to break this strange, heated atmosphere.

"Oh, I'm not, Miss Greaves," he murmured. "I'm just looking forward to feeling them on my skin. This time when you know I haven't really passed out."

She could feel the heat drain her face. He'd known? He'd been awake when she'd touched his chest, when she'd pressed her lips against his on that very first night in his household? And then the heat returned, and she wanted to crawl under the table and slink away.

Denial was the only way to handle it. "I have no idea what you're talking about." Her voice was stalwart.

"Then why are you blushing?"

"You can't see that!" she said, and then could have kicked herself. She'd just admitted to it, whether he could see it or not. She soldiered on. "Besides, the very mention of me touching you is indecent."

"Not nearly as indecent as what we did in my bed last night."

She tried to rise, but he caught her wrist and pulled her back down, his strength gentle but inexorable. "Stop running away from me, Bryony. There's only so far you can go."

"Don't call me that. And I believe I can go anywhere I please. I can leave your employment—"

"But then you won't have accomplished what you want to accomplish."

She froze at his gentle tone. What exactly did he know about her? She pulled herself together, but even the small amount of cognac she'd drunk before he'd come in was having an unsettling effect on her. It warmed her bones, heated her flesh, stirred strange things inside her. Or maybe, to be truthful, those strange things had been stirring for days. Since she'd met Adrian Bruton, the Earl of Kilmartyn.

"Again, I don't know what you're talking about. I needed a position, and—"

"And what? You weren't sent by any reputable employment agency. You sent a letter to my idiot wife, requesting an interview. A very simple way to infiltrate my household."

She was feeling a little desperate. "Why would I want to do that?"

"You tell me."

Before she could come up with an answer he picked up his glass, as if the subject no longer interested him. "You can scarcely warm the glass if you're wearing gloves, my pet."

She swallowed nervously, pulling herself together. "Another reason women shouldn't drink hard spirits. In society women wear gloves."

"But we're not in society, are we? We're sitting in a kitchen, you in your nightdress, me not much better, and we're drinking cognac together. No one to watch, no one to know." The smile he gave her was peculiarly sweet. "Pick up the glass and hold it."

She did. The weight of the heavy crystal, the movement of the liquid, the way her heat moved to the glass, caught her attention, and she stared into the golden color, lost in it, forgetting about the man beside her. Almost.

"Very good," he said softly. "Now lift it to that charming nose of yours and breathe it in. Let the aroma play with your senses. Seduce you with its strength."

For a moment the spell cracked, and she shot him a wary glance, but he simply ignored her. "Then bring it to your mouth and take the tiniest of sips. That's right, just a bit, and then hold it on your tongue. Play with it. It's hot and dangerous, like my tongue in your mouth, but it's what you want, isn't it?"

There was no way she could protest, not with the small amount of cognac on her tongue, no way she wanted to protest. The fiery taste of the cognac was divine, full of notes of apple and honey, and she savored it, closing her eyes for a moment, before swallowing.

She opened her eyes to find him staring at her, an intense, heated expression on his beautiful face. *Beautiful,* she thought. He was beautiful. What would he want with someone like her?

"Do you have any idea how erotic you look when you do that?" His voice was low, as seductive as the cognac. "And I like the way you swallow."

Why did that seem to mean more than the simple words? Before she could question him he took her hands and wrapped them back around the glass, and the touch of his skin against hers set off all sorts of clamoring need, need she refused to identify. "Another small sip, darling girl. Don't worry, I'm not planning to ply you with cognac and seduce you—there's not enough to make a rabbit drunk. This time let it roll around in your mouth. Let it dance against your tongue."

She could do nothing else. She was caught, hypnotized by his voice, his words, by the book, the instructions, the warmth of him beside her, the heat of the cognac in her belly, the longing for what she could never have.

"Did you like the book I left for you, my precious?"

She almost spat the cognac out again, and she only barely managed to swallow it on a choked protest. Her eyes were watering from her suppressed coughing, and she met his gaze defiantly. "What book?"

He laughed. "You know what book. I collected that when I was sent on the grand tour. It's quite rare and valuable. Usually the art in these things is a great deal shoddier."

She could see those pictures in the back of her mind, so clearly that she had to fight the need to push back from the table and run. She had to pretend that the book had had no effect on her. "The writing was excellent as well," she said, aiming for a disinterested voice. "It was both instructive and poetical."

"You can read Italian, Miss Greaves? You intrigue me. But then, you already know that, don't you?"

She should never have admitted to that, she thought, but the cognac and his intoxicating presence were destroying her better judgment. And then she remembered her lies. "I lived in Italy with my former employer," she said defiantly.

"Yes, my love, but that's Renaissance Italian, not street argot or the stuff of polite conversation. Even I had a hard time translating."

"Even you," she echoed, letting a trace of mockery into her voice. "You find it surprising that a lowly female could reach your lofty intellectual understanding?"

"I find it surprising that a shopkeeper's daughter could."

She was making too many mistakes. She was used to being cool and hardheaded, but he seemed to have an innate ability to get inside her thoughts. Get inside her. *Inside her.* She shouldn't be thinking like that.

"Why are you blushing, my dear Miss Greaves? Is it in shame over your many arrant lies, or is it something else?"

"I do not lie," she said with dignity, taking another sip of the cognac. He was right, it was so much better this way, savoring it, letting it roll around in her mouth. Like his tongue, he'd said. *Oh, God.*

She set the glass down with a snap, and for a moment she was horrified she'd broken it. She hadn't, thank God. Bad enough pilfering the master's brandy—breaking his crystal would be beyond the pale. The master. He wasn't her master, no matter what role she was playing.

She should get up, leave him. He wouldn't stop her, wouldn't force her, she knew that much. But she didn't want to. She wanted to stay here in the warmth with his eyes watching her with slow, slumberous arousal, and she wanted this. Wanted him. One glass and two sips of cognac and she was losing all her common sense, that was fine with her. She reached for the cognac bottle, ready to pour herself more.

He put his hand over hers, stopping her. "I think you've already had quite enough, my girl." There was laughter and something else in his rich, slow voice.

"I've barely touched it. You were the one who told me I needed to master it."

"You're a fast learner." He pulled the bottle out of her way. "So what do we do now?"

"I should go to bed."

"Excellent idea. Here?"

"Please," she said, no longer sure what she was asking for.

"Please," he echoed, his voice soft and seductive, and she raised her eyes to meet his.

A mistake. She, who knew far too well the emptiness of physical beauty, was enrapt by his beautiful face, his forest green eyes, his tawny mane of hair and seductive, cynical mouth. He was beautiful, and he wanted her. And God help her, she wanted him. Not because of his beauty, but because of the odd gentleness in his manner when she didn't expect it, because of the lost look in his green eyes, because of the way he made her feel with just a few words, because of the way he made her melt when he touched her. The jaded rake he presented to the world was just as much a mask as her own was.

"P-p-please what?" she stammered, losing the train of thought.

"We need to go to bed," he said in a soft, practical voice. "Do I need to ply you with more brandy before I get you there? Because I'm not going to do so. You'll have to decide on your own."

"I don't know what you're talking about."

"Of course you do. You feel it too. You can pretend all you want, but I've had a vast deal more experience in things like this, and I know when the need, the interest, the desire is mutual. I doubt you could want me as much as I want you, but I expect you want me more than anyone you've ever wanted in your life."

"You are so vain!" she protested, trying to ignore the fact that he still held her hand.

"Not vain, Bryony. Realistic." He was too close, but he didn't touch her. "Now come with me to my bed. I don't have to take your virginity— there are ways around it, leaving you technically pure in case you decide to marry."

Whether it was the small amount of brandy, or whether she was using it as an excuse didn't matter. She had decided. She wanted him. Her body cried out for him, her heart cried out for him, and this could be her only chance to have a taste of what had always been denied her, and she wanted more than a taste.

"You can't take my virginity," she said in a choked voice.

"Darling, I'll do whatever you let me do, up to and including that. There's a limit to the small amount of honor I still possess."

She shook her head, and she could feel tears prick at her eyes. That damned cognac. "You can't," she said again. "I'm not a virgin."

He stared at her for a long, heated moment. "Good enough," he said, pulling her into his arms.

CHAPTER FIFTEEN

HE WAS A RIGHT royal bastard, in word and deed and birth, Kilmartyn thought as he pulled her slight, warm body against him. If he had any kind of decency at all he'd let her spend the night dreaming of the book of erotic drawings and his kiss on her mouth, and then simply start anew tomorrow. He wanted her to come to his bed with clear intentions and informed agreement, and he'd always planned to have her that way. It didn't matter that she was a lady—he would treat a courtesan the same way. You didn't coerce, you didn't force, and you certainly didn't drug an unwilling female into your bed. Although if she put up any more resistance he was going to look for the laudanum.

He needed this woman, no matter who she was or what she wanted from him. He needed the sweet comfort of her skin next to his, her long legs around his hips. He needed to lose everything in the sweetness of her body, he needed to forget, needed to wash himself clean, and he needed her. No one else would do. And thank God she wasn't a virgin—he wouldn't harm her if he was careful.

She was shaking slightly in his arms, and she had her face tucked down against his shoulder, against the skin beneath his opened shirt. He reached his hand under her chin and tilted it up, to see her eyes full of unshed tears. "Are you crying, my dear Miss Greaves? Surely not. Tell me you don't want this, be honest just this once, and I'll release you. You can make your delectably tipsy way back up to the attics and we'll never speak of it again." He was lying to her, of course. Nothing could keep him away from her indefinitely. But maybe, just maybe he could keep Bryony for a better time, untainted by the bleakness of the last day. He could take her in sunlight and a field of flowers, no darkness and pain and death.

He realized with a shock that her arms were around his waist, holding him. Maybe she'd had more to drink than he'd thought. And maybe he was needier than he thought.

Her eyes were closed, the tears seeping beneath them, and he cursed the fact that his cock was so damned hard he could come just from looking at her, cursed the fact that he could never do the right thing. He needed to carry her up to her own room, settle her in her bed, and leave her with a chaste kiss on the forehead.

And that was the very last thing he was going to do. "Open your eyes, Bryony," he murmured, and to his surprise she did. He kissed her then, putting his mouth on hers as he'd been wanting to do again since he'd had her in his bed and he'd foolishly let her go. But then, he hadn't known what he'd find the next morning when he found the clothes bundled beneath his bed, what he'd find in his wife's apartments.

Bryony tasted of cognac and salt tears and sweet, untutored lust. She tasted of the redemption he could never have, the fiery hell he was heading for. She tasted of everything he had ever wanted, and he lifted her up against him, so she was pressed against his erection. He slid one arm under her bottom, supporting her, and by instinct she wrapped her legs around him, not noticing he was lifting the fine linen nightdress up her long legs so that he could feel the sleek skin of her thighs. He set her on the table, sweeping the decanter and brandy snifters crashing to the floor, and the pungent scent of the spilled liquor added to the night air, added to the smell of her skin and the taste of her mouth. He broke the kiss, pushing her back on the scrubbed wood, and she went willingly, staring up at him as his hands slid up her legs, moving between them. He wanted to unfasten

his breeches and slam into her—thank God she wasn't a virgin, didn't need
to be wooed or treated tenderly. He could just fuck the hell out of her, hard
and fast, as he desperately needed to, and wipe out the last twenty-four
hours. He needed Bryony, nothing but Bryony, breathing her, taking her,
drowning in her.

He looked down into her face, the indigo blue eyes and small nose, the
lush lips that would feel so good wrapped around him, sucking him. Her
tawny hair was loose, spread out behind her, and she looked delicious,
irresistible, and her eyes closed. She knew what she was doing, and he
thanked his stars. He pushed the night dress up to her waist, and she
reached down in sudden shyness, trying to cover herself up again. *Not a
virgin, but not much more than one,* he thought, ready for her, catching
both wrists in his hand as he dropped to his knees on the hard stone floor
and put his mouth between her legs.

He hadn't done this to a woman in a long time, and he'd forgotten
how much he loved it, the honey and sweetness of her. She was still making
some kind of fuss, but he simply licked his way up to the tight little nubbin
at the top of her sex, sucking at it while he used his other hand to trace her
wet, silken folds. She'd had so little experience she most certainly hadn't
had this particular delight. He slid a finger into her, testing, and she let out
a small cry, one of shocked pleasure. She was tight, too damned tight, and
she was going to need to be a lot more relaxed or he'd hurt her, and he'd
never enjoyed hurting women, even those who enjoyed being hurt. He suddenly realized she wasn't struggling. Her hips were arching up against his
hand, seeking completion, and he pulled out his finger and slid in two.

Tight, so deliciously, damnably tight, but he knew where to touch her,
where to rub inside her, and he used his teeth on her, biting just enough
that she arched off the table, spasming in hoarse, gasping response as he
pumped his fingers, feeling her clench around him.

He didn't want to stop, but she was panting, shaking with reaction,
and he rose up, standing at the edge of the table, looking down at her as she
lay spread out for him. "Wait," she said in a raw voice. "I should tell you . . ."

If she was about to confess who she was she'd picked a hell of a time
for it. "No," he said. Her shawl had fallen and the nightdress was rucked

up beneath her bottom on the hard wood table. He took the fine material in his hands and tore it up the front, to the row of tiny buttons that popped off as the material ripped beneath his strength, and her breasts were small and hard and perfect—she was perfect. He slid his hands up her body to cup those breasts, plucking gently at the hardened nipples, and she sucked in her breath as another ripple of response danced across her skin.

"More?" he said, barely recognizing his own rough voice.

She closed her eyes again, arching into his touch. "More," she whispered. "Please."

He wanted to lick her breasts, but the angle was too difficult, and getting inside her was more important. After the first hard, fast fuck he could take his time with her, explore her, treasure her sweet body. But right now he had to shove inside her or he'd die.

He unfastened his breeches and released himself, and she was wet and slick beneath his questing fingers, ready for him, wanting him, thank God, and he rubbed the head of his cock against her, spreading his dampness and hers, and she let out a little moan of anticipation. He held his cock and began to push inside, into her glorious sweetness, trying so damned hard not to slam inside and hurt her, when he suddenly froze.

He stared down at her, the beauty of her imperfect face, her gorgeous mouth, the pale, aroused body waiting for him, ready for him, and he wanted to ignore everything but the roaring need inside him.

He couldn't do it. He pulled back out, groaning, and shoved his damned cock back in his breeches, not caring if he hurt himself. Her eyes had flown open in surprise, and she rose on her elbows, staring at him.

From somewhere inside he found the ability to smile at her. "You little liar," he said softly. "Didn't you know I can tell you're still a virgin?"

"You can?" she sounded slightly dazed. "It doesn't matter. Don't stop. Please, don't stop!"

But that was exactly what he was doing. "Hush, love," he said, pulling her torn nightdress around her. He only wished he had a blanket as well, the more layers between her body and his, the better. "You don't take a woman on the kitchen table for her first time. You take her to a bed with fine linen sheets and you do it slowly, carefully, so it doesn't hurt, and she feels like the treasure she is." He pulled her forward and picked her up, cradling her against him. She was shivering, and he didn't know if it was cold or reaction. He damned well wanted to shiver and cry as well.

"You've had that many virgins?" she said in a small voice, not denying the truth.

He shook his head. "I'd rather not take a woman's innocence when I can't offer her anything in return except pleasure. A man knows certain things by instinct, and I'm not deflowering you when you've had too much cognac."

"I didn't!" she protested. "And I want it. I want pleasure. I want someone to love my body despite my face."

Someone. Anyone? It wasn't going to be him. Not tonight. "Hush," he said again, cradling her slender body in his arms. "Hush, sweet love." And he headed for the stairs.

She was asleep by the second floor. He hesitated about taking her up to the servants' attics—the last thing he needed to do was run into one of the inquisitive maids—and there were a number of smaller rooms on the third floor that would do. But that was far too close for comfort. He'd managed, just barely, to stop himself from taking her, one of the few decent gestures in his life. If he went back on it now he would have gone through all that pain for nothing.

The attics were still and silent as he carried her upstairs, just barely managing in the darkness of the unlit hall. He'd need to install gas lighting up here as well, he thought absently. Assuming he was going to stay here for much longer and not find himself on trial for his wife's murder.

She looked so peaceful as he laid her down on the narrow, sagging mattress. They needed better beds up here as well. At least the maids didn't have to share beds, as they did in most other houses, but one could hardly manage a decent night's sleep on ticking like this. Bryony's torn nightdress fell open, and he sucked in his breath. The moon was bright that night, shining in her window, illuminating her far too well, and he gave himself a mental kick in the arse. If he didn't take her when she was drunk and awake he was hardly going to deflower her while she was sleeping so heavily. He wasn't sure how much she'd had to drink before he'd found her, but it had hit her hard, and she was almost passed out. With luck she wouldn't even remember what had happened down on the kitchen table—he'd go back down and clean up the mess and try to forget it himself.

He slipped off her clothes, tossing the torn nightdress out the open door before going in search of another one. She made soft, unintelligible noises as he dressed her, and at one point she simply curled up against him, breathing in deeply as she fell back into sleep, and he wanted to groan. She wasn't making this any easier on him.

Lifting her up, he tucked her beneath the covers, and did just what he'd sworn he wouldn't do. He kissed her on the forehead, and then on her soft, sweet, dreaming mouth.

"Sleep well, darling one. Dream of the good man who'll take you with love, and forget about a right bastard like me."

He stepped back, before he could think better of it, and left the room, closing the door behind him.

He picked up her ripped nightdress and headed back to his makeshift room. He was still hard, and at this point he decided he'd probably stay that way until he damned well died of it. He started to strip off his clothes, then paused, staring down at his white shirt. He must have brushed against something as he searched through Cecily's room. There was dried blood on the sleeve.

Had it really been the daughter of Eustace Russell, cleaning and scrubbing and trying to disguise his possible guilt? It could have been Collins, of course. The man was clearly loyal, and he'd be the first to cover up any misdeed. At times like these the Irish stood together, be they man-servant or lord of the manor.

But he didn't think it was Collins. It had to have been Bryony in there, scrubbing on her knees, straightening the chaos, hiding the truth of what had happened. Thank God.

Because when a wife went missing, and turned up dead, there was usually one man the gentlemen of Scotland Yard looked at: the husband. And while some of society was under the impression that he and Cecily were happily married, there were enough people who knew the truth.

He shoved the telltale shirt and Bryony's nightdress in the pile in the back of his closet, hidden with the other blood-soaked clothes. He'd burn them later when he had a chance, that or simply get Taggart to get rid of them. Taggart would do anything he asked without question.

Or he could take Bryony's torn nightdress to bed with him and take care of his current condition in a few moments, he was so damned hard.

But he wasn't going to. He was going to be the saint he'd suddenly decided he was, and go to sleep.

And with a bed-shaking punch of his pillow, he did just that.

CHAPTER SIXTEEN

THE CRUSHING PAIN in Bryony's head woke her, that and the raucous cries of the birds. She tried to open her eyes, but it felt as if there were lead weights on her eyelids, and she rolled over, burying her face in the soft pillow, trying to shut out the incessant noise. Her entire body hurt, her skin was on fire, her teeth itched—everything was wrong. And if the birds were singing it was past time to get up and face whatever fresh disaster the day would bring.

Slowly, carefully, she rolled over again. She wasn't certain what part of her body hurt the most, and she had no idea why. The last thing she could remember was going down to the basement after hearing Kilmartyn's muffled curses.

And then she remembered the cognac! Good God, what had she done? She tried to scour her brain for details of the night before, but it simply made it ache more, and she put her hands to her head with a groan. She didn't want to think about it, refused to think about it. If drinking spirits did this to you then she was never touching the foul stuff again.

At least she must have managed to get back to her own room safely enough. With great care she pushed herself up, swinging her trembling legs over the side of the bed. Her entire body felt tender, from her breasts to between her legs to the soles of feet to her scalp. Sitting motionless on the side of the bed wouldn't fix anything, however, and she could scarcely spend the day in her room. The only way to get past this was to get through it, and she pushed herself to her feet, swaying for a moment before moving to the wardrobe.

Stripping off her nightclothes, she dressed as quickly as she could, trying to ignore the fiendish screeches of the normally twittering birds outside. On top of everything else her stomach was queasy, and the thought of one of Mrs. Harkins's grand fry-ups was daunting. There must be some way she could avoid looking at eggs while they were staring back at her.

She'd washed her hair in Kilmartyn's impressive bathtub last night, and she'd fallen asleep before it had dried properly. Dragging a comb through the tangled mess had tears springing in her eyes, and there was no way she could bring it under complete control. By the time she'd managed to plait it and pin it down at the nape of her neck she was ready to go back to bed and be damned to the consequences. She pinned a black lace cap to the back of her hair, trying to blink away the tears that filled her eyes, and then she straightened her shoulders and started down the endless flights of stairs. If she was lucky no one would have any knowledge of those missing hours. If it was up to her she'd just as soon not remember them either.

For some reason Mrs. Harkins had decided to make an extreme racket as she capably handled her pots and pans. She gave Bryony a comforting look. "Slept in, did you? Well, you needed that. And not to worry—Emma saw to the master's morning tray and he'll probably want to see you later. He was asking about the mistress's rooms—apparently he knew they were in a mess. I just hope it wasn't another knockdown, dragged out fight." She slammed a cast-iron skillet onto the hob and tossed some butter in. Even the sizzle made Bryony's ears itch.

"Do they have knockdown, dragged out fights?" she said, the sound of her voice echoing inside her head. She needed tea, strong tea with loads of sugar and cream, quite badly. She sat at the table and poured herself a cup, then paused, staring down at the clean, scarred surface. There was something about the worktable, something about the kitchen, something she needed to remember. No, something she didn't want to remember. She looked up quickly.

"Occasionally. I don't think he hits her—he's the only one who's ever seemed to have bruises. She screams and rages and throws things, and I expect he goads her. There's no love lost between them."

She wasn't sure whether this knowledge pleased her or frightened her. On the one hand, she was illogically happy that he didn't care for his wife, and she wasn't going to consider why. On the other, if what she suspected had happened in that room, his dislike of his wife wasn't a good sign.

She brought the cup to her lips, trying to disguise the fact that her hands were shaking. The first sip was ambrosia, and she felt her world begin to fall back into order. Another, and the incessant pounding in her head quieted. Whether it was the tea, the sugar, or simply the ritual of it all, she was coming alive again. With the sense that something was dreadfully wrong.

Was it just the disaster in the countess's apartments? Or was there something else, something possibly catastrophic, that she couldn't remember? Didn't want to remember.

"Are you quite all right, Mrs. Greaves?"

She looked up at Mr. Collins and managed to shake off some of her dark doubts. "Of course. Why do you ask?"

"I simply wondered if something had gone on last night. I found bits of glass on the floor down here, and the bottle of cognac is missing."

Hell's bells, she thought miserably. Her sins were coming home to roost. She must have dropped the bottle—that was the catastrophe her mind refused to recall. "My fault, I confess," she said easily. "I thought I heard a noise and I came down to investigate, and I'm afraid I knocked over the tray in the pantry."

"You should have come and got me and some of the menservants," Collins said severely. "It could have been an intruder. I've heard stories of bad things happening, even in this part of town, and you can't be too careful."

"Next time I'll be certain to call for you." She took another deep gulp of tea, grateful to note that her hands weren't shaking, grateful that

Mr. Collins didn't question why the tray he'd left in the butler's pantry had been broken in the kitchen. She could have come up with a convoluted excuse but right then her brain was too tired to think.

"He's in a right foul mood," Bertie said as he came into the kitchen. "Something must have tweaked him real bad." He spied Bryony. "Begging your pardon, Mrs. Greaves."

"He's probably suffering the ill effects of overindulgence," Mr. Collins said smoothly from his spot beside Mrs. Harkins, and Bryony's sense of impending doom increased. "Not that it's our place to criticize our betters. But drinking too deeply can wreak havoc with the mind and constitution. Take that as a lesson well learned, Bertie."

"Yes, sir, Mr. Collins," Bertie said respectfully, as Bryony ducked her head. Collins was a great deal more observant than was entirely comfortable. "And he's asking for you, Mrs. Greaves. Said as how you should bring a fresh pot of tea and two cups and meet him in the library."

Mrs. Harkins threw her a look. "He certainly spends more time with you than other housekeepers we've had. It's not my place to say anything, but you have a care. It's clear to all of us you're better bred than our usual run of housekeepers. You may not be aware of the dangers. Lord Kilmartyn is a very attractive man, with strong appetites and not much care for what society thinks. You could get into trouble quite easily if you're not careful. He's always had an eye out for a pretty girl."

Bryony stared at her in astonishment. "Mrs. Harkins, do you have trouble with your eyesight? I'm a far cry from a pretty girl."

"Nonsense," the woman said comfortably as she watched the bubbling contents of her frying pan. "You've got a few marks on your face, that's all. In truth, you've got a quiet sort of beauty, and a graceful way about you. You're quality, in every sense of the word, and his lordship is well aware of it. I'm just being bold enough to warn you. We like having you here, and I, for one, wouldn't want you to come to no harm."

Harm? What kind of harm? The kind of harm that had befallen someone in Lady Kilmartyn's room? Or some other kind of harm that she couldn't remember?

She barely managed her calm smile. "You're very kind, Mrs. Harkins, but I believe I'm well aware of his lordship's . . . attractions. Trust me, I'm the last person he'd be interested in seducing. He's much more likely to turn to someone like Emma."

"Oh, goodness, no!" Emma squealed. "He scares me."

"There's nothing scary about him," Bryony said crossly, and then could have bit her tongue. "He's a man like any other," she continued evenly, "despite his title."

"And you've known so many men, Mrs. Greaves?" Mr. Collins asked. "Begging your pardon for the impertinence, but Mrs. Harkins is right concerned for you. You don't have the air of someone who's been . . . well, in the company of men much."

Bryony straightened. She was supposed to be a woman of the world, a capable, mature housekeeper, not some sheltered ninny. Even if that was what she was feeling like at the moment. "No, Mr. Collins, I have not known many men. Not in the biblical sense, certainly, and not particularly in the social sense. My previous mistress and I lived a secluded life in Italy and here in England. Nevertheless, it's been my responsibility to see to the gentlemen's well-being when they visit a household I have charge of, and they're really not so different."

Something that sounded suspiciously like a snort came from Mrs. Harkins, but she said nothing, simply turned to the butler. "Mr. Collins, would you be good enough to make up a tray for Mrs. Greaves to take to the master? He likes things delivered promptly."

Bryony drained her tea, shuddering. Was she one of the things being delivered to Kilmartyn? Of course not—where did that thought come from? So he'd kissed her, touched her when he'd had her in his bed a few nights ago. He'd probably do that to anyone who ended up in his bed. And he'd let her go quite easily.

She started to reach her hand up to touch her scars, but she stopped herself. It had turned into a nervous habit—using her hand to cover the half of her ruined face—but she'd forced herself to stop. She needed to accept herself the way she was, not fuss over something that couldn't be changed.

She rose. "Let me do it, Mrs. Harkins. After all, it appears I'm the one on the chopping block today."

She moved through the halls, carefully balancing the heavy tray, trying not to jar it or her still-aching head. Most of her other ills had improved, save for a strange tenderness between her legs, but she certainly wasn't going to be thinking about what she might have done to herself in her fit of drunkenness. She had experimented with pleasuring herself but had stopped in a fit of embarrassment. And why was she thinking of that now?

The closer she got to the library the stronger her sense of dread grew, though she couldn't imagine why. As she'd told Emma, there was no reason to be frightened of Kilmartyn, despite the rare mood Bertie had warned her of. She could handle him—she'd handled him before. But the closer she got the more her heart began to pound, and the tray trembled slightly in her formerly steady hands.

When she arrived at the door she stood there in a quandary. She could try to balance the tray on one knee while she knocked . . . no, scratched on the door. She could set it on the floor, but then, how in heaven's name was she going to open it? She didn't want to face him anyway, though she wasn't sure why. Perhaps it was simply that she, like Kilmartyn, was suffering the aftereffects of too much indulgence . . .

A sudden panic washed over her, and she whirled around, ready to run, when the door was flung open and she heard Kilmartyn's distinctive voice. "What are you doing, creeping about? Why didn't you bring the tea in?"

It took a great deal of effort but she pulled herself together, turning back and showing him an impassive face. "I didn't know how to carry the tray and scratch on the door at the same time, much less open it."

For a moment he said nothing, just looked at her, and she wanted to squirm beneath his searching gaze. "Of course you don't," he said obscurely. "I'll take the tray."

He reached for it, but she held on. "Don't be absurd. I'm your employee—"

"If you don't let go of it it's going to splash all over us."

"If you don't let go of it I'll dump it on you," she shot back, and then was silent, horrified at her words.

With a sound of exasperation he let go, and she moved past him into the room, her clothes brushing against him. A frisson of reaction swept over her body, stronger than ever, and she remembered that damnable book hidden beneath her bed. She'd forgotten all about it. The wretched thing had taken her from a harmless, almost juvenile longing for the beautiful, unattainable male, to a case of steaming lust.

She looked around her, uncertain where to put the tray, but he must have read her mind. "Put it on the desk, Bryony," he said, sounding weary.

She didn't like the sound of her name in his rich, seductive voice. It was too intimate, when she desperately needed formality and distance before she made a complete fool of herself. "Mrs. Greaves, if you please, my lord," she said as she set the heavy tray down, straightening up without showing any of the ache the tray had caused.

"Bryony," he said firmly. "Sit in that chair."

She looked at it. It was one of a pair of huge leather club chairs, much too comfortable for a servant. "I believe I'll stand, my lord."

"I believe you'll sit," he said. "With or without my help."

Alarm swept through her at the thought of him putting his hands on her, and she sat quite quickly, perching on the edge of the chair, hands folded in her lap, feet neatly together on the floor. He stood at the desk, his back to her, and he was pouring the tea. She started to protest, then shut her mouth again.

He was wearing trousers and a white shirt, but no tie and collar and no vest or coat, and she could see the lines of his body clearly. She could dwell on them. His legs were very long, which made sense, since he was a tall man. He was more wiry than muscled, though she knew he was quite strong. He could pick up . . . her mind went blank, and she started to rise.

"Sit, Bryony," he said sharply, like a master to a dog, she thought, trying to dredge up a righteous anger to overcome her nervousness. She stayed where she was.

He turned with two cups of tea in his hand, and he simply gave her a warning look as she started to rise. "Sit back in the chair and get comfortable, my very dear Miss Greaves. Because you and I are about to have a long, interesting talk."

CHAPTER SEVENTEEN

BRYONY STAYED EXACTLY as she was, the cup of tea balanced carefully on her knee, because her hand was still trembling. She summoned up a reasonable facsimile of her immutable housekeeper expression, keeping her eyes politely lowered.

"Look at me."

His peremptory tone made her lift her head, and she didn't bother to disguise the flash of annoyance. "Yes, my lord?"

"We have a problem that needs to be addressed." He took the seat opposite her, but left his tea on the table. He paused, looking at her strangely. "Exactly how much of last night do you remember?"

Hell's bells, she thought. *How bad could it have been?* "I don't believe I understand you, my lord. What do you mean?"

"If you call me 'my lord' one more time I'm going to . . ." He appeared to think about it for a moment. "I'm going to do something that you probably won't like at all. So stop it and answer my question."

He must know she'd gotten into his cognac, she thought. But surely he wasn't hypocrite enough to fire her over one misdemeanor. "I heard someone crashing around and I went to investigate. I discovered it was you, so I continued on to the kitchen where I admit I helped myself to a bit of your cognac. And then I went back to bed. I do realize that was a grave act of misconduct, and I do promise that it won't happen again. The after-effects are very unpleasant."

He stared at her in what might almost be amazement. "That's what you remember? Nothing more?"

That pain in her head was growing worse, and her entire body was going into an uproar. Her breasts felt odd, sensitive against the plain cotton chemise, and there was a clenching feeling down low, and this man . . .

No! "I had very disturbing dreams, my . . ." she let the words trail off. She didn't want to give him any excuse to touch her.

"I expect you did," he said obscurely. "Very well, we'll get back to that later. I have another question for you. Who cleaned my wife's rooms yesterday?"

That one was easier but just as disturbing. "I did," she said with deceptive calm, when she wasn't feeling very calm at all. "I thought it might be politic for me to take care of the mess, rather than have gossiping maids to do it."

"And did you happen to notice anything peculiar?"

"You mean apart from the ripped curtains and torn-up bedding and smashed scent bottles? No, my lord." She used the term defiantly.

"Not even a large, peculiar stain beneath the window? Difficult to remove?"

She could still see it, smell it, the blood that had pooled beneath the window and she'd scrubbed and scrubbed. Why was he asking her? If he knew about it then he must have had something to do with it. Had he? Had he hurt his wife? But no, he couldn't have. She cleared her throat. "If I did, my lord, I'm certain I did my best to clean it up. Stains like that are difficult to remove but I believe I did a fair job."

"Why?"

She tried to look unconcerned, raising her eyebrows. "Because it's my job, my lord." There was a certain pleasure in annoying him when he couldn't make good on his threats. "I would be interested in learning what caused that stain, and whether there's any reason to worry about someone's health." Why was he asking her these questions? He could have no more

181

killed his wife than she could, she was certain of it. But a tiny, niggling doubt teased at her.

"I imagine you would," he said, a grim tone in his voice. "But that's something else you'd be better off forgetting. In fact, I think I'm going to have to send you away."

Her blood ran cold. "You're dismissing me, my—" She stopped short of using the word. Annoying him probably hadn't been the smartest move. "I do promise I won't touch your cognac again, and I'll be—"

"I like you when you're half-tipsy on my cognac," he said. "And I didn't say I was firing you, I said I needed to send you away. Just until things get sorted out."

"Things? I don't understand." She was truly bewildered. "How can I be a housekeeper here and not be on the premises? It's impossible."

"You know as well as I that you're not a housekeeper," he snapped. "I've put up with it, because it amused me, but now that—" He stopped as he heard the front doorbell peal, and an odd expression crossed his face. They waited, in silence, listening to the muffled footsteps of the well-trained servant who answered the summons, listening to the quiet conversation and the heavy thud of official-sounding footsteps as they approached the library.

The rap on the door was loud enough to make Bryony startle, and she spilled some of the hot tea on her dress as she jumped to her feet. Kilmartyn stayed where he was.

"Yes?"

The door stayed shut, but Collins's imperturbable voice came from the other side. "My lord, there are some gentlemen here who wish to speak with you."

"I'm busy."

"I'm afraid this can't wait—" There was the sound of a mild scuffle, and then the door opened, revealing two very officious, very menacing gentlemen of the constabulary.

If the elegant room awed them they didn't show it. The smaller one stepped forward, a pugnacious expression on his face. "Are you Adrian Bruton?"

She'd never seen Kilmartyn display such hauteur. He could have frozen water in the hot July sun. "Yes, I'm Kilmartyn. Lord Kilmartyn."

The chilly emphasis on the title didn't faze the officer. "We've orders to bring you down to Scotland Yard. There've been questions about the disappearance of your wife."

"My wife is in the country visiting friends."

"Not according to a report laid against you."

"By whom?" He still hadn't risen, and he had one leg crossed over the other, perfectly at ease.

"I'm not at liberty to say," the first man said, but unfortunately the second one spoke up at the same time.

"Anonymous, my lord."

The first man glared at his partner before turning back to Kilmartyn. "That's neither here nor there, my lord. Questions have been raised and you'll need to come with us."

"In fact, I don't," Kilmartyn said lazily. "Your superiors should have come to me, discussed the matter in civil tones in the privacy of my home. However, I'm always in favor of cooperating with the local police services, so I'd be more than happy to accompany you. Mrs. Greaves, I'm afraid we'll have to put off our discussion until later. It shouldn't take long to resolve this, and then we'll make arrangements for your journey when I get back."

She kept her face impassive. What journey? What was happening? Did they really think he'd done anything to hurt his wife? Despite everything she knew he couldn't have. He simply couldn't.

He rose, taking his time, as Collins hurried into the room, a jacket and cravat over one arm, a hat and walking stick in his hand. Kilmartyn dressed in a leisurely fashion, and Bryony didn't move. She ought to excuse herself, but she couldn't move. Would he ever return to this house?

He pulled on his gloves and tucked the walking stick under his arm. "I believe I'm ready, gentlemen. Mrs. Greaves, tell Mrs. Harkins I should be back in time for dinner."

"I wouldn't count on it," the first man grumbled.

Kilmartyn raised an eyebrow. "I would." He turned, about to head for the door, when at the last minute he leaned down toward her, close enough to whisper words only she could hear.

"By the way, Bryony. You taste delicious."

And then he was gone, and she was alone.

The room spun, and she collapsed back in the chair, holding her head, shock and rage and shame sweeping through her in continuous waves as her memory came back full force. She was still sitting there when Collins peered back in the room, took one look at the expression on her face, and quickly shut the door.

She had no idea how long she sat, conflicting emotions running through her. Fury that he'd touched her. Shame that she'd let him. And the most disturbing reaction of all. Anger that he'd stopped.

The details were still fuzzy, but she could remember the feelings, her body tight and hot with longing. She could remember the explosion of pleasure he brought forth in her, she could remember the clawing craving for more that he'd inexplicably denied her. And that craving still threaded through her body, which was the most infuriating part of the entire, disturbing recollection.

She pushed herself up, trying to focus on her rage and not the strange desires whirling inside her. She hoped Scotland Yard hanged the bastard before she had to see him again. She finally had access to his library, and she'd find proof today, no matter what. Once she did she'd leave this house and never have to see him again. Maybe her instincts were all wrong. He could have killed her father and then murdered his own wife, and if so he deserved the coals of hell heaped upon his beautiful head.

She stopped herself. No, he didn't murder his wife. No matter how much he disturbed her, annoyed her, she couldn't believe he'd done such a thing. It was neither in his nature nor a reasonable assumption given the other occurrences that night. Her other moment of stupid weakness. There had to be some other explanation.

Not that she cared, she reminded herself. No, she was going to leave the house in Berkeley Square and never return. As long as he hadn't been complicit in her father's death she could then forget all about him, and the shocking things he'd done to her, the shocking way he'd made her feel.

It took her more than three hours, going through every drawer, sifting through the books, the papers, the files, and she found absolutely nothing. No telltale note, no sign of a recent influx of money, no mysterious correspondence, no hidden compartment behind the paintings. She wasn't sure what she had expected to find. Surely if a man had stolen a massive sum of money and blamed it on another man there'd be some trace of it.

But there was nothing. She sank down in the chair behind his desk, and then jumped up again. It was a leather chair, and the seat had conformed to Kilmartyn's admittedly shapely backside. Not that she should be thinking of such things, particularly after last night. She should be disgusted, and she was. But she still couldn't banish that note of almost wistful longing.

How could wistfulness and rampant lust abide in the same soul? Apparently it could in hers. She sank back down in the chair and let herself relish the feel of the worn leather around her. It was almost like a phantom embrace, the chair that had conformed to him now holding her body.

She was being a moonstruck idiot. It was a good thing she was done here, or she might make an even bigger fool of herself. There was nowhere else she could search, nothing more to gain, and everything to lose if she stayed here one more day. She had no doubt the police wouldn't keep Kilmartyn—in truth, she was surprised he wasn't home yet.

She needed to get out of here. There was only one problem. She had no money, at least, not enough to get to Devonport and somehow insert herself into the doubtless ramshackle household of Captain Thomas Morgan, the former pirate.

There was the household cash, of course, under her lock and key, but if she took that she'd be a thief just as she suspected Kilmartyn of being. She'd have to figure out some other way of getting out of here, some way to get money. Selling herself on the streets would get her nowhere, she thought with dark humor, when a sensualist like Kilmartyn didn't even want her for free.

There were her grandmother's pearls. She could probably sell them for enough money to pay for a train ticket to Devonport. It broke her heart, but if it rescued her from the danger Kilmartyn presented then her beloved grandmother would approve and it would be money well spent.

Because if she stayed, and Kilmartyn changed his mind, she'd end up in his bed with or without the benefit of cognac. There was no use denying it, she was a fool for the man, a total, witless ninny. He saw her as a plaything, and she was so besotted with him she was willing to be just that, willing to do anything if he'd kiss her again. Much as she hated being a coward, her only choice was to run.

She'd get over it. After all, he was the first man she'd ever spent much time with, and he had the misfortune to be beautiful. Though admittedly the delicately handsome face of Lady Kilmartyn's cousin Rufus had left her entirely unmoved, and the footmen's excellent physiques held no interest. No, it was Kilmartyn, with his wicked humor and his sly, teasing ways, his mouth, his eyes . . .

And she needed to get out of there before she saw him again. Because even if he'd changed his mind last night and decided she wasn't worth the trouble, there was no guarantee he wouldn't change it again, if he was bored and drunk and randy.

She checked the small watch pinned to her black-clad bosom. It had been more than four hours, the midday meal already past, and she hadn't eaten anything since last night. Up until now the very idea of food had made her gag, but the influence of the night before had passed off enough for her to realize she was hungry.

First things first. She would fetch the pearls, and anything else she could carry, and make some excuse to leave the house, never to return. She hurried up to her room, searching through her meager belongings.

Where was her other nightdress? And then memory came back, of him ripping it in half and gazing down at her, not with boredom but fierce need, and she felt herself grow hot with her own kind of longing once again.

But in the end he'd changed his mind. He hadn't wanted her. The details of that rejection were hazy, but the truth was plain. She wasn't worth his time or even his random lust.

What had she done with the torn nightgown? She assumed she'd somehow made her way back upstairs after he'd walked away from her, because she'd woken up in her own bed, dressed in her other nightgown. But where was the torn one? It had been very expensive, once upon a time, one of the few things she'd been allowed when the creditors had taken everything, including most of their lace-trimmed underthings, and anything could be mended. Indeed, it had been an older piece, the fabric soft with age, but she'd loved it, and she wasn't leaving it behind.

It was nowhere in her room. She already knew it couldn't be in the kitchen—Mrs. Harkins would have said something. There was one more place it could be.

As a housekeeper she wore no hoops, only the stiffness of her crinoline keeping her skirts away from her body, but there was still enough room to tuck a few of her belongings into the pockets Maddy had cleverly sewn into it. She tossed a few more things in her shawl and then twisted it into a tie. It wasn't large enough to cause notice, and even if it did she doubted anyone would say anything. They were probably too busy discussing the fascinating happenstance of their lord and master being dragged off by the police.

She started down the narrow servants' staircase, stopping on the third floor to emerge from the baize door in the hallway. She froze. *He* was there again, like a recurring ghost, except he was very real.

"Mrs. Greaves," said Mr. Brown with a pleased smile. "How lovely to see you again! I hadn't expected you'd still be here."

CHAPTER EIGHTEEN

Bryony was instantly wary. He was Lady Kilmartyn's cousin, and presumed lover, so why was he here in Kilmartyn's house when the woman was gone, unless he knew more about her disappearance and the blood that had covered the floor? No—he struck her as someone far too precise to ever soil his hands with blood. She was imagining monsters everywhere, when the only monster had probably been a huge rat. Or so she kept wanting to believe.

"Good afternoon, Mr. Brown." The perfect housekeeper mien was in full force. "Why would I be anywhere else?"

"Well, the Kilmartyn housekeepers seldom stay for very long. I imagine Adrian's advances aren't always welcome."

The words stung, and she could feel heat flame her cheeks. He was telling her she was only one in a long line of easy women, but in the end she hadn't passed muster. Had she truly expected anything else? "May I help you, Mr. Brown? I imagine you know that Lady Kilmartyn is in the country, visiting friends. Indeed, I assumed you were with her." She could sting back as well, and she was beyond caring about proper deference.

"Now why would you think that?" he countered. "In truth, Cecily's disappearance came as a great shock to me, since she was promised to spend an afternoon at the regatta with me yesterday. I was most disturbed. But I presume Kilmartyn knows where she is."

"He hasn't mentioned it."

Brown looked at her for a long, contemplative moment. "You may trust me, Mrs. Greaves. I know we are not well acquainted, but I promise you I can prove a steady friend if you find yourself in need."

He looked so handsome, so earnest, so winning, with that elegant curl centered on his high forehead. Just the sort of man she had always dreamed of when she'd been younger. So why wasn't she melting with longing for him? Why didn't she trust him?

"You're very kind, sir. I cannot imagine being in such a circumstance, but I will remember your generous offer. And indeed, how may *I* assist *you*?"

"In no way, Mrs. Greaves. I was merely here in search of my cousin, but I found nothing. Unless you know anything about her sudden departure? Did she leave a note in her room, perhaps?"

She shook her head. It surprised her how easy it was to lie nowadays. The falsehoods rolled off her tongue. "I'm afraid she left no note, but as we both know the Kilmartyns do not share the warmest of relationships. I gather Lady Kilmartyn is prone to spur-of-the-moment departures. I'm certain she'll be in touch with you when she wishes to."

In truth she was certain of no such thing. If the countess was still alive, and please God she must be, then she had some reason for keeping her presence a secret from everyone, including her lover.

Mr. Brown inclined his handsome head. "I'm certain you are right. But if you hear anything, perhaps you might let me know." He held out an engraved calling card.

She didn't want to take it, but she had no choice. She tucked it inside the apron she still wore and gave him a brittle smile. "Perhaps I can show you out? Lord Kilmartyn is out for the afternoon, as I imagine you know, or you'd hardly be wandering the corridors."

His smile was both abashed and winning. "I confess I've been watching, and I did see that bastard leaving with two very unpleasant gentlemen."

"You don't care for Lord Kilmartyn?"

"How could I? Not when I consider the brutality he's shown my cousin over the years. She stays secluded so that no one can see the bruising, but I'm afraid that sooner or later he might—" He stopped, as if he'd said too much.

It was an excellent performance. Bryony wasn't sure how she recognized it as such. A great many men beat their wives—it was their legal right to do so. But Kilmartyn, for all his supposed wickedness, didn't strike her as a man who'd hit someone smaller and weaker. "I don't expect his lordship to be gone that long, so if you wish to leave without being seen I'd suggest you go now," she said, trying to sound encouraging rather than annoyed. He was keeping *her* from escaping, and she couldn't afford to run into Kilmartyn again. Not with the memory of last night between them.

He took her unwilling hand and pressed it. "You're very good, Mrs. Greaves. I won't forget your kindness."

She watched him disappear down the hallway, staying motionless for a long time after he'd left. She'd hardly been kind—the man was a charming snake, and she was much more likely to believe he knew more about Lady Kilmartyn's disappearance than Kilmartyn did.

The warning she'd given him held for herself as well. She needed to fetch her cape and leave this place. She simply had one more thing to check.

His temporary rooms were spotless. She searched under the mattress, half afraid she'd come up with another salacious volume of drawings, but there was nothing there. The drawers and cabinets were all devoid of anything interesting, including her torn nightdress, and she'd begun to believe it had probably gone out with the dustbin when she noticed the cupboard door was ajar. She opened it, peering inside. The tiny room was filled with an array of day and evening wear, boots and day shoes and evening slippers, and she stared at them for a moment. They smelled like Kilmartyn. Wool and leather and something else indefinable, and she could remember the taste of his mouth on hers. For a moment she closed her eyes and buried her face against one coat, breathing it in, letting the longing suffuse her. And then she pulled back, about ready to close the door when she noticed the faint splash of white at the very end of the space, almost out of sight. It could only be her nightdress, and she knelt down, reaching for it and drawing it out. And then dropping it with a muffled cry of horror. Her torn nightdress was there. So were the blood-soaked clothes of a man, and there could be only one who would wear them. Only one man tall enough and with arms long enough to fill the sleeves of the shirt.

She sat back on her heels, shivering in horror. *Stupid, stupid man! What had he done?* She glanced around her, finding nothing, and as a last resort she grabbed the thin silk dressing gown that lay across the bed, waiting for his return, and bundled the clothes inside. She didn't stop to consider why, she simply acted on impulse, adding her own torn nightdress to the bundle.

She could hardly waltz through the kitchen carrying such a load—someone would be bound to ask, so she moved to the window that overlooked the back garden, opened it and let the parcel drop, watching with relief as it disappeared into a blossoming lilac bush. She went back to the cupboard, trying to get a good look at the floor, but if the blood had stained through she couldn't see it, and with luck neither could Scotland Yard. He was safe, at least for now. She'd done everything she could for him. The rest was up to him.

The kitchen seemed warm and cozy when Bryony stepped inside. She pulled her half cape from the hook by the door and tied her reticule around her wrist. "I'm going out," she said, sounding brisk. "I thought I'd look for those spices you were missing, Mrs. Harkins, and see if I could order new uniforms for the household. The ones we have are getting shabby. I'm certain his lordship will return soon, and in the meantime we need to continue as we mean to go on."

"Very wise," said Mr. Collins, never taking his eyes from Mrs. Harkins's sturdy figure while he rubbed at the silver candlestick, slowly, almost sensually, and Bryony paused for a moment.

Oh, my, she thought. Surely love wasn't blooming in her very kitchen? If the butler fell in love with the cook then it brought a certain stability to the household. Mrs. Harkins had almost managed to run the household—with Mr. Collins's help she'd be easily able to do so, with Bryony gone.

The thought should have cheered her as she moved on. Kilmartyn would be fine, Lady Kilmartyn would reappear sooner or later, and no one would miss her. It was time to go home.

Except she had no home, apart from refuge with their old nanny, who was already supporting Maddy and Sophie. She could only hope they hadn't been too much of a burden. She'd sent them a note, assuring them all was well, but they could scarcely write back. Nanny Gruen would take good care of them—at least she could count on that much. Right now all she had to worry about was Kilmartyn, and what had happened to his wife. She was a fool to ignore the obvious, a fool to try to protect him. If he truly was responsible for the death of his wife then her meager efforts wouldn't save him for long.

Either he'd left the bed he'd briefly shared with her and gone and brutally murdered his wife or someone was trying to make it look as if he had. And if he were truly guilty she should never have tried to cover it up.

She would leave the bloody clothes where they lay, hidden beneath the lilac bush. If the police had any real cause to suspect him they would come and search the place. She would leave the rest up to fate.

· ·

The day was crisp and overcast, and she forced herself to walk easily, moving through Mayfair at a brisk clip. If she stopped to think about what she was leaving she would weep, so she simply squared her shoulders and strode onward, her head clearing in the cool spring air. There was an odd prickling sensation in the middle of her shoulders, as if someone was watching her, following her. While her first instinct was to head straight to the moneylenders, she forced herself to move as if she were simply out on a housekeeper's errands.

She dealt with the markets quite handily, finding Mrs. Harkins's missing herbs, arranging for a delivery of fresh fish and poultry. City living was very different from country living. At Renwick, the eggs and dairy and most of the meat were produced on the estate. One only had to plan. Here in the city arrangements must be made, and the Kilmartyn household's arrangements had been extremely haphazard. The deliveries were hit-or-miss, the quality unreliable, forcing Mrs. Harkins to be extremely creative.

She could take care of this—it was one thing she could do before she disappeared into the night. She knew the best suppliers, having dealt with them via the steward of her father's household on the few times she came to town. She had already dismissed the current vendors—no more improperly aged beef or chicken with a bad odor to it. No more curdled milk or rancid butter or wheat with bugs in it. She would leave his house well ordered.

She'd finished her needless errands, including a visit to Mr. Peach to get the assurance that the rooms would be finished by the next morning, and she was moving toward the shadier area where the moneylenders plied their trade when the most extraordinary thought struck her, so shocking that she stopped where she was on the sidewalk, forcing a large gentleman to move around her, tipping his hat politely as he went.

The entire day, as she dealt with strangers and friends—and she considered the staff at Kilmartyn's house to be friends—as she walked on the crowded streets and in and out of shops, no one had stared at her scarred face. No one had even looked twice, and not once had she been aware of it. The young man at Mr. Peach's emporium had even flirted with her, and she'd tentatively flirted back, without once ducking her head.

She reached her gloved hand to touch her cheek in wonder. Life and death and falling in . . . developing an inappropriate passion for someone tended to put things in perspective, and her scarred face was of small importance in the larger scheme of things. It was an astonishing thing to consider.

By the time she found the moneylender she was feeling an odd combination of elation and tearing grief. She wasn't going to examine the latter—there was no reason for her to regret leaving Kilmartyn and every reason to count her escape a fortunate thing. Exchanging the pearls for money proved surprisingly easy, and though the amount she received was pitiful it was enough to buy a train ticket to Devonport and purchase a few of the necessities she'd left behind. She wasn't sure how she was going to talk herself into Captain Morgan's household, but she wasn't going to think about it. She was famished, and the train didn't leave until the evening, so she found a small café near the train station and ordered a cup of tea and sandwiches.

She sat alone, her head bent, sipping at the strong tea, and told herself she was certainly not going to cry in public. That could wait until later, perhaps when she was on the train. She needed to distract herself from the memory of his green eyes, watching her, the unexpected sensation of his touch on her skin, his long, elegant hands, his mouth, on hers . . .

She dug into her purse, pulling out the crumpled scrap of paper. This was what she needed to concentrate on, not foolish maunderings. She stared at the familiar words, looking for answers that eluded her.

Don't trust any of them. Someone's stealing money, and it looks like Kilmartyn's in league with them, no matter what excuses he makes. Don't trust Morgan either. Never trust a pirate. Something's going on, and I'll get to the bottom of it, or

Had it been a message to someone, a scrap of a letter, or simply a note to himself? She had viewed it as holy writ, words from beyond the grave, and she'd done everything she could to find proof of Kilmartyn's involvement. If she'd hired a professional then perhaps he might have found proof, but he wouldn't have been able to get inside the very household of the man, search his desk, his drawers, beneath his mattress. She still couldn't rid herself of the notion that there was more to his involvement than she could find, but she couldn't do anything more. With the police breathing down his neck any guilt over her father's death would be likely to come to light. Maybe she should simply join her sisters at Nanny Gruen's and wait a bit, see what happened. She'd already bought her ticket to the coast, but she could cash it in for a train to Somerset. She needed time to think, to force some reason into her stubborn brain when it came to Kilmartyn. He was more than likely a murderer, and there was no reason in the world why she kept coming up with excuses, reasons to trust him.

Except that she did, she realized, putting down the sandwich uneaten. No matter what he said or did, deep inside her heart cried out for him, and her heart had never been foolish. She wouldn't, couldn't feel this way about a ruthless murderer.

Had the police released him? Were they wondering where she was? It stayed light quite late these days, but she checked her watch and found it was almost dinnertime. In an hour her train would leave. In an hour her absence would be noticed and commented on. In an hour she could make her way back to the house on Berkeley Square with acceptable excuses.

She would be putting herself in every kind of danger. If he were a madman, a charming killer, and he suspected who she was he would kill her as well. If he were simply Kilmartyn he would take her, sooner or later, because he wanted her, and because, God help her, she couldn't resist him. Didn't want to. She was so awash with confused emotions that she was afraid to examine, afraid of what she might find. That it was more than infatuation, more than impulse, but something stronger, deeper, something that wasn't going to break, to shatter, even when he put her away from him, as he'd inevitably do.

When she stopped long enough to think about it she knew the wanting ran through him as deeply as it ran through her. It wouldn't take mild inebriation to get her back into his bed. All he had to do was hold out his hand and say her name in his deep, warm voice, look at her with that single-minded intensity, and she'd be lost.

Rampant insanity had never been a family affliction; she must be the first to suffer from it. She paid her chit and rose, gathering her packages around her, and started the long walk back to Berkeley Square.

She was being extremely tiresome, Rufus thought from his stance across the street from the little tea shop. He'd been following her all day, and she'd gone from shop to shop, always staying in full view of people, and there'd been no way to get closer. Shoving her under the wheels of a carriage had seemed too haphazard, and his previous failure had irritated him, so this time he was leaving nothing to chance. He had a loaded pistol and a long, thin knife that apparently had once belonged to an Italian assassin. He could use either, or his bare hands. No matter what, the job would be done, and the observant Mrs. Greaves would never make it back to Berkeley Square.

At one point as he followed the tedious bitch around town he wondered whether she had any plans to return to her employer. A housekeeper would have no need of a moneylender unless she'd been filching baubles from her employer, and a smart woman—Mrs. Greaves struck him as unfortunately far too intelligent—wouldn't risk returning after robbing someone like Kilmartyn. When her next stop was the train station he was certain she planned to make a run for it, and he considered the possibility of simply letting her go.

If she disappeared she'd hardly be likely to return to tell the police about the strange gentleman wandering the halls of Kilmartyn's town house. If she did, she'd have to explain why she'd left, and they didn't treat thieves kindly.

In the end he decided that unfortunately Mrs. Greaves couldn't be trusted. Despite her current thieving activities she had the look of a boringly honorable woman, someone with a conscience, God help him, and she might very well throw herself on the altar of truth. Besides, he'd noticed her reaction when he mentioned Kilmartyn. She was besotted with the man.

No, he would board the train, follow her to her carriage, lean over to greet her with surprise, and slip the thin knife into her heart. It would be instantaneous—he'd gotten quite good with it, and had the position and timing down perfectly. No one would even notice.

She really was the most annoying woman. Just when he thought everything was settled she rose from her seat, gathered her parcels, and Rufus was ready to strangle, stab, and shoot her immediately. He wanted to be in his club, reading a freshly ironed newspaper and drinking a cup of tea. Instead he'd spent the day in parts of London he never wanted to see again, hiding behind stalls of smelly fish as he stalked the blasted woman.

While he had a personal abhorrence for physical imperfections, he had to admit that the plain housekeeper was far prettier than he had supposed the first time he saw her. When she smiled her entire face lit up, and she definitely had very fine eyes. Too bad the scarring marred her so dreadfully. In truth, he'd be doing her a favor. It must be painful to be imperfect.

She seemed to have no idea she was being followed, lost in her own thoughts. He hadn't thought this particular move out, trusting that he'd know what to do when the spirit moved him, and indeed, the gods answered his request.

The streets of London in this thirty-second year of Queen Victoria's reign had undergone a transformation. All sorts of new areas were being reclaimed from the squalid human rats who had lived there, and Mayfair was no longer the only place to live.

"The useful thing about that, Rufus," he muttered beneath his breath, "is that the rats still border the better areas. And she'll have to come close to one to get home."

He'd wait till then. But he was getting more and more irritated with the entire situation. So irritated, in fact, that when the tall, spare figure of Mrs. Greaves crossed a dark group of streets on her way to Grosvenor Square he looked around him, saw no one, pulled out the gun, and shot her.

CHAPTER NINETEEN

BRYONY FELT SOMETHING LIKE a bee rush past her and slam into the wall. Very odd—it was too early for bees, and whatever creature it was it had flown alarmingly fast. She moved to the wall to examine the hole. It looked as if some kind of pellet were lodged there. She shrugged, turning around, when she felt something knock against her arm.

But there was no one there. For a moment she had the strange, fanciful feeling that the ghost of her father was throwing rocks at her, trying to get her attention. More likely a neighborhood boy playing pranks, but this wasn't the best bit of street to be walking through, and she sped up, moving into the brighter lights of the street up ahead. Her arm was curiously numb, and for some reason she was feeling a bit light-headed. Thank goodness she was at the edge of Berkeley Square, and the house loomed up in the gathering darkness, looking oddly welcoming. She shouldn't be going back, of course. The place was starting to feel like home—a natural enough reaction when she was taking care of it. But those were dangerous thoughts.

She paused a moment to catch her breath, leaning against a lamp-post. Her arm was beginning to hurt quite dreadfully, and she needed to get home and put a cool compress on it. She closed her eyes for a moment, and when she opened them again she saw dark spots dancing in front of her.

For some odd reason she didn't know if she could make it that far. She'd had a decent tea, there was no reason for her to feel dizzy, but when she pushed away from the lamppost she swayed before she managed to take a step. *One at a time,* she thought dazedly, but why did her arm feel numb?

She felt someone coming up behind her, moving fast, and a trickle of unease ran down her spine. Had someone actually hurt her while she'd walked by that dark alley? Were they coming after her to finish the job?

But that was ridiculous, theatrical, she must simply have a cramp in her arm, she'd done too much . . .

She couldn't do much more. This time there was no lamppost to hold on to for support, and she swayed, afraid she was going to fall to the sidewalk when he came up behind her, catching her, holding her while she looked up at him through blurry eyes. It was the devil himself, Kilmartyn, and he looked furious, terrifying. Had he been the one? Had she doomed herself by going home? Was he going to finish what he started?

There was only one thing to do. "Oh, bugger," she said weakly, letting the darkness close in.

· ·
· ·

Kilmartyn felt her body go limp, and he hauled her up into his arms. Bystanders had been watching her erratic pace surreptitiously, doing not one damned thing about it, but now that he'd finally managed to reach her they were all solicitude. He was well known in the square, and even if they disapproved of him they knew the kind of power a man of his wealth could wield. It was all he could do to answer them civilly as he strode the rest of the way to his house, taking the front steps two at a time. She was too light, he thought. She needed to eat more.

Collins was already on the front portico, reaching for her, a horrified expression on his face, but Kilmartyn had no plans to give her up. "Get the doctor," he said roughly, starting up the stairs.

It wasn't until he reached the first floor that he realized he had no idea where to put her. Without thinking he bounded up the flights to the third floor, but his damned rooms were still in disarray; the room he'd chosen near the servants stairs was too small.

After three tries he found a bedroom that hadn't been affected by the renovations, and he kicked it open. He'd expected cobwebs and dust, but the estimable Mrs. Greaves had made her mark, and the room was spotless in the waning daylight. He set her down carefully on the bed and pulled off her hat, tossing it to the floor. Her face was paler than usual, with an almost bluish tinge. He reached to unfasten the cape-like thing she wore, and then he looked at his hands.

His gloves were stained red with blood, and he swore, ripping them off. Too much blood. By that time the cook had appeared, accompanied by the three maids, Mr. Collins, and the boy . . . what was his name? Jem? The women looked worried. The men looked . . . guilty? No, that made no sense.

"What's happened, my lord?" the cook demanded in not very subservient tones. "How did she take ill?"

"She's been hurt," he said roughly, beginning to unfasten the buttons of her dress when Mrs. Harkins, that was her name, skillfully and effectively moved her sturdy form between his housekeeper and him. "We'll get her undressed, my lord," she said in a firm tone. "It wouldn't do for you to be present until we got her fixed proper-like."

All he could think of was preparing a corpse for burial. All proper-like, cold, and bluish like his mother had been, and he wanted to hit someone, to scream, to beat against the walls.

"You should leave, sir," Collins said quietly. "Come with me and I'll get you a brandy."

Damn, and he needed one. His stained hands were shaking, by God, and she looked as if she were going to die. "I'll wait in the hall," he said tersely. "And I'll take some tea." At least that wouldn't dull his reaction time. He had to make certain she would be all right. He had to.

"Tea, sir?" Collins looked surprised. He was looking almost as shaken as Kilmartyn felt, and for a moment a primitive, jealous streak washed through him. Had Collins been courting her? Because if he had, he was going out of the house tonight.

On what pretext? he reminded himself. But then, an earl didn't need a pretext, now did he?

He was about to go searching for someplace to sit when one of the footmen appeared, carrying a heavy club chair as if it weighed as much as a loaf of bread. He set it quietly outside the door, then greeted Kilmartyn with a bow. "Is there anything more I can get your lordship? Would you like me to bring you some wine?"

Why the hell was everyone trying to push liquor on him? Probably because that was his usual response to everything. He managed a civil tone. "No, thank you. Collins is bringing me some tea."

He sat. He waited. He drummed his bloody fingers on the arm of the chair. The new footman appeared again, without the doctor but with a bowl of water and a towel, offering it to him.

"I think they might need it more in there," he said, nodding toward the closed door.

"Jem's already bringing it, my lord."

"Where the hell is Bertie?"

The new footman looked at him uneasily. "He should be back at any moment."

He washed his hands, frowning as the bowl of water turned red, and then he heard a quiet moan. Enough was enough. He rose and pushed open the door, ignoring Mrs. Harkins's hiss of outrage.

She lay there, her eyes closed, her face creased in pain. His little spy, Russell's daughter, moaned softly. Bryony. Was Bryony Russell going to die in his bed?

Mrs. Harkins had removed her hideous dress and most of the ridiculous undergarments women found it necessary to wear, and she lay in her blood-stained shift, her left arm on a layer of toweling that was soaking up the steady flow of blood. He stared at the wound in disbelief.

"Someone's shot her!" he said, moving to her side and staring down in shock.

"So it seems, my lord," Mrs. Harkins said. "Would you have any idea how this came to happen?"

He jerked his eyes up to look at the woman. Anyone else would fire her for her impertinence. "Of course not!" he snapped. "Why would you ask?"

Mrs. Harkins didn't answer, turning to one of the maids. "Emma, you take her clothes down and have Becky start soaking them in cold water. Her underthings are of very fine quality—it would be a shame to have them ruined."

He spared a moment to imagine those very fine underthings on her body, taking them off one by one, and then concentrated on the business at hand. "I don't think we can wait for the doctor," he said, ignoring Mrs. Harkins's efforts to get between him and Bryony. He simply moved her out of the way very gently before he took the seat someone had pulled up next to the bed. "Where's Jem with the water?" he demanded.

"Right here, yer lordship," the boy announced from the door, carrying a large, steaming pot of water. One of the new maids followed with a pile of fresh toweling and a large bowl.

"Bring them here."

"Your lordship, you can't—" Mrs. Harkins said.

"Be quiet. I might need your help, but I'll have you bodily removed if you get in my way."

Mrs. Harkins subsided with a sniff.

He washed the blood away, taking a good look before it welled up again. As unlikely as it seemed, it appeared his little spy truly had been shot.

Whoever had done it had been at a fair distance, or the bullet would have gone straight through her arm. As it was, the blasted doctor was going to have to dig it out, and it was going to hurt like hell. At least the man had been a poor shot—he hadn't managed to hit any vital organs. That still didn't mean she was safe—more people died of the infection that could follow such an injury rather than the injury itself.

He wiped the blood away again. The bullet was lodged in her upper arm, and he couldn't tell whether it had broken the bone or not. He pressed the cloth against the wound to slow the bleeding and she moaned again. He glanced up, and found she'd turned to look at him, her eyes full of pain.

"What . . . ?" The word was choked out.

"Don't talk," he said, his voice steady. "It'll only wear you out, and you're going to need all your strength. The doctor is coming, though I have no idea why it's taking him so bloody long, and he'll get the bullet out and you'll soon be right as rain."

"Bullet?" she gasped.

"Didn't I tell you to be quiet? Yes, you've been shot, and when you're feeling better you're going to tell me whom you've annoyed so much that they decided to take a gun to you. In the meantime be still, and if the saw-bones doesn't come soon enough I'll dig the bullet out myself." He wasn't ready to consider the fact that she was lying there because of him. More than likely there was some connection between this and Cecily's disappearance. And he'd wanted to get her away from him, away from danger. He simply hadn't had the time.

He turned his head. "Collins!" he shouted. "Bring me the goddamned brandy."

Collins had just appeared with the tea tray, and he started to turn back, when Kilmartyn snapped, "Leave the tea. That's for me. The brandy is for Mrs. Greaves." Funny how easily that false name came to him. Maybe he was better off thinking of her by that name. Because Bryony suited her too well. Bryony was soft and sweet and delicious. Mrs. Greaves was dangerous.

"Yes, my lord." Collins set the tea tray down on the table.

He turned back to the woman lying in the bed. "I thought that I'd better stay sober in case I'm the one who's going to operate on you."

She managed a hoarse cry, and he reached over and touched her face, stroking the side of it with a gentle hand. "Don't worry, my angel," he said under his breath, for her ears only, "I promise to take good care of you."

Mrs. Harkins moved closer, a suspicious look on her face. Damn, she was a protective old bat. "I think brandy is a good idea, don't you, Mrs. Harkins?" he said in a louder voice.

"Unless the doctor brings ether," the cook replied, and he noticed she didn't say "my lord" this time.

"I don't know when the goddamned doctor plans to get here," he said harshly. He expected the cook didn't like his language, but that was something she was used to. When it came to her pet lamb she was willing to break all generations of training and stand up to him, but with everything else she was the perfect servant. The more champions Bryony had, the better.

The towel he was holding against her arm was soaked, and he tossed it on the floor, grabbing another and holding it against the wound. That bullet had to come out, and soon. He'd removed bullets before, when he'd traveled in India and run into trouble, but the thought of digging around in her tender flesh made him feel slightly ill. He'd do it if he had to . . .

"Doctor's here," Bertie announced from the door to the room, slightly breathless.

"Then where the hell is he?" Kilmartyn roared.

"He's climbing the stairs, my lord. He's not as young as I am."

"No excuse," Kilmartyn said, rising from beside the bed. Bryony had closed her eyes again, but he was pretty sure she was still conscious. Unfortunately.

A moment later the stocky figure of Dr. Brattle appeared in the doorway. "What's all this?" he said, surveying the sickroom. "I hear your housekeeper had some kind of accident. And who's this young woman?"

"She's the housekeeper," Kilmartyn said. "And she's been shot."

Dr. Brattle knew him too well to stand on ceremony. "Awfully young and pretty to be a housekeeper."

Kilmartyn shrugged. "She needed the work."

Brattle had already removed his coat and rolled up his shirtsleeves as he surveyed his patient. "So who shot her?"

"I have no idea. And if you've finished this endless discussion perhaps you'd consider getting the bullet out of her arm?"

Kilmartyn's acid tone had no effect on Brattle. "Don't rush me. I need to see whether I can use ether to knock her out."

"Why couldn't you?"

"Because it would take me too long to render her unconscious, and judging by the look of that arm, the sooner I get it out the better. It's a simple enough extraction," he continued, sitting down in Kilmartyn's vacated chair and examining the wound, "and I might be better off just going in and getting it, quick-like, before it has a chance to fester." He leaned over. "Young lady, can you hear me?"

Bryony opened her eyes for a moment, staring at the doctor with hazy eyes. "Who . . ." she managed one word, and Kilmartyn broke in roughly.

"This is the doctor, Mrs. Greaves. He'll tend to your arm. He's good at what he does—you may trust him. He's going to take the bullet out, and he's going to do it right now, without ether. Or we can wait until an anesthetic takes effect."

He saw her strong little jaw firm. "Now," she said.

Brattle nodded. "My lord, if you will hold her down, and Mrs. Harkins, you could hold her legs. That's right. Put your arm across her, my lord, and keep a strong hold of her arm."

Kilmartyn had taken the seat on the opposite side of the bed, and he leaned over her, sliding one arm beneath her to hold her still, wrapping the other one around her, just below her breasts, to clasp her forearm. She let out a strangled cry—the pain must be radiating down her arm—and he felt his stomach twist. "For God's sake, man, get the bloody thing out. Fast," he growled.

Brattle had pulled out a variety of lethal-looking instruments, and he'd put on a thick pair of glasses, further endangering Kilmartyn's peace of mind. "Don't rush me, young man," he said sternly. "My lord," he added belatedly.

The next five minutes were some of the worst in his memory. She fought him, fought the doctor, and he held her fast, murmuring in her ear, soft, comforting words, endearments, praise for her bravery. He could sense she was trying very hard to hold still, but the pain was simply too much, and for some goddamned pathetic reason he wanted to kiss away the tears that ran down her face.

"Got it," Brattle announced, holding the bullet up in his forceps, and Bryony slumped back against him. He didn't let go of her, didn't stop his soft, soothing litany, some in English, some in the old language his mother had used when he was a baby, and he stroked her forearm with the gentlest of touches.

"About time," Kilmartyn said, even as he whispered in her ear.

"It was a bit more complicated than I expected. The good thing is she hasn't broken any bones, and the torn flesh should heal quite well. I expect she'll regain full use of her arm."

"You'd best hope so." There was no mistaking the menace in his voice, but Brattle was unimpressed.

"I'm going to have to wash out the wound and disinfect it, and I expect she's going to find that just as bad. Keep a hold on her, or she'll probably punch you in the jaw."

"She'd be more than happy to, even in the best of times," Kilmartyn said. He whispered in her ear. "One more time, lass. It'll hurt, but this time I promise it'll be over quickly, or I'll throw the bloody sawbones out the window."

Did he see the faint trace of a smile on her face? He almost thought he did. Until she screamed as the doctor poured alcohol on the wound, her entire body arching, rigid in pain. And then, finally, she fainted.

"About time," Brattle said. "I'm going to sew her up and she won't like that either. Keep holding her, just in case she comes to."

Kilmartyn had no intention of giving her up. He'd asked for her the moment he walked in the door after the police finally let him go, but she was nowhere in the house. When she hadn't returned in an hour he'd gone looking for her. It was sheer luck he'd come across her as she stumbled home. Home. To him. Perhaps she trusted him after all.

At last the surgery was over. "She'll do," Brattle announced, washing his hands in a fresh basin of water. "Make sure she keeps her arm in this sling for the first few days, and have her rest. This kind of thing takes a toll on the body, but I see no reason that she won't be back on her feet in three or four days."

"And when will her arm be healed enough for work?" It wasn't work he was interested in, of course. He wanted to know how long he had to wait before he could get her into his bed.

Not that it had to be his bed, of course. The top of his desk, up against a wall, on the carpet, anywhere he could think of would be acceptable. Except that he liked the idea of curling up on a soft mattress with her, which was strange. He always hated it when his current paramour spent the night. He was a light sleeper, and he couldn't sleep with someone else in the room.

He wanted Bryony in his room, in his bed. It was illogical, and presumably only a passing fancy, but he looked down at the warm figure in his arms and resisted the impulse to pull her closer.

Brattle looked at him with disapproval for his heartless ways. "She'll be ready when she tells you so. People heal at different rates, and you'd best leave her be to do so. I've brought laudanum for her. She'll be in pain, and there's no need for her to suffer."

Kilmartyn didn't even notice when the doctor left. Slowly, carefully he let go of Bryony, letting her slip back onto the mattress. He turned to look at Mrs. Harkins, who was now sitting on the edge of the bed. "She needs all that blood washed off her. I don't suppose you're going to let me take care of it."

"You ought to be ashamed of yourself, your lordship!" Mrs. Harkins puffed up in indignation, for all the world like a ruffled chicken. "I won't be having such goings on, and I'll tell you that direct. No one's taking advantage of the poor thing while she's so bad off."

"And when she's better?" he asked with a faint smile.

"It's a good thing I know you're funning me," Mrs. Harkins said with the disapproval of a long-term retainer. "That poor girl hasn't done you any harm, and I won't be having you ruining her reputation."

He glanced back at Bryony. Done him no harm? She'd destroyed his peaceful way of life, confused him, filled him with so much ridiculously impossible need that he was half-mad from it. He took a deep breath. "She's lucky to have such a fierce protector in you, Mrs. Harkins."

It was most definitely the right thing to say. The bristles vanished, and she began to look at him with a hint of, was it possible, approval?

"You'll want to bathe her and change the sheets," he said, finally pulling himself out of the strange bubble that had seemed to surround his head. "I'll administer the laudanum as needed, and we'll leave her in this bed for the time being. That will make it easier on everyone."

"Yes, my lord," Mrs. Harkins said in a properly servile voice. She rose, looking at him. Waiting for him to leave.

He wasn't going to win this particular battle, but there'd be plenty of time in the future. "Very well, Mrs. Harkins. I'll be in my library."

"Emma," the cook said, and one of the maids emerged from the shadows. He hadn't even realized she'd been there all along. "Go up to Mrs. Greaves's room and fetch a clean chemise and see if she has a nightdress with loose sleeves."

"Yes, Mrs. Harkins," the girl said, moving toward the door.

Kilmartyn rose, and the girl politely stepped out of his way. He, master of his house, was being dismissed by his servants, and he was allowing them to do so.

All for the sake of the spying Miss Russell. He really must be out of his mind.

CHAPTER TWENTY

SHE HURT. THAT WAS all Bryony could think as her mind went swirling around in brightly colored circles. That pain was all through her, but most of all her arm. She tried to sit up, but someone had tethered her to the bed, and through the bright daze all she could think of was Kilmartyn.

She opened her eyes, but that didn't help. The room was very dark— only the glow of a fire at the far wall provided any light. Not her tiny attic under the eaves, then, unless someone had set the house on fire. She was ready to believe anything.

She closed her eyes again, trying to fight her way through the crippling dizziness. She knew what it was—laudanum. She'd been dosed with it enough when she'd been sick that she'd never forgotten the taste of it. She hated it, and its efficacy against pain seemed just about nil at that moment. If she was going to hurt like hell she'd just as soon be awake for it.

It took a few moments of intense concentration, but slowly she pushed past the smothering mists of the drug, like someone fighting through cob-webs covering a doorway. And she'd been spending too much time clean-ing this wretched house if she started to think of things in terms of cobwebs and dust.

She counted in her head, forcing herself to concentrate on pragmatic, mathematical issues. Common sense began to drift back in, and she realized she wasn't alone in this strange, dark bedroom. Someone was in the chair beside her, and she knew who it was. No one she should find safe and comforting. It was the devil himself.

Her eyes fluttered open, and she turned to look at him. He was asleep, stretched out in a club chair, his long legs propped on a stool. Why had he fallen asleep in her room? Did he think she was going to die? To run away? For some reason his voice echoed in her head, insisting she'd been shot. That was absurd! Why would someone want to shoot her?

She opened her mouth to speak, but nothing came out but a harsh croak, and she realized she needed water quite desperately. The tiny sound had woken him, though, and he sat forward, his feet hitting the floor as he looked at her.

"You're awake, then. Obviously. What do you need?"

"Water." It was so raw and garbled it was amazing he recognized the word, but he nodded, rose, and crossed the room. A moment later he was back with a tall glass of barley water. He sat down on the bed beside her in a matter-of-fact manner, slipped his hand behind her neck and pulled her up to drink, holding the glass against her mouth.

It was cool and refreshing, flavored with lemon and mint, and she drank it gratefully until Kilmartyn pulled the glass away. "Don't overdo," he said. "You'll end up throwing it all up and I don't fancy changing my clothes again."

He set her head back on the pillow, slowly, and his fingers lingered as they pulled away from her neck, offering a quiet, soothing stroke before leaving her. "Did I throw up on you before?"

"You did not."

She tried to shrug, but her left shoulder didn't work, strapped down as it was. "One can only hope."

His soft laughter was like a puff of springtime. "You are the most refreshing female I've ever met. There are not many women who would lie in my home, recovering from a gunshot wound, and insult me with such equanimity."

"I didn't insult you. I just said I wouldn't have minded throwing up on you."

"You said you hoped you'd thrown up on me. A very slight difference, I grant you, but a difference nonetheless. How are you feeling?"

She could think of several terms she'd heard in the stable but Kilmartyn was not someone to bandy curses with. "Words fail me."

"One can only hope."

She was surprised to find out she could laugh. It hurt, and she groaned in the midst of her chuckle, and she could feel unexpected tears fill her eyes. With luck he wouldn't be able to see them, but luck had hardly been with her recently, and he'd already proved to be far too adept at seeing in the dark. *Like a cat,* she thought. Not a tame tabby, but one of those long, sleek jungle creatures she'd seen in books.

"Do you remember what happened?" he asked in his indolent fashion.

She tried to think. "You said I'd been shot," she said after a moment. "But that's impossible."

"Since I watched Dr. Brattle dig a bullet out of your arm I assure you it's not impossible at all. Did you happen to see anyone when this happened?"

"No one," she managed to say. "I don't even remember it happening. Did you shoot me?"

For the briefest moment she saw shock in his eyes, but he covered it quickly, and there was a faint flash of a grin in the darkness. "Now that would be a terrible waste of female flesh."

It was wasted anyway, she thought with a trace of self-pity, her eyes filling with tears. She was young and strong and her body would wither and die without ever being touched, loved.

It was the laudanum, of course, making her maudlin, and she tried to ignore it. She really didn't want anyone touching her.

She closed her eyes again, drifting into the pain. She could feel the tears slide down her face, and her misery only increased. She didn't want to cry in front of him, be it from pain or weakness or both, but she couldn't even blink it away. She was alone, abandoned, and she hurt, and the misery encircled her like a cocoon, smothering her.

"Poor darling girl," she heard his voice, a lilting, gentle croon, and the tears kept flowing, just as she was hoping to regain control. She didn't want him being kind to her. She couldn't accept pity from him, not from him.

The mattress dipped, and she distantly realized he'd climbed onto the bed with her. She should order him away, but her tears only came more heavily as she felt him slide one arm underneath her, so carefully that she barely felt it in her trussed arm. He put his other arm around her waist, and instead of trying to pull her against him he simply wrapped his strong, warm body around hers, tucking her head against his shoulders. He was wiping her tears away with something soft, but there were always more coming, and he whispered to her, words she didn't understand. She didn't need to. They were words of comfort, and he called her his darling, his love, his sweet, precious girl, and the colors swirled down around her once more. He had put laudanum in her barley water, she realized belatedly, feeling the last bit of her mind slip away. His long fingers were on her cheeks, brushing the tears away, and at the very last, just as she was sinking into sleep once more, she opened her eyes to see him looking down at her, such honest emotion in his eyes that it stripped the lies from her.

"Did you kill him?" she whispered.

CHAPTER TWENTY-ONE

HE SLEPT BESIDE HER, a fact that astonished him. It was far from a comfortable position, half wrapped around her body. Dr. Brattle had tethered her arm to a board that was strapped to the side of the bed, to keep her from reopening the wound, and he'd simply had to move around her, arranging himself carefully. Her final words had been the ultimate mistrust, though they'd come as no surprise. She thought him capable of the most heinous crimes, of murder and embezzlement, of leaving his former business partner's daughters destitute. With his wife's bloody disappearance she might very well think him capable of even worse.

His mind should have been a whirl of questions, and instead he'd simply held her, offering her the warmth of his body, the strength of his arms, the shelter of his protection, and the comfort of his . . .

He wasn't sure what he was offering her. Certainly nothing more than temporary surcease of pain and despair. And he expected he would be handsomely rewarded eventually. If he were a decent human being he would be lying beside her with only caring thoughts in his head, the wish to provide comfort for one in distress. Unfortunately he was a very bad man, his cock had been hard for so long it ached, and it was all he could do to keep from sliding his arm up to rest against her small, lovely breasts.

And they were lovely. He could remember from the shadowy kitchen, when she lay stretched out in front of him, ready for him, hot for him. Tipsy, and a virgin. And he'd been a damned gentleman for once in his life, the ultimate act of stupidity. He wouldn't make that mistake again. He'd have to wait, of course. It would be all the lovelier when she was awake, alert, and bared herself to him knowing what she was doing. He'd never been fond of unconscious partners.

Sex was about give and take. Desire and retreat, need and generosity, control and abandon. He'd never waited so long for a woman, which amused him, considering it had only been four days. In his experience most women fell at his feet. And if they didn't, there were always other women available. Unfortunately, at least for the moment, no other woman would do.

Bryony. He liked it. His very dear Miss Greaves was Bryony Russell, eldest daughter of Eustace Russell, a woman who was purported to be an invalid, one who was judged too frail to appear in public. He'd snorted with laughter at that one. Bryony Russell was about as frail as a steamship. She'd stormed through his house like a typhoon and swept everything in front of her. It had been days since he'd seen so much as a speck of dust.

He didn't want her weak, broken like this. He wanted her strong, fighting back, and he wasn't going to consider why, or whether it had anything to do with this strange fascination she held for him. Indeed, he should probably just take her and get it done with. But she was going to have to be feeling just a little bit better before he became the complete villain he knew himself to be.

He woke up before she did, a knot in his neck, the arm beneath her numb. He slid from the bed, careful not to wake her. Her skin was cool, her color good. She hadn't taken on an infection, and since the bullet had thankfully landed in a fleshy part of her arm she should be up and about in a few days, a week at most. In the meantime, he had things to do.

If Collins was surprised to see him strolling from the housekeeper's bedroom he didn't show it. "I'm afraid Mr. Peach's men are here again, my lord. Would you like me to send them away?"

"How noisy are they?"

"Not very, my lord. I shouldn't think they'd disturb you, and they've promised to finish today."

He grimaced. "It was Mrs. Greaves I was concerned about. She'll need peace and quiet while she recovers."

"I don't believe they'll present a problem, my lord. Your rooms are at the opposite end of the house. If they disturb her we could always see they're sent away to a more opportune time."

He nodded, dismissing him, but Collins wasn't so easily dismissed. "Might I be bold enough to inquire whether your lordship might like assistance with his toilette this morning? I am accounted an excellent barber—my gentlemen always said I had a most delicate hand with a razor."

He was damnably tired. "I prefer to shave myself. In fact, I believe I'll take a bath first, unless the workmen are mucking about in the bathing room." He was very fond of the huge copper bathing tub and the hot water that traveled by pipes directly into it.

"Not at the moment, my lord. Allow me to draw one for you."

There was an odd note in Collins's voice, and Kilmartyn looked at him sharply. The imperturbable Collins was looking decidedly perturbed, almost . . . guilty. Odd. And interesting. Instead of sending him about his business, Kilmartyn nodded. "Do so then. And I believe I'll sample your skills with the razor after all."

Collins bowed, and most men wouldn't have noticed any difference in his behavior. But Kilmartyn wasn't most men. Something was off. Was Collins going to cut his throat when he shaved him? He could try, of course, but he wouldn't get very far. If he were dealing with the gently reared son of a British lord then he might succeed. But Kilmartyn hadn't been gently reared, he was Irish, and even if he hadn't developed an unexpected distrust for his butler-cum-gentleman's gentleman it would require someone of great cunning and skill to best him.

A man of great cunning and skill wouldn't be letting his current agitation show. Something was disturbing Collins, and Kilmartyn had every intention of finding out what it was. His initial thought, that Collins harbored romantic feelings for the housekeeper, had evaporated. There was nothing of the worried lover in the man's bearing. Something else was troubling his manservant, the one who had been thrust upon him despite his protests.

There was a logical conclusion. Collins arrived soon after Bryony, at her behest. There was a strong probability that they were in this together. But he didn't think so. For one thing, what would a gentleman's gentleman care about an embezzlement scheme? There was no doubt that was exactly what Collins was—he was too good at his vocation to be an imposter. And Kilmartyn had sensed no collusion between them. His housekeeper had secrets, and he'd known that, but Collins came as a surprise.

The bathing room was large, a converted bedroom at the back of the third floor, a fact which had annoyed his wife to no end.

He shook his head. He really was a heartless bastard. He'd been so worried about Bryony that he hadn't given a thought to the fact that the woman he'd been married to for almost ten years, the woman he'd once loved to distraction with all the passion of a twenty-year-old, was almost certainly dead. They'd hated each other so intensely that it was impossible to summon the grief he knew he should be feeling, but at least he should remember she'd been murdered. Unless she was perpetrating some complicated sham as revenge.

He didn't think so. He was Irish enough to trust his instincts on this. Cecily was well and truly dead. He was now a widower. Whether he could prove it, and whether that proof might send him to the gallows, was another matter entirely.

He saw the merest shadow out of the corner of his eye as he walked down the hallway, but he moved quickly, grabbing the child by the scruffy shirt he wore and holding him while he struggled.

"And what are you doing on this floor, young Jem?" He gave him a gentle shake. "Are you spying on me?"

The child looked both indignant and guilty, and Kilmartyn remembered with a flash that his reaction to Bryony's being shot had been similar to Collins's. Remorse.

"Am not, guv'nor. Me lord," he amended hastily, his dark eyes shifting. "I was just wanting to make sure Mrs. Greaves was all right."

"Why should you care?"

Again the guilt. "She hired me, didn't she?" he said. "No one ought to have shot her. He said . . . I mean, she should have been safe."

Kilmartyn froze. He forced himself to take a slow, calming breath. "He said?" he prompted gently. He'd known boys like this, rough and desperate and determined not to show it.

"Nuffin," the child said stubbornly.

"You said, 'he said.' Exactly whom are you talking about?" The child was squirming, trying to get away from him, but Kilmartyn's fingers tightened on the collar of his shabby shirt.

"Nuffin!" he shouted, and yanked. The shirt tore, and the child, Jem, was off, disappearing through the door to the servants' stairs in a flash.

He could have caught up with him. Despite his generally indolent air he could be as fast as any street rat, something that would have shocked his titled friends. But he let him go. Time enough to deal with him later. He had Collins to deal with, Collins who would undoubtedly know more, and it wasn't going to be pretty.

● ●
· ·

Bryony blinked rapidly, trying to clear her brain. It was one of those rainy, gloomy days that plagued London, and the light in the room was so murky she had no idea what time of day it was. She lay very still, trying to assess her surroundings.

Her head ached abominably. She tried to move, but for some reason she'd been tied down, and the pain that shot through her arm was almost as bad as her headache. That's right, someone had shot her. Or so Kilmartyn had insisted.

Though she couldn't quite remember when she'd seen him. Had he been there when she'd been brought back? And who had found her? Perhaps she'd made it as far as Berkeley Square, collapsing at the servants' entrance in a dead faint. It was all a blur. But she could hear his caustic voice, telling her to lie still.

Had he been in the room last night? She turned her head automatically, and the pain slammed through it. They'd given her laudanum again to help the pain. She hated the stuff—it always made her ill the next day, dull and foggy, with a thundering pain in her head, and the only cure was fresh air. She tugged at her arm, letting out an unbidden cry of pain as it held.

She could see him in that chair, stretched out lazily. But that was ridiculous. Why in the world would he be in her room in the middle of the night? Well, there was one obvious reason, but with a gunshot wound she was hardly a good candidate for bed sport. Perhaps he thought that once she was tethered she wouldn't be able to fight him off.

No, that wasn't Kilmartyn. He would never resort to force—careful seduction was more his style. Had he been the one to shoot her? No. If he'd wanted her dead he'd had time enough to finish her, alone in the room with her. Instead he'd curled up around her, held her like she was a precious, delicate creature. Like she mattered to him.

Which was, of course, impossible. At the very best he was involved in his wife's disappearance, and her own father hadn't trusted him. At worst, he was a murderer twice over—his wife and her father. And why should he stop at two?

Why in heaven's name hadn't she simply gotten on the train and disappeared? What had made her come back here, to a house of secrets and lies? But she knew the answer to that, fool that she was. Whether she trusted him or not, she came back for Kilmartyn. She couldn't leave him, not yet.

• •

Rufus walked through the burned-out ruins of the Russell house on Curzon Street, the devastation calming his tumultuous thoughts as night fell on the city. He'd failed again. No, it hadn't been his fault—he didn't make mistakes. But that whore had managed, by sheer luck, to get away from him with only a bullet in her arm. Just a few inches to the left and she would have been dead, no longer a problem.

But then, perhaps things had worked out for the best. Having informants in the household served him better than he imagined. He'd merely expected them to keep track of the housekeeper's movements; he'd never hoped for the added information. Collins had spied her searching Kilmartyn's office, rifling through his papers. Had she been selling information rather than baubles when she disappeared among the warrens of the moneylenders? Had Kilmartyn already been destroyed?

No. Kilmartyn was barely aware of his existence—they'd met once or twice on social occasions. He would have no idea that Rufus was behind the satisfying destruction of Eustace Russell and everything that was dear to him, including his reputation, his house in London, his daughters. He would have no idea that own his wife had helped him, and therefore had to be silenced. And that he was about to become the perfect scapegoat for the entire affair.

Except Russell's daughters were going to be more of a problem than he'd thought. Poverty and disgrace should have been enough, but he shouldn't have counted on it. Collins had searched the woman's room thoroughly and come up with the most interesting information. The woman who'd inserted herself into Kilmartyn's household was none other than Russell's eldest daughter, Bryony, doing her own form of investigating.

Stupid bitch. If she'd just known her place and kept it she wouldn't have had to die. Kilmartyn was going down for embezzlement and the murders of Russell and his own wife. Bryony Russell's questions would have an answer. Her quest for revenge, if that was what it was, would be satisfied, and he could have left her alone.

Not now. She'd seen him, twice. She'd been through Kilmartyn's papers—she'd know when proof showed up that it hadn't been there before. There were so many reasons to silence her, and yet she'd avoided his attempts twice now, something that infuriated him.

He took a deep breath, calming himself. He was a man of certain strong passions, and he didn't dare give in to them until this was accomplished. He only had a few stray details to clean up, and then it would all be done. Three of those details were Eustace Russell's daughters. Because if the eldest had started on this crusade there was little doubt the other two knew about it.

He should have recognized her immediately—he had to admit to that mistake. He'd known that the eldest of Russell's daughters was hideous, scarred, and so unsightly that she hid herself from society. The woman he ran into so unfortunately in Kilmartyn's hallway was pretty enough, the scarring faded and barely noticeable. If he'd put two and two together he could have strangled her then and there. It would have been a risk, but one worth taking.

Now life had become a great deal more complicated.

Returning to the ruined house on Curzon Street always soothed him, reminded him of all he'd accomplished. He'd not only taken Renwick back, the house his father had lost in a stupid wager to that ignorant *merchant*, he'd destroyed their other home as well. It was a shame only servants had been in residence to perish in the fire, but he was a man who could deal with challenges.

The front half of the house had collapsed after the fire had been put out—the back still stood, with the remnants of a roof and walls and even doors. Some of the floors remained, others were gaping holes. It was a good place to lose a body. Sooner or later the rest of the house would fall in, someone would buy the land, clear it, and build anew. Over the bodies of Cecily and her officious French maid, and possibly Miss Bryony Russell. He hadn't had time to find out where the other two sisters were, but there was no hurry. He didn't like to be rushed. He took things one at a time, and right now he was focused on murdering that interfering bitch before she could cause any more trouble.

Too bad his informants balked at the idea of murder and even his most devious threats couldn't move them. The Irishman could have put poison in with the laudanum they were doubtless using, but he flat out refused. He was feeling guilty for informing on her—never a good sign. Never trust a man with a conscience.

As for the boy, he was no more than a courier. He still had possibilities, and he could be a pretty thing when he was properly washed. No, the boy still had uses. The Irishman would have to be disposed of as well.

Life was such a trial. So many loose ends to tie up, just when he thought he was finished. It was a good thing he'd discovered he found a certain pleasure in snuffing out a life. A godlike thrill. He'd never hunted when he was young—a fox or a bird seemed a pitiful enough victim. But people were much more of a challenge, and in truth, he never liked things to be too easy.

He pushed through the charred back door, using his handkerchief to keep his black clothes from getting sooty. The front half of the gardens had been destroyed by the heat of the fire, but toward the back daffodils were blooming, and the mews were intact. He would bring her in this way, though the front stairs remained as well, and in somewhat sturdier condition. Because, in fact, poison was too good for her. She'd been too much of a cock-up, and he was going to take his time with her and enjoy himself. Practice his artistry.

Because he had the other two sisters to deal with, and he wanted to give them his very best work.

CHAPTER TWENTY-TWO

IT WAS RAINING when Kilmartyn returned to his upended household that night. His housekeeper was in bed with a gunshot wound, his valet was tied up in one of the bedrooms, the cook was sulking, the footmen looked at him warily, the boy was gone. There was no change in the maids' demeanor—they'd always been half-terrified of him.

Not to mention that his wife was missing and Scotland Yard was watching the house. Somewhere along the way things had taken a bad turn, and he didn't know how to change things back.

Not that he wanted to fix everything. Finding the blood-soaked clothes had been a shock to his system, but he couldn't truly grieve for his wife. She'd hated him, used him, cuckolded him, and blackmailed him, and he'd been trapped, tied to her through the almost unbreakable bonds of marriage.

Which were now effectively broken, assuming they ever found her body. As it was, he couldn't be sure she was dead, though given the amount of blood it was a reasonable supposition. Not that it should matter—he would never make the mistake of marrying again. He could stay the

husband of a missing woman for the rest of his life—he didn't give a damn
if they found her body.

Unless, of course, it led to her murderer and the author of all this disaster, including Russell's downfall. All the evidence pointed directly at
himself, and Kilmartyn knew that was no accident. Someone was doing
their best to paint him as a thief, a murderer, a man who'd betray a friend
and mentor. He needed to find out exactly who that man was.

Unfortunately the duplicitous Collins knew almost nothing about
the man who'd hired him. Not a name or direction, and he'd met the
man in darkened alleys, so there was no way he could describe him. Collins
had been surprisingly forthcoming, and Kilmartyn, tempted though he
was to turn him over to the police, had simply left him trussed in a back
room until he decided what to do. Collins clearly had had no idea that
his mysterious employer had meant to harm anyone—he was just supposed to keep track of things and send Jem to report back. His family
in Ireland were among the starving, the desperate, and he'd taken the
money for them. Kilmartyn hadn't doubted him. If he didn't know his
own holdings and tenants were being well provided for there was no ac-
counting for what deals with the devil he might make, in order to provide
for them.

He could understand that kind of deal—he still bore the weight of his
own responsibility in the deaths of so many in the Fenian bombing. Was
he any less guilty than Collins?

He couldn't discover anything at the club, despite his very delicate questions. His fellow club members knew his wife was missing
under mysterious circumstances, knew he'd been taken to Scotland Yard
for questioning, but such matters were too ill-bred to discuss, so instead he
held murmured conversations about the derby and the Russell debacle that
had set off the one-day financial panic, causing two banks to fail.

And he'd come away with exactly nothing. Barely even a scrap of information about the daughters, though his friend Barlow had remembered
the lies about the poor, half-mad, invalided eldest daughter, and there was
something about a broken engagement for the middle child.

Russell had been his friend, his confidant, and he'd done nothing for his children, Kilmartyn thought, tossing back his glass of whiskey. Nothing except plan on seducing the eldest. The poor, half-mad invalid who was the strongest female he'd ever known, who drove him wild with inappropriate lust. The one he had to keep his damned hands off.

Then again, why should he? He was no damned saint, nor had he ever pretended to be one. He'd let her go, twice now, when he'd wanted nothing more than to shove inside her and lose himself.

But in truth, what was the worst that could happen? She had no father, no protector to call him to accounts. He could hardly be forced into a marriage if he compromised her—to the world he was still a married man, not a widower. He could take her, enjoy her, part ways with a sufficient financial gift, as he did with all the other women.

Except that he couldn't do that to her. He wasn't sure why or how, but he . . . cared about her. He could be the worst possible bastard, but something stopped him from being that callous, and the thought disturbed him. Was he growing soft? Becoming kind?

Of course not. He'd developed an odd sort of attachment for the girl, that was all. It had nothing to do with kindness, it was his own comfort. He simply preferred her safe and happy, and he intended to see to it. He would send her off, as soon as she was well enough to travel, and make certain she and her sisters were provided for.

A sudden spike of fear went through him—what if she'd caught a fever after all? Things like that could happen—a patient could be recovering nicely when they were brought low by an infection, and they could die quickly. Very quickly.

He took the steps two at a time, his heart racing. It was too dark, too quiet. Had they called in the doctor? The undertaker?

He saw the form of one of the maids, sound asleep outside Bryony's door when he reached the top of the stairs, and he felt a cautious relief sweep through him, calming him down. He started toward her, and she woke, jumping to her feet and bobbing a curtsy.

"Beg pardon, your lordship, but I was just—"

"Shhh," he cautioned her. "How is she?"

"Fretful. Doesn't like being sick, doesn't like taking the laudanum, but her color's good and she ate something. But she's not happy."

He didn't let his relief show on his face. "Very good. You can go to bed, Emma, is it?"

"Yes, sir. But Mrs. Harkins said I was to stay in case she needed something."

"Do you take your orders from Mrs. Harkins or me, Emma?"

"Begging your pardon, sir, but Mrs. Harkins."

"And who gives Mrs. Harkins her orders?" he said, controlling his frustration.

"You do, my lord."

"Then do as I say."

She hesitated, then bobbed another curtsy. He didn't bother to wait until she was gone; he simply opened the door and went inside.

Bryony was awake. She lay in the bed, her eyes dark with pain, watching him warily as he closed the door behind him.

The first thing he did was pour her a glass of the barley water, bringing it to her. He sat down on the bed, and she tried to scoot away from him, but she was still strapped to the board and immobile.

"What are you doing here?" Her voice was thin and weak, but her eyes flashed.

"Still full of fight, I see," he said pleasantly. "I came to see how you were doing."

"Recovering." The word was flat.

He strolled over to the chair, pulling it close. "I'm enchanted to hear it. Are you ready to talk?"

"About what?" She eyed him suspiciously.

"About what happened."

A deep color suffused her too pale skin, and belatedly he realized she was thinking about those moments on the kitchen table, not being shot. Interesting priorities. "When you were shot," he clarified, allowing himself a faint smile, which clearly failed to endear himself to her.

Only a little of the color began to fade. "I don't remember. I didn't even realize I'd been shot. I was walking just past Stratton Street and I felt something knock against my arm. I turned to look, but there was no one around, so I kept walking. Until I felt too weak to go any farther."

He nodded. "That's when I found you."

Her eyes flashed open in clear distress. "You found me? I thought I'd made it as far as the servants' entrance."

"I'm afraid not. You were about to collapse on the street, right at the edge of the square, when I caught up with you."

"You were following me?" Her thin voice was slightly stronger.

It should have amused him, her clear lack of trust, but he was having trouble finding anything amusing nowadays.

"Not with a gun, Miss Russell. I do my hunting in the countryside." He waited to see if she'd react to her true name, but she didn't notice. "In the meantime, can I get you something?"

"There's nothing you can get me," she said, and he recognized the slight grogginess in her voice from the effects of the laudanum. Clearly someone had managed to get some in her, probably in the barley water he'd given her.

"Try me."

She was too groggy to appreciate his double entendre. "I want my arm freed from this damnable board. I don't like being trussed up. I want a bath—my hair is caked with blood, and I want people to stop giving me laudanum. It gives me a headache. Most of all, I want this to have never happened."

He surveyed her calmly. "I can't do anything about the last—even I can't turn time around, but I expect I can manage the rest."

Her eyes were drifting closed. "Just let me sleep," she murmured, closing her eyes.

He allowed himself the odd pleasure of watching her. She did look terrible—her hair had dried blood in it, her skin was parchment white with a blue tinge to her eyelids, the smallpox scars were turned toward him, and he surveyed her dispassionately. Why had she allowed such a minor imperfection to control her life? The Bryony Russell he knew was no fainting violet, content to hide away from life. She was a fighter.

And yet she'd done just that.

There were still a great many mysteries to unravel about his little spy. He only hoped he'd have the time to do so before he did what he had to do, the absurdly decent thing, and send her away.

••••••••••••••••••••••••••••••••
....

Someone had given her laudanum again, and she wanted to scream. Her head was pounding, her body aching, and something was tugging at her arm. She opened her eyes and turned her head, only to see Kilmartyn there, untying the knots that kept her strapped to the board and to the bed.

She was so relieved she didn't say anything, simply watched him as he went about the business with surprising efficiency. And then she remembered she didn't trust him.

"What are you doing?" she croaked.

"Following your orders."

What orders? What was he talking about? Her arm came free, and a momentary shaft of pain slammed down on her, leaving her breathless, sweating.

"Just breathe," he said. "I promise I'll be very careful."

Careful doing what? Murdering her like he had his wife? They'd left her alone with him—how did she know he wouldn't finally finish her off? If he killed once, killed twice, then he could easily kill again.

He'd discarded his coat and cravat, dressed simply in a white shirt with the sleeves rolled up. He came around the other side of the bed and gently slid his arms underneath her, lifting her effortlessly. It wasn't the first time he'd carried her, she thought, though she could barely remember the other occasions. She only knew that she'd felt safe in his arms, held high against his warm chest, his beating heart. She tried to keep her neck straight, but her head hurt, and it felt so much better to let it rest against his shoulder as he carried her through the dark hallway.

He pushed open a door, and suddenly she was enveloped in heat and light and a warm mist, and she lifted her head, looking around her in shock.

"Milady said she wanted a bath," he said. "Do you think you can stand for a moment? I'll catch you if you fall."

She nodded, even though the move hurt her head, and he slowly set her down, letting her slide against his body, and if the aftereffects of being shot hadn't made her knees weak the feel of his body would have done so. She stood in the circle of his arms, and it took her a moment to realize what he was doing. He was unfastening the buttons at her throat.

"No," she croaked, but the way he held her, good arm trapped against her side, gave her no way to fight. He undid them quickly, efficiently, then slid the nightdress down.

"Don't be juvenile, Bryony," he said in a comfortingly matter-of-fact voice. "You can't bathe in your nightdress—it's the only one you have left."

That was the last thing she wanted to think about. "The shift stays on," she said. It provided scant modesty, but she'd take what she could get.

"Whatever you say, Bryony." He picked her up and carried her over to the deep, steaming copper tub, started to put her in. At the last minute he somehow managed to pull off the shift, just as she was sinking into the blissfully warm water, and she had to swallow her instinctive shriek of protest.

The warm water felt so good she didn't bother to argue. He'd held on to her bandaged arm, letting it rest carefully on the high side of the tub, and there was nothing salacious about his expression. She might have felt better if there was.

"Are you going to drown me?" She hadn't meant for those words to come out, but she was still groggy from the drugs.

He laughed, though there wasn't much humor in it. "No, I'm not going to kill you. I'm not a murderer, no matter what it looks like."

She sighed, sinking further into the lovely water. Too late she realized her hair was flowing around her, and she tried to sit up, but he pushed her back, gently. "If you want the blood washed from your hair you're going to have to let me do it."

She considered it. But he was viewing her with all the passion of a man surveying a suet pudding, and though she couldn't remember the details of that rapturous time on the kitchen table, she knew that she'd ended the night the way she started it, still a virgin. So clearly he'd lost interest in her. He was merely doing this out of the kindness of his heart.

Then again, she was under no illusion that Kilmartyn had a kind heart. Nevertheless, the warm water was drugging her far more pleasantly than the laudanum had, and she wasn't going to fight. "Go ahead," she said ungraciously. "Just don't take the occasion to drown me."

He made a sound of disapproval. "When will you learn to trust me, Bryony?"

"When hell freezes over," she murmured, as he moved to the end of the tub and his hands cupped her head. "And don't call me Bryony." She felt faintly uneasy, but she had no idea why.

"What do you prefer?" he murmured, pouring water over her hair, carefully keeping it from her eyes. She closed them anyway, relaxing into the sensation. Her injured arm was throbbing, and she didn't care, as long as his fingers were caressing her scalp, rubbing the soap into it, threading through her hair.

"Mrs. Greaves will do," she said dreamily. She could lie like this forever, she thought. Besides, getting out of the tub would expose her body to his critical gaze.

"I like Bryony better."

She purred as he poured fresh water over her hair, rinsing it. And then he lifted the length of it and draped it over the back of the tub, pouring more water to wash the suds away.

"You're not letting that water get on the floor, are you?" she demanded suddenly.

"You're not the housekeeper here anymore, Bryony. But there's a basin behind the tub for just such a purpose."

"Very clever." And then his words penetrated. "Of course I'm the housekeeper here."

"I'm afraid not. Mrs. Harkins has taken over."

"Then I must leave."

This time his snort of laughter was genuine. "And just where would you be going in your current condition? Besides, I'm not letting you out of my sight. Someone's trying to kill you, and I don't intend to let that happen. You're not going anywhere until I can make proper plans."

"Who's trying to kill me?" She focused on the most important part of all this.

"I'm damned if I know. Presumably the same man who killed Cecily." His voice was blunt, matter-of-fact, with no sorrow in it.

She turned her head to look at him. "If you didn't kill her then why were your clothes covered with blood?"

"Ah, so you're the one who moved them. You relieve my mind—I was afraid the police had somehow gotten hold of them. My clothes were covered in blood, my precious, because someone took them and dowsed them in it. Presumably whoever killed her."

"Why didn't you call the police?"

"You didn't . . . don't know Cecily that well. She's entirely capable of buying gallons of pigs' blood to set me up like that. I have no guarantee that she's not enjoying herself in Paris, laughing at my expense."

"Do you really think so?"

"No." He moved around to the side, a cloth and a bar of sweet-smelling soap in his hand. "Let's wash the rest of you."

She sat up, so quickly her arm went into a painful spasm, so quickly the water slopped lower, exposing the tops of her breasts. "I can wash myself."

"I'm sure you can. Are we going to have a wrestling match? Because I intend to win, and I don't mind getting wet."

"No."

"Yes," he said, and she felt the bar of soap brush against her collarbone. "Close your eyes, Bryony. I'm not going to hurt you."

"I don't trust you."

"I know you don't. But right now you're injured and you have no choice."

He was right. His hand was moving lower, over her stomach, and she realized he'd skipped her breasts entirely, thank heavens, except they were tight and aching and she wasn't quite sure why as his soapy hand traced leisurely circles on her stomach. He moved closer, his other hand behind her back, supporting her, and she let herself lean into him, letting him touch her, giving in to the pleasure of his hands.

His hand slid lower, brushing against the soft hair between her thighs, and she jerked for a moment, then calmed. What could he do to her in a bathtub, for heaven's sake? And why would he want to?

And then, to her horror, he moved his hand between her thighs, touching her intimately, and she let out a strangled cry, arching up.

"Hush, sweetheart. I know, it's unfair. But the problem is, I can't resist you. I've been trying very hard, but I'm not the kind of man who's made for noble sacrifice, and I think I've about reached my limit."

She opened her eyes to look at him, aroused and frightened and longing. "I don't . . ." she began, knowing she should protest, knowing it wouldn't do any good. "I don't think . . ."

"Don't think," he said, and covered her mouth with his, swallowing her arguments, as his fingers delved deeper. She jerked against him, startled, and the water splashed up against them, but he simply held her still with one arm around her shoulders, cupping her neck with his hand, while he began to rub against her sex, sliding in the deep, warm water, slippery, seductive, moving inside her, and she arched her hips against his hand, reaching for him, wanting more of him, letting him do whatever he wished, as shameful as it was.

It didn't feel shameful. She couldn't understand the heat building inside her, the fierce, gnawing need that was taking over, filling her with raw wanting. She'd seen lust in Kilmartyn's eyes, and she wondered what it would look like in her own. Because this was the only possible explanation for the powerful longings arching through her body, the only possible explanation why she slid her tongue against his when he kissed her, why she didn't fight against him, but fought to get closer.

And then she stopped thinking, only felt, as she gripped the side of the copper tub with her one good hand and dissolved into sensation, a shiver, and then an explosion, and there was water everywhere and she didn't care, she just hid her face against his damp shoulder and let the feelings ride her, a cataclysm of impure delight that stole her breath, her will, her heart.

"That's my girl," he said in a low, hypnotizing voice. He took his hand from between her legs, trailing it up her body in the warm water, moving it to brush against one tightly beaded breast, and she jerked again, squeezing her thighs together as still another explosion rocked her. He moved on, pushing her wet hair out of her face, cupping her chin as she hid against his shoulder and she made a sound of protest.

He laughed softly. "Don't worry, I'll give your perfect little breasts the attention they deserve. I'm saving them for my mouth." She made another sound again, a moan of mortification and desire. "Now I'm going to pick you up, wrap you in a towel, and carry you back to my bedroom. And then I'm going to do a proper job of taking the virginity you lied about, and you're going to say yes. I told myself I wouldn't, I'd be a gentleman, but I'm afraid I'm simply too weak to resist you."

She tried to find her voice, her pride. "No, I won't," she managed to choke out.

He smiled at her, a smile of peculiar sweetness. "Yes, you will. Because you want me just as much as I want you. Your mouth may be full of lies but your body betrays you."

"I don't lie," she said weakly.

"Of course you don't," he said softly, scooping his arms under her and picking her up, setting her on her feet.

"I'm making you wet," she said, as he wrapped a towel around her.

"Don't worry. I don't plan to be in these clothes for long." He picked her up again, and she knew she should protest, even when it was the last thing she wanted to do. She wanted to go to his bed, she wanted him to take her, show her, love her, even if it was temporary, a physical lie. "And I have every intention of making you wet," he said.

She knew what he meant—she'd read enough Italian to understand that part of his wicked book, the long list of elaborate techniques to ready a woman for the intimate act. She already felt hot, liquid inside, ready for him, and he carried her through the hallway, into his newly refurbished bedroom.

The gaslights were turned low, the wide bed turned down by one of the maids, and he put one knee on the mattress, lowering her down, pulling the covers over her before he took the towel away. "You're going to catch a chill and we can't have that," he said. "Just lie there and get warm while I start a fire."

She wanted to protest. She knew she should scramble out of the bed the moment he turned his back, and she knew she wouldn't. For one thing, her legs wouldn't hold her, not because of the gunshot wound, but the wicked thing he'd done in the bathing room, turning her every bone and muscle to jelly. For another, she didn't want to. She wanted to finish this, her one chance at experiencing what most women took for granted. What most women avoided, if she were to believe the stories she'd heard. What women craved, if she were to believe her own body.

The fire had already been laid, and it was the work of a moment to turn it into a warming blaze. And then he turned to look at her. The white shirt was plastered against his chest, and he began to unbutton it in a leisurely fashion, his eyes never leaving hers. A moment later he'd pulled it over his head, and there was nothing but skin underneath, shocking in itself. He reached for the fastening of his trousers, and she turned her face away quickly, and he laughed softly.

"It's not that terrifying, angel," he murmured, and she heard the sound of fabric dropping to the floor, his footsteps coming closer to her. "Half the population possess one." She felt his hand on the covers, lifting them. "Move over, precious. It's chilly out here. Unless want me to . . ." She tried to scoot out of his reach, but her arm got in the way and she let out a cry of pain.

In a moment he was in the bed, pulling her gently into his arms, exquisitely careful of her wound. "Poor baby," he murmured. "I'm a bastard and a half to even touch you while you're still hurting. We should wait until you're better."

She turned to face him. It was growing warm from the fire, the spring chill leaving the room, and the dim light cast his face in shadows, and she believed he'd do just that. Except that he was warm and naked in the bed, his legs brushing against hers, his arms reaching for her, and she felt that hard part of him against her thigh. "If you do, I'll die," she said simply, her eyes looking into his with no artifice, no guile. "You've brought me too far to simply leave me again."

His smile was crooked. "The only reason I stopped last time was because you were both tipsy and a virgin, two rules trained into a gentleman from early on."

"I never thought you were much of a gentleman."

"You were right," he said, covering her mouth with his. It was a long, slow, deep kiss, leisurely, as if he was ready for this to take all night. His tongue danced against hers, and he nibbled on her lower lip, biting, and the sensation exploded inside her. *Heat,* she thought dizzily, *and damp.*

She was breathless when he lifted his head, and she could feel him all around her, the rough texture of his legs, the smoothness of his chest, the pressure of that strange, unknown part of him against her. He kissed her eyelids, her jaw, then fastened his teeth on her earlobe, making her jerk in reaction.

"You need to lie back, sweetheart," he whispered. "I don't want to hurt that arm any more than necessary, but I have to touch you. Taste you." He gently pushed her onto her back, arranging her painful arm on one of the pillows before leaning over her. "Your job is to try not to move too much. You'll like it better when you can move, but I promise you'll like this well enough to want to try again."

Try again with whom? she thought, but then pushed the thought away. She would leave tomorrow, hurt arm or not. She'd been a fool to come back. She needed to get away and hide, from Kilmartyn, from whoever had tried to kill her, whether they were two or simply one deranged person.

He was arranging her with such care that she didn't even notice that he'd moved between her legs, pushing them apart, that he was kneeling there, watching her with an intensity that only made the fires burn hotter. She looked at him, and then looked down at his sex, and she let out a little screech.

"Oh, no," she cried, trying to scoot out of the way. "That's impossible."

He laughed, pulling her back. "You're going to hurt yourself, love. And trust me, it's very possible. Just relax and let me take care of things."

"Relax?" she echoed, not bothering to hide her skepticism. "You're out of your . . ." the word trailed off as his hands covered her breasts, and she swallowed a groan of intense pleasure. "This is a terrible idea."

"Of course it is," he said, bending down, and she felt the wetness of his tongue dance across her nipple, and everything inside her seemed to contract. "But we're going to do it anyway." And then he fastened his mouth on her breast, sucking and pulling at it while his fingers toyed with her other hardened nipple, and she began to shiver in response.

This was desire, this was madness. Lust and insanity, wrapped together into a tight grip of impossibility, but she no longer cared. His hair fell over her as he sucked at her, and that impossible part of his body seemed to twitch and grow larger still against her, and she knew he lied, knew it would kill her, and she no longer cared. She'd gotten past the point of worrying, she was nothing but need incarnate.

He lifted his head and blew on her damp breast, and she cried out again, this time a moan of pleasure and dismay that he'd stopped, until he caught her other breast in his mouth, swirling his tongue against the tight nipple, and then she felt the soft brush of his teeth, and another flurry of pleasure shook her.

She was panting, the room was now warm, and he'd shoved the covers back. He was levered over her, and he took her hand and drew it down, down, to touch that part of him. She tried to yank away from him, but his grip was unbreakable. "It's a cock, love. A John Thomas, a member, a dick. Whatever you want to call it, it's nothing to be afraid of. Touch me. Yes, like that. Oh, God, yes, like that," he whispered, wrapping her fingers around the smooth length of him. He was like iron beneath the silken skin, and he moved her hand up and down, slowly, pumping at him, and he was shivering too in the hot room. He released her, but she didn't stop. She let her fingers play with him, touch him, learn him. He was damp too, the head of his . . . cock was damp, and she remembered the night on the kitchen table. What would he taste like? Would she ever know?

He groaned, catching her wrist and pulling her gently away. "Too much of that and it'll be over before it begins," he said wryly. "We need to dispense with your tiresome virginity before I have one of my rare attacks of conscience again. Lift your hips just a tiny bit, love. I'll try not to make it hurt too much."

He was brushing against her sex, and she remembered then, the wonderful feel of him, filling her emptiness, and the dampness of both of them easing his way, and she wanted to hold on to him, but he was holding her bad arm down against the pillow, very gently, and there was nothing she could do. With a sharp jerk of his hips he pushed in, and she felt a tearing inside her. She cried out, and he covered her mouth with his, silencing her, holding very still within her, letting her get used to the feel of him.

It hurt. It burned. He lifted his head, and she stared up at him in accusation, her desire momentarily banked. "You lied," she said. "It doesn't work."

"Yes, it does. And that was the worst part. From now on it's all pleasure." He pushed, and she felt him slide in deeper yet. He lied again, it still burned, but not as badly as that initial thrust. In fact, she could feel the first stirrings of pleasure return. "Look at me, Bryony."

She did, her eyes staring up into his dark ones. She could feel herself slipping away, and she made one last attempt. "I still don't trust you."

He smiled down at her, so tenderly. "I know you don't, love." And he began to move, slowly thrusting into her.

She sucked in her breath. She could feel him everywhere, he possessed her, owned her, and she wanted to weep with the beauty of it. Because as she was his, he was hers, shaking in her arms, thrusting, a deliberate pace that began to grow faster. She was shaking again, and she waited for that wondrous little explosion he'd brought from her before, in the tub, in the kitchen, but it eluded her, and something else was taking its place, something darker, more powerful. She was right not to trust him—this was no simple pleasure, this would destroy her, and she had no defenses. She was losing herself, completely, to the steady thrust of him, the tension in his muscles as he held himself above her, and yet he managed to keep his fingers gentle on her bad arm. It was blazing hot, their bodies were covered with sweat, sliding against each other, and she was trembling, wanting to cry, to scream, to beg for something she didn't understand, and he was shaking as well. She couldn't breathe, couldn't speak, as tears poured down her face in the darkness, and she wanted to beg him, but she didn't know for what.

He cursed, a low, guttural sex word, and twisted his hips against her, and the darkness hit, turning everything into a cataclysmic explosion that rocked every inch of her. She was barely aware that he'd pulled out of her, that warm wetness spread over her belly, and she would have cried out, but her voice was strangled in her throat, and then he covered her mouth with his, swallowing the last of her protest, the last of her passion, and she wanted him back inside her. And then he collapsed against her, shielding her left side, breathing roughly, shaking.

"Jesus, Mary, and Joseph, Bryony," he whispered. "It's not supposed to feel *that* good." A moment later he rolled off her, and she wanted to hold him, pull him back against her, into her. She wanted to curl up into his arms, to weep against him.

It was too dark for him to see her clearly, but she felt his fingers brush the tears away from her face. "Did I hurt you?"

"Yes. No. Yes," she said.

"Poor little love." He didn't sound particularly remorseful. "It will be better next time."

"Oh, God," she muttered weakly. "I don't think I could survive better than that."

She felt the bed shake slightly with his laughter, and he kissed the tears from her face, her chin, then kissed her mouth once more, a sweet, almost playful kiss. "I need to clean us both up, my darling. And then I'd better check your arm and make sure you're not bleeding again."

He was so matter-of-fact about it all, as if the world hadn't just tilted on its axis. "Yes," she said meekly, thinking she shouldn't admit such a thing.

"Good. I'll take care of things, then sneak down to Mrs. Harkins's kitchen and find the bandages and something decent to eat. You know, that woman was ready to wrestle me to the ground when it came to looking after you. She frightens me."

Bryony managed a watery chuckle. "If I didn't frighten you then I doubt Mrs. Harkins can do so."

"Oh, my love," he said softly, "you terrify me. Stay put."

"I don't think I'll ever walk again."

"I'm not *that* big, love," he said, and a moment later she heard the door click behind him.

She wanted to roll onto her stomach and bury her face in the pillow. She wanted to weep, this time from guilt and confusion. She'd told him nothing but lies, and he had no idea who she was. If he did, he never would have touched her. If being tipsy and being a virgin were enough to rouse his latent conscience, the fact that she was a properly reared young lady would have stopped him cold. There was no way she could tell him, no way—

The truth hit her so hard she sat up, stifling a cry of pain as her arm protested. Miss Russell. He'd called her Miss Russell. The . . . the son of a bitch really had no conscience at all. He knew exactly who she was, and it hadn't stopped him from ruining her. So much for his latent nobility.

Thank God he had none. She lay back down, carefully, favoring her arm, and thought about it, and a slow smile spread across her face. She had been most carefully, beautifully, deliciously ruined, and she wouldn't have wanted it any other way. So he knew who she was, and he was playing games. She could play games as well; in fact, she had been since she entered this house.

She closed her eyes. She still felt faintly dizzy from the laudanum, but she didn't blame that for her fall from grace. She had entered into that willingly, as he said she would. And given the chance, she would do so again.

The door opened, and he came back into the room carrying a basin of water. He was wearing a robe, but he stripped it off as he came back to the bed, and she let herself look at him again. Looking at the part she wasn't supposed to look at—his cock. The part that was so very different from her, and yet, despite the odds, somehow made her complete. He still didn't look like a Greek statue.

He sat down on the bed and pulled the covers away, then took a warm, wet cloth and began to gently clean her stomach, between her legs, and the slow strokes shouldn't have been arousing. But then, everything he did, even the way he looked at her, was arousing.

"I don't understand the Elgin Marbles," she said suddenly.

He laughed softly. "What a completely random observation. What made you think of that?"

She looked down at him. He wasn't as large as he had been, but he was still very different than the Greek statues. "Your . . . cock is so much bigger." She felt odd using the word. "Even when you aren't about to . . . I mean . . ." She let the words trail off under the sudden heat in his gaze, but when she lowered her eyes she found the member in question had grown larger.

"Actually, I am about to . . . I mean . . ." he mocked her gently. "And I'm afraid you saying the word 'cock' does powerful things to me."

"Really?" she said faintly.

"Unless you're averse to the idea."

"Oh. No." She could feel heat wash through her.

"That's no, we're not going to fuck again, or no, you're not averse?"

That word, that indecent word, seemed to have the same effect on her that "cock" had on him. "Oh, no, I'm not averse."

He smiled, putting the basin to one side. "A good thing. I think we'd better get creative with that arm. I don't want to do it any more damage."

"Creative?"

He grinned at her, a wicked, carefree grin that caught her heart and broke it at the same time. Because he could never be hers. "I can be extremely creative, my love. You'll be impressed."

And she was.

· ·

His darling Bryony lay half curled around her bad arm, a delicious, sleeping bundle of femininity, but even he couldn't get it up a fourth time in that many hours, though his cock was doing its best. He left her in an exhausted little heap and bathed and dressed. At the last minute he remembered Collins, sitting in the storeroom, tethered, and he grinned. He'd better let the bastard out or he'd wet himself.

Apparently Collins was more adept than he'd thought, or his miniature confederate had come back and untied him. There was no sign of him in the room, the bonds lying loose on the chair, and Kilmartyn cursed beneath his breath. He had more questions to ask the man, but once released he was going to disappear into the vast populace of London, never to be seen again.

Bryony's arm seemed to be in good shape despite their exertions—there was no sign of fresh blood, but he decided he'd better rewrap it anyway, once she woke. He was starving, though as far as he knew all his servants had decamped along with Collins. Maybe they were all in the pay of the mysterious mastermind. No, that was hardly likely—Mrs. Harkins had been in residence for more than ten years, and the head footman, Bertie, had been there almost as long.

He didn't bother ringing for anyone. He descended the winding servants' staircase, pushing open the door to the basement kitchen, and watched with amusement as everyone froze.

Mrs. Harkins was at the stove, which made sense, and whatever she was cooking smelled delicious. The rest of the staff had been sitting around the table, including, to his astonishment, Collins, though there was no sign of the boy, and they all leapt up as if he were the grim reaper himself.

"I see you decided to stay with us, Collins," he said, his voice laconic. "Who untied you?"

"I did," Mrs. Harkins announced, once meaty hand on her hip. "Everyone makes mistakes. Let he who is without sin cast the first stone."

"Well, we certainly know I'm not without sin," he said easily enough. "Any sign of the boy? Or Scotland Yard? Or my missing wife?"

"No, sir," Collins said, the perfect manservant once more.

He made no comment. "Mrs. Harkins, I'm starving. Please send a massive breakfast for two up to my room in about an hour, and in the meantime I'll take coffee and pastry in my library."

"For two, sir?" Collins questioned.

"Don't be disingenuous, Collins. Nothing happens in this household that you aren't all aware of, and you know Miss Russell spent the night in my bed."

Mrs. Harkins's look of deep disapproval changed to confusion. "Miss Russell? Where is Mrs. Greaves?"

"Same person, I'm afraid. Our housekeeper hasn't been completely honest with us. Which makes her fit right in with the rest of you."

Mrs. Harkins cleared her throat with awful menace, but he wasn't interested in placating anyone. "In the meantime, everyone keep away from the third floor," he continued. "She needs her sleep."

"My lord . . ." Mrs. Harkins began, and then she trailed off, clearly uncomfortable.

"Yes, Mrs. Harkins?" he said wearily.

"Would you be so good as to tell us what's going on?"

Normally he would have put them in their place, but he'd never really been a man to stand upon ceremony, and he was the one who'd invaded their sanctuary. Besides, it would be easier to protect Bryony if they had an idea of the danger she was in.

"Miss Russell is the daughter of my business associate, Eustace Russell—" he began, but Mrs. Harkins interrupted him.

"That terrible man," she said. "Do you know how many people lost their money when the banks failed . . ."

"I suspect Russell had nothing to do with it. Whoever was behind it murdered him, and seems to think his daughter should be his next victim. Right, Collins?"

Collins shifted his weight uneasily. "I was told to watch her, and send word when she was going out, nothing more. I didn't figure it was my business, as long as he paid me enough money to send back home."

"You have a wife and children back there, Collins?"

"No, my lord. I've never married." The man couldn't help but cast a longing look at Mrs. Harkins's sturdy figure, and Kilmartyn could practically see her preen.

"Any more questions?" he said acidly. "Or may I retire to my library? And will my servants answer the bell when I summon them?"

"Yes, sir," Bertie said nervously. "Begging your pardon, your lordship, but it wasn't my idea to—"

"Bertie," Collins said in a warning voice, and the young man flushed.

"Never mind, Bertie. Just behave from now on so I don't have to turf you out. Miss Russell wouldn't like it." He gave Mrs. Harkins a speaking look. "Coffee and pastry. I'm . . ." He froze as he heard the heavy pounding on the front door, and sudden dread washed through him. He knew exactly who would make such an indelicate racket on his front door—he should stay where he was and force the men to use the servants' entrance.

He sighed. "I believe that might be Scotland Yard again. Perhaps they have word of Lady Kilmartyn. Mrs. Harkins, I'm afraid I'm going to have to make do with a cup of your tea and a slice of your excellent bread. And let Miss Russell sleep another two hours. I expect I'll be back by then."

Bertie looked doubtful. "You want I should just ignore it, my lord?"

Kilmartyn gave him a faint smile. "Tempting as that thought is, I'm afraid the gentleman of the Yard are notoriously tenacious. They won't go away, so I may as well face them. Take them to the library and tell them I'll be right there."

"My lord . . ." Mrs. Harkins paused, and then steeled herself. "Is her ladyship dead?"

"I don't know, Mrs. Harkins," he said absently. "One can only hope."

CHAPTER
TWENTY-THREE

BRYONY MOVED CAREFULLY, looking at her arm. It was heavily bandaged, but to her amazement there was no fresh blood, despite their exertions, and the pain was almost . . . bearable.

She managed to sit up on her own, though she hissed in pain, biting her lip. A lip that felt swollen, sensitive, reminding her of things she needed to put out of her head.

Cradling her arm, she looked around her. It was hard to decide which hurt worse—her head or her arm. Most people had thought it was strength of character that had enabled her to get through a broken leg and a case of fever without resorting to laudanum, but they hadn't understood the vicious effect it had on her.

She waited until the dizziness passed, then swung her legs over the side of the bed. Everything about her felt slightly abraded, her breasts, between her legs. And wicked girl that she was, she liked it. She managed to find his discarded robe and pull it around her, and by the time Mrs. Harkins pushed open the door she was sitting in a chair by the open window, breathing in the rain-drenched air.

"My goodness, Miss Russell, what are you doing out of bed!" she cried in a voice just a trace too loud for Bryony's aching head.

She winced. "Getting some fresh air."

"Well, you get right back in bed, young lady," the cook said sternly. "His lordship said I was to let you sleep, but I was thinking you might be hungry. I've got some beef broth, and another dose of laudanum might do you some good."

Did Mrs. Harkins know how she'd spent her night? Of course she did. She was in Kilmartyn's bedroom, now decorated in a deep blue that supposedly matched her eyes, wearing nothing but his robe. Bryony started to shake her head and then thought better of it. "His Lordship has no idea how quickly I heal," she said. "I have every intention of getting dressed, and I'm starving. No beef broth, and definitely no laudanum." To prove her point she rose, able to hide the slight unsteadiness of her legs. "Perhaps you would be good enough to tell me where my clothes are?"

"Not the ones you wore when you were shot," Mrs. Harkins said, not in the least bit cowed. "You're going to need new sleeves on that one. And don't be thinking of getting those clothes yourself. I'll send Emma," she added with a sniff. "Otherwise you'll be back in bed in a trice, wishing you hadn't been so stubborn. And let's just hope you don't take a fever and die from getting up too soon. Then you'd be sorry."

"At that point I'm not certain I'd notice," she said in a practical voice.

"Oh, his lordship would notice all right. He said I was to bring you breakfast, and he'd be back in an hour or two. Personally I think they might hold him a bit longer this time, but—"

"Hold him?" she echoed, filled with sudden panic. "Where is Lord Kilmartyn?"

"Why, Scotland Yard came and got him again," Mrs. Harkins said. "Didn't I tell you? Though why they're making such a fuss of it I'll never know. That Lady Kilmartyn goes off whenever she pleases, never leaving so much as a word for the staff or her husband. Why they think she'd been murdered is beyond me."

Maybe because they know about the destruction I hid, the bloody clothes I threw away, she thought guiltily. *It couldn't be Kilmartyn—he couldn't make love to me like that, kiss me, days after slaughtering his wife. He'd have to be some kind of monster.*

Then again, making love to her was a sure way of sealing her lethal case of infatuation, so that she'd never say anything. Making love . . . no, he'd called it fucking . . . was more enjoyable than killing. At least, to some people. Why would he want someone like her, why . . .

She stopped. Foolish, hurtful thoughts. Why was it that she was the one who was so cruel to herself? No one else, save perhaps her mother, long ago, had ever made her feel ugly. And last night, this morning, Kilmartyn had made her feel . . . radiant.

"Emma will bring your clothes, and she'll assist you in bathing and dressing, though she has little training as a lady's maid." Mrs. Harkins's bearing was stiff, affronted, and too late she realized how she'd addressed her. Miss Russell.

"Mrs. Harkins," she said tentatively, "I'm so sorry I lied to you."

"That's neither here nor there, miss. We're here to serve, whatever you might need." There was no change in her affronted dignity.

"I need your friendship."

Mrs. Harkins unbent, just the tiniest bit. "Quality and staff aren't friends, miss."

"They are if they want to be. We've worked side by side. We scrubbed pots, I peeled carrots and potatoes for you, I drank tea at your table." That wasn't all she'd done at her table, but she wasn't about to tell the woman about that.

The cook eyed her doubtfully, and Bryony couldn't blame her. She'd lied, and lies were hard to forgive. After a moment Mrs. Harkins gave a slight nod, not a full acceptance, but it was at least a crack in her armor. "Emma will be with you shortly. And his lordship will be back soon—he's already been gone longer than he expected. I know he'll want to see you."

"Thank you, Mrs. Harkins," she said meekly.

"And I'll have her bring you tea, and some of those little cakes you like," she said, unbending a little further. "You must be hungry, and a little solid food won't do you any harm." Mrs. Harkins looked at her for a long, considering moment, and then she nodded. "You'll do," she said obscurely.

She was gone before Bryony could ask her what she meant. She waited until the footsteps died away, and then, holding on to the window sill, she pulled herself to her feet, standing for a moment as she pulled her strength back in. She'd told Mrs. Harkins nothing but the truth—she healed quickly, and despite the pain in her arm and the emptiness in her stomach she felt almost normal.

And the panic in her heart. What were they asking him at Scotland Yard? What had he told them? She needed to go outside and see if those bloody clothes were gone, she needed to check the rooms and make certain everything looked normal.

It took her a ridiculously long amount of time to traverse the hall and make it up the narrow servants' stairs. Her clothes were where she'd left them when she'd begun her ridiculous attempt at flight. What would have happened if she hadn't turned back? Would she have been safe? Or was the man who shot her following her even back then? Would he have tried to shove her in front of a train? Was he responsible for her tumble in front of the carriage?

But Adrian had been there. He had made her say his name last night, over and over again, rewarding her in deliciously sinful ways each time she said it aloud. Adrian. He was always there, to rescue her, perhaps. Or to pretend he was doing so if there was an inconvenient witness. Was he a murderer, a liar? Was she a blind fool?

She brought the clothes down with her, trying to move a little faster. The last thing she wanted to do was depend on Emma for help. Emma, who'd been her friend as well. She could manage on her own.

She washed thoroughly, wishing she could manage a bath on her own. Her hair was a mess, and all she could do was try to wind the unruly mass in a coil at the base of her neck and pin it there, hoping it would stay. She was just finishing, buttoning the front buttons of the ugly dress, when the door to the large bathing room opened, and she looked up, relief and welcome overshadowing her doubt, expecting Adrian to walk in, to kiss her, to quiet her fears and doubts.

But it wasn't Adrian. She looked up, into the charming, handsome face of Rufus Brown, Lady Kilmartyn's cousin, and she quickly yanked her bodice together, outraged. "I beg your pardon, sir . . ." her stiff voice trailed off as she got a clear look at him.

He lounged against the door, a smile on his face, a small pistol held negligently in one hand. "Oh, don't mind me, Miss Russell. You may continue getting dressed before we leave. Indeed, I do think you'd be better off with shoes, because I'm certainly not going to be heroic like Kilmartyn and sweep you into my arms. But then, I have different plans for you than Kilmartyn did."

She slowly finished fastening the row of tiny buttons, trying to force her mind past the shock that left her frozen. Should she scream? Would the staff hear her in time, or would she be calling them to rush up and face a bullet?

"Did you shoot me?" she said finally, once her voice came back to her.

"I would think that would be a reasonable assumption since I'm now holding a gun on you. I'm usually a much better shot, but you were moving at such a determined pace it was hard to draw a bead on you. Most unladylike, I must say. You were practically running back to the arms of your lover."

"He wasn't my lover."

"Not then, perhaps. But he is now. This house practically vibrates with sex." He gestured with the gun. "Go ahead with the stockings and garters. I have to admit that lovely young women and their limbs hold no interest for me at the moment. I have more important things on my mind."

Being missish was a waste of time when she was looking into the barrel of a gun. "I can't put my stockings and shoes on with only one working hand," she said flatly.

"Then barefoot it is. Get up."

She hesitated. "Was I wrong then? You weren't having an affair with your cousin?"

He laughed. "Cecily? That tedious tramp isn't related to me, thank God. And yes, I fucked her. It was the only way to ensure her cooperation and get into the workings of the shipping company. And it kept her quiet long enough, but I really hate to perform on cue."

"You killed her."

He sighed dramatically. "Must we have a full recitation of my crimes while we're sitting here? If you think Kilmartyn is going to return and rescue you if you stall long enough I'm afraid you'll be disappointed."

She stared up at him, at his handsome, slightly impatient face, so normal, so charming, so deadly. "Who are you, really? What do you want?" There was no disguising the thread of fear in her usually strong voice.

"I'll be more than happy to entertain you with the scope of my genius once we get to where we're going. The only problem with this brilliant endeavor of mine is that there's no one else to appreciate its complexity."

"But you'll tell me?"

"Of course, my dear. You're going to die. What could be the harm?"

She'd thought that clawing in her stomach was hunger. It was fear, cold and stark. "And after you kill me?"

"Why, then, you'll be dead."

"And Kilmartyn?"

"Still worrying about your lover, are you? You shouldn't. As I said, he'll be in custody when you're killed, providing him with a perfect alibi. You really should have stayed wherever you were, Miss Russell, and not gone poking into your father's death. I had arranged everything so carefully, and then there you come, upsetting everything."

Of course! Why hadn't she realized it sooner? "You . . . arranged it?" she demanded in a raw voice. "You killed my father?"

"Not now, Miss Russell," he said impatiently. "I'll answer your questions when we get there. In the meantime, you're throwing me off schedule."

"Should I say I'm sorry?" She didn't bother to hide her hatred or her bitterness.

"Indeed you should. Stand up, Miss Russell. I don't want Kilmartyn to change his mind. Men can get foolishly sentimental once they've bedded someone, and I don't want him thinking there's any way he could have his cake and eat it too."

"What do you mean by that?"

"Why, that's he my confederate, my partner in crime. He killed his wife on my orders, and he was supposed to kill you, but instead he allowed a bit of lust to get in the way. I think it'll be much easier on him if we're simply gone if he happens to be released. You want that, don't you?"

"I don't believe you," she said flatly. He couldn't have lied to her, made love just days after slaughtering his wife.

"Women are such fools—they'll believe anything a man tells them. It would have been far better for you if you'd simply gotten on that train— yes, I was watching you then. I could have taken care of this business neatly and quickly, but instead you go running back to him. I imagine he finds it almost as tiresome as I do, though he did have the advantage of your pussy. Which must be quite remarkable, to keep him so enchanted. I never could understand why men got so entranced with feminine parts—there must be some magic spell on yours."

She hid her expression. What the hell was he talking about? Magic body parts? At least it settled the question of whether she'd foolishly returned to face her own demise. He had been ready to kill her on the train. Coming back hadn't made any difference.

"Why don't we wait until Kilmartyn returns?" she said in a reasonable voice. "If he's your confederate then he should have some say in the matter." Was it possible that she'd be wrong, that her blind faith had, in fact, been blind? Could Adrian look at her and sentence her to death? Would he be the one to kill her?

"You surely don't think I'd listen to what he has to say? To be more accurate, he's not my partner in crime, he's my minion, and he'll do what I say. There's too much money involved for him to be sentimental."

A spark of hope suddenly appeared in the bleak, empty landscape of the future. Adrian was nobody's minion, especially not this smiling, prancing lunatic. She tried to think of something, anything to distract him, slow him down. Scotland Yard couldn't keep a peer of the realm, even a lowly Irish one, without just cause, and he would come straight back to her, she knew he would.

Wouldn't he?

"Time to go, Miss Russell," Rufus Brown said cheerfully.

"And if I refuse?"

He moved with such grace she didn't realize what was coming until he slammed the gun against her wounded arm, slapping a hand across her mouth to muffle her scream of pain.

Everything went black for a moment, and she was afraid she was going to vomit from the pain. His hand was smothering her, but she stayed very still, and after a moment he stepped back. "I trust you understand me," he said in his light, charming voice.

"Absolutely," she said grimly, trying to catch her breath.

"Then get up."

"Give me a minute."

"Get up."

She rose. She'd overestimated her strength, or maybe it was simply the aftereffect of the blow against her recent wound. It was bleeding again—she could feel the blood beginning to run down her arm, and she let it drop, painful as it was. If she could leave a trail of blood Adrian would come after her. He would save her.

Or he would kill her.

She swayed slightly, then stiffened her back. "May I ask where we're going?"

"Certainly, my dear. You're going home."

"To Renwick?" she said, astonished.

She didn't even see the blow coming, his hand holding the gun, slamming it across her face, knocking her against the wall, and it was sheer force of will that kept her standing. That, and the small chair she clung to. Pretty Mr. Brown was ugly now, red and blotched with rage, spittle flying from his mouth.

"Renwick isn't yours. It's never been yours, your father stole it!"

He was mad, she reminded herself dazedly. He was making no sense at all. "What does Renwick have to do with anything?"

His laugh was just slightly off. "That proves what a fool you are. Renwick is everything. That's what this is all about."

He was making no sense, and she didn't want to give him another excuse to hit her. She wasn't quite certain how much more she could stand.

"Then where are you taking me?" she asked in what she hoped was a soothing voice.

He calmed himself, and while his smile was strained, it was an attempt at his usual insouciance. "To Curzon Street. To the burned-out ruin of your old house."

"But . . . but there's nothing there," she protested.

"Oh, that's not true. Lady Kilmartyn and her obstructive maid are there. And that's where I intend to leave you. It's an excellent spot, and eventually it will be demolished and be covered over completely. Maybe a hundred years from now someone will find your bones and little scraps of your clothing and wonder who you were, but that's the best you can hope for."

She would vomit, she absolutely would. "And Kilmartyn? What happens to him?"

"I told you, he's my confederate. He gets to live out his life mourning his missing wife, who will be seen in Paris and Vienna once I make the proper arrangements, and he'll enjoy his share of your father's money. You'd like that, wouldn't you? You want the man you love to be happy."

She looked at him, calmly, steadily. "I'll see you in hell."

"Ah, but you'll be there first, my dear. Move."

CHAPTER
TWENTY-FOUR

THEY WEREN'T GOING to let him go. Kilmartyn paced the luxurious office he'd been shepherded to, a nod to his title and position, but there was a guard outside and no easy escape in sight. Every now and then another of Scotland Yard's detectives came in to talk to him, to ask him the same damned questions, but as far as he could tell they had not one new scrap of evidence. Someone was feeding them accusations, but there didn't seem to be a thing to back them up.

It was growing later—if he could judge by the color of the sky it was getting close to early evening, which meant he'd been gone for at least six hours. Six hours in this stuffy office, being offered tea and biscuits, with the most deferential of inquiries, but no one was letting him out. Which meant Bryony was home alone.

There was nothing to worry about. The servants were there—Collins was so awash with guilt he would protect her with his own life, and he could count on Mrs. Harkins to scare off any but the most hardened villain. But whoever he was, he'd killed two women and had tried to kill a third, which didn't argue for a gentle soul.

And he hadn't the faintest idea who could be behind it all.

When Russell had first come to him, accusing him of falsifying shipments and tampering with the books the only thing that had kept him from decking the blustering old man was his age. The trail of larceny apparently led straight to his door, and he was never sure whether he'd convinced Russell of his innocence or not.

The hell with it. It was Russell's problem, not his, and he was damned if he was going to be accused like a common thief. He'd thought differently when Russell turned up dead two days later, supposedly on the run with his ill-gotten gains. Kilmartyn could have believed it, if those ill-gotten gains hadn't managed to disappear along the way. The whole thing was too convenient.

He'd been an idiot. It had taken him long enough to guess who his little in-house spy actually was, when he should have known right off. Should have offered to help her, not gotten her shot and then seduced her. She'd be safe in his house; she had to be.

He didn't know if he could wait much longer. Uniformed officers had been coming in and out at regular intervals, asking him if he wanted anything, polite and unhelpful, and by the time the shadows were growing longer he started watching them a bit more closely, waiting till someone his approximate size and build appeared. It was a long wait. He was taller than average, and while he was built along spare lines he had a fair amount of muscle. He couldn't just grab any spindleshanks who happened to walk in.

By the time a suitable offering arrived he'd been ready to throw a chair through the window just to get out of there. The uniformed officer backed in, kicking the door shut, carrying another inevitable tray of tea and biscuits. Kilmartyn had to piss like a racehorse. If he ever got out of here he was never touching a drop of tea again.

"Sorry for the delay, your lordship," his sacrificial offering said in a genial cockney accent as he set the tray on the desk, conveniently turning his back on Kilmartyn. "It shouldn't be too much longer. Detective Inspector Pierson is conferring with his superiors, and he—"

The police officer dropped like a stone beneath Kilmartyn's blow. He moved fast, dragging him out of sight of the window and stripping off his jacket and trousers. He didn't dare waste the time in re-dressing him—it wouldn't do any good, and he needed to get home. They would come after him again, and they'd view this as another sign of guilt, and he didn't give a rat's arse. He needed to get home.

The hat was a little large, but he tilted it on the back of his head, and backed out of the door while carrying on an imaginary conversation with the trussed-up man in the faded red combinations.

"You just enjoy your tea, yer lordship," he said, using a strong cockney accent. "They'll come ter get you before long." And keeping his head down, he walked straight out of the main office at Scotland Yard, with no one giving him a second glance.

· ·

It was growing dark, and a storm was brewing. Bryony surveyed the darkening sky, felt the wind pull at her loosely coiled hair, tugging at it. She was walking barefoot through the streets of London, arm in arm with the man who was going to kill her. She could feel the muzzle of the little gun against her ribs, and she had no doubt he'd do just as he promised and shoot her in full view of the public. He had every certainty that he could simply run away before anyone realized what had happened, and whether he could or not didn't matter. What mattered was his belief in his invincibility.

The house on Curzon Street looked even more derelict than it had the one time she'd driven by it. The houses on either side had suffered significant damage, and they were abandoned as well—there was no chance of anyone hearing her if she had a chance to scream for help.

She could only hope her Hansel and Gretel–like trail of blood might lead Adrian to them. The blood dripping down her arm had stopped, but there'd been a broken jar at the side of the road, and she'd deliberately stepped on it with her bare foot, not changing her expression as she felt it slice into her. It was her only chance. Unless, of course, Brown wasn't lying, and Adrian was part and parcel of the whole thing.

"Hurry up, dear," Mr. Brown said in fond accents. "I do believe we're due for a storm."

She sped up, forcing herself to walk normally despite the bloody footprints she was leaving. She didn't want anything to call her kidnapper's attention to them—he'd drag her onto the grass to hide any bloody trail.

It was already too late. He was pulling her down the narrow passageway between houses, and the smell of burned wood and damp assailed her nostrils. People had died in this fire. Three servants in their household, and a child in one of the adjoining households. This man had already killed many times over. Nothing would keep him from doing it again.

"Don't you have a conscience?" she said in a lower, bitter voice.

He glanced at her, delight in his strangely pale eyes. "Are you about to give me a lecture about my evil ways, Miss Russell? Oh, please do. It will be a waste of time, but it might enliven things. Why do you ask?"

"Four people died in this fire. A fire I presume you started."

"I did indeed. Well, not me personally—you can really hire someone to do just about anything in London if you have the money. And your father's money paid for the arsonist—an amusing piece of irony, don't you think? And do I lament the loss of life? Why should I? People die every day. I didn't know them—to pretend sorrow would be hypocritical."

"And God knows one should never stoop to hypocrisy," she muttered.

"You really are entertaining," he marveled. "Here I am, about to kill you, and you're being positively confrontational. No wonder Kilmartyn was so fond of you. He didn't want me to kill you, you know. He thought he might keep you around for a few weeks longer. I know it will make you feel better to know that he found you quite enjoyable. But in the end he agreed with me that you were . . . shall we say . . . de trop?"

"I don't believe you." She looked up at the back of the house. It seemed like only a frame of the place, though the last time she'd been here the front staircase had remained, leading upward into the ruins. The back looked only slightly more sturdy—the framework reached the full four stories, though the windows and doors were wide open to the elements.

"Of course you don't, my dear. And I'm perfectly happy to have you die with your illusions intact. We do have a problem though. This place is littered with broken glass, and I don't want you cutting your feet to ribbons on the way in."

"We're going in?" she said, startled. "I thought you'd simply strangle me in the back garden and have done with it. I do understand that a gun might be too loud, though considering how deserted this particular area of the square is, you might very well get away with it."

"Of course we're going in. I have no interest in hauling your body around—do you have the slightest idea how much a dead body weighs? It's quite extraordinary; even someone as light as Cecily's scrawny little French maid seemed to weigh twice as much once I'd stabbed her. By the time I finished moving the bodies from Kilmartyn's house I was so prostrate with exhaustion that I couldn't move."

"You have all my sympathy. Why do you care whether I cut my feet or not? If I'm about to die I wouldn't think you'd be that concerned for my comfort."

"Oh, it's not your comfort, my dear. It's the fact that you might leave tracks." He peered upward, into the rapidly darkening sky. "However, it does look like rain, and a good London soaking will wash any telltale blood away. Come along." He dragged her forward.

It could have been worse, she told herself, trying not to weep. If she wasn't going to cry over dying she certainly shouldn't cry from her feet being cut. She needed to get things in perspective.

The charred wood crunched beneath her bloody feet as he pulled her inside, and she shook herself free from his tight, smothering grip. He laughed softly. "Why, it appears you aren't fond of my touch, Miss Russell. I'll have to take that into account."

"Why?"

"Because I'm planning to take my time with you. You've caused me no end of aggravation, and I promised myself a little treat when it came time to finish with you. And if I can perform with a foul cunt like Cecily then I can certainly perform with you. Particularly since Kilmartyn has already broken you to the bridle, so to speak."

She almost screamed then, but he moved the gun front and center. "I wouldn't if I were you. You never know whether some miracle might happen and you might be saved. Why throw away your life before it's absolutely certain?"

"To avoid a lot of pain and degradation?" she said caustically, knowing she wasn't going to do it.

"Oh, I'd shoot you in a spot that was extremely painful, I do promise you that. And just because you're dead doesn't mean I can't degrade your body. I told you, there's nothing that can keep me from performing if I have a good enough reason. And I must confess that hurting you is a very good reason indeed. Start climbing. We'll take the servants' staircase—you should be used to that by now. I'm not certain how it'll hold up, but we can consider it an adventure."

She had no choice—she started up the narrow, winding staircase ahead of him, the only light coming in from above, where the roof had already collapsed.

The first drops of rain splattered down on them, and she heard Brown curse behind her. By the time they reached the first-floor landing her feet were becoming numb—she should count that as a blessing. The doors and most of the walls were gone, and she could recognize the blistered outlines of the wallpaper her mother had chosen, before he jabbed her with the gun once more, and she continued upward, higher and higher.

There were more walls on the second floor, and part of the floor remained. "Keep climbing, my dear. I have just the place for us. Out of this wretched rain, where we can be quite cozy, you and I."

She kept climbing. The stairs felt spongy beneath her feet, and the entire staircase seemed to sway as they climbed steadily upward. Was it going to hold up long enough, or would it collapse beneath them? If she was going to die she wanted him dead too.

Maybe she could kick back when he wasn't expecting it, sending him tumbling down the stairs? But then, where would she go? He was blocking the only way out, and he was the one with the gun.

"I do have a little treat for you," he said in a merry voice, sounding slightly breathless as they neared what remained of the top floor. Clearly he hadn't been in service or he would have built up more stamina, she thought sourly, thinking of those endless trips up and down Adrian's stairs. "Just to provide the coup de grâce to the day."

"And what exactly is that?"

She'd just reached the top floor, when she saw the shadow beneath what was left of the eaves. A shadow that moved out into the storm-infused light, a tall, lean form that was instantly recognizable, despite the incongruous policeman's jacket he wore.

"Is that you, Kilmartyn?" Mr. Brown called out, as she froze, blocking him. "I thought young Jem would be able to lead you here. He didn't want to, if that's any consolation."

"It's not," Adrian snarled from across the darkness. "Who the fuck are you?"

"You don't have to play the game anymore. She knows the truth, don't you, my dear? Now don't keep the man waiting. I'm sure he'd love a kiss good-bye." He put his hand in the middle of her back and shoved her, and she went sprawling on what was left of the attic floor.

"No!" Adrian shouted, moving toward her, but then he stopped, holding motionless, as the floor beneath her shifted and creaked.

"I'm afraid the floor might not be strong enough for you over here, Kilmartyn." Mr. Brown hadn't emerged into the light, his voice eerie and disembodied. "That's why I sent you that way. You won't be able to reach her. I didn't want you to change your mind."

"Change my mind? What are you talking about?" Adrian's voice sounded almost unnaturally calm.

"Tsk-tsk. You don't have to pretend anymore. She knows you're working with me. Don't become tiresomely sentimental, old boy. We've planned this for too long to let a little bit of crumpet interfere."

She heard the words with numb dread. It couldn't be possible. She had gotten to her knees, looking at Adrian from across the gaping chasm of the missing floor. He looked the same, beautiful, cynical, though in the shadows his eyes were dark and unreadable.

"Tell me you don't believe him, Bryony," Adrian said. "But of course you do. Your face says it all. You think I'm a thief and a murderer who fucks his victims before he sends them to their death. You'd believe your unseen friend before you'd believe me."

"Why should I believe you?" she cried out, knowing Brown was behind her, the gun trained on her. She could feel the floor shifting beneath her, creaking dangerously. *At least this way it would be fast,* she thought miserably, and she might take Brown with her.

"I haven't the faintest idea," he said, his voice cool and emotionless. "But you're going to—"

There was a sudden terrific creaking noise behind her, and Brown's high-pitched laugh was eerie. "I do believe we're running out of time. I had hoped for more heartwarming theatrics, but I'm afraid this place isn't going to be standing for very much longer. If you won't shoot her, Kilmartyn, then I will."

Bryony didn't move. She could see that Adrian held a gun, and it was pointed in her direction. Or was he pointing it at the man who stayed at the top of the stairs, still in the shadow, her body shielding him?

"I'm not going to shoot her," Adrian said flatly.

"You don't need to pretend anymore, Kilmartyn. I've told this little fool the truth."

"What truth?" Adrian snarled.

"That you were using her. That you lied to her, seduced her, while all the time you were covering up your involvement in her father's murder."

"And why would I do that?" Adrian sounded very calm, and through the miasma of doubt and pain Bryony felt the faint flowering of hope.

"For entertainment, of course. But this grows tedious, old man. Enough is enough."

She heard an ominous clicking sound, and she froze, knowing she was going to die, when another gust of wind hit the side of the house, shaking the entire building. There was a sudden great rending noise, as if the world were being split in two, and then his scream, high-pitched and panicked. She whirled around, looking for the monster who'd brought her to this death trap, but the stairs were empty. In fact, the stairs were gone, taking Brown with them, and she stared in horror, feeling the floor shift beneath her feet.

"What was that?" Adrian snapped, moving closer.

He was still holding the gun, she realized. Would he be able to hit her from across that open stretch of flooring? Would it matter? There was no way out for her.

"The stairs have collapsed," she said in a dull voice. "I'm afraid your friend is gone."

"He's not my goddamned friend. I have no idea who that man is, and I don't care. If he's gone then there's nothing to stop you from coming over here."

She gave him a look of stark disbelief. "Are you mad? There's a gaping hole between us that goes all the way down to the basement and the bodies of your wife and her maid. You'll just throw me down there anyway—why not save you the trouble and wait for the floor to finish collapsing?" Her voice was bitter.

"If you keep talking we won't have long to wait," he snarled. "You have to trust me. In truth, I don't care whether you do or not, I'm not going to stand here and watch you plummet to your death. Get on your feet and jump, damn it, or I'll come over there and get you."

"Even if I wanted to I don't think I could," she said, and the numbness that plagued her feet seemed to have traveled to her heart. She no longer cared what happened to her, what happened to him. She'd given up fighting. She sat back, sticking her bloody feet out in front of her. "You were supposed to follow my bloody footprints. If I knew you were going to be here anyway I wouldn't have gone to so much trouble to slice up my feet."

"Get up," he said, his voice so cold and lethal that she found herself reaching for a handhold automatically, starting to pull herself up, only to feel the fragment of floor tip forward, a few remaining pieces of charred furniture sliding down the angle and plummeting into the darkness. "Now move as far back as you can go. Carefully."

For a moment she didn't move, staring at him. "You must be mad."

"You have no choice, Bryony. You can trust me, or you can take your chances on the house not falling down." There was no gentleness in his voice, no persuasion. Simply a statement of fact. "Which do you think is more likely?"

"Give me one good reason to trust you," she said, gimlet-eyed.

"I can't think of one," he said. "Except that I love you. Now run, damn it, and jump to me."

She stared at him, shocked. "Now's a fine time to tell me," she finally managed to snap back.

"I've been busy," he growled.

"I suppose you expect me to tell you I love you too."

"You could," he agreed. "I'd much rather have you move your bloody arse and get over here and we can argue about the details later."

"Let me think about it."

He cursed, the words so foul she was impressed. "If you don't move now you won't have a chance to ever have a thought in your clever little brain again."

"You're right," she said judiciously. "Besides, it's really very simple."

"It is?" He sounded no more than slightly harassed.

"Of course. If you want to kill me then I'd just as soon be dead. So either catch me or you're lying and you'll let me fall, but make up your mind."

"There was never any question on my part," he said. "Trust me, Bryony."

It was the third time he said it, and that third time gave her wings. She took a running start and leapt across the cavernous hole, closing her eyes and praying as she went sailing through the air.

She crashed into him, and he went down beneath her. Catching her in his arms, he rolled them both away to the far wall, keeping her still beneath him as the building creaked and shifted ominously. The remains of the house across the divide began to crumble, and a moment later it collapsed into the basement with a thunderous noise and a huge cloud of dust and soot, burying her would-be murderer. Slowly, slowly he loosened his death grip on her. She opened her eyes to look up into his blazingly furious ones.

"I don't know whether to kiss you or strangle you," he muttered.

"I thought you told me I could trust you?"

"That doesn't mean I'm not tempted to beat you within an inch of your life. 'Let me think about it,'" he mimicked. "I'll give you something to think about, my girl."

"Let's wait until we get out of here, shall we?" she said. "Or aren't there any stairs left?"

He stared at her in disbelief. "You mean you jumped across that gaping hole and you didn't even know whether or not there was a way to get down?"

She smiled up at him, and finally her eyes began to fill with tears. "I love you too."

CHAPTER TWENTY-FIVE

THREE DAYS LATER Bryony Arielle Josephine Russell Bruton, Countess of Kilmartyn, stretched out in the bunk, warm and catlike. "Thank God I don't get seasick," she said. "It's bad enough that I can't walk and can't use my left arm—if I'd been casting up my accounts all over the place I really couldn't bear it."

Her husband gave her an indulgent smile from across the wide cabin. "I rather like it that you're currently forced to stay in bed. It's the best way to enjoy a honeymoon, such as it is."

"It's lovely!" she protested.

"Well, running from the law and leaving everything behind and not knowing if or when we can ever return isn't quite my idea of lovely," he said. "And you're worried about your sisters."

"I know, but I needn't be. I sent them a letter telling them that we know father wasn't responsible, but the man who was is dead and we can't prove anything. Not good news, and I expect they'll be horrified that I'm married."

"Horrified?" he echoed, affronted. "Why?"

"Because I told them I was never going to marry. I was going to live in happy seclusion in a little cottage for the rest of my life once everything was settled."

"You can live anywhere you want as long as the seclusion includes me." He crossed the room in a few strides and caught her face in his hands. "Foolish girl," he whispered, and deliberately turned her face to one side to kiss the scars. "You are such an idiot for such a smart woman." He kissed her eyelids, and then her mouth, a deep, possessive kiss that had her rising up to meet him. He climbed onto the bunk with her, tucking her against him, and she felt that strange, wonderful calm envelop her once more.

"It's actually the staff at Berkeley Square that I'm worried about," she said after a few quiet moments. "I hate it that we just abandoned them without a word."

"They have word, darling. My lawyer has seen to it that Mrs. Harkins . . . or for all I know she's Mrs. Collins by now . . . has charge of the household money, and they're taking good care of Jem. I imagine they'll have a lovely time having the house to themselves and not having to look after anyone."

"I hope they all get a chance to use the bathtub," she said. "You really should put one up in the attics as well."

"We will. When we get back."

She was silent for a long while. "Will we get back?"

He slid his arms around her waist, leaning over and giving her ear a tiny bite, sending shards of warmth through her. "You know we will. We have the Pinkerton Agency's best man in England working on it. If the man survived they'll find him. If he crawled off to die they'll find him. Either way, they'll find out who he is and get the proof they need so we can return home."

"What if he is still alive? What if he goes after my sisters?"

He kissed the side of her face tenderly. "Why would he? And how would he even find them? They're buried in the countryside somewhere, aren't they?"

She nodded, still uneasy. "Nanny Gruen won't let anything happen to them."

"They're with your old nanny? Then I tremble to think of anyone interfering."

She turned her face to smile at him. "You know nannies very well."

"Fiercest creatures on the face of this earth," he said promptly. "So they're safe, the staff at Berkeley Square is safe, and we're going to travel to Venice and France and Vienna until Scotland Yard gets the proof that I never killed anyone . . ." He hesitated. "Well, that at least I never killed my wife and her maid."

She turned completely, ignoring her healing arm, and held him. "You weren't responsible for the bombing," she said fiercely. "You didn't know."

His laugh was without humor. "Ignorance is a poor excuse."

She gave him a tiny shake, the best she could manage given how much bigger he was. "Being a martyr is annoying. You told me that when the captain married us and I wanted to keep my face covered. So if I'm not allowed to be a martyr then neither are you."

This time his laugh was real. "All right. We'll be two completely unmartyred vagabonds for the time being. Until we get home."

She kissed him, sweet and full. "Until we get home," she echoed.

ABOUT THE AUTHOR

ANNE STUART is a grand master of the genre, winner of the Romance Writers of America's prestigious Nora Roberts Lifetime Achievement Award and survivor of close to forty years in the romance business—and she still just keeps getting better.

Her first novel was *Barrett's Hill*, a gothic romance published by Ballantine in 1974 when Anne had just turned twenty-five. Since then she's written more gothics, as well as Regencies, romantic suspense, romantic adventure, series romance, suspense, historical romance, paranormal, and mainstream contemporary romance.

She's won numerous awards, appeared on most best-seller lists, and speaks all over the country. Her general outrageousness has gotten her on *Entertainment Tonight*, as well as in *Vogue, People, USA Today, Woman's Day*, and countless other national newspapers and magazines.

When she's not traveling, she's at home in northern Vermont with her luscious husband of thirty-eight years, an empty nest, three cats, and four sewing machines, and when she's not working, she's watching movies, listening to rock and roll (preferably Japanese), and spending far too much time quilting.